THE BLACK ORCHID MYSTERY

James R. Nelson

Copyright © 2013 James R. Nelson
All Rights Reserved

ISBN-13: 978-1483904719

ISBN-10: 1483904717

Chapter 1

Archie Archibald lay flat on his back, his arms outstretched as if he were ready to make a snow angel. As his eyes slowly opened, he saw only a black expanse of nothing. He blinked several times and tried to focus. Gradually, thousands of tiny yellow dots started coming in and out of view. He tried to shake his head, but a stabbing pain immediately stopped him in his tracks. There was movement about twenty feet above his head, and he could see a brown palm frond spinning slowly in the breeze. *Stars*, he thought. *Those yellow lights must be stars.*

He reached out with his right hand and tapped the area next to his body. He grabbed hold of something that felt like wet cardboard. He cautiously extended his hand farther until something sharp sliced into his finger. He pulled his hand back and tried again to sit up. Another pain shot through his neck.

There was a noise that sounded close. He slowly turned toward the sound. The back of his head felt as if a concrete block had bounced off it. Again, something rattled near him. This time, he shifted his eyes to the right and peered into the darkness. He caught a quick burst of movement close to his face and bolted upright. A rat!

Another jolt of pain shot through his body, and suddenly he felt sick to his stomach. Everything around him started to spin in a slow clockwise direction. He reached down to try to steady the motion and felt his hand settle into a pile of thick, slippery liquid. Pulling his arm back, it dawned on him that he was sitting on top of a huge mound of garbage. *A dumpster! I'm sitting in a damn dumpster!*

Archie carefully flexed his arms. First the right one and then the left. They felt stiff, but nothing seemed to be broken. He repeated the exercise with his legs and winced as he straightened out his right leg. Nothing too surprising there.

He twisted his body to the right and then to the left. He was sore and his muscles felt tight, but other than the throbbing pain in his head, he seemed to be okay.

He crawled over a mound of tin cans, paper, and cardboard until he got to the green metal rim of the dumpster. He grabbed hold of the side and let himself down. Another wave of pain jolted through his body as he landed on the cracked blacktop.

Archie stared into the shadows to make sure he was alone. The few overhead lights that were still working in the front parking lot did little to illuminate the alley he found himself in. He listened for any ominous sounds but heard only the wind high up in the palm trees. Dark clouds were moving fast above his head, blocking out the dim light from a quarter moon.

Wiping bits and pieces of garbage off the front of his shirt, he limped over to a dark puddle and rinsed off his hands. *God only knows what's in this water.* Walking over to a pile of wooden pallets, he sat down and tried to remember where he was headed when he left his office earlier that evening.

Archie jerked his head toward the darkened alleyway. There was a sound of rustling paper, and it was getting louder. Something was coming his way. He stood up and glanced around for something to pick up. The sounds were getting closer. In desperation, he snapped off a small piece of wood from the pallet and turned toward the alley, his arm ready to strike. A black cat stepped from the shadows and looked over at him. Archie breathed a sigh of relief. The cat came over and started to weave in and out of his legs. He could hear a loud purring noise. He bent down and scratched the cat behind the ears. "Nice kitty."

Everything started coming back. Two days earlier, in the middle of the afternoon on Monday, October 17th, a short Hispanic man, wearing a brown striped suit that seemed a little too big for him, had walked into his office looking for a private detective.

Archie had laughed to himself because the man looked like a darker version of Danny DeVito. Turned out, the guy, Fernando Mendes, owned a strip mall over on Oakland Park Boulevard, and he asked Archie to do a little leg work for him. According to Mr. Mendes, a group of punks were shaking down his shop owners, asking for protection money. His tenants were complaining, and he wanted Archie to look into it. Archie told Mr. Mendes that he was busy for the next day or two, but he'd run over there and see what he could find out as soon possible.

    Archie looked down at his watch. It was hard to read in the dim light, but it looked like twenty minutes after three. He walked along the back of the building, listening for any signs of gang members. Several fifty-five gallon drums were lying on the ground next to a car that had been stripped of it's hubcaps and tires. Mounds of garbage littered the alley. Ft. Lauderdale was a far cry from the sleepy beach town he remembered seeing in the movie *Where the Boys Are* so many years before.

    Archie slowly walked out from behind the mall, staying close to the building as he made his way to the front parking lot. He glanced around to make sure he was alone. The last thing he needed was another beating. He understood only too well that this one was to teach him a lesson. Go away. He may not be lucky enough to walk away from the next one.

    Archie tried to remember of where he had parked his car. *Oh, yeah. It was in front of that dumpy indoor flea market.* He had been walking around the complex when he turned a corner and walked right into five of them. La Frios Gang members. He tried talking his way out of a confrontation but it didn't work. As he limped over to the sidewalk, his right leg was getting worse and his head continued to throb.

A cab was heading east down Oakland. Archie stepped onto the dead grass in the swale and waved his arm. The cab slowed down and pulled up to the curb. He walked over to the driver's side door and leaned in. "I need to get to Commercial and North East Twenty-Eighth Avenue.

The cabbie jerked his head back from the window with a look of disgust. "Take a bath, buddy. I don't give rides to no bums."

"I'm no …"

The cabbie threw the car into gear and took off, spinning Archie onto the ground.

He stood up and limped back over to the sidewalk as he watched the cab's taillights disappear into the darkness. Again, he tried to remember where he had parked his car.

A voice called out from the far side of the shopping center. "Mario, él está allí!"

Archie turned and saw a man pointing at him as another guy stepped out from the shadows. Archie started running down the sidewalk. His back was stiff and he felt like he couldn't get going. It reminded him of trying to run in a dream. He turned. They were young, in much better shape than he was, and they were gaining on him fast.

Archie jumped off the sidewalk and sprinted, as best he could, into the parking lot of El Grande Flea Market. He wasn't covering much distance. His right leg felt like it was about to buckle. Twenty years before, he had taken a bullet in the thigh. It left him with a permanent limp and a resolve to not stop any more bullets.

The pain in Archie's back was getting worse. He stopped for a moment and bent over to try to catch his breath. The sweat from running seemed to activate the layer of garbage that was clinging to him. He coughed and stifled a gag. *Hiding from a gang at this point in my career is not really what a slightly overweight 53 year old should be doing.* Archie looked over to the right and saw three cars parked at the far end of the lot. His car, a seven-year-old, green Miata, was sitting between a tricked out El Camino and an old van. He fumbled in his pocket for the keys and made a dash for the car. He heard footsteps closing in behind him as he jammed his key into the lock and pulled open the door.

Archie felt a hand grab his left arm. He threw himself into the driver's seat and stuck the key in the ignition. He looked over and recognized the kid who was trying to pull him out of the car. He was the same guy that had approached him a few hours before, wanting to know what he was doing in their 'territory.' His muscular friend, who looked younger, had stood in the shadows, arms crossed, with a disgusted sneer on his face.

Archie lashed out with his left leg and connected with the kid's knee cap, sending him rolling backwards onto the pavement. As Archie turned the key, he glanced into the rear view mirror and saw the other kid running toward him. He threw the car in reverse and stomped on the gas pedal. The car flew backwards and almost smacked into the younger gang member, who dogged away just in time.

Archie shoved the car into first gear and headed toward Oakland Park Boulevard. He glanced in his side mirror and saw the first guy reach down, grab a rock, and hurl it at the car. He heard a sharp crack on the plastic window behind his head as he squealed out of the parking lot. He headed east on Oakland until he got to US 1.

A thick ocean mist was rolling in from the Atlantic as Archie pulled into the parking lot behind his office building on Commercial Boulevard. He let himself in the back door and walked over to his desk. He picked up a manila folder and thumbed through the pages. The owner of the strip mall had given him a $200 retainer. Archie tossed the folder down on the desk. It just wasn't worth it. *This damn town's going to hell,* he thought.

He walked over to a small room in the back of his office. After spending so many nights there, Archie finally wised up, and added a single bed into a small room that was normally used for storage. He was lucky. Before he had rented the place, the former tenants had added a tiny shower to the bathroom that was already there. A battered wardrobe from the Salvation Army held several changes of clothes. Archie stepped into the bathroom and pulled off his shirt and pants, trying to avoid touching any of the residual garbage that still clung to him. He took a long, hot shower. The steam felt good on his battered body.

    Archie sat on the edge of the bed, rubbing his thigh. The nerve damage caused by the bullet so many years before was making his leg tingle. Rubbing it seemed to help. He eased himself into bed. The bed felt welcoming and familiar. Unfortunately, he had spent way too many nights in it.

Chapter 2

Stephanie Woods swung her aging Lexus into the parking lot and noticed Archie's car. *Must have spent another night at the office*, she thought. That's the only time he ever arrived before she did. She unlocked the door, walked over to her desk and deposited her purse in the bottom drawer. She sniffed the air. *No coffee, he must still be sleeping.* Stephanie walked over to the alcove where the coffee pot was, scooped some coffee into a filter, and flipped the switch to brew. She tip-toed over to the doorway to the spare office and looked through the half opened door. She saw Archie sprawled out on the bed, sleeping soundly.

Stephanie crinkled up her nose. *What's that awful smell?* She looked down at the pile of clothes next to the bed. *What has that man gotten into?* she wondered. She turned around and walked back to the coffee pot. *Whatever it is, it's not my problem. I'm the secretary, not the maid.*

She had worked for Archie for almost six years. She had originally worked next door as a receptionist for a hair salon. That business closed at the same time Archie was looking for someone to replace his old secretary. The transition was easy, she just picked up her desk items and moved them from one office to another, not missing one minute of employment. She walked back to her desk and started working.

Archie rolled over and opened his eyes. No darkness this time. He recognized the familiar swirl pattern of his office ceiling tiles. He slowly stretched his arms and felt the muscles in his back tighten. The back of his head was still tender. He glanced down at the floor and saw a pile of filthy clothes. The dumpster memories hit him like a bad dream. Archie pushed off the covers and sat on the side of the bed, trying to remember everything that happened the night before. He walked over to the closet and pulled out a spare set of clothes; brown slacks, blue shirt, and a brown sport coat. Archie struggled to get dressed, each movement introducing him to muscles he never knew he had. Archie made his way over to the coffee pot and poured himself a cup. He walked out to the main office and limped over to his desk.

Stephanie stopped typing. "So, what kind of adventure did you have last night? Smells kind of bad. I'm not sure I even want to know."

Archie took a sip of his coffee. "Remember that guy who has the strip plaza down on Oakland Park?"

Stephanie gave him a puzzled look. "Mr. Mendes?"

"Yeah, that guy. Well, he's getting all his money back."

"He is?"

Archie nodded. "Yep. Another gang. Remember back in April when I spent two days in the hospital from that beating I got from that other bunch of punks?"

Stephanie frowned. "I sure do."

"Same type of deal. A bunch of tough guys shaking down the tenants in his plaza. Protection money. He knows it, I know it…there's nothing much I can do." Archie paused and arched his back. "Except, maybe land in the hospital again."

Stephanie sighed. "Why?"

Archie got up and walked back over to the coffee pot. "Want a refill?"

"No, thanks."

"My clients are changing. I can't talk to half the people that come in the front door because I don't speak Spanish. How can I be effective?"

"Ah, maybe take a class?"

Archie spun around, almost spilling his coffee. "You know, if I was twenty years younger, I'd do that. But, not at this stage of the game. It's just not the clients. It's the jobs." He thought for a moment. "Where are all the old staples? The messy divorces, the bar owners wanting to find out who's skimming from the till, the…."

She interrupted him. "It's a changing world around here, that's for sure."

"And that's the problem. Everything's changing but me."

Stephanie looked puzzled. "What does that mean?"

"It means, if I want to continue this detective business, I'm going to have to move."

"Move?" she asked with a look of shock. "Where are you going to move to?" She didn't give Archie time to answer. "What about the rent? I don't want to be brash, but you're barely covering your bills now. Don't forget, I write the checks every month." She got up and walked to the front window. "I know this neighborhood's getting a little seedy, but at least the rent is reasonable. You move over to US 1 or A1A and I can't even imagine what you'd have to pay."

"I know, I know, but that's not the change I'm talking about." Archie paused for a sip of coffee. "I'm talking about getting out of South Florida altogether."

Stephanie turned from the window. "What? Where would you go?"

"Remember Luther Johnson?"

Stephanie was still trying to process the idea of Archie leaving the area. "Ah, sure. Luther, the maintenance man for our plaza."

"Yeah, good old Luther. We still keep in touch. When he retired, he moved up to the Vero Beach area."

"I remember now. Central Florida. He couldn't wait to get up there. He was a fishing nut, wasn't he?"

"Still is. I've driven up there to go fishing with him a few times. He's got himself a little place just west of Vero, and he loves it. The pace is quiet, traffic's manageable, great fishing and the weather's a lot cooler than down here in this tropical oven."

"So that's where you're thinking of retiring?"

Archie looked over at Stephanie. "Retiring? I wish. No, I'd have to start up another agency. I can't give it up yet. I just think the caliber of clients would be a lot different."

"From what I hear, there's a lot of money in Vero Beach."

Archie nodded. "That's what Luther tells me. I'd probably pick up a lot more of those genteel jobs. You know, jobs where you don't get punched out. Rich husbands cheating on rich wives."

"So, what you're telling me is, you're looking for a better class of criminal."

He laughed. "Yeah, I guess that's what I'm hoping for."

Stephanie frowned, "You're serious about this, aren't you."

Archie saw the look of alarm on her face. "I am. To tell you the truth, I've been thinking about this ever since I got out of the hospital in April. I think last night just made my decision for me." He paused. "But your job is still there, if you'd like to move, too."

She shook her head. "Thank you for that, but with Mother and everything, I can't leave. I've lived here for twenty-seven years. I'm not about to pick up and start over at this stage of the game."

Chapter 3

Luther P. Johnson stepped back and watched the glazier finish applying gold letters on the large plate glass window facing 21st Street. He read them aloud, "A. Archibald, Private Investigator." He turned to Archie, "Why did your parents give you the same first and last name?"

Archie smiled. "Not too creative, I guess. Do you know how many times I've been asked that question?"

Luther laughed. "Plenty, I'm sure. " He slapped Archie on the back. "Man, I'm so happy you got up here. Here it was, only a month ago you called me and asked me to start looking for a building, and now you're all moved in. I think we should probably go fishing, you know, to celebrate."

"Sounds good to me. I remember those days when we'd go out to Loxahatchee. Big gators and great fishing." Archie glanced at his watch. "But not today. First, I have to hire a secretary. I've got some interviews starting in ten minutes. Come in the office and hang around for awhile. You can help me out."

They walked into the building. "Everything smells new in here," Luther said, sniffing the air. "New paint, new furniture."

"Let me give you a tour," Archie said. He pointed to an open foyer directly in front of them. "I've got new leather couches over here. This is where my clients can wait if I'm busy in my office. They can see my assistant's desk over here." Archie walked Luther twenty feet to the left. "I have a nice new desk and chair for my soon-to-be-hired assistant. Brand new computer with a printer over here and two filing cabinets behind her desk."

"Looks nice, Archie. Looks very classy."

"Hey, it's Vero, what do you expect," Archie said with a laugh. "Cost me a bundle. You see this corridor behind the assistant's desk?" he continued. "That leads to a small coffee area and the bathroom. Come on, I'll show you."

He marched Luther down the hallway. "Want coffee? I'll put on a pot"

"No thanks. I see you got a lot of storage back here." Luther stopped. "What's all this stuff?" He pointed to several shelves filled with all kinds of gadgets and devices.

"The tools of the trade, my friend." Archie picked up a small round clock. "See this?"

"A clock?"

"You're right. It's a clock with a small pinhole camera built in."

"No kidding!" Luther said, handing him the device.

"We've got magnetic bugs that will ping a signal every few seconds, listening devices so small you'd never spot them, night vision glasses, the works!"

Luther stared at all of the hardware. "Just like James Bond!"

Archie laughed. "We're more advanced compared to the first Bond movies. It's a new digital world out there."

"See this door?" Archie asked. "This is the back way into my office. You can go in from the main door in front but I can also come out this way and go out the back door, if I want to."

"Sneaky," Luther said. "Let's take a look at your office."

Archie opened the door and they stepped inside. Luther saw a set-up very much like what Archie had in place for his secretary.

"Very impressive!" He plopped down in Archie's tall leather chair and leaned back into the soft padding. "Hmm, now that's comfy!"

Archie laughed, "Don't want it to be too comfortable. I need to get some work done."
Luther got up and they exited the office from the front door and ended up back in the open foyer area.

"Now I've got to start paying for it. I hope I can find a secretary soon." Archie took out his wallet, pulled out a business card and tossed it to Luther. "Here you go. My business card. Brand new. Just picked them up this morning."

As soon as Archie finished his sentence, a tall woman, who appeared to be in her early twenties, approached the building. She had short black hair combed into a peak on the top of her head. The sides of her head were shaved close, and her left arm was covered in a colorful tattoo sleeve. She had a piercing in her nose, and both ears sported silver earrings which ran from the tops down to her lobes. She looked over at the gilded lettering on the window and opened the door. She glanced at Luther and then looked over to Archie. "Which one of ya'll is Mr. Archibald?"

Archie stepped forward. "That's me." He picked up a manila folder from the coffee table and pulled out a piece of paper. "Ms. Scroggins?"

"Yeah, but you can call me Tonya, honey."

Archie motioned, "I'd like you to meet my friend Luther. Come with me, Ms. Scroggins, we'll do the interview in my office, if you don't mind."

Luther stood up. "Hello, nice to meet you."

Archie walked slowly toward his office. He didn't like strangers to notice his limp. Halfway to the door, Archie turned back to Luther and said, "We'll be out in about twenty minutes. Let the next candidate know if they show up before I'm finished."

"Will do, Archie," Luther said, sitting back down on the couch.

Twenty-five minutes later, another woman approached the building. She pulled open the door and looked in. Luther stood up.

"I'm here to see Mr. Archibald."

"Hello. Mr. Archibald's busy with an interview. He should be out shortly. Please have a seat." He motioned for her to sit down in a chair next to the couch. Luther leaned over and extended his hand. "Luther P. Johnson."

"Candace Muldoon," she said, shaking his hand. Candace studied Luther's face. "Don't you coach ball down at the Fellsmere Park?"

"Yes, I do," Luther said, taking a closer look. "Oh, you're Evan's mother, right?"

"Yes, I am. How nice to see you. Do you work here?"

He laughed. "No. Mr. Archibald's is a good friend of mine."

Candace was dressed in a conservative business suit. Her hair was black and cut short. She stood about five-feet six, and she was wearing two inch heels.

The door to Archie's office opened, and he and Tonya Scroggins walked out. "Thank you for your time, Ms. Scroggins. I have several more interviews scheduled for today. I'll give you a call by the end of the week to let you know my decision."

Archie escorted Tonya out the main door and turned to Luther.

Luther stood up. "I'd like you to meet Candace Muldoon." Candace rose and reached for Archie's hand.

He just stood there for a moment. "Ah, oh yes...Archie...Archie Archibald. Nice to meet you. I hope you weren't waiting too long. Let's step into my office. Could I get you a cup of coffee?"

Thirty minutes later, Luther heard the door open and Archie and Candace walked out. Archie walked her to the front door. "Thank you, Ms. Muldoon. As we discussed, I have a few more candidates to talk to. I'll call you before the end of the week."

Candace walked out to the sidewalk and Archie closed the door. He and Luther stayed at the window and watched as she walked across the street.

"I know her boy," Luther said. "He comes down to the field and helps me out."

"No kidding," Archie said. "Is he on a team?"

"No. He's in a wheelchair." Luther paused, "How did she do?"

"She did just fine. Only problem is, she used to be the personal assistant to the president of a big orange grove that just closed up. Selling the land for development. I doubt if she'd want to work for what I'm offering."

Luther said, "Depends on how bad she needs a job."

"I guess."

Luther stopped talking and stared out the window. "There he is now."

Archie watched as Candace walked across the street. As she stepped onto the sidewalk, another woman came around the corner of the building, pushing a small wheelchair. The other woman was taller than Candace but they shared similar features.

"That's got to be her sister," Archie said.

Candace had bent down and was speaking to the child when the kid started to cry. The other woman also knelt down and started talking, but it only seemed to make matters worse. The kid's face was getting red, and they could hear the crying all the way across the street.

Luther took a step closer to the window. "Yeah, that's Evan all right."

"I wonder what's got him so upset."

"He's a good kid. He comes down to the ball field and helps me out all the time. He's a baseball fanatic. Knows every statistic you can think of."

"Let me see if anything's wrong," Archie said. He pushed open the door and stepped outside. Luther followed behind.

The two men crossed the street, and Archie asked, "Is everything okay?"

Candace looked up and said, "Oh, Mr. Archibald. Yes, yes…everything's fine. My son's just a little upset. He'll be okay in a moment." She turned back to the sobbing child. "Evan, please. It's not that bad."

Candace's sister pulled Archie aside. "I'm really sorry for the commotion. I'm Candace's sister, Estelle."

"Nice to meet you, Estelle."

"It's just that we've had to stop Evan's therapy for now. You know, with Candace not

The Black Orchid Mystery

working. The poor little guy. He wanted to know if she got the job, and she tried to explain that she'll know by the end of the week. Evan really doesn't know how it works and all, so he just knew she didn't say yes. I'm sorry if we caused a scene."

Luther bent down and put his hand on the boy's shoulder. "Hello, Evan. What's the problem?"

The boy looked up and tried to stop crying. He wiped his face with his shirt sleeve. "Hi, Coach." He wiped his face again and looked down at the ground.

Archie turned from Estelle and looked over at the boy. "Well, we can solve this problem right here and now." Archie walked back to Candace, "Ms. Muldoon, would it be possible for you to start working tomorrow morning, say ten a.m.?"

Candace stood up. "What? I thought you had several other people to interview?"

Archie smiled, "Why waste time with that when I'm sure you'll be perfect for the job."

"Really? Are you sure?"

Archie smiled. "Yes."

Candace kneeled next to Evan, "Did you hear that? I got the job, just like you were hoping for."

Candace stood back up and shook Archie's hand. "Thank you, Mr. Archibald. You…you won't regret it."

Archie turned to Luther, "Come on, I've got some appointments to cancel."

Once they got back to the office, Luther said, "That was a surprise. Do you really think she's going to work out?"

Archie laughed. "I hope so. She did really well in the interview. I'm sure she'll be making quite a bit less money working here. I just hope she sticks around."

Chapter 4

The Silverman Estate sat on a sixty acre peninsula that jutted out into the blue-green waters of the Atlantic Ocean just north of Vero Beach. Franklin Silverman started building the mansion in 1951 as a Florida retreat for his beautiful young wife, Clara.

When Franklin was scouting around the acreage looking for the perfect place to construct the house, he discovered several rare black orchids growing on the property. He made note of their location and hired a horticulturist to start propagating them while the house was under construction.

Franklin came from old money that could be traced back to his great, great grandfather in Fairfield County, Connecticut. He dabbled in several occupations but his fascination with the entertainment business allowed Franklin to use his family fortune to set himself up as a popular game show producer in Hollywood, California.

Television audiences were enthralled with game shows during the fifties, and his shows became very popular. Blessed with good looks and the confidant charm that being rich provided, Franklin fit in very well with the more established directors and producers of the time. And, his reputation of taking full advantage of the casting couch ritual, didn't hurt with the major players, either. Some said he built his Florida retreat as far from Hollywood as possible to keep his beautiful young bride from keeping track of him.

It took two years to construct the ornate fifty-two room mansion. The house was constructed with marble brought over from France, and the grounds resembled a scaled down version of the famous Chateaux-viex.

Once the estate was finished, Franklin dug a canal across the front of the heavily wooded property, turning the peninsula into an island. He had a drawbridge and large stone walls constructed in order to keep out what he called 'the bad elements'.

He named the property Black Orchid Island after the rare plants that populated the swampy areas throughout his land. Many artifacts of Spanish settlements had been discovered when the mansion was being constructed. While the house and grounds were very important from both an architectural and historical perspective, most people had only heard of the place. Very few had actually seen it.

Recently, the site gained the potential of even greater historical value when some historians theorized that the Estate was the spot where Ponce De

Leon had actually landed in Florida, far to the south of the more recognized St. Augustine landing. There was also a huge natural spring on the property, and some suggested that this was the original fountain of youth Ponce De Leon supposedly discovered.

If that was the case, it wasn't doing much good for eighty-four year old Clara Silverman who was lying upstairs in an ornate bed in the largest of 14 bedrooms the mansion contained.

Clara had lived alone in the mansion, not counting the help, since 1955 when a disgruntled contestant from one of Franklin's shows went to authorities and provided evidence that the games on the show were fixed. Franklin's sponsors immediately demanded that their million dollars be returned. After a very public trial, Franklin was convicted and ended up being sentenced to five to ten years in the infamous Rikers Island Prison with its dank view of the East river.

At the start of the investigation, Franklin was smart enough to transfer all of his money to his wife. Unfortunately, three years into his sentence, Franklin contracted pneumonia and died alone in his cell. With Franklin's death, thirty year old Clara, became one of the wealthiest women in America.

After Franklin's death, Clara took to wearing long black dresses that trailed behind her; and whenever she was seen in public, she wore a veil over her face. As she got older, her hair turned to a silver gray. The contrast of the long, silver hair against the darkness of her veil and dress was quite startling.

She hadn't left the mansion in ten years, but during her last outing, a young photographer in New York had managed to take a picture of her when she attended an award dinner in her honor. She had contributed two million dollars to the International Orchid Society when they renamed the black orchid found on her property Oncidium silvermanium. That gala event was the last time she had been seen in public. A quick photograph snapped by an Associated Press photographer, featuring her long silver hair and dark veil, became the image the world would forever associate her with.

Over the years, interest in Clara came and went, but with rumors spreading that a new wing of the huge Saint Francis hospital in Los Angeles was to be named in her honor, more stories about her were appearing in magazines and television.

Clara tried to sit up in bed. She struggled as she reached for a glass of water. *This getting old was for the birds*, she thought. Eighty-four was not turning out to be a good age for her. The year before, she was sharp and full of energy. Now, she found it was almost impossible to get out of bed. She picked up a pill from the nightstand. *Maybe it was this new medicine?* She tried to remember if she had had more energy before she started taking those pills. She struggled to remember just how long it had been. Her mind was in a fog. She lay her head back down on the pillow and tried to clear her mind.

Clara saw the bedroom door slowly open. She saw a dark figure come close to the bed. Clara tried to see who it was, but the light was too dim. She felt as if she were being lifted up from the bed. *Was it a dream?* she wondered.

Chapter 5

Sonny Porter grimaced as the buzzing tattoo gun traced the outline of an iron cross on his chest. The rail-thin young man standing next to him looked down at his own arms which were covered with tattoos. "How you gonna explain this to Francine when you get home?"

"Shut up, Billy. Maybe that's what you have to do at your house, but I don't have to explain nothin' in mine."

Billy laughed. "Okay, okay...I just know Francine's gonna throw a fit about you spending more money on another tattoo is all."

Sonny jerked like he was going to get up.

"Settle down, Sonny," the tattoo artist said. "Ya want me to screw up or what?"

Across town, Sonny's wife walked into Gray's Drugstore and looked around. She walked down aisle 3 and paused in front of a display of pregnancy test kits. She glanced behind her and then reached over and picked one up.

"Well just look at that, Francine. Is there going to be another addition to the family? Oh, your father will be so happy!"

Francine threw the kit back into the bin and spun around. She was horrified to see Ardell Hayes standing there. Francine grabbed her by both arms. "Please, Ardell. Don't say anything about this to no one. Especially not my father. I need to talk to Sonny first."

Ardell's eyes got wide. She shook herself out of Francine's grip. "You know me better than that, Francine. If you don't want nobody to know, then you can count on me. I'll be as quiet as a church mouse. But I'd say it's way overdue for little Ronnie to have a brother or sister to play with. What is he, about nine years old by now?"

Francine gave her a weak smile, "He's twelve, and thank you, Ardell. I know I can count on you."

As she walked away, Francine wondered how she was going to break the news to Sonny. It had to happen that night after supper. With Ardell in the picture, she knew she didn't have much time.

Archie drummed his fingers and looked out the window. "This is ridiculous. We've been here over a week now, and the only person who's walked in tried to sell me a magazine subscription."

"Did you ever consider placing a few ads?" Candace asked.

"Where?" Archie asked. "The radio? The newspaper? I can't afford television. I need to watch my cash flow. Where do you suggest?"

"Maybe you should start with those freebies that people can pick up. I'm sure it's not very expensive to take an ad out there."

He glanced over at Candace. "We've got to do something. I can't keep paying out rent money for an empty office. Maybe this isn't the right location."

"What do you mean? The rent's reasonable and the street gets some traffic. Does a detective office really need a special location? I thought people needing your services would go to the trouble of finding you. Don't forget, you're new to this area."

"I know. But it didn't seem like it took this long to get going in Ft. Lauderdale." He paused. "Maybe it did. It was a long time ago."

"This town's full of old money. They stick together. Since nobody knows you, it could take awhile for you to 'break in,' so to speak."

Archie tossed down his newspaper. "I don't have time to wait to be discovered. Why don't you find a few of those papers and get some ads placed this afternoon."

Candace turned back to her computer screen. "I'll look them up right now." Ten minutes later she turned to Archie. "Okay, that's done. They should show up by the middle of next week." She walked over to the coffee pot. "Ready for a refill?"

"Sure," he said, holding up his cup.

She brought Archie a new cup and sat down in the chair across from his desk. "What brought you to the Vero area, anyway? Didn't you have a thriving practice down in Ft. Lauderdale?"

He laughed. "Not sure if you'd call it thriving. I did have steady work, but things were changing." Archie related his last few encounters with the South American gangs and why they had made him change his mind.

Candace thought for a moment. "I can see why you'd want to get out of there. You got any family around here?"

He frowned. "No. I was married when I first moved down to Fort Lauderdale, but it didn't last."

"How long ago was that?"

He paused. "It has to be about twenty some years ago, now. Time sure goes by fast." Archie took a sip of coffee. "We had a little girl. Not long after that my, wife started getting homesick, and she begged me to move back to Dayton."

"Dayton?" Candace said, "I had an Uncle stationed there in the Air Force."

"He must have been at Wright-Patterson. I didn't want to move back to Ohio. Put up with that snow and cold, and get some factory job. My business was starting to pick up. The last thing I wanted to do was go back up North."

"So what happened?"

"I got home late one night after a stake-out, and the place was empty. She packed up all their things, and she left with the kid."

"Just like that?" Candace said, raising her eyebrows.

"Just like that. I tried to keep in touch. I visited my daughter during the summer but then my ex met some biker guy and they made it known I wasn't welcome anymore. I mailed my support checks every month until my daughter turned eighteen, but I haven't heard from her or seen her since she was fifteen."

"That's sad," Candace said. "What's her name?"

"Amanda. I tried to find her a few years ago. I drove back to Ohio, but my ex told me she had moved out, and she wasn't going to tell her I was in town because she didn't want to see me anyway."

"What did you do?"

"I just turned around and drove back to Florida."

Candace twirled her hair. "Well, that was your bitter ex talking. Maybe Amanda would have wanted to see you."

"I didn't get that feeling."

Candace leaped up. "I know! You should try to find her on-line."

"I've thought about that," Archie said. "I tried a few times but never really got anywhere."

She let out a laugh. "And here I thought you were a detective!"

Archie looked embarrassed. "Yeah, I know. I'm pretty good with the computer, but I'm not up on all this social media the kids are using these days. Maybe if I was thirty years younger." Archie paused.

The Black Orchid Mystery

"Wait a minute. I'm sure you're a lot more versed in that stuff than I am. Maybe you can find her for me. It's not like you've got a ton of caseloads to keep you busy."

Candace smiled, grabbed a piece of paper and scribbled down some of the things Archie had told her. "Maybe I can. By the way, since you don't have any family around here, do you have any plans for Thanksgiving?"

"Thanksgiving?" Archie asked.

"Yes. It's this Thursday, you know. I'm not planning to be in the office."

"I don't know," Archie said. "I never gave it any thought. I'll probably see what Luther's doing. Maybe we can go to a restaurant someplace around here."

Candace turned up her nose. "A restaurant? Who wants to do that? You and Luther should come over to my place. I'm cooking a turkey and my sister's bringing all the fixin's."

"Oh, I don't know about that," Archie said. "I don't want to be a bother."

"Bother? Are you kidding? Anyway, I need someone to pick out a few bottles of wine." Candace stopped and thought for a moment. Suddenly her face lit up. "Maybe we can go on an airboat ride?"

Archie laughed. "An airboat ride? On Thanksgiving?"

"That's what Estelle does. She has an eco-tourist business and gives airboat rides out in the swamp just west of here."

"Who drives the thing?" Archie asked.

"I told you, Estelle and a few of her employees."

"Are you kidding? She looks so…um…feminine."

Candace laughed. "I know. But, she's a tough one. You wouldn't think so from looking at her, but she can hold her own out in the swamp. We're so different. I have a fit when I see a bug!"

"That's amazing," Archie said, conjuring up an image of Candace's sister. "About Thanksgiving, let me see what plans Luther has." Archie heard the front door open. He glanced up with a look of hope. "Speak of the devil!" Archie said.

Luther walked in, stood in the middle of the floor and looked around. "Looks nice. Even better than before. Now you got plants and pictures. Hey, did you call me a devil?"

"I did. We were just talking about you when you walked in." Archie looked around. "It does look pretty good, doesn't it? Didn't think we'd get this far so fast. But it wasn't me, Luther. It was Candace. She was able to add all the finishing touches. Now all we need is some clients. In fact, I was hoping you were one when I heard that door open."

Luther laughed. "I'm sure they'll be coming. Just you wait and see." Luther looked over at Candace and then glanced back to Archie. "There's a great diner just down the street. Anyone interested in having some lunch?"

Archie stood up and hesitated. His leg was hurting again. "Might as well. Nothing's going on

The Black Orchid Mystery

here." He turned to Candace. "Come with us. We can put an out-to-lunch sign up for half an hour."

"No thanks, Archie. You know that's when our first client would show up. Anyway, I brought my lunch today."

Archie slowly headed toward the door, trying not to limp. "Okay, I'll be back in about half an hour." Archie paused. "Just in case anyone's looking for me," he said with a smirk.

Candace waved her hand. "Yeah, right. Oh, Archie, before you leave, what year did your daughter graduate from high school?"

Luther held open the door for Archie. "Two years ago. I sent up a nice gift and never heard a thing."

"Okay, enjoy your lunch," Candace said, as she turned back to the computer.

As Archie and Luther were heading out the door, Candace got up and walked over. "Oh, I just remembered. My sister may stop by with Evan this afternoon to see the office. Would you mind?"

"Mind? No, not at all."

"Thank you. When Evan found out I was working at a detective office, he almost came unglued. He's been begging me to let him come by and see the place."

Archie let out a laugh. "He's been watching too much TV. I'm afraid he'll be bored silly after a few minutes here."

"Knowing Evan, probably not. He's got such an active imagination, I'm sure he'll dream up something."

Archie and Luther crossed the street, meandered one block east and walked into the Alligator Tail diner. It was only a few years old, but it looked as if it had been built sometime in the fifties. The outside was covered in chrome, and all the booths had the red vinyl covering that was so popular back in the day.

As they slid into a booth, Luther grabbed a menu but didn't look at it. He stared out the window instead. He turned to Archie. "Look how nice it is today. If you ask me, it looks like a fine day to do a little fishin'. What you say after lunch we both take a ride out to Blue Cypress Lake and give it a try?"

Archie looked up from his menu, "I wish. Sorry, but I need to generate some business, Luther. I can't be taking the afternoon off."

"Didn't look like you were generating anything but some small talk when I stopped in."

"We're in the process of putting together a new website. I'm so glad I found Candace. From working at the grove, she's got some great marketing ideas. I'm lucky to have her."

"I'm glad she's working out."

The waitress came by and they both ordered.

"Oh, by the way, Candace wanted me to ask you if you have any plans for Thanksgiving?"

Luther scratched his chin. "That's coming up this Thursday, isn't it? I hadn't paid it no mind."

"To tell you the truth, neither had I. With setting up the new office and everything, I never even thought about it. Anyway, if you don't have any plans, we've been invited over to Candace's place."

"Really? Luther thought for a minute. "That sounds like a great idea. What can I bring?"

"Don't ask me. You'll have to ask Candace when we get back to the office."

Sixteen blocks away, Sanford Leeds' corvette flew over the Merril P. Barber Bridge and turned left onto Ocean Avenue. Three miles later, he slammed on the brakes, made a hard right turn, and raced down a narrow lane that seemed to meld into the thick surrounding tropical foliage.

Sanford drove about a quarter of a mile and squealed to a stop in front of a huge wrought iron gate festooned with mermaids and manatees. He pushed a button in his car, and the gate slowly swung open. Sanford continued along the driveway as it wound through a dense tropical hammock. He loosened his tie and unbuttoned the top button of his shirt. He could feel the humidity rise the farther he drove down the lane. The sides of the road were lined with wild coffee bushes. Their thick, shiny, green leaves made an impenetrable wall, broken now and then by the red peeling bark of tall Gumbo Limbo trees. Florida Oaks spread their giant limbs over the road, blocking out most of the bright sun.

Finally, Sanford's car left the shaded tree covering and broke into an open meadow. Acres of close clipped St. Augustine grass formed a green blanket that lead up to the Silverman estate.

Sanford had been Clara Silverman's lawyer for the last four years, ever since his father passed away. Having one of the richest women in Florida as your client did wonderful things for your business and reputation. The last thing he needed was to have something happen now. He got out from the car, walked up to the massive oak front doors and pounded on the solid brass knocker. Three trips to the gym each week and almost daily runs along the beach gave him a much younger look than one would expect for his 53 years. Sanford pounded on the door again. He could hear waves from the Atlantic Ocean crashing on the beach behind the house.

The right door swung open, and Enrique Vasquez, Mrs. Silverman's chauffer and part-time body guard, motioned for him to enter.

Sanford walked into the foyer and, without stopping, said, "Go get Gloria and James and meet me upstairs in the study."

When Enrique, James Harrow, and Gloria Rodriguez entered the room a few minutes later, Sanford was pacing back and forth in front of a floor to ceiling bookcase overflowing with first editions and assorted rare volumes. He heard them enter and spun around. "Are you sure about this? Where haven't you looked? She's eighty-four years old, and the richest woman in Florida! How could this happen?"

Gloria stood five feet four with dark hair streaked with gray. She was wearing a black smock with an apron tied around her waist. Gloria had come to this country from Cuba when she was sixteen, but she still had a Spanish accent. She was the first to speak. "I don't know, Mr. Leeds. Three hours ago I went to her room to check on her like always, and she was not in her bed. I think maybe she could be in the bathroom, so I sit on the edge of the bed and waited. I don't hear nothing. So after ten minutes, I tap on the bathroom door and call out her name. When she not answer me, I get scared and open the door. She not in there. Then I called Enrique and James. We started checking the house. With all these rooms, it took a long time. We were looking everywhere. Still, we no find her. Then we go all over the house. We no find her again, so then I call you."

"Did you check all the other floors?" Sanford asked. "My God, there's over fifty rooms here."

"Yes, sir," Gloria said, nodding her head.

"What about the guest compound?"

"We look there, too."

Sanford turned away from Gloria. "James? What do you think is going on?"

James Harrow was a slight man in his late fifties. He was always impeccably dressed, and his salt and pepper hair was close cut, never a hair out of place. He had a small moustache that was much darker than the hair on his head. For years he had been a cook at a mansion Mrs. Silverman owned in Devonshire, England. He used to accompany Mrs. Silverman to whatever house she was staying in, but since she hadn't traveled in over ten years, he had remained in Florida.

James coughed discretely into a monogrammed handkerchief and said, "Well, sir, as Ms. Rodriguez explained, I joined Enrique in the search as well. I checked all the bays in the garage and then I went through the four guest suites."

"What about the area above the suites? Did you look in the recreation room and the offices?" Sanford asked.

"Yes, yes. I checked those, too. She wasn't there, and I didn't see anything that looked out of place. That's when we called you. It is puzzling, sir."

"Puzzling! It's a damn abomination! She must be outside. Maybe she wanted to get some air. Did you check the grounds?"

"No," Enrique said. "Mrs. Silverman would sit on the porch off her bedroom when she wanted to be outside. As you know, that's on the second floor. Besides, I don't think she could have walked more than a few feet without someone's help."

James added, "We checked all the doors and they seemed to be in order. Properly locked, you know."

Sanford ran his fingers through his hair. "I know, I know…but we have to do something. Come on, let's take a walk around the grounds."

Forty-five minutes later the group met back in the foyer. Sanford had draped his suit coat over his shoulder; he was perspiring heavily. "Did you find anything?"

Enrique, James, and Gloria all shook their heads. James took out his handkerchief and wiped the tops of his shoes. Sanford looked exasperated. He tossed his coat over the back of a chair. "Did you see anything at all that looked out of place? Footprints, tire tracks, pieces of clothing?"

"No, I didn't see anything like that," Gloria said, glancing over toward Enrique. She paused. "But I did see an alligator in the pond over by the gardens."

"He's been there for more than a year now," Enrique said. "I don't think he's the reason Mrs. Silverman's gone missing."

"Wretched creature. It should be removed, but she would never agree to it," James said, with a disgusted look on his face.

Sanford picked up his coat and headed toward the study. "Come on, let's check the answering machine." On the way, he asked Gloria, "Tell me again how long it was from the last time you saw Mrs. Silverman until you discovered she was gone."

"I peeked in last night around eleven and she was sleeping. I get up today, make some breakfast, get her tray ready, and walk up to her room. When I open the door, she wasn't in bed. Like I told you, I think maybe she's in the bathroom, so I waited. Then I don't hear no sounds, so I tap on the door. She not in there."

Sanford turned to Enrique, "Has anyone visited the Estate today? Any vendors, sales people, maintenance men?"

"No, sir. Nobody's been on the property. I heard the alarm sound when you opened the gate. That's the only time it's gone off today."

"What about in the last few days?" Sanford said.

"I had to throw that photographer off the property again," Enrique said.

"Russell Craig? Is he still coming over here?" Sanford asked, with a look of amazement.

"Yeah, it seems like he goes in spurts. I don't see him for a few months, and then I catch him two or three times in a row."

"I told that jerk I was going to get a restraining order on him. Looks like I'm going to have to do it. He didn't get any pictures, did he?"

"Not of Mrs. Silverman," Enrique said. "He could have taken some of the estate."

Sanford turned to James. "What about you? Did you notice anything unusual?"

"I've been in the kitchen most of the morning, sir," James replied. "I helped them look through the house. But I didn't run across anything that looked out of the ordinary."

Sanford nodded. "Well, if you don't have anything else to tell me, James, you can go back to whatever you were doing."

"Certainly, sir." James turned and walked down the hallway. Sanford looked at Gloria. "Have you been giving Mrs. Silverman her medicine like I've asked you to?"

Gloria nodded. "Yes, Mr. Leeds."

"Good." Sanford walked over to the answering machine and saw the light was blinking. He pressed the play button.

"Gloria, its Nancy Abbott. This message is to remind Mrs. Silverman I'll be coming by tomorrow for our three o'clock appointment. I'll have the two paintings we discussed last week. She's expecting me, but I thought I'd call and remind her. Oh, could you be a dear and have the gate open for me? Thank you."

Sanford's face turned to a scowl as he looked up at Gloria and Enrique. "If Clara's still missing tomorrow, not a word of this to Ms. Abbott, or anyone else. Is that clear? She can be quite a gossip."

They both nodded.

"We have to find Mrs. Silverman, that's all there is to it. Enrique, I want you to go back outside and check around the grounds again. Start at the front door and walk around in larger and larger circles. Search the perimeter of the woods if you have to, and keep an eye out for anything that could help us. Do you understand?"

Enrique shot Sanford a glare as he headed back to the front door. He looked back, "There's over fifty acres here and about forty of it's woods and wetlands. It would take an army to look through all that."

"I can't believe she'd walk into the middle of the woods," Sanford said. "I just spoke to her yesterday, and she didn't exhibit any signs of dementia. Quite the contrary. Take the golf cart and check what you can."

He turned toward Gloria. "Go get James. I'm going to search the second floor again. You cover the downstairs. James can look at the third and fourth floors."

"But you closed off those floors. Why do we need to check them?"

"Because we don't know where Mrs. Silverman is, that's why," Sanford said, trying not to sound irritated.

Gloria didn't respond. She just looked tired.

Outside, Enrique slowly walked around the grounds, keeping his head down, looking for anything out of the ordinary. *I'm not going into those woods*, he thought. He had seen four foot black snakes out there, and once he had killed a pygmy rattlesnake out by the pool.

Back at the office, Candace looked up when Archie and Luther walked in from lunch. "Did I miss anything?" Archie joked. Candace ignored him.

"Did Evan stop by?" Luther asked.

"Not yet. My sister called. She's picking something up at Neisner's Toy Shop. They should be here in a few minutes."

"Luther, did you know Candace's sister drives an airboat out in the swamp?"

"What?" Luther asked. "An airboat?"

"Yes, can you believe it? She runs an eco-tourist company somewhere west of here."

"Out at that place called Gator Junction?"

"That's it," Candace replied.

"I should have known that," Luther said. "I've seen her ads on TV. She looked much more, how should I say this…citified, when we saw her the other day."

Candace laughed. "I know. I won't let her walk around Vero wearing the safari suit and pith helmet she wears at work."

Archie said. "By the way, Luther and I talked about it at lunch, and we'd be happy to come over for Thanksgiving. What can we bring?"

Candace thought for a moment, "Like I said, some wine would be nice?"

"I make a mean sweet potato casserole," Luther said. "I put those little marshmallows on top, the whole works."

Candace's face lit up. "That would be perfect. You bring the casserole and Archie can bring some wine. How about coming around three o'clock?"

Just then the front door swung open and Evan entered the office, pushing the wheels of his wheelchair. Estelle followed behind. Candace took one look at her son and burst out laughing. "Evan, what do you have there?"

Evan looked slightly embarrassed but quickly recovered. "Aunt Estelle bought it for me," he said with a serious look on his face. He was holding a huge magnifying glass in his right hand. He had a black curved plastic meerschaum pipe in his mouth, and he was wearing a plaid deer slayer hat on his head.

Archie bent down to get a closer look. "I do believe we've got a miniature Sherlock Holmes right here in the office." Archie reached over to shake Evan's hand. "Welcome to the office, Evan. Looks like we'll need to make you an honorary detective in the firm!"

Evan's face beamed. "Really! That's cool! What's my first case, Mr. Archibald?"

Archie thought for a moment. "Good question. Since we just opened a few days ago, we're still waiting for one. But, I'll tell you what, that big magnifying glass of yours could come in very handy. Once we get a case, you'll be the first to know."

Evan pushed himself up and stepped out of his chair. "I want to walk now."

Candace stood up from behind her desk. "Are you sure, Evan?"

Evan nodded. "I'm okay."

Candace looked over at her sister. "Okay. Come on. I'll give you both a quick tour." It was all she could do not to laugh every time she glanced down at her son as he was examining every surface with his magnifying glass.

Once the tour was over, Estelle said, "Thanks, everyone. He's been talking about coming over here non-stop ever since he found out where Candace worked. We're going to head back to my house." She stopped and thought. "Hey, maybe he can find out who's been stealing my paper every night."

Evan climbed back into his chair. He looked tired.

Once they left, Candace turned back to Archie. "Thanks for letting him come by. Did you see how excited he was?"

Archie smiled. "I'm happy they stopped in. Now that I think about it, maybe I should get a hat like that."

"Not a bad idea," Luther chimed in. "You get yourself a hat like that and then I can be your Doctor Watson." Luther glanced around the empty office. "Hey, Archie, looks like this may be a great time for you to sneak out for a little fishing. You know, before it starts to get busy."

Archie shrugged out of his sport coat and tossed it onto the sofa. "You never give up, do you? Not going to happen. You never know when a potential customer may come walking in."

"Okay, okay. Some other time," Luther said, heading for the door.

Archie waited for Luther to leave and then turned to Candace. "Can I ask you a question?"

"Sure."

"Evan. I noticed he got up from his wheelchair."

A look of concern came over Candace's face. "It's strange, Archie. Evan started needing to use that chair about seven months ago. His legs started to get weak, and he would get real tired."

"Seven months ago?"

"Yes. Since then he's had every test you can imagine. They've got a few ideas, but nobody's come up with a definitive cause. I'm taking him in next week to see another doctor."

Archie didn't know what to say. "Well, don't worry about taking time off work. We're not exactly busy. Let me know if there's anything I can do to help."

"Thanks, Archie. I will."

Chapter 6

Twenty miles northwest of Vero Beach, Sonny Porter's shaved head was glistening with sweat. He was running down a narrow trail in the middle of a thick tropical forest. His camouflaged army fatigues were starting to stick to him, and there were growing dark green stains under his arms. He turned to the two men running behind and shouted, "Come on, only three more miles till we get to the pond!" Sonny ran for another ten minutes and then turned and looked behind him. "Billy, keep up. Don't fall behind!"

After another ten minutes, they slowed down to a fast walk until they could catch their breath. All wore green and brown camouflaged clothing and army issued sand colored boots. An M-16 was strapped over their shoulders.

The Black Orchid Mystery

Suddenly, Sonny grabbed his rifle, spread his legs, took aim and squeezed off a few rounds into the pond. The other men spun around. "What the hell was that?" shouted the tall, lanky man behind Billy. He pulled off a green baseball cap and started to fan his face with it.

"Gator," Sonny said. "Don't get so jumpy, Skip."

"Don't you be killing any gators out here," Skip said. "You know they're protected, and we don't need to be calling no attention to ourselves."

"And just who the hell's gonna find a dead gator way the hell out here?" Sonny asked. "My father-in-law's got twelve hundred acres, and we're smack dab in the middle of it." Sonny spit on the ground and wiped sweat off of his shaved head. "Come on, let's get over to the range."

The men followed Sonny single file down an even narrower trail that led to an open clearing with a four foot mound of dirt at one end. Rows of targets were lined up in front of the dirt. Some of the targets were bulls-eyes but most of them where either human silhouettes or detailed graphics of various ethnic types. Starting at the left was a row of targets depicting black men in various menacing stances. The next group was made up of pictures of Hispanic looking gang members. Finally, at the far right was a group of oriental men, all in various karate stances.

"Take your places!" Sonny shouted. The men crouched down and aimed their rifles. "Fire!"

A blast of bullets streamed down range and tore the targets to shreds. Lead could be heard thumping into the dirt and trees at the end of the field. After several minutes of continuous fire, Sonny stood up and yelled, "Stop!"

The group put down their rifles and walked over to examine the targets. "Not bad...not bad at all," Sonny said, staring at the tattered remains. "Ok, let's put up a new batch and do it all again."

After an hour of shooting, Sonny signaled the others to stop. "Okay, boys. Enough for this week. Let's go. Step it up. We're going to do a forced march back to the truck."

Luther walked out of Archie's office and got into his car. He headed north on US 1 until he got to the small community of Wabasso. He turned left on County Road 510 and drove to Fellsmere Road. He glanced over to the back seat to make sure his gear was still in the car. He was disappointed that he couldn't talk Archie into going fishing. Luther glanced out the window. It was a beautiful day. Since he already had his tackle box and rod, Luther decided he would do a little fishing, even if he had to do it alone. He drove past the road that would take him home and continued through the farming community of Fellsmere. Luther slowed as he passed the Little League Park. He glanced at his watch. He needed to be back in two hours so he could coach his latest batch of up-and-coming baseball players.

Luther continued driving west for another four and a half miles on CR 512 until he came to a large pond that was one of his favorite fishing spots. He pulled the car over to the side of the road and was

The Black Orchid Mystery

relieved to see that nobody else was fishing there. He gathered up his gear from the back seat, walked over to the side of the pond, and started casting into the still blue-green water. There was a three foot alligator basking in the sunlight on a muddy bank over to the right, and a smaller gator was swimming in the middle of the pond. Luther was careful not to get his lure anywhere near them.

He heard the crunch of tires on gravel and looked over to see that a truck had pulled up and parked next to his car. Three men jumped out and started walking his way.

"Hey, boy, I do believe you're fishing in our spot," one of them called out.

"You tell'em, Sonny," another man called out.

Luther ignored the comment and threw out another cast.

"Did you not hear me, boy?"

"Plenty of people fish out of this spot, Mister. I'm sure there's enough fish for everyone," Luther said calmly.

"I do believe your type do their fishing down by Suckermouth Creek, don't they?" Sonny asked.

Luther stared at the man. "My type? Maybe fifty years ago, my friend, but that's all ancient history now."

"Maybe for some." Sonny walked closer. His two buddies stayed back a few steps. "I guess you didn't hear me the first time. This here's our fishing spot, and we're not in a sharing mood."

"Since this is county property, we all have the opportunity to use it," Luther said.

Sonny took a step closer. "And I'm telling you, old man, you got about two seconds to get your black ass back in your car and hightail it outta here, if you know what I mean."

He saw the shaved headed man spit on the ground next to his feet.

Luther slowly reeled in his line and then turned toward him. "I'm not going anywhere, Mister."

Sonny lunged at Luther, hitting him in the chest. Luther spun around and shoved the handle of his fishing pole into Sonny's stomach. Sonny let out a yelp and gasped for air. He took a wild swing at Luther and missed. Immediately, Sonny's other friend, Skip, jumped into the action. Luther didn't have time to think. He turned again and landed a blow on the side of Skip's head. Sonny jabbed at Luther's head. His Army training kicked in and Luther snapped his head back, just dodging Sonny's punch.

"Get him, Skip!" Sonny called out. Skip lunged at Luther from the side. Luther spun around in a quick arc and kicked him square in the knee cap. He heard a sharp crack followed by a high pitched scream as Skip rolled in the dirt clutching his leg.

Sonny's other friend, Billy, took one step toward the fighting, saw Skip rolling in the dirt and decided to stay where he was.

Sonny screamed, "You bastard!" and ran up to Luther from behind. He wrapped his arms around him and tried to wrestle him to the ground. Luther spread his legs wide and balanced his weight as best he could. He drove his left elbow deep into Sonny's ribcage and felt Sonny let go. Luther spun around and slammed the heel of his hand just under Sonny's nose. Sonny fell to his knees, blood pouring from his face.

Luther looked at the third man who was now kneeling over Skip. "What about you? You want to kick my black ass, too?"

Billy looked up in fear. "This ain't my fight. Hey, man, I don't even like to fish. It's cool, man. It's cool."

"You stay over there with your friends. Looks like they're going to need some medical attention," Luther said, as he bent down and picked up his fishing pole, which was now dangling in three parts. He walked over to his car and tossed the pieces into the back seat. He reached into the car, popped opened the glove box, pulled out his cell phone and dialed 911.

Twenty minutes later, a black Florida State Police car pulled up and parked behind Luther's car. A stocky trooper climbed out and surveyed the scene. He was wearing a tan smoky-the-bear hat and silvered sunglasses. From what he could see, two white men had obviously been beaten up. A third was sitting on the ground cradling his friend's twisted leg. An older black man was standing in the middle of all of this, holding a cell phone. The trooper rested his hand on his holstered revolver and slowly walked over to Luther. "Looks like someone's in a little bit of trouble here."

Billy jumped up. "Ya'all got that right, officer. This damned nig..." He stopped for a second. "This old lunatic attacked us 'cause we was at his fishing spot. This ol' boy needs to be locked up."

"Is that right?" the trooper asked, slowly taking a step closer to Luther. He moved his hand to his billy club and looked over at Sonny.

"Yes, sir!"

The Trooper took another step closer to Luther and asked in a loud voice, "How old are you now, Mr. Johnson?"

Luther looked puzzled. "What?"

"How old are you now?"

"I'm sixty-seven, Trooper Stephens."

"Ya hear that fellows," the trooper said, glancing over at the three men. "You got your asses kicked by a sixty-seven year old man." He let out a little chuckle. "Can you believe that?"

Billy said, "But wait..."

Trooper Stephens interrupted. "There's special laws in this state about messing with the elderly. The way I look at it, you're all in a heap of trouble."

Skip tried to stand up but took one step and tumbled back to the ground. "You gotta be shitting me. Look at us. This guy ain't got a scratch on him and we're all busted up. He's the one that should be in trouble."

Trooper Stephens walked over to the three men. "Boys, I've helped Mr. Johnson coach little league over at the park for six years now, and I've also fished with him right here at this location on many occasions. He's never had a problem with anyone else sharing this space." Stephens paused. "Oh, I'm also quite familiar with your buddy, Mr. Porter, over there and what he stands for. Looks like today you're all getting arrested for assault and battery on the elderly."

Billy scrambled to his feet. "Hey, wait a minute. We're the victims here. Just look at us."

Trooper Stephens moved his hand back down on his holster. "Sit down. For once you guys picked on someone who could handle himself. You're lucky Mr. Johnson didn't kill you all. I know his background. He's quite capable of that. If I were you, I'd do a little thinking about who your friends are. I imagine you'll have plenty of time to do that when this is all over."

Trooper Stephens looked at his watch. "You okay, Luther?"

"I'm fine. These amateurs didn't hardly land a blow." He walked over to the trooper and asked, "What did you say that guy's name was just now?"

Trooper Stephens glanced over at the three men sitting on the ground. "You mean Sonny Porter? The guy with the shaved head?"

"Yeah. Porter? I think his kid's on one of my teams."

"He's got a son about twelve years old. I've had to go over to his place a few times."

Luther frowned. "I bet Ronnie's his boy. Ain't that something. Sure explains a lot."

"What's that?" Stephens asked.

"I've never seen any kid so young with so much hate. I've been working my tail off trying to get to him, but I don't think I've even made a dent. I about tossed him out of the program twice, but then I knew if I did that, he wouldn't have a chance."

"Not surprised," Trooper Stephens said. "But I'm glad you're still trying. You've got the kids coming down to the park pretty soon, don't you?"

"Yeah, I should be heading over there about now." In the distance, Luther heard the sound on sirens heading in their direction.

"Ambulance will pick up these two. I'll take the other guy down to the station, and I'll swing by the field later and get your statement."

Sonny took his hand away from his bleeding nose long enough to shout, "Watch out, old man. We ain't done with you yet."

Trooper Stephens pulled out his notepad and scribbled down some notes. "Hmm, sounds like threat and intimidation of the victim to me."

Luther got into his car, pulled out of the county park, and headed back to Fellsmere. *Victim,* he thought. *I don't think I was the victim here."*

Chapter 7

The next day, Archie sat at his desk paging through a Nifty Thrifty magazine. "It's not in here," he said.

"Today's Wednesday, Archie. I only called it in yesterday. It won't be in there until sometime early next week. Oh, by the way, I think I made some progress finding information about your daughter."

Archie's eyes got wide. "You did?"

"I think so. Let me tell you what I found, and you can be the judge of if it's right or not. Come over to my computer. I'll show you."

He walked over to Candace's desk with a feeling of anticipation. She sat down at the computer and started hitting the keys. She opened up an email account and started reading. "Looks like your daughter's living in Sandusky, Ohio."

"How did you find that out?" Archie asked.

"Remember yesterday I asked you what year she graduated from high school?"

"Yes."

"Well, I went on a few sites and pretended to be one of your daughter's girlfriends from high school."

"Really!" Archie said.

"Here's the picture I posted," Candace said, pointing to the screen.

Archie bent down to take a look. He jumped back. "My, oh my," he said, picking up a piece of paper and fanning himself. "Now, that would get some attention."

Candace gave out a low wicked laugh.

Archie looked down again and saw that she had taken a very provocative picture of herself with her hair piled up on top of her head. She was wearing a low cut top, and at the angle the picture had been taken, there was very little left to the imagination.

She looked over at Archie. "Oh, come on now. It's not as bad as all that. I did it on purpose. I wanted to make sure I got some attention from some of the boys in your daughter's class."

"I have no doubt you succeeded," Archie said, bending over to take another look.

"Well, guess what? It worked. I heard from two different guys that graduated that year and another guy who graduated the year after," Candace said, looking up at Archie with a smile.

"No kidding," Archie said.

"And they were all very interested in trying to help me out with information about your daughter."

"I bet they were. What did you find out?"

"She's living in Sandusky, Ohio with someone named Travis Gibson. I did a little search for him, and he's probably not the kind of guy you'd want living with your daughter. Unfortunately, none of the guys that contacted me thought much of him, either."

Archie frowned. "Really, why is that?"

"He seems to be quite the loser. Petty theft, domestic violence, drug possession."

"Wonderful," Archie said. "Even more reason why I need to get back into her life."

"I've got her phone number," Candace said, handing Archie a piece of paper.

Archie took the number and stared at it. Candace walked over to the coffee area and started to brew a new pot.

"How did you find this?" Archie called out from the office.

"One of the guys from her class gave it to me. They still keep in touch. Just to make sure it was her, I called and told her I was conducting a consumer survey, and if she answered a few questions, she would be sent a check for ten dollars. It's her all right, and we need to send her ten bucks."

Archie just stood there. "Well, I can't believe it. This is amazing! In no time at all you were able to find out where she lived, who she lived with, get her phone number, and even talk to her." He looked down at the paper in his hand again.

Candace laughed. "Ah, I work in a detective agency. Did you forget?"

"Oh. Right." Archie said with a grin, as he stuffed the number in his pocket.

Sanford paced his office. He had just put down the phone. According to James, nothing was new. There was still no sign of Mrs. Silverman. Sanford looked up as his secretary walked in.

Jennifer Taylor took one look at him and said, "Okay, what's going on. You've been moping around since yesterday. You're not yourself, Sanford. What's the problem?"

"It's Mrs. Silverman."

"What about her? Is she sick?" Jennifer asked.

Sanford walked over to a window and gazed out at the ocean. "No, she's gone."

A look of shock crossed Jennifer's face. "She died!"

He turned. "We don't know. She's disappeared."

"Disappeared? What do you mean? Did she go someplace? Take a trip somewhere?"

Sanford walked back to his desk and sat down. He motioned for Jennifer to take a seat across from him. "Remember when I tore out of here yesterday morning?"

"Yes, I never saw you move so fast."

"Well, I got a call from Gloria over at the estate. She told me that they couldn't find Clara. I thought that she probably had just taken a walk and maybe fell down or something. But when I got there, they had already searched the whole house and all around the grounds. Just to be sure, we did it all again when I was there."

"And she wasn't there?" Jennifer asked, astounded.

"No. Nothing looked out of place. No windows had been broken, no doors were damaged, no strangers had been around, nothing."

"Did you call the police?"

Sanford put his head in his hands. "Not yet. I thought we'd find her right away. I have to be really careful with this. You know Clara. She hates publicity." He sighed. "I guess I need to call them."

"Would you call her disappearance publicity? It could be a crime."

"I know. I guess I was hoping we'd find her."

"You know they'll be poking into everything," Jennifer said.

Sanford didn't respond.

"What about a private detective?"

"I thought of that. But Frank Conway likes to drink. I wouldn't trust him to keep his mouth shut."

"How about Mitch Rosen? You've used him before." Jennifer asked.

"I thought of him, but he's so connected to most of the lawyers and cops around here, it would be impossible to keep this quiet if I got either one of them involved."

"I guess you're right," Jennifer said. "Wait a minute. There's a new guy in town."

"What?"

"Yeah, my boyfriend's father just rented him

an office. I think he came up from South Florida. Fort Lauderdale, I think."

"And he's a detective?"

"That's what he said. He just got here, so he probably doesn't know anybody."

Sanford walked over to the coffee pot, poured two cups and sat back down at his desk. He pushed a cup over to Jennifer. "I really should get the police involved in this."

"It's your call," Jennifer said. "But, are you ready for everyone and their brothers looking over Mrs. Silverman's net worth and all her charitable contributions? You know how she never wants to get any credit for what she does. I can think of at least two million dollars she's given away just this year, and nobody knows about it but you and me." Jennifer took a sip of coffee. "And don't forget about the foundation you run. You think they won't be looking into that?"

Sanford winced. "You're right. Who knows, maybe she decided to go to Palm Springs for a few days."

"Really?" Jennifer asked with a look of disbelief.

Sanford rubbed his temple. "I doubt that's the case, but if it was, and we brought all these people in here…the newspapers and everything, well, I'd be fired on the spot."

"Maybe you should give that guy a call?" Jennifer suggested.

Sanford picked up his cup and thought for a moment. "That's a risk, too. Who is this guy? He could be some shyster that got run out of Fort Lauderdale. I need my name out of this."

He stood up and walked back over to the window. "How about this? You take a ride over to his office. Look around his office and ask him a few questions. See what you think about him. If he looks halfway decent, tell him you work for Mrs. Silverman and you're concerned because she's gone missing. Make sure he understands that this has to be kept quiet."

"What if he starts asking me questions?" Jennifer asked with a frown.

"You've worked with me on this account for a few years. You've been to the estate countless times and you know everyone who works there. That shouldn't be a problem."

"Yes, you're right. Okay, I can do that."

Sanford pulled open a drawer, opened a metal box and pulled out some money. He counted the bills and put them into an envelope. "Here, give him this. If he's new in town, I'm sure he's not very busy. This should get his attention and give him something to do for a few days. By that time, we'll know something, good or bad."

Candace heard the door open and looked up. It was Luther. She sprang up and ran over to him. "What happened to you?"

"What?" Luther asked. "What are you talking about?"

"Your face. You've got a lump on your head, and your face is scraped up and swollen."

Luther waved his hand. "It's a long story. It ain't nothin.' Is Archie in?"

Archie, hearing the concern in Candace's voice, stepped out of his office. "Luther, looks like you've been in a fight!"

"Fight? Naw, maybe a little dust up. Come on, let's get some lunch. I'll tell you all about it over a cup of coffee."

"Bring me back a salad, will you?" Candace asked.

"Sure," Archie said, walking Luther out the door. "So, tell me what happened."

Forty-five minutes later Candace heard the door open. "Did you remember my salad?" she asked, staring intently at her computer screen.

"What?"

The voice didn't sound anything like Archie's. Candace looked up and saw a woman standing in the doorway. "Oh, I'm sorry. Can I help you?"

The woman shifted from side to side. She was about 5'7," thin, and had her blond hair pulled back into a stylish ponytail. She was wearing a form fitting dark gray suit. She glanced back toward the window. "Is Mr. Archibald in?"

Candace approached her and extended her hand. "I'm Candace Muldoon, Mr. Archibald's assistant." She glanced at her watch. "He stepped out for a quick lunch, but he should be back any moment. Perhaps I can help you?"

The Black Orchid Mystery

Candace watched as she spun around and took a step backwards toward the door. "Um, maybe I'll just come back. It's kind of private."

Just as she was turning to leave, Archie and Luther walked in.

"Oh, there he is now," Candace said. "Archie, this woman would like to speak with you."

Archie stepped forward and introduced himself. He motioned toward the office. "Let's go back here and you can tell me what's on your mind."

Archie escorted the woman into his office and offered her a chair. "What can I do for you?" He paused. "Ms? Mrs?"

A look of panic crossed the woman's face. "I'm, um, my name is Gloria. Gloria Rodriguez."

"Okay, Ms. Rodriguez. Just relax and tell me what I can help you with today."

Jennifer smiled. "Well, I have a problem, and I may need the services of an investigator."

"You've come to the right place. What's the nature of your problem?"

"Can I ask you a few questions first, Mr. Archibald?"

Taken somewhat aback, Archie said, "Certainly."

"From what I hear, you're new to the area. Is that correct?"

"Yes, we just opened the office a few days ago."

"Can you fill me in on your background? You know, how long have you been in this business, things like that?"

Archie gave her the condensed version of his twenty years in the business.

"And what brought you to the Vero area? Friends? Family?"

"Did you notice the man I walked in with?"

"The black gentleman?"

"Yes. Well he's a wonderful friend of mine. I knew him back in Fort Lauderdale. He retired up to this area, and I always envied him when I would come and visit. So, I decided to close my practice and move it up here." Archie was getting tired of this grilling. "Any more questions, Ms. Rodriquez, or can we move on to what brought you here?"

"No, I think you have told me all I need to know." Jennifer leaned in and lowered her voice, "Well, this must be held in the strictest of confidence, Mr. Archibald."

"That's not a problem. That goes without saying in my kind of work."

"Yes, I'm sure it does, but it's doubly important with what I'm going to tell you."

He nodded his head. "I understand."

"You see, I'm a guardian for a very prominent woman, Clara Silverman. I'm sure you've heard of her."

Archie thought for a moment. "I'm sorry. The name doesn't ring a bell. But, like I said, I'm new to the area."

"Oh, well, welcome to Vero. Just so you know, Mrs. Silverman's probably the wealthiest woman in Vero Beach."

The Black Orchid Mystery

"I see," said Archie. "And what can I do for you, Ms. Rodriguez?"

"I'd like you to see if you can find her."

"Find her?" Archie asked. "Has she gone somewhere?"

"We don't know. She just disappeared. We really don't want anyone to know about this. It's quite embarrassing and all."

"Maybe she took a trip somewhere. You know, Paris, Italy? Maybe a nice little jaunt over to Europe, perhaps?"

"I don't think so. Mrs. Silverman is eighty-four years old and almost an invalid."

"How's her mind?" Archie asked. "Does she suffer from dementia? Could she have wandered off someplace near the house?"

"That's what we thought may have happened, but we've searched everywhere and we can't find her. Her mind is usually just fine." She paused for a moment.

Archie tapped his pencil on the desk. "Okay. So, let me ask you, Ms. Rodriguez. What do you think happened to her? Do you think she just wandered off? Is there a possibility she may have been kidnapped?"

She bolted from the chair. "Kidnapped! Oh, heavens no. I mean, there hasn't been any kind of demand or anything."

"How long has Mrs. Silverman been missing?"

"Since yesterday morning."

Archie looked surprised. "That's over twenty-four hours now. Have you notified the local authorities?"

Ms. Rodriguez looked down at the floor. "I'm afraid we have not." She looked back up at Archie. "But, Mr. Archibald, this is a very sensitive situation. That's why I'm speaking to you. You have no idea. Could you just please take a look at this for us."

"Us?" Archie asked.

She looked puzzled.

"You asked if I could look into this for 'us'…you said 'us'."

"No, no. It's just me. I'm sorry, and like I said before, this has to be done discretely. Please, no mention of my name."

"How many other people work at the house?"

"Just me, a young man named Enrique Vasquez, and a gentleman, James Harrow."

"What do they do?" Archie asked.

"I guess Enrique could be called the chauffer, though Mrs. Silverman never goes out anymore. He's a big guy, so he makes sure nobody's snooping around the place."

"And Mr. Harrow?"

"He's the cook. He used to accompany Mrs. Silverman wherever she went. She has houses around the world. But he's been here in Florida for years because she hasn't visited any of her other places for quite some time."

Archie scribbled down some notes in a spiral bound pad. He looked up. "How long have you all worked for Mrs. Silverman?"

"Me? I've been there going on…" She paused. "Ah, about twelve years now and Enrique started helping out when he was sixteen, so that means he's been there about seven years."

"What about Mr. Harrow?"

"I'm not quite sure. Much longer than me, but since he was hired over in England, I'm not quite sure when he was brought on."

"Any chance one of these gentlemen could have something to do with this? Enrique, does he use drugs? Does Mr. Harrow gamble? Any problems you know of?"

"Oh, no, Mr. Archibald. Enrique spends a lot of time at their gym. He's a health nut."

"How about Mr. Harrow?"

"Certainly not. Like I said, he's been with Mrs. Silverman for years.

Archie scribbled a few more notes down and then paused.

"What about spouses or girlfriends? Are there any hanging around the Estate?"

She let out a snicker.

Archie gave her a look. "And?"

"Enrique has a revolving door of girlfriends, but he never brings them over to the place. And James…well, let's just say he's not a big fan of women."

"Okay," Archie said. "Does Mr. Harrow do any entertaining? Does he have visitors?"

"Now and then, not very often because it's frowned upon by Mrs. Silverman."

"What does Mrs. Silverman do with her money?" Archie asked.

"What do you mean?"

"Other than the numerous houses you mentioned and the taxes and upkeep associated with them, what does she spend her money on? It seems like she doesn't travel."

"She has foundations and charities she donates quite generously to."

"Is everyone happy with the money they get? Are you aware of any person or group who may feel like they didn't get their share? Has she cut any group out recently?"

Jennifer thought for a moment. "Only Doctor Garneau."

"Oh? Who's he and why do think he's not happy?" Archie asked.

"I'm not sure I'd say he's not happy. He runs a halfway house for people getting out of prison. It's here in Vero, over on 41st Avenue. He had plans to expand this year; but, because Mrs. Silverman was donating quite a sizable amount of money for a wing on the St. Francis Hospital in Los Angeles, all of her other annual donations were cut by ten percent this year."

"Wouldn't that upset all the others, too?"

"I'm sure it did, but Doctor Garneau was the most vocal. Please Mr. Archibald, I'm not saying I think he had anything to do with this."

"I know. It's just that I need some direction to start looking," Archie said with a sigh. He looked around his new, unpaid-for office. "My fee is five hundred dollars a day plus expenses."

She reached into her purse and pulled out a thick envelope. "This should be enough to get you started."

Archie opened the envelope and quickly glanced inside. He slid open the top drawer of his desk and put it away. "Thank you. But, you have to promise me, if nothing turns up in a day or two, we need to consider going to the authorities."

"Certainly."

"Since time is of the essence, Ms. Rodriquez, I'd like to drive over to the estate this afternoon and have a look around."

She hesitated. "I guess that would be okay."

"Can you tell me how to get there?"

"Go east on Route sixty until you get to A1A. Go about three miles north. There's a very narrow driveway that goes into the woods. It's not marked, and it's real easy to miss. Take that until you get to a big gate. Push the button on the gate, and someone will let you in."

Jennifer stood up and extended her hand. "Thank you, Mr. Archibald. Here's my cell phone number. Let me know immediately if you find out something."

Archie scribbled her number in his notebook. "I'll do that."

He showed her out of his office and walked her to the front door. When he turned around, both Luther and Candace were sitting with looks of anticipation on their faces.

"Well?" Candace said. "Do we have a client?"

"I guess so," Archie said. "But probably not for very long."

"What does that mean?" Candice asked.

"This is something the police should be looking into. It's more of a missing person case. Seems like the old lady she works for disappeared," Archie said.

"Disappeared?" Candace asked. "Who disappeared?"

Archie looked down at his notes. "Clara Silverman."

"Are you kidding me?" Luther said, with a look of complete surprise. "The Black Orchid? Well, leave it to you! When you finally get a client, you don't fool around."

"Can you believe it! The Black Orchid!" Candace repeated.

"A black orchid? Where did that come from? Some old lady is missing, not a plant," Archie said.

Candace laughed. "Damn, Archie. She's probably the wealthiest of the wealthy around here."

"That's what I was told."

Candace continued, "Yeah, they say that woman's been in seclusion for the last ten years. She's got places all around the world but hasn't set foot in any of them for years."

Archie looked over at Luther. "Why did you call her The Black Orchid?"

"Everyone calls her that," Luther said. He thought for a moment. "For a couple of reasons, I guess. First, her mansion's on Black Orchid Point."

Candace interrupted. "Oh, and then they call her that because she dresses all in black, like the orchid."

Luther turned to her. "I was getting there."

"Sorry!"

"Really?" Archie said. "How do you know all this?"

Candace laughed. "Don't you read the tabloids? Every couple of years they run an article about how nobody's seen the little rich girl for years."

"Tabloids?" Archie scoffed. "Who believes them?"

Candace's eyes got wide. "But it's true, Archie. Geeze, how do we know anything about anyone in town? Gossip! Everyone talks about everyone else around here. This isn't a huge place like Miami, you know. Word gets around."

Luther looked over at Candace. "Do you know Frank Bowman down at the paper?"

Candace shook her head no.

"Well, anyway, Frank's a friend of mine, and he tried for over five years to interview Mrs. Silverman for a feature article. Her people always said no. No pictures and no interview. Too bad, because according to Frank, she was doing a lot of nice things around the community with her money, including the ball field where I coach in Fellsmere. I guess she just doesn't want anyone to know about it."

"This is really a case for the authorities, and I told Ms. Rodriguez that. She about begged me to at least look into it. I imagine she's worried about losing her job." Archie said. He repeated what she had told him.

Archie continued, "If we're going to look into this, we can't be going on what the tabloids and local gossip say. Candace, put together a file on Mrs. Silverman based on her actual history, not this other fluff and innuendoes. I'm going to head over to her estate and take a look around. When I get back later this afternoon, let's review what you come up."

Luther stood up and took a step toward the door. "All I can say, Archie is, if you find this lady, you probably ain't got to worry about any more cases. With all her millions, I'm sure you'd get paid handsomely, and it sure don't look like you're going to be doing any fishin' today!"

"Not today. I've finally got something I can sink my teeth into. Oh, before you go, Luther. Have you ever heard of a Doctor Garneau?"

Luther laughed. "Yep, sure have. You'd know him too if you'd been reading the local paper for the last six months."

"Why is that?"

"The man runs a halfway house for ex-prisoners, and he's been fighting the neighborhood and city hall to expand. People who live around his place aren't exactly thrilled with who stays there. It's a pretty rough crowd, and they sure don't want more. Why are you asking about him?"

"His name came up when I asked about what charities Mrs. Silverman contributes to."

"You think he had something to do with this?" Candace asked.

"I doubt it, but who knows? Probably a long shot. Maybe I'll stop over there and see what I can find out."

Luther thought for a moment. "Ah, if you do, I'll go with you." He gave a little wave, pushed open the door, and stepped out onto the sidewalk.

"He's funny," Candace said. Then she paused. "Um, can I ask you a question?"

Archie looked up. "Sure."

"Should we be discussing cases in front of him? How do you know him?"

Archie waved his hand. "Don't worry about Luther. I've known him for years. He's got an amazing background in Special Forces. He's completely trustworthy."

"I'm sorry, I just wanted to be sure."

"No, I'm glad you asked. Luther was the facilities manager for the strip mall down in Ft. Lauderdale where my last office was. Let's just say that he was underutilized, based on his background, but that's how he wanted it. He told me several times, he was ready for a job where he just had to do physical labor. You know, a job that he didn't have to take home with him."

"Sounds like you've known him for a long time."

"That's right. He'd stop in every now and then, and we became good friends. We were both in the army so we had a lot to talk about."

Candace pulled out a blank manila folder and wrote 'Silverman, Clara' on the tab. "How do you want to start this case?"

"I told Ms. Rodriquez that I'd drive over to the Estate and start looking around," Archie said.

Sanford reached for his phone. "How did it go?"

"Pretty good. I asked him a few questions first. Looks like he really doesn't know anyone around here except for one friend from Ft. Lauderdale. I made sure he understood this had to be kept quiet. He's going to ride over there this afternoon and look around. That's okay, right?"

"Sure. That's what he's getting paid to do. There's no link to me, right?"

"No. I told him I was Gloria from the Estate, and I was worried about my employer." Jennifer paused, waiting for a comment. "Hello? Sanford, are you there?"

"What name did you give him?"

"Gloria Rodri…. Oh, wait a minute."

"Jennifer, sometimes I wonder about you."

"Shit. I never thought of that. What's he going to think when he meets the real Gloria?"

"Damn it, Jennifer. Well, too late to worry about it now. Let's see what he finds out. Call Enrique and let him know this guy's coming."

The Black Orchid Mystery

Archie walked out the back door, hopped into his Miata and headed down 34th Avenue. His car was seven years old and needed a paint job, but the engine ran great. He hated how the car looked, but he had a hard time convincing himself to invest money for a new paint job on a car so old. *Maybe I'll just get a brand new one after this case*, Archie thought to himself with a smile.

Driving down Ocean Avenue, Archie marveled at how different Vero was compared to South Florida. Traffic was light and there was no concrete corridor of huge condos blocking out the sun and ocean view. The atmosphere just felt nicer. He looked around and thought about what Luther told him. This definitely was a playground for old money.

Archie flew right by the narrow entrance that was the road leading to the Silverman Estate. He did a quick U-turn and drove into the narrow tree-shaded lane. As soon as he pulled into the wooded drive, he noticed how the air seemed to change. The thick trees and lush vegetation of the tropical hammock engulfed him. Almost immediately, no traffic noise could be heard from the street. The air felt humid and a rich smell of soil and decaying leaves surrounded him. Archie slowed down as he approached a large iron gate. He pulled his car up to a metal box and pushed a button.

A voice from the speaker said, "Yes?"

"My name's Archie Archibald. I'm here to…"

Enrique interrupted him. "I was told you were coming, Mr. Archibald. I'll meet you at the front door."

Archie watched as the gate slowly swung open. It was at least twelve feet high and was connected to a ten foot stone wall that disappeared in both directions into the woods. He peered into the forest floor, looking to see if he could see any of those black orchids.

He pushed the stick shift to first gear and drove onto the property. Archie followed the narrow lane through the woods for another few minutes before the landscape opened up to a large, perfectly manicured lawn. He could see a pond to the left and a huge mansion in the distance. As he drove closer, he could see there was another set of buildings to the left of the main house. *This was real money*, Archie thought as he got closer to the mansion.

He noticed that some of the structures looked like they needed to be repaired. Large vines were growing up the sides, and spots of green mold or some kind of moss were spreading over the bricks.

Archie turned into a wide brick driveway, stopped the car, and slowly approached the ornate front door. He grasped a large iron hoop that hung down from a metal lion's mouth and knocked. Almost immediately, the door swung open, and Archie was staring at a young Hispanic man who appeared to be in his late twenties.

"You must be Enrique," Archie said.

The Black Orchid Mystery

"Yes, please come in." Enrique said, motioning Archie toward the foyer. "Can I get you something, Mr. Archibald? Coffee, tea, a soda?"

"No, but thanks anyway. I take it you know why I'm here?"

Enrique nodded.

"Good. Would it be possible to meet the other members of the staff?"

"Sure, let me find them," Enrique said.

Archie walked around the foyer area. It was huge. The floor was a highly polished marble; there were tapestries and old oil paintings hanging on the walls. Antique furniture was scattered around the perimeter of the room. He spotted what he thought may be one of those black orchids Candace and Luther were talking about. He walked over and looked at it.

He heard a soft cough behind him and turned around to see a slightly built man approach him with his arm outstretched.

"James Harrow, Mr. Archibald. Pleased to meet you."

Archie shook his hand. "A pleasure."

Enrique walked in from another doorway followed by a woman. "I couldn't find James…oh, looks like he beat me to it. Mr. Archibald, this is Gloria Rodriquez."

Archie tried to hide the startled look he knew must have been on his face. "Ah, excuse me, what was your name again?"

The woman stepped in front of Enrique. "My name is Gloria. Gloria Rodriquez."

"Okay, that's what I thought you said," Archie replied with an embarrassed smile. He looked around. "Will the others be joining us?"

"What others?" Enrique asked.

"This place is so huge," Archie replied. "Don't you have additional people on the staff?"

James laughed out loud. "Now that's a very good question, Mr. Archibald. We used to. But Mr. Leeds, the gentleman who's in charge of Mrs. Silverman's expenses, has deemed it unnecessary, and he has let quite a few people go over the last few years. What you see is what you get."

Archie thought about the dilapidated look of the buildings and grounds he had noticed when he drove in.

"I see. There's not another caretaker by the name of Gloria working here?"

A puzzled look appeared on all of their faces. "No, sir," Gloria responded. "Just me. Why do you ask?"

He thought for a moment. "Just some bad information, I guess. Anyway, can you please tell me how it was that you discovered Mrs. Silverman was missing yesterday?"

One by one, the members of the staff told Archie what they had experienced the day before.

Archie pulled out a small notebook and scribbled down a few notes. "I'd like to see the grounds. Walk the perimeter and take a look at the other buildings. After that, I'd appreciate a tour of the house."

Enrique stepped forward, "I'll take…"

The Black Orchid Mystery

    James took Archie by the arm. "I'll do it, Enrique." He guided Archie toward the kitchen where they walked down a long hallway to a huge glassed-in room. "This is the solarium. Mrs. Silverman liked to sit out here when she was able. Unfortunately, for the last month or two, she was confined to her room. She didn't have the strength to come down here."

    Archie looked around. The room was filled with green plants and wicker furniture. It was beautiful. "It sounds like she would not have been able to just wonder off somewhere. Is that what you're saying?"

    "Exactly." As James opened the door, Archie could hear the roar of the ocean. Fifty feet beyond the house, waves from the Atlantic could be seen stretching all the way out to the horizon. James walked Archie across the driveway to a building that was constructed with the same dark marble as the main house. "This is the guest compound. There are five suites here, each with two bedrooms and two baths. Upstairs, there's a recreation room and a small suite of offices that come with their own tidy living quarters." James pulled out a set of keys from his pocket. "Come on, I'll show you."

    He guided Archie through one of the suites. "They all look the same. Unfortunately, Mrs. Silverman no longer gets any visitors, so they don't get used. Let's head upstairs."

    James unlocked a door at the head of the stairs. They stepped out into a large open area. Archie could see a pool table, a big screen television, and some video games. Several card tables were set up around the room. "This was built for us," James said. "Mrs. Silverman didn't want us to get bored. Just like the rooms downstairs, this area almost never gets used."

He pointed to a door at the end of the cavernous room. "Two office suites are back there with another small apartment. We walked through this whole place and didn't see any signs of Mrs. Silverman or anything that looked out of the ordinary."

"I saw a large pond when I drove in. Can we check that area out?" Archie asked.

"Oh, that hideous alligator lives there. I hate to go near it," James said. "How about I point you in the right direction?"

"Fine," Archie laughed. "They're not my favorite thing, either."

As Archie and James walked out of the guest suites, Archie saw a van pull up in the driveway. "Who's that?"

James stared at the van. "That would be Nancy Abbott. She sells Mrs. Silverman paintings."

Archie and James walked down the stairway. James followed Archie until he got about thirty feet from the pond. "I hope you don't mind, but this is about as close as I want to get to that wretched water."

Archie laughed. "Not a problem. I'll just walk around the perimeter for awhile."

The Black Orchid Mystery

Nancy Abbott pulled her new Lexus LX Sports Utility vehicle up to the Silverman mansion and stepped out. She stopped to look at her new purchase. It was perfect! Classy looking, but it had enough room for moving paintings and sculptures around when she needed to. It had pained her to have the 'Abbott Galleries' decal put on the sides, but that's what she bought the vehicle for in the first place.

Nancy was wearing a designer suit, and her long black hair was cut in the latest style. She looked in the back at the two paintings she had for Mrs. Silverman and decided that Enrique could carry them in. She wanted to remain fresh for her next appointment.

She knocked on the door and stood waiting on the steps. After a few minutes, the door swung open a few inches.

Nancy waited for the door to open, but Gloria said, "Oh, Ms. Abbott. I'm sorry, but today…"

Nancy pushed the door open and rushed past her as if she wasn't even there. "Hello, Gloria. Please find Enrique to help me get some paintings out of my van. My goodness, it's hot out there."

Gloria tried to interrupt, but Nancy kept talking. "Do you have something to drink? Lemonade would be wonderful."

"Ah, no. We don't have any lemonade…and I'm afraid I'm going to have to…"

"No lemonade? Such a shame. How's Mrs. Silverman? I hope she's feeling a little more with it today." Nancy stopped talking and looked around.

"Where's Enrique? I'm in a hurry, and I don't have all day for her to approve these paintings or not."

Gloria just stood there.

"What's the problem? Can you get Enrique, please?" Nancy said, with a look of impatience.

"I'm afraid Mrs. Silverman is not going to be able to look at your pictures today, Ms. Abbott."

"These aren't pictures, Gloria. They're priceless works of art, but that's beside the point. It will only take a moment. All she has to do is take a quick peek and then sign the sales form. Really, it won't take but a second. Please, let's get Enrique over here so I can get to my next appointment."

Gloria put her hands on her hips and didn't move. "It no happen today. I'm sorry but you need to come back some other time."

"That's ridiculous. Didn't you hear me? This will only take a minute. Look, I'll run out and get the paintings. Tell Mrs. Silverman I'm here." With that, Nancy turned, pushed the heavy oak door open and stomped outside.

Gloria muttered something in Spanish, walked into the kitchen, picked up the phone, and dialed Mr. Leeds's number.

Sanford picked up his phone. "What is it?" Sanford asked. "Any news?"

"It's that picture woman."

"Who?" Sanford asked.

"Mrs. Abbott," Gloria said. "I tell her Mrs. Silverman can't see her today, but she don't listen. She's outside getting her pictures now."

"That woman's insufferable," Sanford said. "Okay, I'll deal with her. Put her on the phone."

Gloria walked back out to the foyer and said, "Mr. Leeds would like to talk to you."

Nancy looked down at her watch. "Honestly, I'm in a hurry. Is this necessary?"

Gloria didn't respond. She just headed toward the kitchen.

Nancy grabbed the phone. "Sanford, what's this all about? I've got an appointment with Mrs. Silverman and I'm running late."

"We should have called you, Nancy. I'm so sorry. I'm afraid Mrs. Silverman's not in any condition to meet with you today. Perhaps you can leave the paintings?"

Nancy stopped and thought. "I don't know. We're talking about three hundred thousand dollars here."

"You're not doubting she'd be good for it, are you?"

Nancy laughed. "Of course not. But who's to know I dropped them off?"

"Stop by the office this afternoon. I'll sign for them," Sanford said. "After all, I am her executor."

"All right," Nancy sighed. "How's she doing, anyway? I've noticed see seemed to be declining the last few times I've been here."

Sanford frowned. "I think she caught a little bug. Nothing serious, but yes, I think you're right. She is eighty-four, for goodness sake. I hope I'm half as sharp as she is when I get that old."

"Sanford, you'll never get that old. You'll be shot by a jealous husband."

Sanford smiled. "Really! Are you trying to tell me something?"

"Off to my next appointment," Nancy replied. "I'll see you this afternoon." Nancy hung up the phone and turned to Gloria. "Could you be a dear and have Enrique come and help me with the paintings?"

Archie walked around the pond as far as he could. The ground was starting to get very wet. He turned around and retraced his steps. As he approached James, he said, "You can go back to the house, if you'd like. I'm going to walk around the grounds for a little while. I'm sure you have things to do."

"Actually, I do need to start preparing something for supper."

"I'll only be a short time. Maybe Enrique can walk me through the house when I come back in."

"I'll tell him to be ready," James said.

Archie spent almost an hour walking around the other side of the pond and surrounding areas. He spotted the alligator right away. It was about an eight footer. Luckily, it stayed in the center of the pond.

Archie walked back to the main house and found Enrique waiting for him in the foyer. Together they walked the empty corridors of the first and second floors. Archie went into Clara's bedroom and looked around. The bed was still unmade. Gloria had wanted to make it, Enrique told him, but James said to leave everything as it was in case there were some clues they didn't notice.

"What about floors three and four?" Archie asked.

"They haven't been accessible for about a year. Mr. Leeds told us since nobody was using them, to shut them up. Guess he wanted to save money on cooling them."

"What did Mrs. Silverman think of that idea? I would imagine she has enough money not worry too much about the electric bill."

Enrique laughed. "He told us not to tell her. She hadn't been up there in so long; I don't think she would ever know."

"But you did say you searched those floors looking for Mrs. Silverman, didn't you?"

"Oh yes, before Mr. Leeds got here and after. Do you want to go up there?"

Archie gazed up the staircase. "Probably not right now. If it's been looked at twice, I doubt if I'd find anything. And you said you didn't see anyone trespassing on the property, correct?"

"Not yesterday," Enrique said.

"What does that mean?"

"Every now and then someone will wander up from the beach, and we have to ask them to leave; but a few days ago, I caught that damn Russell Craig sneaking around here again."

"Who's that?"

"He's a paparazzi who keeps trying to get a picture of Mrs. Silverman."

"A paparazzi? You've got to be kidding. What's he want her picture for?"

"I guess cause nobody's seen her in ten years. And before that, the only famous picture of her is when she was with the Rat Pack," Enrique said.

"The Rat Pack? You mean the Sinatra and Martin Rat Pack?"

"Yeah! Can you believe it. Mrs. Silverman ran with quite the crowd in her day."

"Does she still have famous friends?" Archie asked.

"Not so much. From what James tells me, he's been with her the longest, she got tired of the entertainment crowd and pretty much turned into a recluse a long time ago. Other than Mr. Leeds, I can't remember anyone coming to visit her as long as I've been here."

"What about that Russell guy? Could he have anything to do with her disappearance?"

"I don't think so. He's a persistent dude, but I can't see him getting involved in anything as serious as taking her or anything like that."

As they were talking, Archie and Enrique had worked their way back down to the main foyer. "I appreciate the tour. Tell Gloria and James I said 'thank you'." Archie pulled out one of his business cards and handed it to Enrique. "If you think of anything at all that may seem helpful, no matter how unimportant it sounds, give me a call."

Enrique took his card. "I'll do that."

As Archie walked back to his car, he noticed the Abbott Gallery van was gone. He wondered what kind of art Mrs. Silverman was buying.

Back in the kitchen, James busied himself making preparations for the evening meal. Even though Mrs. Silverman wasn't there, they still had to eat.

James checked the oven. Another forty minutes until the seafood casserole would be done. He walked over to the refrigerator and took out some fried chicken from the day before. He made a basket of leftovers and stepped out into the hallway. He glanced to the right and left. There was nobody around. James walked to a side door and looked outside. Again, he didn't see anyone. He pushed the door open and quickly walked across the driveway to the guest suites. He looked back several times to make sure he wasn't seen.

Chapter 8

A television set was playing in the living room, but nobody was watching. The volume was low, which forced John Barrington, who was sitting at the kitchen table, to cock his head in order to hear what the weatherman was saying. John listened for a few minutes and then stood up from the table and walked over to the coffee pot. He filled up his cup and took the pot over to his wife, Kit, who was standing next to the stove, and poured her a refill. "Looks like we're going to get hit with a good snow tonight."

"How bad?"

"Three to six inches. A storm's heading our way across Lake Superior. They think it's going to start snowing sometime around midnight."

John and Kit Barrington lived in a house John had inherited from his Aunt Thortis the year before. Locals referred to the house as *The Four Chimneys* due to the four distinctive chimneys perched on top of the structure. It was built on top of a hill and could be seen for miles rising above the surrounding forest. The house was in the middle of ninety acres land on the south-eastern side of Upper Michigan's Garden Peninsula. It had been built by Aunt Thortis' grandfather, a wealthy lumber baron, over one hundred years before. The heavily wooded peninsula extended fifteen miles into Lake Michigan with Little Bay de Noc to its west and Big Bay de Noc to the east. Lake Superior was located about fifty miles due north, and that seemed to be the direction the worst storms always came from.

The eastern shore of the peninsula was dotted with camps and cottages, but the western shore, where the Four Chimneys was located, was quite remote. There were a few farms scattered among the woods, but the harsh winters made the growing season much too short for farmers to compete with their Lower Michigan and Wisconsin counterparts. Several of the larger fields had been abandoned, while the remaining ones were worked more as hobby farms.

John sat back down at the kitchen table and flipped open a page in the Escanaba *Daily Press*. He glanced down and started to read an article. "I can't believe this!"

Kit was frying whitefish in a pan on the stove. "What? I can't hear you."

She wiped her hands on a dish-towel, walked over to the table, and sat down across from John. "Okay, what were you saying?"

"This article," John said, pointing to the paper. It looks like the state is moving ahead to build that maximum security prison over at Fairport."

"Oh, no," Kit said, glancing across the table at the newspaper. "What are they thinking?"

John shoved the paper over to her. "I don't know. I'm sure it's all about jobs, and they probably think Fairport's the perfect location, since it's so isolated from anything."

Kit scanned the article. She sighed. "I guess. I mean, jobs are important, especially around here. But this will change everything. Traffic, all the lights, the environment, everything."

"We have to do something," John said. "We can't just sit here and let our way of life just slip away."

"I wonder if they're going to talk about this at the Garden council meeting next week," Kit asked. "Let's plan on going. I know the council's not for this, but if the county wants to turn this land over to the state for jobs, I'm not sure what exactly it is we can do." Kit got up and walked over to the kitchen window. "Guess what? Snow's starting to fall already."

Sanford Leeds stared at the man sitting on the other side of his desk. "How many times have we had this conversation, Dr. Garneau? Mrs. Silverman has reduced all of her contributions this year by ten percent. I understand you're doing good things. So are all of her other charities."

"But, I assumed we'd be getting our normal contribution. I've signed contracts. We're about to start construction early next year. Sanford, after all the things I've done for you…"

Sanford's phone buzzed. "Mrs. Abbott is waiting to see you."

Sanford stood up. "Look, here's what I can do. I appreciate what you've done for me. You know that. Okay, I'll do a little creative financing and get you your money. But Mrs. Silverman can't hear about this." He thought for a moment. "Nobody can know about this. If word ever got out, I'd have every charity and organization knocking down my door. Understand?"

"Completely."

"Good. I'll have a check out to you in a few days."

A light rain was falling outside as Sonny's wife sat on a gray metal chair and looked around the stark cinderblock waiting room of the Indian River County Jail. She could hear the sound of airplanes as they took off and landed from the nearby Vero Beach Municipal Airport. *A lot of rich Vero businessmen who had way too much money to invest in their expensive hobbies.*

Francine remembered going there with her father on many Saturdays. They would climb into his small plane and head to Ft. Lauderdale or Orlando for the day. Several times he took her and her mother all the way to Key West. When she was fourteen, they had to ditch the plane in a cow pasture west of Jupiter. Her father sold the plane the next week-end.

Francine thought about those childhood memories. They seemed as if they were from a hundred years ago. It had been a fight trying to convince her father to hand over Sonny's bail money. If it wasn't for her breaking down and telling him about the new pregnancy, she doubted that he would have given in and handed her the money.

As her father pointed out, the bond money was just a temporary solution, and Francine knew it. Since Sonny was on probation, she knew this charge was going to be serious. Maybe Sonny could plea bargain down to something less than aggravated battery. She understood one thing, there would be no more money coming from her family. They wanted Sonny to go away, and they made no attempt to hide it. She rubbed her tummy and wondered if Sonny would even be around when she had the baby.

Suddenly, a large deputy appeared at the door. He motioned for her, and she walked out to the booking area. Sonny was in the lobby looking a mess. He had a two day growth of whiskers, and it looked as if he had slept in his clothes, which in fact, he had.

"What the hell took you so long?" Sonny snarled.

"Daddy. It's a miracle he even gave me the money," Francine replied.

Sonny took a step toward her. "Come on, let's get outta here," he said, looking as if he was about to spit on the floor next to the deputy. He pushed the door open and pulled Francine outside.

"Gimmie the keys," Sonny barked, as he climbed into the driver's seat. As they pulled out of the walled compound, Francine started to cry. "What are we going to do, now?"

Sonny turned and glared at her. "What do you mean?"

"You're on probation. I'm going to have another baby and now this new charge. Daddy said they could charge you with being a habitual felon or something like that."

"Screw your old man. He don't know shit. That's what he's hoping, the old bastard. First off, you need to get rid of that kid like we talked about. Don't worry about nothing else. I just need to get that old black man to drop the charges, that's all. Then everything goes back to normal."

"Would he do that?" Francine asked.

Sonny smiled. "I think it's a good possibility." Sonny turned right at the intersection of 43rd Avenue and 49th Street.

"Where are you going?" Francine asked.

"I need to see that lawyer, Sanford Leeds."

"We can't afford him!" Francine said, with a surprised look on her face.

"No shit! We don't have to. Don't worry about it and don't ask any questions." Sonny turned to glare at his wife. "And forget we ever went to see him. You got that?"

From the look on his face, Francine knew he wasn't kidding. "Okay," she said. She turned and looked out the window, tears streaming down her face.

Sonny pulled into a parking spot next to the Leeds Building and turned off the engine. "Stay in the car. I'll be right back."

Sonny jumped out and hurried across the parking lot. It was raining harder than he thought. He stepped into the lobby and walked over to an elevator and pushed the button for the penthouse. Sonny looked down and watched as water pooled under his feet. The water made the colors of the polished terrazzo tile look even brighter.

As Sonny stepped into the elevator, he saw two men dressed in business suits approach. They looked in and both stopped just outside the open door. *Good move*, Sonny thought. The door slowly closed and Sonny felt the car jerk upward. He looked down and saw that there was dried blood on the front of his shirt. He hadn't slept much the night before, and he hadn't taken a shower in the morning. Francine was right. He was a mess.

The elevator slowed to a stop and Sonny stepped out into a plush lobby with a polished teakwood reception desk and a beautiful dark haired receptionist sitting behind it.

"Can I help you?" the woman said, somewhat taken aback at his appearance.

"I need to see Sanford Leeds," Sonny said, combing his hair back with his fingers.

"Is he expecting you?"

"Naw, but he'll see me if you let him know I'm here."

The receptionist looked at Sonny over the top of her reading glasses.

"Go ahead, give him a call," Sonny said, trying to move the process along.

The receptionist picked up the phone. "Your name, please?"

"Sonny Porter."

Jennifer Taylor was freshening her lipstick, when she took the call from the receptionist. "Sonny Porter!" She made a face. "Let me see if Sanford's got time to meet with him." Just to be sure, she quickly scanned Sanford's appointment calendar. She returned to the phone. "Mr. Porter's not scheduled, and Sanford's got someone in the office with him right now."

The receptionist looked down and whispered, "I know, but he insists Mr. Leeds will see him."

"Oh, all right," Jennifer said, putting her on hold.

She didn't like Sonny Porter and never felt at ease when he was in the office. She buzzed Sanford and told him Mr. Porter was in the lobby and wanted to see him.

"Okay, send him in," Sanford replied.
Surprised, Jennifer told the receptionist to let him in.

Sonny walked into the outer office where Jennifer had her desk and stood in front of her. She reached over, pulled out her bottom desk drawer, picked up her purse and quietly set it in the drawer.

"What are you doing?" Sonny asked.

"Putting my purse away, why do you ask?"

"Cause you think I'm going to steal it, right?" Sonny said with a smug smile on his face.

She blushed and tried to remain calm. "No, that's ridiculous. I'm supposed to keep it in the drawer, and sometimes I forget."

"The last time I was here you remembered to stick it away, too," he sneered. "You ain't fooling me none."

The door to Sanford's office opened and he stepped out. He walked over to Jennifer's desk. "Everything okay?"

She nodded. Sanford motioned to Sonny and ushered him toward his door. Jennifer looked surprised. She asked Sanford, "What about Nancy?"

"This will only take a minute. She'll be fine."

Once in the office, Sanford walked Sonny over to his desk and pulled up another chair. "I'd like you to meet Nancy Abbott."

Sonny mumbled, "Hello."

"Nancy runs an art gallery on Cardinal Drive. You should stop in there sometime."

Sonny glanced over at Nancy. "Yeah, I'll do that."

Nancy gave Sonny a reserved smile and moved her chair a few inches away.

"What brings you here? We don't have a meeting scheduled," Sanford said, glancing down at his appointment book.

"Uh, can we talk alone?"

"It's okay, Sonny. Nancy and I go way back."

Sonny didn't look pleased. "I need some dough."

Sanford reached into a desk drawer and pulled out a journal. He thumbed through the pages. "Didn't I pay you two months ago? Looks like you're not due more money until the middle of next month." Sanford looked up at Sonny. "What the hell happened to you, anyway? You look like shit. Is that blood on your shirt?"

"I just got out of jail. Didn't sleep much. Look, can you just advance me next month's money? That would really help me out."

Sanford thought for a moment. "That's never a good idea."

Sonny clenched his right hand into a fist and moved as if he was going to stand up. Nancy got up from her chair and walked over to the far side of the room.

"But in this case," Sanford said, as he fished his wallet out of his pocket, "I'll make an exception." He pulled out some bills and handed them to Sonny. "Here you go."

Sonny pushed the money into his jeans. "Thanks."

Sanford pulled out a few more bills. "Here's a few extra bucks so you can go get yourself cleaned up. And buy a new shirt while you're at it."

Sonny turned to leave.

"Oh, wait a minute," Sanford said. He leaned over close to Sonny and whispered, "Maybe you can help me out. A rich old lady's gone missing, probably wandered off like they do all the time. But, do me a favor. If you hear any talk about this out on the street, let me know right away, okay? You never know about these things."

"What old lady?"

"I can't go into details right now, but just remember what I said." Sanford stood up; signaling his meeting with Sonny was over. "Oh, about this old lady. You don't need to be out there asking questions. Just let me know if you hear anything."

Sonny nodded. "Will do, boss." He left Sanford's office and walked by Jennifer's desk. He looked over at her and smiled. "Your purse still there?"

When he walked out into the lobby, Jennifer stormed into Sanford's office. "That guy gives me the creeps! I hate it when he comes here. Why you let that freak in here is beyond me." She looked over and saw Nancy at the window. "Oh, Mrs. Abbott. I'm so sorry. I forgot you were here."

Nancy walked back to Sanford's desk. "That's okay." She stared at Sanford. "She's right. That guy is creepy. I thought he was going to deck you for a minute."

Sanford laughed. "Sonny Porter? He's harmless." He thought for a moment. "Well, probably not harmless, but he does serve a purpose."

"What could that possibly be?" Nancy asked.

"Information. Feet on the street. I need to know what's going on out there. The DA's office has investigators helping them. I need a few well-placed informants helping me out. You know, to even the playing field."

"If you say so," Nancy said. "How did you ever meet him? He certainly doesn't fit your typical client's profile."

"His old man. I helped him out a long time ago when he was growing weed way back in the swamp. He was a big player back then. He died in prison about ten years ago, but the kid keeps in touch and actually comes up with a few good tips every now and then."

"I've got a good tip for him," Jennifer said.

"You do?" Sanford asked.

"Yeah, tell him to stop messing with me. I'm not taking any more of his shit!"

A concerned look came over Sanford's face. "Watch out for him. Fact is, he's a low-life criminal, and he'll probably die in prison someday. He's got a hair-trigger temper, and I don't need you setting him off. I can deal with him, but I'm telling you…be careful when he's around."

Archie was surprised to see Candace at the office. "What are you still doing here? Don't you need to pick up Evan?"

"Oh, what time is it?"

"It's quarter after six."

"It is? Already? No, my sister was getting him tonight. She's taking him to her friend's daughter's birthday party. I'll pick him up at her house around eight. How did it go?"

"You were right. It's quite a place. A huge house with a big guest quarters. Five or six car garage. It sits right on the ocean. But, it's looking kind of run down. They only have three people on the staff. I don't see how it's possible to keep something so big running with so few people."

Candace looked puzzled. "Only three people? Why is that? Is the old lady running out of money?"

"I don't think so. Have you ever heard the name Mr. Leeds?"

"Are you kidding? Sanford Leeds? Sure. He's a big time attorney here. From what I hear, he's quite the ladies man. Why?"

"One of the help told me Mr. Leeds was the person cutting back on the staff. It really doesn't make sense to me. He's even had them board up the top two floors."

"Maybe he gets a percentage of all the money he can save or something," Candace wondered.

"Maybe, but the place is starting to look like it needs some work. Oh, and guess what?"

"What?"

"Remember Gloria Rodriquez?" Archie asked with a smile.

"Yeah."

"I met another Gloria Rodriquez at the Estate. This one was about twenty-five years older than the woman who showed up here."

"Was it her mother?"

"I don't think so. They didn't look anything alike. Something's not adding up here," Archie said, shaking his head.

Candace handed him a manila folder. "I've put together that file on Mrs. Silverman for you. Do you want to go over this stuff now or wait till tomorrow morning?"

He glanced down at his watch. "I don't mind doing it now if it's okay with you."

"Fine with me. I don't have to pick up Evan until eight. Okay, I started with some background on her husband, Franklin Silverman. He came from a very wealthy Connecticut family. His father and grandfather were northeast industrialists. Franklin never worked in the family business. From what I read, it seems like he was quite the playboy. You know, too rich to work. Anyway, he ended up in Hollywood, and he went on to become a producer of popular television game shows in the fifties."

"Sounds like he was living quite the life," Archie commented.

"That he was. Until there was a big scandal with one of his shows."

"Scandal? Oh, this sounds interesting. What happened?"

"Seems like some of the contestants were getting the answers before the show went on the air. It was a big deal, and his sponsors weren't too happy to have their brand tarnished."

"I heard about that," Archie said. "I think a couple of shows got busted."

"Old Franklin ended up in jail where he died of pneumonia a few years later. His wife wound up with most of the family fortune. He was an only child."

She paged through her notes. "Oh, there was a huge age difference between them. She was twenty-one when they got married and he was forty-seven. After his death, she inherited fancy houses all over the place. One in California, the English countryside, Connecticut and a few more."

"Did she ever remarry?" Archie asked.

"No, and I was wondering the same thing. She was a very rich, attractive woman, and I thought it was kind of strange that she never remarried. But, like I told you, as the years passed, she became more and more reclusive. It's a shame because she had some really famous friends around the time her husband died."

"Famous like Frank, Dean and Sammie?"

"How did you know?" Candace asked with a look of surprise.

"One of the staff told me. How did she meet her husband?" Archie asked. "Did she come from a wealthy family, too?"

"I don't know. The earliest I could find was an article in the New York Times social section about Franklin getting married. The article listed Clara's maiden name as Thorsen. I haven't had time to look into that yet."

Chapter 9

Clara Silverman's gray hair stood out in strong contrast against the dark blue pillow-case beneath her head. Her eyes fluttered open when she heard the door to her darkened room open. She tried to sit up but felt weak and tired. A shadowy figure approached. Clara reached out. "Please, where am I? I want to go home." She blinked and tried to focus as the person got nearer to the bed, but the room was very dim. She could see what appeared to be a woman's silhouette.

"You're in a safe place, Mrs. Silverman.
"Am I in the hospital? Did I have a stroke?"
"No, dear. Please, I brought you some oatmeal and orange juice. Just try and eat something, and then you can lie back down."

Clara picked up the glass and took a sip. It was cold and tasted as if it were freshly squeezed. "I want to go home." She handed the glass back to the woman.

"I know you do, dear."

The old woman picked up the spoon and ate a few bites of the oatmeal. She was feeling tired again. She pushed the bowl away and snuggled back down into the covers.

Sonny pulled his pickup into a dirt field and parked it next to a jeep that was painted in Desert Storm camouflage. He looked over at Ronnie. "Now you just listen and don't talk. Do you understand?"

Ronnie nodded.

"Do you understand?" Sonny asked again, this time louder.

"Yes, sir."

"That's better."

As they walked through a field toward a big tent, Sonny looked over and said, "I thought I asked your mother to iron your uniform."

"You did."

"Then why does it look like you just slept in it?" Ronnie hesitated. "Well?"

"Ma, doesn't like it."

Sonny stopped and glared at his son. "Did she tell you that?"

Ronnie looked down and kicked a clump of dirt with his black shoe. "Ah…ya."

"No shit. When she met me, she used to like it just fine. If you ask me, seems like her whole damn attitude's been changing lately. Well, you need to look sharp when you wear the White Brigade uniform. A sloppy uniform tells everyone you ain't got no discipline."

Sonny bent down and pulled Ronnie's shirt tight. "Don't ever wear the uniform like that again. If your Ma won't make it look nice, then you gotta iron it yourself. Got it?"

"Yes."

"What did you say?"

"Yes, sir."

The crowd was roaring as they approached the tent opening. Ronnie saw a man standing on a makeshift stage. He listened as the man spoke.

"Do we want to be the minority, my Brigade brothers?"

The crowd roared, "Nooo!."

"Do we want to give up our rights as the white race, my brothers?"

Again, the crowd responded with a loud, "Nooo!"

"Do we need the sick, the crippled, the weak and the Jews watering down our power?"

The crowd screamed back,"Nooo!"

Chapter 10

Thanksgiving morning started out rainy and gray. A thick salt fog blew in from the Atlantic Ocean and covered everything in a swirling mist of salty droplets. Archie grabbed the four bottles of wine he picked up the night before and looked at the clock. If he left the house immediately, there would be just enough time to stop by the office. He wanted to review the file Candace had started on the Silverman case, and he also wanted to see if there were any messages on his answering machine. He was hoping another potential customer may have seen his name on the office window and decided to call, or maybe Gloria or Enrique had something new to tell him.

Archie unlocked the main office door and stepped into the foyer. He flipped on the lights and walked back to his office. He glanced down at his answering machine. The light indicating new calls was not lit. He grabbed the Silverman folder on his desk and started reading. Candace had added some additional information about Mrs. Silverman's holdings, including a complete list of the houses she had all over the world. Archie glanced down the pages and saw summaries which included a penthouse in New York City overlooking Central Park, a lavish place in England, an oceanfront house in La Jolla, California, and a few others.

Archie finished reading and set the folder back down on his desk. He reached into his pocket and pulled out the number Candace found for his daughter. He stared at the paper for over a minute. *What the hell,* he thought as he pulled his cell phone out of his pocket and dialed the number. After five rings, a man's voice said, "Yeah." Archie wasn't expecting a male voice.

Again he heard, "Yeah?"

"Ah, hello. My name is Archie Archibald. I'm trying to reach my daughter, Amanda."

"Amanda's old man's dead. Is this some kind of sick joke?"

"No, no…please! I am her father, and I can tell you, I'm very much alive. Can I speak to her please?"

"She ain't here."

"Really? Well, with it being Thanksgiving and everything, I thought I'd call and try and talk to her."

"She's over at that bitch of her mother's place."

"I see. Well, if you don't mind, I'd like to leave my number."

"Don't bother. Like I said, her old man's dead. Anyway, the answering machine's grabbed the number."

"All right then. Well, you have a nice Thanksgiving, and please tell Amanda that I called."

The phone clicked and Archie hung up. He looked at the number again. Candace was correct. This guy wasn't going to win any personality contests. She may have found Amanda's number, but based on the tone and duration of the call, he didn't have a very good feeling he'd be hearing from Amanda anytime soon.

He walked back to the lobby, turned off the lights, locked up the place, and drove over to Candace's house. As he got closer, the sky started to lighten up. The rain had temporarily stopped, but fast moving dark clouds indicated it could start up again at any moment.

As Archie pulled up, Luther and Evan were playing catch in the front yard. Evan's wheelchair was sitting on a small mound of dirt surrounded by a thin puddle of rain-water. Evan was standing next to it, waiting for Luther to throw him a ball. Archie could see little sprays of water fly up when Luther's feet hit the grass. Archie grabbed the wine and walked over to Luther as he tossed an underhand pitch toward Evan. Archie could see Luther was careful to direct the softball slowly and precisely toward the boy. Evan reached out with both hands and firmly caught the ball. "Good job, Evan!" Luther shouted. "Come on, send it back to me as hard as you can."

As the ball sailed back to Luther, he caught it with an exaggerated motion. "Oh man, that one really stung. You're nailin' them now, kiddo." Luther held on to the ball and turned to Archie. "It's about time you got here. For a minute there, I thought you had stood us up."

Archie glanced down at this watch. "Oh, I had no idea it was so late. I stopped back at the office and the time just got away from me. I'm going inside and drop off the wine."

"You're gonna love the smell coming from that kitchen," Luther chuckled. He turned to the boy. "Okay, slugger. Get ready for this fast ball!"

Archie walked over and stepped into the house. Just as Luther said, the house smelled wonderful. Aromas of roasting turkey, fresh bread, and assorted spices washed over him as he walked through the living room to the kitchen.

Candace and Estelle were busy and didn't notice Archie at first. "Hello, ladies. Where do you want me to put the wine?"

Candace turned around. "Archie. It's about time you got here! Just set it on the counter over there." Candace pointed to the only empty space left on the countertop. "What took you so long?"

"I stopped over at the office. I wanted to review my one and only case."

She laughed. "Not much to review. Did you see the update I stuck in the file?"

"I did. Thank you for doing that."

Archie glanced into the living room and saw two little girls coloring.

"Aren't Estelle's girls darling? Can you run out and get Evan and Luther?" Candace asked. "Things are getting manageable in here. Let's get everyone in the living room and have a drink."

He walked outside and saw Luther was picking up the ball and glove. "Time to come in, guys. It sure smells great in there."

"Want a ride?" Luther asked Evan, as he grabbed the handles of Evan's chair.

"No, Coach. I can walk." He grabbed a side of the chair and held on to it as they both headed into the house. Archie followed behind.

The afternoon went by quickly. Archie was amused to see the interaction between Candace and her sister. He was a little disappointed that there was no mention of an airboat ride, but from the looks of the weather, he understood why. He had actually been looking forward to seeing what that swamp looked like. He had visited Everglades National Park several times when he lived in south Florida. He wondered if it looked the same.

The Thanksgiving meal was wonderful, and Archie could see Evan was very happy to have Coach Johnson spending time at his house during the holiday.

Archie and Luther helped clear the table. They both offered to help wash, but Candace insisted she and her sister would do the rest. Just as Archie was about to leave, his cell phone rang. He pulled it out of his pocket and glanced down. It was an Ohio number. From the look on Archie's face, Candace could see Archie needed some privacy. She pointed him to her bedroom, and when he walked in, she shut the door.

"Hello…" Archie answered.

"Um, hello?"

"Yes, Amanda. It's me."

"Kind of surprised to hear from you."

"Well, I'm not dead, if that's what you thought."

"Dead?" Amanda asked, with a shock in her voice.

"That's what the gentlemen said when I told him who I was. I know it's been about five years since we talked, but it wasn't because I had passed away. You know I tried to reach you."

There was a pause. "That not what Mom thinks."

"Why do you say that?" he asked. Again, silence.

"Whenever I'd ask about you, she'd say you weren't interested in me."

Archie felt his face flush. He thought about the best way to answer that. "Honey, that's just not true, and it's never been true. I've tried to get in touch with you many times, but your mom and her husband always put me off."

"Ex-husband."

"What?"

"They got divorced. Mom threw the creep out."

Archie sat down on the edge of Candace's bed. "Oh. Anyway, I wanted you to know that I recently moved the office from Fort Lauderdale up here to Vero, and one of the first things I did was ask my new assistant to see if she could track you down. She understands that social media stuff a lot better than I do. Finally, she was able to find your number." Archie paused. "You don't mind that I called you, do you?"

"I...I don't know. Mom said you didn't like us and you didn't want to talk to me anymore."

He tensed. "Amanda, that's just not true. You know what can happen when two people get divorced. Sometimes unkind things are said in anger. I've always wanted to keep in touch, but your mother made it impossible for me to contact you. Now that you seem to be out on your own, I'm hoping we can get to know each other again."

He held his breath and listened for a response. After quite some time, she replied, "Really? This is just so different from what I thought. Can I think about it for awhile?"

A jolt of panic swept through him. "Ah...sure you can. Take as long as you need. Well, I hope that's not too long. Oh, can I ask you a question?"

Another pause. "Yeah..."

"Are you married?"

"What?"

"You know, married. Some guy answered when I called you."

"Oh, that was Travis. No, we're not married. Not yet, anyway. But he does live here with me."

Archie sighed. "Okay, well I was worried you went off and got married and didn't let me walk you down the aisle."

"No, that didn't happen. Look, I need some time to figure this all out."

"Okay, Amanda. Thank you so much for calling me back. Please don't ever forget I love you."

"Bye."

Archie stuffed the phone back into his pocket and fished out his handkerchief. He dabbed his eyes a few times and thought how wonderful it had been hearing his daughter's voice. He could never thank Candace enough for all the work she did tracking Amanda down.

He opened the bedroom door and walked out into the living room. Candace and Estelle were talking to Luther. Candace looked up with a puzzled look.

"Amanda," Archie whispered.

From the look on his face, it was clear to the group that questions were not an option. "Nice, Archie," Candace said, with a wink. "Very nice to hear."

Luther stood up. "Thank you, everyone. It's been wonderful." He turned to Evan. "Keep using that pitching arm of yours, Evan. You about knocked me over a few times out there."

Evan laughed. "Okay, Coach."

Archie stood up. "Time for me to head home, too. That was a fantastic meal. Thank you both for inviting us over." He walked over to the front door and stopped. "Oh, remember. We're off tomorrow.

Didn't want to interfere with you ladies and your shopping. I'll see you back in the office on Monday."

"We still going fishing tomorrow?" Luther asked. "You're not getting up at three in the morning to hit the malls, are you?"

Archie laughed, "Not a chance. Pick me up at six o'clock like we talked about. Don't worry, I'll be ready."

Chapter 11

Luther knocked on Archie's door exactly at six in the morning. Archie walked out carrying his fishing gear and a small cooler. "Morning, Luther. Looks like we got a nice day."

"A lot nicer than yesterday," Luther replied, his eyes scanning the sky. He helped with some of Archie's gear and tossed it in the back of his bass boat.

They headed west out of Vero on State Road 60. Forty-five minutes later, they were pulling into Middleton's Fish Camp, the only fish camp on Blue Cypress Lake. Luther skillfully backed the boat down the ramp, and Archie marveled at how perfectly smooth the lake looked as Luther floated the boat off the trailer. He threw Archie a rope attached to the boat. "Hold on to this. I'll park the truck and be back in a minute." Soon they were in the boat, skimming across the flat surface of Blue Cypress Lake.

The sun was a ball of orange as it peeked over the horizon. Archie saw alligators floating on the surface on both sides of the boat. Every now and then one would sink down below the surface as the boat came too close. As they approached the middle of the lake, Luther slowed the boat down, and they both grabbed fishing poles and started casting.

"We got seven miles of the cleanest water in Florida," Luther beamed, as he tossed out his line. "Ain't this something!"

Archie marveled at the beauty of the lake. It was easy to see where the lake got its name. The water was truly blue, and a thick ring of Cypress trees lined the shore. Archie looked up to see two ospreys circling overhead, calling to each other.

"It doesn't get much better than this," Archie said as he felt a pull on his line. He set the hook and reeled in a good size bass. They fished for two more hours, enjoying the sun, the scenery, and the quiet solitude of the lake.

Luther pulled out a thermos. "Coffee?"

"Sure, that would be great."

They both sat in the bobbing boat, enjoying the view. "Gator!" Archie called out as an eight foot alligator floated near them.

"This lake's full of them," Luther said. "A few weeks ago, I had twelve swimming around the boat."

Archie took a sip of coffee. "You know my daughter called last night when we were at Candace's."

"I was wondering if that's who called," Luther said.

"That Candace is something. I asked her if maybe she could look into finding Amanda's number, and in no time at all, she had it. I've been trying to find it for a long time with no luck. Candace jumps on it, and before you know it, she's got the number."

"That's amazing."

"Well, she did resort to using a secret weapon that would have never worked for me."

"A secret weapon?" Luther asked. What's that?"

"She posted a sexy picture of herself and claimed to be Amanda's friend from high school looking for her. She targeted the boys in Amanda's class, and it worked out pretty good. You should have seen that picture. Let's just say, she took advantage of all of her assets."

Luther laughed. "I wish that picture had been in my yearbook!"

"I don't think it would have been allowed in mine," Archie replied. "But who cares! It worked, and I got to hear my daughter's voice for the first time in a very long time."

"I'm glad for you."

"Now I just have to wait and see how much my ex has poisoned her about me. I sure hope she calls me back."

The calm of the water was interrupted by a large splash as a huge gator dove underwater.

"Did you see that one?" Luther asked.

"What a monster!" Archie said. "I'd hate to fall off this boat. God knows how long you'd last."

Archie and Luther fished for several more hours before heading back to Vero. It was six-thirty when Luther pulled up to Archie's apartment.

"That was amazing," Archie said, as he lifted his fishing gear from the boat. "I sure can understand why you moved up here. Thanks for taking me with you."

"Anytime, Archie. You know me; I'm always up for fishing. I'll try and stop by and see you at the office sometime next week."

Nancy Abbott heard her cell phone ring just as she pulled into her cobblestone driveway. She was exhausted from shopping, and her car was filled with Black Friday bargains. She glanced down at the dashboard clock. It was quarter to six. She kept the car running as she fished her phone out of her purse. *Sanford? What could he want this late in the day?* Nancy had a look of irritation on her face as she answered the phone. "Yes?"

"Nancy, it's me."

"I know. What's going on?"

"You need to get over to my office right now. It's very important."

"Now? Sanford, this isn't a good time. My husband's home and..."

"It's not about that. Something's come up, and it's important that we talk. Where are you?"

"I just pulled up to my house. I've been shopping all day. I'm exhausted…"

Sanford interrupted her. "Look, you can be here in ten minutes. I'll see you then."

Nancy heard a click as Sanford hung up. She sighed, put the car into reverse, and backed out of the driveway. *What in the world could be so important?* she wondered.

Jennifer Taylor walked into Sanford's office and started to cough. "You can't smoke in here!"

Sanford spun around holding a cigar in his teeth. He pulled it out of his mouth and exhaled a large cloud of smoke. "This is my building. My father built it, and I pay taxes on it. If I want to smoke in my office, I'm going to smoke in my office."

"Suit yourself, I guess, but Mrs. Abbott's waiting for you in the lobby, and I'm sure she'll be thrilled to have her beautiful Donna Karan suit smelling like an old cigar." Jennifer said. "By the way, she doesn't seem to be in a very good mood. Just so you know."

"I really don't care. Send her in, will you? Oh, you don't have to stick around. You can go home."

Jennifer walked back to the lobby and ushered Nancy into Sanford's office.

Sanford stubbed out his cigar, brushed past Nancy and closed the door. Nancy waved her hand in front of her face, as she walked over and tried to open a window. "This is disgusting, Sanford. How can you stand it?"

"Don't bother. They don't open. Stand it? That was a twenty dollar cigar!"

She turned to him. "So what's going on? You seemed a little agitated when you called."

"We got a problem," he said, taking a seat behind his huge mahogany desk. "Sit down."

"Okay, okay," Nancy said, glancing at her watch. "What is it?"

Sanford looked across the desk. "Clara's disappeared."

She thought for a second, not comprehending. "Disappeared? I thought you told me the other day she wasn't feeling well."

"Unfortunately, that wasn't the case. Gloria called me all in a panic a few days ago and told me she couldn't find Clara. I rushed over and thought she must be wandering around the grounds somewhere. We looked everywhere and couldn't find her. The next day you showed up. I was still trying to get a grip that this really was happening, so I couldn't say anything when we talked on the phone."

Nancy stood up, walked over to a window, and thought for a moment. "So, what happened? Clara's gone. You couldn't find her on the grounds. Has she been kidnapped? Has anyone called and left a message?"

"No," Sanford said. "You would think by now someone would have contacted me if that's what was going on."

"What about that cook, Harrow?'

"What about him?" Sanford asked.

"I think he's creepy. If anyone was behind something like this, I'd put my money on him."

Sanford laughed, "He's been with Mrs. Silverman longer than any of the others. Gloria and Enrique don't care for him, either. I think they're jealous because he seems to have a special relationship with the old lady. She doesn't treat him like servant. He comes and goes as he pleases, at least once the cooking's taken care of."

Nancy turned to him. "What are you going to do? She's either been kidnapped or she walked into the woods or the pond and is dead by now, and you just haven't found her yet. In her frail condition, what else could it be?"

"I think you're right," Sanford said after a moment. "Enrique and I are going to have to check the property again."

"Can I ask a question?"

Sanford walked over and put his arm around Nancy. "Certainly."

She pulled away. "You said this happened Tuesday, right?"

"Yes."

"So, why haven't you gone to the police?"

Sanford stepped back, a look of irritation on his face. "Do you have any idea of how this would look? I'm the guy in charge of her and something like this happens? I could be ruined!"

Nancy shot Sanford a look. "Well, you have to do something. You can't go on forever pretending nothing's happened."

"I'm not pretending anything. For God's sake, Nancy, I'm trying to protect the golden egg we have here. Do you want to lose the best client you've ever had?"

Nancy laughed, "I hate to break the news to you, but I think she is lost. And I doubt this is all about me. I'm forking over quite the percentage of my sales right back to you. I can only imagine what you're skimming off the Estate every year for yourself."

Sanford grabbed her by the shoulders. "Stop it. This has worked very well for both of us for quite some time. And I am doing something. I just need a little more time to find out what's going on. Nobody knows anything about this, so I figure I have a few more days. I've retained a private investigator to look into this. He's already been over to the Estate. Now, don't you go talking to anyone about this. Not even your husband."

"A private investigator? Isn't that a little risky? How are you going to keep him quiet?"

"I found a guy who just moved up here from South Florida. He doesn't know anyone around here." Sanford paused. "And...I paid him a hell of a lot of money."

"I don't know...it's still a risk. What about Gloria and Enrique?"

"I told them that I'm working on this, not to say anything to anyone, and I stressed that I'm

The Black Orchid Mystery

keeping them on the payroll. They understand that if word leaks out, the money stops. I don't think I have to worry about them right now."

"Disappeared! I can hardly believe it. I bet she wandered off somewhere." Nancy said, shaking her heard.

Sanford stepped closer to her. "I need to have a drink. Lets go over to The Tides."

A shocked look crossed Nancy's face. "You know I can't. Victor's back in town."

"He is? Well, it won't take long. One drink."

"Sanford, we need to talk about this, I don't think we can…"

With a wave of his hand, he interrupted, "Forget it. Let's not go there now. We've both got a lot on our minds."

Nancy walked over to the couch and picked up her purse. "I've got to go. Let me know what you find out."

Chapter 12

Archie woke up early Saturday morning. He looked at the clock and saw it was only five-thirty. He groaned and dragged himself out of bed. It was no use; he was wide awake. He had been dreaming all night long about searching for Mrs. Silverman. He got up and made a pot of coffee and then walked out to his driveway and picked up the morning paper. It was still dark out, and Archie felt a cold chill in the air. He poured himself a cup, sat down at the kitchen table, and unfolded the paper.

Archie sat up with a start. The headline read *Vero Beach recluse leaves estate in the middle of the night.* There was a fuzzy picture of someone with long white hair slumped down in the back of a dark car. The picture was obviously taken in very dim lighting conditions, and it was impossible to see who was driving. A shadowy figure could be seen in the passenger seat, but it was impossible to make out who it was, or even if the person was a man or a woman. Archie scanned the article.

"Vero's wealthiest resident, Clara Silverman, who has lived in seclusion in her Vero Beach mansion for the past ten years, is rumored to have left her Estate in the middle of the night, November 22nd for an unknown destination, an unnamed source has confirmed.

The spokesperson declined to say exactly when, where, or for how long the 84 year old Silverman would be gone. Little is known of Ms. Silverman's private life for the last forty years, but it is believed that she has not visited any of her many other luxury homes, which are located in the United States and in Europe, in over ten years."

Archie glanced at the clock. It was only 5:52 am. Too early to call over to the Estate. He wondered who the unnamed spokesperson was that provided the story to the press. And where did that picture come from? He tried to remember what the photographer's name was that Enrique had mentioned.

He walked into the spare bedroom, picked up his notebook and thumbed through his notes. There it was, Russell Craig.

Jennifer Taylor was sleeping soundly when the phone rang. She slapped at the nightstand, thinking it was her alarm. When the ringing didn't stop, Jennifer sat up and grabbed for the phone.

Sanford heard something that sounded close to 'Hello.' "Wake up! Have you read the paper this morning?"

"What? Paper? No, I don't get the paper. What time is it?"

"It's six-thirty. We need to talk. This is important, you need to wake up," Sanford said gruffly.

She sat up on the edge of her bed. "Okay, okay. Give me a minute. It's Saturday, isn't it?"

"Yes, it is, but there's an article in the morning paper about Clara, and there's even a picture of her being taken away in a car!" Sanford yelled into the phone.

"What does it say?" Jennifer asked. Sanford read her the article. "And you said there's a picture?"

"Not much of one. It's pretty blurry. Kind of looks like it came from one of those bank video cameras. It shows someone with long gray hair lying in the backseat. I guess it could be Clara, but from the quality of it, it could also be a fake."

"Did you say the article said this was her leaving early Wednesday morning?"

"Yes, that's what it says."

"And that's when Gloria said Clara went missing," Jennifer said. "So how could it not be real? Who took the picture?"

"I don't know. And I'm sure they're not going to tell me anything. I mean, I can't really be calling them up and asking them for information. You need to call that detective right now and let him know about this."

Jennifer yawned. "Okay. But…he's going to know I'm not Gloria by now."

Sanford thought for a moment. "Oh, that. Damnit, just tell him you represent a major interest in the Estate or something like that."

"He's not going to buy it. Don't you think he'll want to know who he's working for? For goodness sake, he could be working for the kidnapper, if there is one, for all he knows."

"You checked him out and think he's okay, right?" Sanford asked, cautiously.

"I think so."

"All right, then. If he starts asking questions, tell him who you are and that you work for me."

Archie was still reviewing his notes when the phone rang.

"Mr. Archibald?

"This is…ah, Gloria Rodriquez."

From the sound of the voice and the lack of accent, Archie knew he was talking to the Gloria that had walked into his office, not the Gloria he met at the Estate. "Er…yes?"

"Do you get the paper?"

"I do, and I've already read the article about Mrs. Silverman."

"We were hoping this information didn't leak out, but as you can see, it has. We have to find out how that picture was obtained."

"I was going to call Enrique this morning. I thought I'd wait awhile, since it's so early."

"I was wondering, when you went over there, did you discover anything that may be connected to that article and picture?" Jennifer asked.

"I may have an idea or two, but first, I really need to know who I'm actually talking with. I presume your real name's not Mrs. Rodriguez?"

Jennifer let out a nervous laugh. "No, it isn't. My name is Jennifer Taylor, and I'm the administrative assistant to the lawyer who is handling Mrs. Silverman's estate, Sanford Leeds."

"Okay, that's better. Why did you tell me your name was Gloria?"

"I'm sorry for being so stupid. It was my fault. Because of the sensitivity of this issue, Mr. Leeds wanted me to check you out before we told you about what's going on. I got nervous and gave you Gloria's name. It was a stupid mistake on my part, and I knew you'd figure it out as soon as you got over there."

"Those things happen, Ms. Taylor. Just to make sure I know who I'm dealing with, why don't I meet with Mr. Leeds in his office in about an hour. Could you arrange that?"

"I'm sure I can. I'll call you in a few minutes and confirm."

Archie walked over to his computer and found the address for Sanford Leeds' law practice. A few minutes later, Jennifer called and confirmed the meeting.

Archie jumped into the shower, got dressed, and headed over to Sanford's office. He was

The Black Orchid Mystery

impressed when he saw that the oceanfront building was named "The Leeds Building."

Archie took the elevator to the fifth floor. Since it was Saturday, there was no receptionist out in the lobby. Archie stood there for a few minutes wishing he had written down Sanford's phone number, when the outer door opened and a tall, athletic man in his mid-fifties walked out.

"Mr. Archibald?" Sanford asked, extending his hand. "Come on in."

Archie followed him into his office. He glanced out the windows and saw a spectacular view of the ocean and A1A.

"Sit down, sit down," Sanford said. "Sorry about the confusion with my secretary using Gloria's name. She was a little confused on how to handle this."

Archie sat down and saw the morning paper spread out on Sanford's desk. "Are you the unnamed spokesperson mentioned in that article?" Archie asked.

"Me?" Sanford said, with a look of complete surprise. "Hell no! We didn't want this to go public."

"That's interesting," Archie said. "Probably something that a kidnapper wouldn't comment on, either."

"And why a picture?" Sanford asked. "It's a terrible one at that, so dark and fuzzy, but it looks like it could be Mrs. Silverman."

"Can I see the paper?" Archie asked.

Sanford pushed the paper over, and Archie bent down to take a closer look. "You're more familiar with the Estate than I am, but it almost looks like this picture was taken when the car was coming around the side of the driveway nearest to the house. Do you agree?"

Sanford got up from behind his desk and leaned over the paper next to Archie. "It's so dark but…yes, I think you could be right."

"And look at the angle," Archie said. It must have been taken from the second floor of the guest suites."

Sanford stared at the picture. "You know, it could have."

"I'd like to head over there and look around," Archie said.

"Good idea. I'll come with you."

When they arrived at the mansion, Enrique was outside walking toward the garage. He looked surprised.

Sanford got out of his car and showed Enrique the paper. "Have you seen this yet?"

Archie stepped out and started walking over to the guest suites. Enrique studied the picture. "No. This is today's paper?"

"Yes!" Sanford said. "Can you believe this?"

Archie climbed the stairs to the second floor of the guest suites and looked over at the driveway. He wished he had the paper so he could take another look at the picture. At the top of the steps, the landing continued to the right for about fifteen feet. A grouping of terra cotta pots filled with assorted plants was clustered at the end of the landing. Archie walked to the end and looked down at the driveway. The view looked very similar. He bent down and peered around the pots. Archie moved several of the smaller ones away and got down on his hands and knees. He pulled out his handkerchief, reached into a thin crevice, and pulled out a small camera that was carefully positioned in the middle of all the grouping

"I found it!" he yelled down to Sanford and Enrique. He held up his hand so they could see what he had discovered. They both turned and ran up the stairway.

"What is it?" Sanford said.

"It's a wireless camera." Archie said.

"Is that an antenna?" Sanford asked, pointing to a fingerlike formation poking out of the back.

"Sure is," Archie said. "It can send a picture to a smart phone or computer."

"That damn Russell Craig!" Enrique said. "It has to be him."

"Didn't you just throw him off the property again?" Sanford asked.

"Yeah! He must have stuck this up there before I caught him."

Sanford turned to Archie. "You need to go talk to him and see what the hell's going on."

"He's got a studio off 12th Street on US 1," Enrique said. "I've stopped in there a few times and tried to put the fear of God in him, but it never did any good."

Archie wrapped the camera up in his handkerchief.

"Let's go," Sanford said. "If you find out he's behind this, I'll sue him for trespassing, breach of privacy, anything I can think of. I've had it with that sneaky bastard."

On the way back to Sanford's office, he told Archie about all the times Enrique had to toss Russell off the property.

"Is a picture of Mrs. Silverman really in such demand?" Archie asked, somewhat skeptical.

"It's hard to believe, but I guess it is. She brings this on herself by being such a recluse," Sanford said. "Word on the street is, some of those disgusting tabloids will pay up to ten grand for a current picture of her."

"No wonder this guy's so interested," Archie said. "I doubt that dark, blurry picture in today's paper would bring that kind of money."

"We're in the wrong business, if it did," Sanford said as he pulled up next to Archie's car. "Let me know what you find out."

Archie got in his car and drove over to 12th Street. He found Russell's studio. It was on the ground floor of a two story building in the middle of the block. He walked up and saw a big red "Closed" sign hanging in the window. He tried the door anyway. It was locked.

Archie walked around to the back of the building and saw a car parked behind the studio. There were steps leading up to a second-floor apartment. The window was open to the right of a blue door that needed a paint job, and he could see curtains fluttering in the breeze. He walked up the stairs as quietly as he could. There were just enough steps to start his leg aching. Archie heard music coming from the apartment. He walked closer to the open window. He could hear voices coming from the interior of the apartment. He banged on the door. The voices stopped, and Archie heard footsteps approaching the door. The door slowly opened and a beautiful young woman stood on the other side. "Can I help you?"

Archie fished out his wallet and showed her his PI license. "I'm looking for Russell Craig."

She looked down at the license and then back to the inside of the apartment. "He's not here."

Archie could tell she was lying. "Come on, I just have a few questions to ask him. I'll be out of here in a couple of minutes."

She turned around and yelled, "Russ, a detective's here to talk to you."

Archie watched through the doorway as a man in his early twenties walked over to the door. He looked wider than he was tall. His hair was long and stringy. It looked as if it could use a good washing. The guy looked pale, like he spent most of his time eating candy bars and playing video games or maybe spending too much time in a dark room. Archie thought, *I'm dating myself. They don't even make darkrooms anymore.*

The guy walked over to the door and took a look at Archie. "You from the police department?"

"No, I'm a private detective."

Russell pushed the door open wider. "Oh. Come in. I knew somebody would probably be coming to see me."

He pushed a big black lab off the couch and motioned for Archie to sit down. Archie looked down at a thick layer of dog hair and wondered how long it was going to take him to brush that off his pants. A cocktail table in front of the couch was covered with empty soda cans, two greasy pizza boxes, an overflowing ashtray, and several photography magazines.

"What do you want with me?" Russell asked, slightly confrontational.

"Why were you expecting someone to come by and see you?" Archie asked back.

"That picture in today's paper. Everyone knows I'm slightly obsessed with getting a picture of Mrs. Silverman. Just ask Enrique."

"So I've heard. Are you responsible for that picture?"

"Naw. Wish I was." Russell reached over, grabbed an opened Coke can from the table and took a drink.

"I'm sure you would have done a much better job as a photographer, right?" Archie asked.

He grinned. "You got that right. That picture was awful."

Archie reached into his pocket and pulled out the wireless camera. "Ever see this before?"

A look of surprise crossed Russell's face for a second, but he quickly recovered. "Ah…no. Where did you find that?"

Archie smiled. "How did you know I found it anywhere? Maybe I bought it on the internet?"

Russell took another sip of soda. "Maybe you did."

"How much did you get for the picture?" Archie asked.

"I told you, I didn't take it."

"All I have to do is go down to the newspaper office and ask to see who they wrote a check to, and I'll bet your name comes up," Archie said.

"Hey, go waste your time if you want to," Russell said with a laugh. "It's a free country."

Archie leaned forward. "We can banter around here for another hour, but let's talk about what you and I both know. You're the only person Enrique keeps kicking off the property. You're the only photographer who keeps trying to get a picture of Mrs. Silverman, and you're the only guy who could have easily hidden this camera on the property if you wanted to. Now let's talk about what you don't know. The picture in today's paper is very important in ways you can't even imagine. I can't go into it now, but if you don't want to talk to me, you'll probably have a roomful of police and FBI going through this apartment with a fine tooth comb. And we haven't even started talking about the trespassing and invasion of privacy charges that I know could be coming at you. Have it your way."

Russell laughed. "FBI because of that picture? Man, you gotta do better than that."

Archie stood up. "Here's my card. I wouldn't wait too long to give me a call."

As Archie headed back to the office, he gave Sanford a call. "I talked with Russell Craig. He didn't admit it, but I'm sure he's the guy that planted the camera. From his demeanor, I don't think he had anything to do with Mrs. Silverman's disappearance. I think he just wanted a picture, and he has no idea what that picture is really about." Archie waited for Sanford to say something.

Finally, Sanford asked, "He didn't admit taking the picture?"

"No."

"Who do you think the unnamed source for the comments about Clara is?"

Archie thought for a moment. "Probably a combination between Russell and some editor down at the paper. They had to say something. They couldn't just publish a photograph."

"I wish that creep had at least owned up to planting that damn camera," Sanford said. "I think he knows a little more about what's going on than what he's saying."

"I gave him one of my cards. Maybe he'll have a change of heart and give me a call."

"Let me know immediately if he does," Sanford said.

Archie drove over to the office and walked back to his desk. He pulled out the Silverman file and started updating his notes. He summarized his meeting with Russell Craig. He pulled out the wireless camera and took a digital picture of it for his files. Archie looked up the manufacturer on the internet and saw that they had twenty four hour customer service. He picked up the phone and dialed. "Yes, this is Russell Craig. I recently purchased a wireless camera from you, model 965 SEC. The antenna has come lose and needs to be replaced. Do you know if you can sell me that part?" Archie heard the customer service agent look up his name. "It's under warranty and you'll send me a new one? Wonderful. Yes, I can verify my shipping address, but would it be possible to hold off for a week or two? I'm going out of town and I won't be here to pick up the package. How about I give you a call next week?"

He hung up the phone. Just as he thought, Russell planted the camera. He stood up and walked over to the coffee maker. As he waited for the pot to brew, Archie heard a faint noise at the front door. He stepped out into Candace's area and watched as a woman quickly kneeled down on the sidewalk in front of his office. He saw a folded piece of paper slip under his door. He ran to the front door and pulled it open. "Can I help you, Ma'am?"

The woman let out a high pitched squeal and spun around. She had a frightened look on her face, as she took a step backwards. She turned and started quickly walking down the sidewalk. Archie reached down, grabbed the folded, and ran after her.

It didn't take him long to catch up with her. "Mrs. Rodriquez! What's going on? Did you want to see me?"

The woman looked up and down the street. "I shouldn't be here. I thought since it was Saturday, nobody would be around."

Archie waved the note. "Well, you must be interested in talking with me, or else you wouldn't have gone to all the trouble of coming down here and leaving me a message."

"Sir, in the note I asked you to call me. I shouldn't be here in person."

Archie unfolded the paper. He read, "Dear Mr. Archibald, I met you when you came to Mrs. Silverman's house. Please call me at 432-8876. G. Rodriguez."

Archie looked back at the woman. "Please, Miss Rodriquez, no one has seen you. Look, you can see for yourself, the street's completely deserted. Let's walk back to my office, and we can talk about your concerns."

As they returned to the building, Archie opened the door and motioned for the woman to enter. She was wearing a plain blue checkered dress with a gray scarf tied around her head.

Archie pointed to his office door. "Let's sit down and you can tell me what's on your mind. Would you like a cup of coffee? I just made a fresh pot."

"No, senor. But muchas…um, thank you." The woman glanced around. Archie could tell she was nervous.

"Not a problem," Archie said. "What can I do for you? Do you have any new information about Mrs. Silverman?"

The woman shook her head. "No, nothing new."

"Okay," Archie said, somewhat puzzled. "What did you want to speak to me about?"

"Mr. Leeds hired you to see if you could find out what happened to Mrs. Silverman, right?"

"Yes, that's correct."

Gloria started to speak, but stopped. She brought her hands up to cover her face and started sobbing.

"What is it? Ms. Rodriguez, what's the matter?"

She suddenly stood up. "I...I...should not be coming here."

Archie jumped from behind his desk, walked over and put his arm around Gloria. "Please, sit back down." He pulled out his handkerchief and handed it to her. "Wipe your eyes. Just sit back and relax. Catch your breath for a moment."

She took the handkerchief. "Thank you, thank you."

He gave her a few moments to compose herself. "Okay, that's better. Now, what was it you wanted to speak to me about?"

She hung on to Archie's handkerchief as if she was going to need it again. Gloria looked up, and Archie could see her eyes were red. "I was hoping you could find some family for Mrs. Silverman."

"Family? Like relatives?"

"Yes...yes. Relations. When you're looking for what happened, I think it would be nice if you could find out about Mrs. Silverman's relations."

"Are you suggesting that they may have something to do with her disappearance?" Archie asked.

"Oh, no…not that," Gloria said, with a look of alarm.

"Okay. So can you tell me why you think this would be a good idea?"

"Everybody should have a family, Mr. Archibald. Mrs. Silverman always tell me she doesn't have one and doesn't want one, but I think it would be a good thing."

"If Mrs. Silverman isn't interested, maybe it wouldn't be a good idea for me to do something she appears not to be interested in."

A profound look of sadness crossed Gloria's face. "So, you think so, too."

"Did you ever think that at her age, maybe her family's all dead?" Archie thought about his daughter. "I don't know, Ms. Rodriguez. I'd hate to go against the wishes of Mrs. Silverman, but if you think that finding her family may help us locate her, maybe I should look into it."

"Mr. Leeds would not be happy. He thinks her family would only want her money. Maybe this is a bad idea." Gloria got up from the chair. "Please, forget I came here. Please don't tell Mr. Leeds about this. I would be fired right away."

"Don't worry I won't say a word to Mr. Leeds. But now that you're here, can I ask you a few questions about how the Estate runs?"

Gloria looked down at her watch. "Really, I should be back by now."

"I'll tell you what," Archie said. "If you stay for another ten minutes and talk to me, I promise I'll see what we can find out about Mrs. Silverman's relatives, and I won't ever mention it to Mr. Leeds. How about that?"

Gloria's eyes lit up. "Really? Oh, yes, I can stay a few more minutes."

"Thank you. I just wanted to double check that it's only you, Enrique and Mr. Harrow that work at the Estate, correct?"

"Yes, there used to be more. Many more. But Mr. Leeds said Mrs. Silverman didn't trust them and he started letting them go. It's very hard for us. We can't take care of such a huge place now, with only us left."

"I can imagine," Archie said. "What does Enrique and the other fellow do?"

"Enrique mostly works outside. He makes sure the lawn men do a good job. He used to drive Mrs. Silverman around, but she never goes anywhere now."

"Okay. So, you do have people come in and cut the lawn and do the landscaping."

"Yes, it's Enrique's job to watch them."

"I see. What keeps you busy?"

"I watch over her, give her medicine, feed her, and I do the cleaning."

"What does Mr. Harrow do?"

A frown crossed Gloria's face, but in a moment, it was gone. "Mr. Harrow. He's the cook."

"How long has he been the cook?"

"He's been with Mrs. Silverman the longest time. He used to work for her in England. He moves with her, where ever she goes."

"He must be a very good cook," Archie laughed.

Gloria did not say anything and her expression remained dour. She turned to face Archie. "And he's working on Mrs. Silverman's story."

"Story? What do you mean?"

"You know. All about her life."

Archie looked surprised. "I thought she was so private? A recluse, in fact."

"Recluse?"

"You know, someone who stays by themselves and shuns other people."

Gloria thought. "That's true, but James has been trying to do this for a long time."

"Mr. Harrow is helping Mrs. Silverman write a book about her life?"

"Yes, like I tell you, her story. James, he keeps telling her that she's not getting any younger, and people should know about her story. I mean her life."

A look of panic crossed her face. "I should not be talking of these things. James told me to not say anything. Not even to Mr. Leeds."

"Mr. Leeds doesn't know about this?"

Gloria's face flushed. "No, and I should not have said anything. Please, forget this." Gloria looked as if she were about to cry again. "I must go now," she said, as she pushed her chair back.

The Black Orchid Mystery

"Don't worry, Ms. Rodriquez. His secret's safe with me. Oh, one more thing. You mentioned one of your duties was to give Mrs. Silverman medicine? What does she take? Is it for Alzheimer's or something like that?"

"Oh, no. Her mind is very good. Mr. Leeds brings it. It's to make her sleep better." She walked over to Archie's door and stopped. "I'll come back with some of Mrs. Silverman's pictures and letters. Maybe that will help you find a relative."

Archie smiled, "That sounds like a good idea. Then I can take a look at what you bring me and learn a little more about Mrs. Silverman."

Gloria whispered, "Nobody must know I have done this, especially Mr. Leeds."

"That won't be a problem. Why don't you come by early Monday morning? I'll be here by seven-thirty. You won't have to worry, nobody's around here at that time."

"Okay, Mr. Archibald, I'll bring them."

He got up from his desk and handed her one of his cards. "If you think of anything, please call me." He followed her out to the lobby. She opened the door, stuck her head outside, and looked up and down the street before stepping onto the sidewalk.

Archie walked back to his office and sat down. He thought about the conversation with Gloria and wondered why she was so adamant about finding a relative of Mrs. Silverman. He pulled out his notes and scribbled down all he could remember about what had just taken place.

He walked over to Candace's desk, found a sticky note, wrote "Candace, See if you can find any relatives for Mrs. Silverman" and stuck it on her computer monitor. When he was finished, Archie reviewed a list of tasks she had been working on. One of them was a group of charities Mrs. Silverman was known to contribute to. He ran his fingers down the list and stopped when he saw one called 'A Second Chance' run by Doctor Garneau. Archie wondered why that name seemed familiar. He flipped back a few pages and started reading his notes on Jennifer Taylor's visit. There it was. Doctor Garneau was the guy Jennifer said wasn't happy with Mrs. Silverman's latest contribution.

Archie felt energized from Gloria's visit. He wasn't interested in going back to his quiet apartment on this long Thanksgiving week-end. Archie looked at the clock. There was plenty of time to pay Doctor Garneau a visit. Archie looked up the address of The Second Chance and headed out the door.

Chapter 13

Twenty miles west of Vero, three dogs, two of them pit-bull mixes, the other one a black mutt, were lying in the white sand and gravel in front of Sonny Porter's singlewide. Sonny's voice could be heard from the open kitchen window. He started yelling and calling Francine just about every nasty name he could think of. The two pit-bulls stood up and found new spots to rest out behind the trailer where thick palmetto bushes grew. The other dog watched them leave, but just put his head back down and stared at the front door. The trailer was parked on a dead-end dirt road, three miles west of Fellsmere. There were no neighbors around to complain or call the police.

A loud slap was quickly followed by a high pitched scream and then a deep thud. The black dog jumped up and ran over to the tall grass next to an abandoned car. Less than a minute later, Sonny Porter flung open the trailer door, stomped down the steps, and marched over to his truck. He turned back to the house, picked up a rock, and threw it at the dog he had just walked past. The dog yelped, ran to the back and crashed through the shrubs to join the other two.

Sonny stood next to his truck for a moment breathing heavily. He slammed his hand down on the hood of the truck and walked back toward the trailer. He bounded up the porch steps, pulled open the door, and stood glaring at his wife, who was still lying on the floor. A thin trickle of blood appeared from her nose.

Sonny yelled, "Damnit, Francine, you were supposed to do something about this, and look at you, it's getting bigger!"

She lay on the floor not wanting to move. Finally, Francine reached over to a chair, which had been knocked on its side, grabbed hold of it for support, and tried to stand up. She didn't look at Sonny. "Like I already told you, it's too late to do anything. The doctor told me it was too late."

Ronnie was in his room with his back pressed hard against the door. He could hear his heart pounding, but he was listening to hear if his father was going to come down the hallway to his room.

Sonny took a step toward her as Francine pulled herself into a tight ball, using her arms to protect her head. "Well, you better figure out something, because we can't afford to have another kid running around. This trailer ain't big enough for what we got now. I told you to tell your dad to put us in a real house, anyway. What's wrong with that bastard? He got all that money, and we're living down here in this dump."

Sonny picked up the chair and set it upright. He reached down for Francine. She grabbed his hand, and he helped her up. "I'm sorry I smacked you. It's just that, I get so worried about how we're going to make it."

Francine's face was burning. She got up and walked toward the bathroom. Her head was pounding. She ran cold water onto a washcloth and wiped her face. She closed the door, sat down on the toilet and started to cry.

Francine knew the reason her father stopped helping them. It was all her fault. She always went after the bad boys, and when it came to bad boys, Sonny was at the top of the list. She met him at a White Forces Brigade meeting right after he got out of prison. He was tough, had great tattoos, and she was sure she could turn him around. Of course, her father couldn't stand him. That was probably a big part of the attraction. He warned her. Oh, how he had warned her. He had even found Sonny a job. Two jobs, in fact. Both times, Sonny had a problem getting to work on time. The first job, it was their car. It kept breaking down. But for the second job, it was all due to Sonny. According to him, the manager was not only stupid, but he was a complete ass-hole, too.

She thought things would change when they had Ronnie, and things had changed, at first. Sonny went out and actually found a job by himself. Things seemed to be going pretty good. Even her father had mellowed. That's when her dad had moved the trailer onto the land he owned and let them stay there for practically next to nothing. The deal was, the rent would be low if Sonny got a job and kept working, which he did…for three months. Then Sonny took a swing at his boss, and it was all over. It was about the same time that Francine found herself moving away from the teachings of the White Forces Brigade. Of course, she didn't tell Sonny this.

Francine stood up and looked in the mirror. Her cheek was red, turning to purple. She hoped it didn't turn into a black eye.

Sonny walked over to the refrigerator and got himself a beer. He knew she would probably stay locked in the bathroom for a couple of hours. That was the way she punished him when he went and lost his temper. He had to take a leak.

Sonny walked down the hall to Ronnie's room and tried to open the door. It didn't budge. He called out, "I'm gonna get the guns. Let's you and me do a little target practice. Meet me out behind the truck."

He walked to the bedroom closet and pulled out a Winchester .22 rifle. From the nightstand he picked up a Colt revolver. Sonny walked back outside and leaned the rifle against his truck. He slipped the revolver into his waistband, walked over to a rusting metal 50 gallon drum they used for garbage, and dug out three beer cans and three bottles.

Ronnie came out of his room and walked over to the bathroom door. "Ma, are you okay?" He asked quietly.

Francine opened the door and tried not to cry. "I think so."

Ronnie stepped closer to his mother. "Can I ask you a question?"

She sat on the toilet and pulled Ronnie close. "Sure, honey. What is it?"

"Am I going to have a new brother or sister?"

She smiled and kissed him on the forehead. "We're not sure yet. It's too early."

He pulled away. "I want a brother. Someone I can play ball with and build forts in the woods."

"We just don't know yet, so don't be too disappointed if it turns out to be a girl."

"Don't want no girl!" Ronnie said. He heard his dad call his name. He looked over to his mother.

"You better go. He's been waiting."

He hesitated and then pushed the front door open.

"What took you so long?" Sonny asked. Without waiting for an answer, he pointed to the bottles and cans. "Put these up on the fence posts over there, and let's see how good your aim is."

Once the targets were in place, Sonny handed Ronnie the rifle, and they stepped back about seventy feet. "You go first," Sonny said.

Ronnie knelt down in a shooter's stance and took aim at the tomato soup can perched on the far right fencepost. He squeezed the trigger. The bullet sailed over the top and thumped into the trees far behind the can.

"What's wrong with you?" Sonny frowned. "That can ain't even movin'. Try it again."

He took his stance and aimed the gun. He pulled the trigger, and the shot went wide to the left.

"Boy, you gotta take your time. You can't just point and shoot."

Once again, Ronnie crouched down. He placed the gun to his shoulder and took aim. He took his time to make sure he lined up the can in the crosshairs of the scope. Remembering what his dad had said, Ronnie waited to pull the trigger. His arms were tired from the previous shots, and the barrel of the gun started to shake. Ronnie closed his eyes and pulled the trigger. This time the bullet hit the dirt about three feet in front of the can.

Sonny screamed, "Are you blind? What's wrong with you? That barrel was waving like it was blowing in a hurricane." He reached down and yanked the rifle out of Ronnie's hands and gave him a shove, knocking him over into the dirt.

"Gimmie that. You're gonna get someone killed shooting like that."

Ronnie clambered back to his feet, wiped dirt off his jeans, turned around and started running for the house. He didn't want to cry in front of his dad. He knew what happened when he did that.

"Boy, you get back here and shoot like a man!" Sonny called after him. "You've gotta be tough, damn-it."

The boy continued to run toward the house. "Ronnie, I ain't lying. When I get up to that house, the switch is coming out. I'll make you tough, one way or another."

Francine watched through the window as Ronnie ran up to the trailer. She watched as Sonny turned back to the fence posts. He started shooting the cans and bottles off the fence posts, one by one. Ronnie threw the door open and ran by his mother, heading for his room.

"Ronnie, what happened out there?" Francine asked.

"Dad says I'm no good. I can't shoot the gun or nothing. Now I'm gonna get the switch."

Francine walked over to the counter and grabbed a set of keys. "Come on, let's go see Grandpa." She bent down and dried Ronnie's face. She wrapped her arms around him. "You're not getting the switch. I think Daddy did enough smacking around for one day."

Francine and Ronnie walked across the driveway and climbed into the pickup truck. Sonny turned around when he heard the engine start. He watched as they headed down the dirt road toward the county highway. He bent down and slid a fresh clip into the rife. He stood back up and took aim at the receding truck. The back of Francine's head was dead center in his scope. Sonny swung the gun toward the trailer and squeezed off three quick rounds.

Chapter 14

"Here's money," Sneaker said, holding up a mason jar stuffed with assorted change and a few dollar bills.

"What's that for?" Kit asked her foster son.

"To buy that land."

"What land?" she asked with a puzzled look on her face.

"You know. Prison. Land for prison."

She bent down and gave him a hug. "Oh, honey. That's very nice of you, but it's going to take a lot more money than that. You take that back to your room. You can help us in other ways."

"How?"

"Well, let's see. You can hold up signs, and you can hand out fliers."

"Okay." Sneaker smiled and headed back to his room.

She couldn't wait to tell John what had just happened. He had taken his daughter, Samantha, down to Escanaba to look for some new music books. She had finished all the violin lessons in her current books, and now she wanted to move up to a more challenging set of instructions.

There were two kids living in the house John had inherited from his Aunt Thortis. Samantha, John's daughter from a previous marriage, and a young boy most people called Sneaker. He was thirteen years old, and up until the year before, he had lived with his alcoholic father over on the next farm. Everyone in the community called him Sneaker. Before he had been taken in by the Barrington's, he was known for roaming the woods and peering out at people from the dense leaf cover of the forest. When it became obvious his father was not capable of taking care of him any longer, the county had worked out a deal in which Sneaker could live with the Barrington family until he was eighteen. Sneaker was autistic. He didn't communicate much with strangers but he had taken an interest in the Barrington family when John and Samantha moved from Chicago. In the year he had been living at the Four Chimneys, Sneaker's social skills had improved dramatically.

Kit watched Sneaker as he walked back to his room. His solution to the problem was typical of the whole community. Too little, too late. The concerned Garden Peninsula citizens had met several times and had even attempted to hold various fund raising benefits to raise funds to purchase the land. They soon discovered it would be impossible for them to raise anywhere near the amount of money that was necessary. John had even discussed the possibility of making another giant corn maze like they had done the year before, but since it would have to wait until the fall of the next year, by then it would be too late. The land would have been sold, and construction would already have been started.

Kit stood at the window and watched as giant snowflakes floated down from thick gray clouds. It was unusual to have weather so calm. No wind was blowing off the lake. That didn't happen very often.

Archie pulled up to the Second Chance sign that stood in front of a two story cement block building. A thick canopy of trees was behind the building and Archie could see several single story structures through the branches. It looked as if at one time they had all been painted a pale green, but now they were due for a new coat of paint.

Archie got out of his car and looked around. The neighborhood surrounding the Second Chance was in a state of decline. The swale area between the sidewalk and the highway was mostly dirt with a small splash of green, which came from weeds, not grass. Across the street he could see a rundown bar, a two-story house that looked as if it were leaning slightly to the left, a pawn shop and a thrift store. Two big dogs stood in front of the leaning house and barked at every car that drove by. He was glad they were on the other side of the highway. It didn't look as if they were chained up.

Archie climbed up a set of unpainted steps to a building that had "Office" painted on the stucco. He pushed open the door and stepped inside. A thin man with a cigarette in his mouth squinted through a cloud of blue smoke. "Can I help ya?"

"I hope so. I was wondering if you had any need for some volunteer work."

The man yanked the cigarette and stubbed it out in an ashtray on the counter. "Are you kidding? We got lots of need, mister."

Archie smiled. "That's great. I don't have anything to do tomorrow. Would it be possible for me to stop by and lend a hand?"

"You damn right. Can you help us serve tomorrow's lunch? You'd need to get here about ten o'clock."

"Ten o'clock it is. I'll see you then."

"Hold on a minute," the man said, pulling out a clipboard. "I didn't catch your name."

"Archie Archibald."

The man scribbled down Archie's name halfway down the paper. "Got a phone number?"

Archie gave him his cell number. "Okay, that's what I need. See you tomorrow."

"Can I take a look around?" Archie asked.

Suddenly, the man at the counter's mood changed. "Why do you want to do that?"

"I'm curious about what kind of operation you're running here."

"First off, I'm not running anything. That would be Doc Garneau. Second thing, not a good idea for strangers to be roaming around. We run a halfway house for ex-cons here. I can't leave the desk, but I'm sure someone will show you around tomorrow, if you still want to come back."

"No, no…that will be fine. I'll see you tomorrow."

The next day, at eight minutes to ten, Archie pulled into the Second Chance compound and parked his car. Gray clouds were low on the horizon and a light sprinkle of rain was keeping the temperature in the high sixties. He checked his car for an umbrella but didn't find one. Archie limped a little as he took the steps to the office. Damp weather seemed to affect his leg. He wasn't surprised to find the office door locked. He walked back down the stairs and followed a gravel path that meandered through a dense canopy of oak trees. Archie could hear voices coming from a low, cement block structure on his left. He walked over to the doorway and looked inside. A strong odor of old grease hit him. Five long rows of tables ran the length of the room. Several groups of men were busily engaged in various tasks. Archie saw several muscular men standing along one of the walls. They were constantly surveying the room, silently observing what was going on. They were all dressed the same, black tee-shirts and dark blue jeans.

Archie looked to see if the man he had talked to the day before was anywhere in sight. He didn't see him. Near the opening to the kitchen, he spotted a man with a clipboard. Archie walked over to the man and said, "Good morning, I'm Archie Archibald."

The man was big. He had a shaved head that looked as if it had just been polished. He was wearing khakis and a blue short-sleeve shirt that looked as if it was about to rip into pieces from the strain of his muscles. He turned toward Archie. "Are you here to volunteer?"

Archie nodded toward the clipboard. "I think my name's somewhere on that paper. Archie Archibald. I talked to someone yesterday about helping to serve lunch."

The bald man glanced down the row of names. "Yeah. I got you. Thanks for stopping by. Looks like you're the only volunteer who showed up today." He stuck out his hand. "I'm Alex."

It felt like a giant vice was wrapping around his hand. "Ah…nice to meet you."

"It's a little early for serving. You good with a mop?"

"I guess." Archie replied.

"Good, we need to get this place ready. Damn syrup from breakfast is making the floor sticky. Come on, I'll get you started." He pointed across the room. "You can help those other guys."

Alex walked Archie over to an area where several metal mop buckets stood in a line. They were all filled with hot, soapy water. "Take a little break when you're done; then we'll put you on the line, and you can help dish out the food."

Archie mopped for about forty minutes and then pulled the bucket back to the staging area where he dumped out the dirty water. He walked over to where several other men who had been mopping were standing around talking. As soon as he walked up, the conversations stopped. Archie walked over to another group, and the same thing happened. Feeling somewhat conspicuous, he walked back to find Alex. He spotted him opening large cans of green beans at a back counter. "We're done with the mopping," Archie said. "What's next?"

Alex glanced down at his watch. "We're in good shape. We won't start serving for another twenty minutes. You want a quick tour?"

"Sure."

"Come on." He led Archie down the middle isle toward the main door. "This place was started about seven years ago by Doctor Patrick Garneau. He had just finished his doctorate degree in sociology. For his dissertation, he compared different work release programs to see how effective they were." Alex stopped at the door. "It's raining a little. Do you still want to see the place?"

"Sure. Those oak trees kept the rain off me when I got here. Let's go." He followed Alex as he turned down a gravel path.

"From what I've heard, the return rate back to prison's about thirty percent. Is that right?" Archie asked.

Alex looked surprised. "Pretty damn close. How did you know that?"

He laughed. "It's kind of my business. I'm a private detective."

Alex stopped. A look of concern on his face. "Does anyone here know that?"

"I don't think so. I didn't mention it yesterday."

"What about the men. Would anyone recognize you?"

"I doubt it. I just moved up from Fort Lauderdale,"

Alex started walking. "Good. I wouldn't let that out, if I were you. These guys don't look favorably on cops and, in their view, you're not much different." Alex pointed to a path that branched off to the right. "This way. I'll show you the church."

"So what's with the guys in the black shirts?"

"Who?"

"Those big muscular guys that were standing along the walls,"

Alex let out a little laugh. "They're the goon squad. The peace keepers. They're all ex-cons, but now they're staff members."

"Are there a lot of problems?" Archie asked.

"Don't forget, some of our guys just got out. They'll spot somebody they knew inside that belonged to the wrong gang. We need to have people watching to make sure fights don't break out." Alex stopped in front of another cement block building and quietly opened the door. He whispered, "I don't want to go in because services are going on, but take a look."

Archie peered inside and saw two rows of pews with a small alter in the front. There were about twenty men sitting inside, each holding a hymnal.

"We run a non-denominational service on Sundays. They don't have to go, but Doctor Garneau encourages participation." Alex closed the door and walked over to another building. "This is one of the dormitories. Two men to a room. We have inspection every morning just like in the army. We have two dormitories now. Doc's trying to find the money to build one more."

"Where does the funding come from?" Archie asked.

"Wherever we can. We get small donations from people wanting to help, families of the ex-cons. A few county groups send us money but most of it comes from a lady here in Vero."

"Who's that?" Archie asked, as indifferently as he could.

"Mrs. Silverman. She put up the money for our second dorm and Doc was hoping she'd spring for the third one."

"But she didn't?" Archie asked.

"I'm not sure what happened. All I know is the date got pushed back a year at least. Kind of disheartening, you know. We could probably fill up a few more dorms, if we ever got enough money."

Alex pointed to another building. "Here's the gym. Usually gets pretty busy, but most of the guys are either in church or getting ready for lunch." Alex pulled out a pocket watch. "Oh, we need to get you back. It's almost time to start serving."

On the walk back to the mess hall, Alex noticed Archie limping. "Are you okay?"

"Yeah. It's the weather. I'll be fine. Oh, I was wondering, will Doc Garneau be here today?"

"Sure. He'll be over at the hall eating lunch. He lives above the office. He takes most of his meals with the guys. That's why they respect him like they do. I'll introduce you. He appreciates our volunteers."

"Thank you, I'd like to meet him."

Alex put Archie to work as soon as they got back to the mess hall. He spent the next hour ladling out mashed potatoes and gravy. He could see why they needed the goon squad. Some of these guys were pretty scary looking. Archie spotted Doctor Garneau as soon as he came through the line. He stood about 6'2", and his gray hair was pulled back in a pony-tail. He was wearing jeans, a black shirt with a brown hound's-tooth sports jacket. He was deep in conversation with another guy when Archie plopped a scoop of mashed potatoes and gravy onto his plate. Archie watched as he made his way through the maze of tables, surveyed the crowd, and picked out a table to sit down at.

Once everyone had been served, Alex told him to make a plate and follow him. They both walked over and took a seat at the table Doctor Garneau was sitting at. Alex nodded toward Archie. "Doc, I'd like you to meet Archie Archibald. He volunteered to help us out today."

The Doctor reached over and shook Archie's hand. "Thank you. We appreciate your support. What brings you to…." The Doctor's cell phone rang in the middle of his question. He reached into his pocket and pulled out his phone. "Hello, Sanford. How are you? What can I do for you?"

When Archie heard the name *Sanford*, he stopped eating and tried to listen to the conversation as inconspicuously as possible. Doctor Garneau stood up and walked over to the kitchen area.

As Archie ate his lunch, he hoped none of the ex-cons asked him what he did for a living. Most of the conversation revolved around sports and the rainy weather, which was just fine for Archie. A few minutes later, Doctor Garneau returned to the table. Everyone talked for another twenty minutes. Once lunch was over, Alex and Archie headed back to the kitchen. Doctor Garneau moved to another table and joined in a conversation with a different group of men.

It took Archie and the rest of the crew another hour to get all the dishes washed and put away. By then the mess hall was empty. Alex walked over and shook Archie's hand. "Thanks for coming by. Maybe we'll see you again one of these Sundays."

"You're very welcome. Yes, I'm sure I'll be back sometime soon." As Archie walked back to his car, he wondered why Sanford had called Doctor Garneau. With Clara still missing, he doubted it was anything to do about financial contributions.

It was almost 3:30 p.m. when Archie pulled up to his apartment. The first thing he did when he walked in was to check his answering machine to see if he had received a call from Amanda. He was disappointed, but not surprised, when he saw he didn't have any messages from anyone.

Archie spent the rest of the afternoon watching sports on television. For supper, he heated up some of the Thanksgiving leftovers Candace had given him. He found himself glancing over at the telephone, hoping it would ring.

Russell Craig heard heavy footsteps coming up the wooden stairs leading to his apartment. He pushed the living room curtain aside and peeked out. Two huge men clad in black tee-shirts and jeans were standing outside his door. Russell muttered, "holy shit," under his breath as he quietly backed away from the window. He ran through the apartment toward the back stairway. As he pushed open the door, another guy, dressed like the others, grabbed him.

"Not so fast, asshole," he muttered as he threw Russell back into the apartment. He landed in a heap on the floor. The man pointed at him and said, "Stay put," as he walked over and unlocked the front door. "I've got him. He's back here."

For one quick second Russell thought about making a run for it, but something about how the guy looked at him when he told him to stay put made Russell think that running would not be a smart move. He was about to stand up when all three men walked in. The man who pushed him reached down, grabbed Russell by the front of his shirt, and yanked him to his feet. One of the other men stepped in front of him. "How about you tell us what you know about that picture in yesterday's paper."

"What picture would that be?"

The man drew back and punched him hard in the stomach. Russell bent over and gasped for breath.

The pain was so intense he thought he was going to throw up.

"Don't play funny with us. We ain't got all day."

Russell was sweating and he started to shake. "Okay, okay. I took the damn picture."

"Why?"

"The *Tribune* said they'd give me a thousand bucks for it."

"Who grabbed Mrs. Silverman?"

Russell thought for a moment. "What do you mean?"

The man drew back his fist.

"Wait…wait…I don't know. I set up a remote camera that was motion activated. I wasn't there when it took the picture. It's all wireless. It sent a few pictures to my cell phone."

One of the other men grabbed Russell from behind, and Russell took another blow to the gut.

"Please!" Russell screamed. "I don't know who they were!"

"Let him go," the man in front said. He stepped toward Russell and leaned in close. Russell could smell a combination of old tobacco and whisky. "If I find out you're lying, we're all coming back here, and next time it won't be so pretty. Get it?"

Russell nodded. "I'm telling you what happened. I don't know who was in that car."

As the three men walked back to the front door, Russell eased himself down onto the couch. He tried to stop shaking. After half an hour he stood up, walked over to his desk, and picked up the card

Archie had left. Russell dialed the number on Archie's card. After several rings, Archie answered.

"Thanks a lot!" Russell screamed into the phone.

"Who is this?"

"It's Russell...Russell Craig. Like you don't know."

"Know what? What are you talking about?"

"Come on. I'm not a total idiot. You come over here and ask me about that picture in the paper, and just now three muscle-bound monkeys barge in my place and rough me up."

"Roughed you up? I don't know what you're talking about," Archie said.

"If you ever pull any shit like that again, I'm going right to the police," Russell said.

"Look, I didn't send anyone over there. When did this happen?"

"About thirty minutes ago," Russell answered.

"What did they look like?" Archie asked.

"What's the matter? Can't remember who you hired to knock me around?"

"Seriously, Russell, I didn't send anybody over. What did these guys look like?"

"Three huge dudes. They all dressed the same. Black tee-shirts and jeans. Right out of central casting."

"Black tee-shirts and jeans?"

"Yep. Ring a bell?"

"I didn't send anyone over to your place, but can you do me a favor?"

Russell paused. "What?"

"If they show up again, give me a call."

"Oh, not a problem. First, I'll call the police, and then you'll be the next to know." He slammed down the phone.

Archie picked up the remote and clicked off the television. *I guess that explains Sanford's call to Doctor Garneau.*

Chapter 15

Archie stood by his office window watching palm fronds blowing back and forth. It was too late for hurricane season, but strong winds were coming in from the Atlantic, and it was supposed to rain before noon. The rainy weather from Sunday was only getting worse. He glanced at his watch. It was five minutes to seven. The early morning street was dark and deserted. The sun wouldn't be rising for another hour. The building on the south-west corner of the block lit up as headlights swept around the corner. He watched as Gloria's car pulled up in front of his office. He set his coffee down on Candace's desk and walked over to the front door.

Gloria got out of the car and opened the rear passenger door. She grabbed a large wooden trunk and tried to pull it off of the seat. Archie walked over and motioned for her to step out of the way. He grabbed the handles and lifted. "That's heavy," he grunted. "How'd you ever get this in the car?"

"Enrique helped me," Gloria said. "There's more back at the house but we need to get up in the attic."

From the weight of it, he thought it must be packed to the top with papers and documents. Gloria held the door open as he carried the trunk into the foyer. He walked back to his office and placed the box on the floor. He turned around and saw that she was standing near the front door. Archie walked back to where she was standing. "Do you want to go through the papers with me?"

"Oh, no. I must get back to the house. If someone sees me here, I can be fired."

Gloria pushed opened the door and stepped onto the sidewalk. Archie followed her outside. She turned and placed her hand on Archie's arm. "Use those papers. Somewhere there must be a relative. You need to find someone. Quickly." She turned and headed toward her car.

Archie called out, "Mrs. Rodriquez!"

Gloria hesitated.

"Can you do me a huge favor?"

Gloria stopped and turned around, a look of panic on her face. "I need to get back!"

"I know, but I need to speak to James Harrow about his work with Mrs. Silverman on her…story. Could you ask him to come and see me?"

Gloria's face fell. "I wasn't supposed to tell you that, remember?"

"I do. But it could be important to finding Mrs. Silverman. I really need to speak to him. Would it be better for me to talk to him at the Estate?"

"Oh, no. I'll ask him to come and see you, but I think he will be very upset with me."

"Thank you."

With that, she stepped into her car and slammed the door.

Archie walked back to his office and pulled up a chair next to the trunk. He opened the lid and stared down at the mound of papers, pictures, and assorted paraphernalia. Archie reached down and picked up a handful of papers. He started sorting. Letters in one pile, documents in another, and pictures stacked on the corner of his desk.

After almost half an hour Archie was surrounded by papers, and the trunk was still almost a third full. Archie stood up and stretched his back. He walked over to the coffee area and started brewing a pot. Archie heard the door open, then footsteps heading his way.

Candace stuck her head around the corner. "Morning, Archie. I smell coffee! How long have you been here?"

Archie poured some sugar into the bottom of a cup and filled the rest with coffee. He poured another cup, black, no cream or sugar, for himself. He walked over and handed a cup to her. "I got here sometime before seven."

She took a sip. "Thanks. Seven! Why so early?"

"Gloria was going to drop off some of Mrs. Silverman's papers. She wanted to stop by when it was still dark. She's very paranoid about someone seeing her here. Come here, let me show you. You won't believe what I've been doing for the last half hour."

She followed him into his office. "Are you kidding me? It's going to take us days to go through all of this."

"Oh, there's more," Archie chuckled, pointing to the trunk.

"Anything interesting?"

"I haven't had time to actually read much of it. I'm just sorting things into piles. I think there could be relatives of Mrs. Silverman we need to try and find. Who knows, maybe they've even heard from her by now."

"Really?" Candace asked. "She's always been such a recluse."

"Probably true, but let's take a look at all the stuff Gloria brought in. Maybe something will lead to a relative or two. Oh, I've got to fill you in on what happened this week-end."

He told her about the picture of Mrs. Silverman in Saturday's paper, his trip to the Estate with Sanford, the hidden camera, his visit to Russell Craig, and his volunteer work on Sunday.

"Wow! You've been busy. I stopped getting the paper about a year ago. I read my news online now. But I was so busy with Evan this week-end, I never got online. I can't believe you didn't call me when you saw that in the paper."

"I almost did, but then I didn't want to interrupt your long week-end."

"That's just crazy, Archie," she said, as she looked around the stacks of paper. "Where do you want me to start?"

Archie picked up a stack of letters and handed them to her. "Here, read these and see what you can find out. I have to pay another visit to Russell Craig."

Sonny stepped into the Eight Spot and looked around. Two Mexicans were drinking beer at the bar, chatting away in Spanish. A pair of good-old-boys were playing pool across the room. The pool hall was located about half a mile outside of Fellsmere. It was known for attracting a rough crowd.

Sonny spotted Skip sitting in a booth near the cigarette machine. He walked over.

"Where's Billy?"

"Probably home nursing that busted leg of his," Skip said, looking over at a pretty young bar maid, bent over, washing glasses behind the counter. "Man, that Jeanine is sure looking hot."

"I told him to meet us here at two o'clock," Sonny said, glancing down at his watch. "We need to make sure that old black man won't testify against us."

Skip jerked his focus back on Sonny. "How we gonna do that?"

"No witness, no case," Sonny smiled.

"Now, wait a minute," Skip said. "Something happens to him, and it won't take two seconds and they all come looking for us."

"Let 'em look. We get the boys to say we was right here all night shootin' pool."

"I don't know about that..."

Sonny sprang from his chair, grabbed Skip around the throat, and bent him backwards over the table. "Did you forget the oath you took when you joined the Brigade?"

Skip was struggling to catch a breath. The girl behind the bar glanced over and then decided to head for the small office behind the counter. She had known Sonny for three years, and she wasn't about to step into the middle of his business.

The two pool players stopped for a moment and then went back to their game.

Skip struggled to say something, but he didn't have enough wind to make a sound. He tried to nod his head. Sonny wrapped Skip's shirt around his fist even tighter. When the shade of red covering Skip's face turned a dark purple, Sonny let go. Skip rolled off the table, bounced off a chair, and lay panting on the floor beneath the table.

Sonny walked to the other side and glared down at Skip. He kicked him with his boot. "Meet me here at eleven o'clock tonight. We're gonna get this done."

Jennifer Taylor walked into Sanford's office and sat down. "What's going on?"

Sanford leaned back in his chair. "I want you to call that detective and let him go."

"Let him go?" she asked with a look of surprise. "Why?"

"Why not? We know what's going on. Clara's been kidnapped. I'll probably be getting a ransom call any time now. We saw her picture in the paper as she was being driven off. What do we need him for, if now we know what happened?"

"If it's a kidnapping, aren't you going to call the cops?"

"Think about it. Nobody knows it's a kidnapping but us. Everyone else thinks Clara's on her way to one of her other places, or maybe she's taking a trip to Europe. I don't say a word when the call comes in, I pay the demand, Clara's returned and nobody knows the difference."

"But the picture in the paper?"

"I've already thought of that. I've written up my response already. I'm sending this over to the *Tribune*." Sanford picked up a piece of paper from his desk and started reading. *"In regards to the picture of Mrs. Silverman in Saturday's paper: Mrs. Silverman has decided to visit another one of her properties. She elected to leave in the middle of the night to avoid publicity. We will not divulge the exact destination of her trip for security reason, and we ask that the press, paparazzi, and general public grant Mrs. Silverman the privacy she values so much. Thank you, Sanford Leeds."*

Jennifer looked amazed. "But that's a bunch of lies!"

Sanford leaped from his chair. "But it does the trick. It takes the heat off me. I'm thankful she's not face down somewhere in the middle of the swamp out there. I just have to pay whatever these people ask for, or negotiate something reasonable, and this whole thing is over."

"What if they kill her?" Jennifer asked softly.

"Stop it! Let's hope for the best. Back to what I called you in here for. Call that detective and tell him we don't need his assistance anymore. Tell him he can keep all the damn money. That should make him happy as a clam!"

Jennifer stood up and walked close to him. "Okay, I'll call him." She twirled around. "Remember this dress? You bought it for me two months ago."

Sanford looked over at her. "I remember."

She pressed herself against him. "It was so sweet of you to remember my birthday. That was quite the night."

Sanford gently pushed her away. "Not now. You need to make that call."

Amanda Archibald pulled up as close to the J.C. Penney store at the Sandusky Mall as she could. The wind from Lake Erie was blowing snow sideways across the parking lot. She pulled up her hoodie and stepped out of the car. Head down, Amanda ran into the mall. She stomped the snow off her feet in the mall entrance and headed over to Penney's. She wanted to do a little Christmas shopping. She hoped to pick up a wallet for her mother, some cologne for her boyfriend, and if the other two items were not too much, something for the gift exchange they were going to have at work.

The Black Orchid Mystery

Getting around the mall was a lot easier than she thought it would be at this time of year. The weather must have kept most people at home. She was lucky enough to find a nice wallet that fit her budget right away. Amanda walked over to the fragrance counter. It didn't take long to figure out that she couldn't afford one of the more familiar names. Reluctantly, she moved over to where the cheaper knock-off brands were displayed. After testing several bottles, Amanda was surprised how nice they smelled. She narrowed her choice and walked up to the counter.

The woman working the cash register smiled and rang up her purchases. Amanda tensed as the prices were entered. The wallet was thirty-five dollars, and the cologne was almost forty. *Well*, she thought, *Christmas only comes once a year*. She reached into her purse and pulled out her wallet. She opened it and gasped. The ninety-five dollars she had put there the night before was gone. She pulled out a five dollar bill and four singles.

The woman behind the counter saw the look of desperation on her face. "Would you like to use your charge card, dear?"

Tears were streaming down Amanda's face. "Ah, no. I'll...I'll just come back later." She ran out of the store and sat down on a bench in the middle of the mall. She put her head in her hands and sobbed. Travis had done it again. How many times had she pleaded with him to get a job? What was she going to do now? This was money she was counting on for presents. Payday wasn't for another week.

Amanda wiped her face and tried to stop crying. She knew she would never get her money back from Travis. He had done this before; and when she'd gotten mad about it, he slapped her and told her to shut up. It had taken her three months to save up enough to buy a few Christmas presents, and now it was only five weeks before Christmas. She could never come up with enough money to replace what he had taken. She put her head down and started to cry again.

Amanda heard someone walk up to her. She looked up and saw a security guard standing over her. "Are you all right, Ma'am?"

She wiped her face and took a breath. "I'm...okay. I'll be okay. Just give me a minute."

The guard stood over her and didn't say a word. She grabbed her purse and stood up. The guard asked, "Can I walk you to your car?"

She shot him a glance. "No, I'll be just fine. Thanks." She walked back to the entrance and stepped out into the cold air. The wind hit her tear stained face, and as she headed to her car, it felt like icicles were forming from her tears. *Can I walk you to your car?* Amanda thought. *In other words, can you get the hell out of the mall because your crying is putting a damper on everyone else's shopping experience.*

On the drive home she tried to think of how she could possibly come up with enough money to replace what he had taken. Suddenly a thought came into her head. Her dad. Maybe it was fate that placed him into her life at this time. Amanda tried to think

The Black Orchid Mystery

of another way. How could she possibly ask for money after just talking to him for the first time in years? What kind of message would that send? She pulled into a parking space and walked into her apartment building. She trudged up the stairs to the third floor, walked down the hallway to apartment 307, and unlocked the door. She saw Travis sitting on the couch watching television. A pile of marijuana was on the coffee table next to some rolling papers. He glanced up. "Where've you been? I've been sitting here over an hour. I'm starving."

Amanda tossed her purse down on a chair and took off her coat. "If you must know, I've been trying to buy a few Christmas presents. But guess what? My money disappeared again, and I ended up standing at the counter looking like an idiot."

He stood up and walked over to her. "Don't start this again. You know how it works around here. If I need money, I need money. Like I told you before, I ain't gonna start begging you for cash. What's mine is yours, and what's yours is mine, got it?"

She didn't stop to think. "Not a bad deal when it's all mine. You need to hang on to a job, at least for a couple of weeks, so what's yours can be mine, too, for a change."

He stepped closer and grabbed her by the shoulders. "You ain't gonna start this shit again."

Amanda didn't say anything. She could see the rage in his face.

"You try and find a damn job with the record I got. It ain't too easy."

"But that money was for Christmas…"

Travis gave her a shove. She fell backwards into a chair.

"This conversation is finished," Travis said, as he headed toward the hall closet. He grabbed his coat and walked over to the door. "Oh, your boss from work called and left you a message." Travis walked out of the apartment and slammed the door.

Amanda pushed herself out of the chair and headed for the bathroom. She stared into the mirror and watched as tears dripped down her face. Her hip hurt from hitting the arm of the chair. She hoped she wouldn't be limping by morning. At least he didn't hit her in the face. The last time Travis hit her, her boss made her take a week off with no pay. Apparently, customers at the diner where she worked didn't appreciate looking at a waitress with a black eye. It was bad for business, her boss had said.

She walked back to the living room and pushed the play button on the answering machine. She heard her boss's voice. "Amanda, this is Frankie. We're running a little slow this time of year with the bad weather and all, so you don't need to come in anymore. If things pick up, I'll give you a call. Thanks."

Amanda stood there, numb. It was Travis. She just knew it. They hated it when he came into the restaurant. Three days before, he had picked a fight with one of the dishwashers because he said something stupid. They had to call the cops, and the dishwasher quit in the middle of his shift. Frankie had told her that Travis was not welcome back; but, sure enough, the next day he walked in, sat right down at the counter and drank coffee for hours. The only reason he was there was to keep an eye on her, to see who was talking to her.

Tears streamed down her face. Her Christmas money was gone, and now she was out of a job. She walked over to the chair and rummaged around in her purse for her phone. She found her dad's number and dialed it.

Archie was a few blocks from Russell Craig's office when his cell phone rang. He reached into the inside pocket of his sport coat, grabbed his phone, and glanced down at the number. Archie was surprised. "Hello?"

"Hi. I hope you don't mind that I called you." Amanda said, trying not to burst into tears.

Archie looked for a place to pull over. "Hold on a minute. I'm in the car with the top down, and I can hardly hear you."

He pulled into an office complex parking lot and turned off the ignition. "There, that's better. It's so nice to hear your voice, Amanda. How have you been?"

She tried to keep it in, but just hearing her father ask about her after so long unleashed a wave of emotion. She started to cry. "I'm sorry to call you like this but…but…"

"What's wrong? What happened?"

"I… I had saved some money for Christmas presents and it got taken and my boss called and I just lost my job. I…I'm sorry, but I don't know what to do. I know this sounds bad. I never hear from you, and then right after I do, I ask you for money. I'll pay you back, honest. I feel so bad about this...."

Archie took a deep breath. "Hold on, honey. Calm down. Let's talk about this. So, what happened to your money?"

There was a long pause as he waited to hear from Amanda. "Um...my boyfriend needed it."

"Okay, but I thought you said it was taken. If someone needed it and you gave it to them, that seems a little different than your boyfriend taking it."

Archie could hear Amanda start to cry again. "Well, he needed it, and he went into my purse and took it. He's done it before, even when I keep asking him not to. So when I got to the counter and tried to buy a few Christmas presents, I opened my wallet and the money was gone."

"Nobody should be going into your purse and taking your money, Amanda. I'm not about to tell you how to live your life, but that's just something that shouldn't be done." Archie took a breath. "How much money did he take?"

"About eighty dollars."

Archie was relieved. "Eighty dollars? Fine, no problem. I'll be happy to send you the money. I'll drop it in the mail today." He paused. "It's been so long since I've seen you; maybe we can turn this into something good. If you're not working right now, why don't you take a little time and come down to Florida for a visit. I'd be happy to pay for everything. It would be so nice to see you. What do you think?"

Amanda thought about the message on her answering machine. She thought about how things had not been going very well with Travis. The cold wind and the snow that seemed to never stop blowing off the lake. She pictured a bright sun shining down on palm trees and blue ocean waves washing up on white beaches. "That would be nice, but…I…I couldn't ask you to do that."

"You're not asking me, Amanda. I'm offering. Why don't you think about it for a day or two, look at your calendar and see when you could come down. I'll send you the money you need today, and I'll have my secretary look into finding you some flights. I'll call you in a few days, and we can figure this all out."

"Okay. I'd really like to see you again."

"Well then, let's make this happen as soon as we can. I love you."

"Bye, Dad."

Archie sat in the car for a few minutes thinking about what kind of life his daughter must be living. *What kind of man would steal money from his girlfriend's purse?* He put the Miata in gear and headed back out to the street.

His phone rang again. Thinking it was Amanda calling him back, he answered, "Hello!"

"Mr. Archibald, this is Jennifer Taylor from Sanford Leeds office."

"Oh, Jennifer. I thought it was my daughter. What can I do for you?"

"Er…Mr. Leeds wanted me to thank you for your work on the Silverman case. He's informed me that your services are no longer required, and he's advised me to let you know that you can keep the initial retainer."

"What?"

"Again, thank you for all you've done. Goodbye." Jennifer hung up the phone.

Archie was still trying to figure out what had just happened when he pulled up in front of Russell Craig's storefront. He sat in the car for a few minutes wondering if he should just turn around. *What the hell, I'm already here.* He climbed the steps up to the apartment. Russell was waiting for him at the door.

"What's this about? You gonna work me over, too?"

"Russell, I didn't have anything to do with that, but I think I know who was behind it. Can I come in?"

"I'm a little busy right now. I'm in the middle of a shoot. When I heard your car pull up, I wanted to make sure it wasn't the goon squad."

"This won't take long."

Russell pushed open the door, and Archie stepped inside. He glanced into the living room and stopped. A beautiful red haired nude model was sitting on a stool. There was a roll of white paper draped behind her and several sets of bright lights pointing at her from several directions. "Ah, you were busy, weren't you!"

Russell yelled over to the other room. "Chrissie, take five in the bedroom. I gotta talk to this guy for a minute." Russell walked over and turned off the bright lights. "Don't worry, she's not going anywhere. So, who was behind it?"

"I can only share that with you if you promise you'll level with me about Mrs. Silverman's picture."

Russell rubbed his soar belly. "Okay."

"Yesterday I just happened to volunteer at a place called the Second Chance. It's a halfway house for ex-cons. When I was there, I noticed there was a group of enforcers walking around who were dressed exactly like the guys who paid you a visit. Not only that, but while I was there, the guy in charge got a call from Sanford Leeds. Now, I don't know about you, but to my way of thinking, that probably isn't a coincidence."

"Yeah, old Sanford hates my guts. I bet he freaked when he saw that picture in the paper."

"So you did take it, right?" Archie asked.

"Sure I did. Like I told those big jerks, I set up a remote camera and it sent a few pictures to my cell phone that night. I picked out the best one and the *Tribune* paid me a grand for it. If I'd a known all this shit was going to happen, I would have asked for a lot more dough."

"What about that car and the people in it? Do you know anything about them?"

"No! Like I keep telling everyone, I just got sent a few dark and fuzzy pictures. I wasn't there." Russell thought for a minute. "If that creepy Sanford wants to play rough with me, he'd better be careful."

"What does that mean?" Archie asked. "He's a powerful man. I don't think I'd want to mess with him."

"Screw him!" Russell walked over to a desk and pulled out a manila folder. "The next time he messes with me, these are the pictures I send to the *Tribune*."

Archie opened the folder and saw a stack of pictures of Sanford in the embrace of several different women. The women weren't completely nude, but they had enough clothes off to indicate what was going on.

"Why do you have these?" Archie asked.

"Insurance. Pure insurance. I knew that bastard was out to get me, so I've been following him around for over a year. It's amazing what a telephoto lens can capture."

Archie looked at the pictures again. "Do you know who these women are?"

Russell looked at Archie in amazement. "Are you kidding? Sure I do." He pointed. "This one's his secretary. These three are that chick that has the art gallery, and these two are of a realtor who rents space in his office building. Look at her. She's a real fox!"

Archie handed the folder back. "If I was you, I'd be real careful with this. Stuff like this can get you killed."

"He better not send any more muscle over here, that's all I can say," Russell said, pushing the folder back into the desk drawer.

"If I'm right, you don't want to mess with those guys who paid you a visit. Do you have somewhere else to stay?"

"I guess I could move over to my girlfriend's place for awhile," Russell said, looking at Archie with concern.

"Probably not a bad idea. At least until this cools down a little." He turned toward the door. "I'm glad we had this talk. Stay safe."

On the way out, Russell called to Archie, "Hey, if you ever need any surveillance pictures, let me know. I've worked with enough private dicks around here to know what I'm doing."

"I'll keep you in mind."

On the drive back to the office, Archie kept wondering why the name Nancy Abbott sounded so familiar. He slammed the steering wheel. Abbott Gallery was the name on the van that pulled in when he visited the mansion. W*ait till Candace hears this!*

Archie parked the car and walked into his building. He looked around for Candace and didn't see her. As he headed to his office, he saw a note taped to his door. *Had to pick up Evan from school. I'm dropping him off at my sister's. Should be back in twenty minutes.*

Just as he finished reading the note, Candace walked in the front door. "Sorry about that, Archie."

He turned around. "Is everything all right?"

"Ah, well...." Candace looked upset. "I think Evan's getting worse. The school called and said he was exhausted. He'd been outside during recess. He wants so desperately to be out of that chair, especially around the other kids. He collapsed on the playground, and I had to run over there and get him. Thank goodness for my sister. He's sleeping at her house now. I called the doctor, and I'm going to bring him in again tomorrow."

"I'm so sorry to hear that," Archie said. "Let me get you a coffee."

He returned from the break area and handed Candace a steaming cup. "Take as much time as you need tomorrow; and, please, if there's anything I can do, just let me know."

"Thank you. I appreciate it." As she took a sip, Archie could see her hand was trembling. "Did you see that paparazzi guy?"

"I did. That guy better be careful. He's got Sanford on his case, and Sanford's sent the ex-con enforcement gang from the Second Chance after him. Those guys don't play around." Archie decided not to tell Candace about Russell's collection of Sanford's pictures.

"What gang?"

"It's a long story. Oh, by the way, I guess you should know, I had a most interesting phone call from Sanford's secretary about an hour ago."

"You did? What did she say?"

"She let me know I was fired and off the case."

Candace slammed her coffee cup onto the desk with a bang. "She did what?"

He laughed. "That was my reaction."

"So what do we do now?"

"Let's keep on digging. She told me to keep the retainer. There's plenty of money to keep us working for another month. Gloria's begging us to find some relatives, so let's do that. Nothing's really changed. Mrs. Silverman's still missing, so I think we should keep plugging away."

"Can you do that? I mean, you just got fired."

"Why not? We've still got a mystery to figure out."

Clara Silverman heard the door open. She watched as a woman came in carrying a tray of food. She struggled to sit up in the bed. "You're going to be in a lot of trouble," Clara said.

The woman set down the tray and turned to her. "And why is that?" she asked.

"Because you're keeping me here against my will. I bet the news is full of my disappearance. Policemen are looking for me, and you're going to go to jail."

The woman ignored her comments and walked over to the bed. "I see you're sitting up now. That's much better. Would you like if I brought in a television set? It's not very big, but the picture's clear."

"You'll bring me a TV? Yes, you do that. Then you can see all the news stories where they must be looking for me. I'm sure my staff and Mr. Leeds are positively frantic by now."

"Here's your lunch, Mrs. Silverman. I'll be right back with the set."

Clara ate half a sandwich and took a few sips of tea. She watched as the woman returned with a small, portable television set. She set it on a table near the door, plugged it in, and turned it on. "Now you can watch your shows. Do you follow any soaps? I love 'The Young and the Restless'. Do you watch it?"

"Yes, I do. But turn it to the news. You'll see."

The woman turned the channel to the local news station. Clara stared intently at the screen. The announcer was talking about a toy drive for the children of migrants living in Fellsmere. Then, his co-anchor talked about a three-car accident on I-95. Next, there was the weather forecast. There was no mention of Clara's disappearance.

Chapter 16

James Harrow was just finishing up packing a roast beef sandwich, some fruit, cheeses, and a thermos of tea into a picnic basket when Enrique walked into the kitchen.

"What you got there?" Enrique asked, peeking into the basket. "Going on a picnic?"

James jumped. "Stop sneaking up on people. You're going to give me a heart attack one of these days."

Enrique laughed. "So, what's in the basket?"

James walked over to the sink and washed his hands. "I'm not feeling well, so tonight I'll be dining up in my room. Everything's ready for supper for you and Gloria. It's in the oven warming. You'll just have to take it out."

"Eating in your room again?" Enrique inquired. "We never see you anymore."

"I'm a little upset with all that's going on around here, and like many limeys, it takes a toll on our tummies."

Enrique acted as if he never heard him. "What's for supper?"

"Pork chops, green beans and mashed potatoes. I'm sure you'll love it."

"Sounds good," Enrique said, as he turned toward the kitchen door. "Hope you're feeling better soon."

James smiled. "Thank you."

Gloria walked in, and immediately James could see something was wrong. She had a worried look on her face. She turned to Enrique, "Please, I need to speak to James."

Enrique felt the tension in the air, and he didn't need an excuse to leave. "No problem. I'll go talk to the alligator out there in the pond. He looked a little lonely this morning."

Once he was out the door, James turned to Gloria. "What's going on?"

She looked down at the floor. "Please, don't be mad. I stopped by the detective's office today to see if he found out anything."

James gave her a surprised look. "You did?"

"Yes. Anyway, I went to talk to him, and he asked me so many questions. I got mixed up, and I told him about how you are helping Mrs. Silverman write her story. That's okay, right?"

James stepped back. "Her story? Do you mean my manuscript?"

Gloria didn't understand what he was asking but she watched as a look of dread washed over him. He took a deep breath. "Please, dear Mother of God, don't tell me that you told some stranger, er.., a detective no less, that I was working with Clara on her biography!"

Gloria's shoulders shrunk down. She looked up at him with troubled eyes and nodded.

James stepped backward and slumped into a kitchen chair. "How could you? This could jeopardize everything. You know how hard I worked to get this far. If word of this gets out, it's all over."

Gloria stepped closer and said, "I'm sorry. I'm sorry. It just slipped out. But the man wants to talk to you about the story."

James rubbed his forehead and then stood up and poured himself a glass of red wine. "I'm sure he does. Gloria, how could you do this?"

She looked back down at the floor and said nothing.

He took a sip of wine. "Well, I suppose I have to speak to him. He's got to understand how sensitive this is. If Clara ever heard this leaked out, my manuscript would be finished. Where's his office?"

She reached into her apron and handed him Archie's card. James read the card and shook his head. She muttered, "I'm so sorry," as she turned and walked out of the kitchen.

He waited ten minutes after she left and then peeked down the hallway to make sure no one was around. He grabbed the basket and walked across the driveway over to the guest suites. He climbed the stairs to the second story and stepped into the huge recreational center.

James picked up a ping pong paddle. It was in exactly the same spot it had been in the last time he was here and the time before that. He remembered Clara's concern that, because of the gates and the canal, the Estate was quite isolated, even though it was close to Vero Beach. She had confided in him that she was worried about making sure the help was happy. She had asked his opinion about building some sort of game room on the property. It sounded like a good idea to him, so she gave him the go-ahead to find a local contractor. James worked with him on the plans, and a few months later a beautiful recreation room and some new office space had been added above the guest suites. The recreation area had a sixty-inch television, a pool table, a card table, and assorted video games. James set the paddle back down. It just never seemed to get much use.

The office space had a main office with a desk, built in teak cabinets, and a fully stocked supply area. There was another small office to the right of the main room for an assistant, a separate conference area with a small apartment attached.

Mrs. Silverman decided to add this when her New York accountant keeled over and died from a heart attack at the age of seventy-two. She had been asking him to move to Florida for years, but he wasn't interested. Once he passed away, she thought, if she had a nice private office complex constructed, it would be easier to find someone, if they needed to move.

As fate would have it, Mrs. Silverman was introduced to Sanford Leeds' father around the same time that the office was being finished; and since he had built a five story complex next to the beach, the office space was never occupied. When he passed away three years later, his son, Sanford took over the account.

James walked down a hallway next to the main office, stopped at a door leading to the living quarters, and pulled out a set of keys. He glanced around to make sure Enrique hadn't followed him. He walked up, unlocked the door, stepped in and set down the basket of food. "Here you are, eat up! I'll be back later tonight."

Chapter 17

Sonny sat in a back booth at the pool hall and stared at the door. It was eleven-fifteen and Skip was nowhere to be found. Sonny stood up, walked over to the bar, and ordered another beer. He glanced over at the front door as he walked back to his booth. *I'll give him ten more minutes*, Sonny thought.

Luther took off his glasses, put down the *Tribune*, and glanced at the clock. It was just after midnight. He thought he had heard a sound outside his window. He turned his head and listened. There it was. It sounded like footsteps. He heard a sharp snap, like a twig breaking, and then silence. Luther switched off the reading lamp next to his couch and walked through the darkness to his bedroom. He

The Black Orchid Mystery

didn't need any lights to know where he was going. He had lived in this house for over seven years. He walked over to the nightstand and pulled out his flashlight and a Smith and Wesson revolver.

Luther crept back to the living room window and pulled the curtain back about half an inch. He didn't see anything. He walked to the back door and stopped to listen. All he heard was the wind rustling through the leaves. After a few minutes, he cocked the pistol and slowly opened the door. A blast of cold air rushed around him. He took a step outside. Without warning, he felt a crashing blow to the back of his head. Luther fell to his knees and rolled sideways into a pile of red cedar mulch. As he hit the ground, his hand squeezed the trigger of the revolver, and a blinding flash of fire ripped from the gun's barrel and illuminated the darkened back yard for an instant.

Sonny felt a hot streak of pain tear through his calf muscle. He fell to the ground and rolled over onto his back. He grabbed his leg and felt sticky warm blood oozing through his fingers. The pain was intense. It felt like a white hot poker had been jabbed right through his leg. Sonny heard something move on the ground near him. Then he heard a low moan. Sonny tried to put the pain out of his mind as he climbed to his knees and felt around for his metal filled leather sap. His eyes started adjusting back to the nighttime darkness. There was just enough light coming from the back porch light for Sonny to make out dim shadows. He saw the leather handle sticking out from beneath a bougainvillea bush. He grabbed the club and crawled closer to Luther.

A flood of light illuminated the neighbor's back yard and a voice called out, "You okay over there, Luther?" Then, a much louder, "Tiny, get over here!"

Sonny heard the sound of paws pounding on the ground, and they were coming closer. He looked up just in time to see a stocky pit-bull clear the neighbor's four foot fence. He heard a snarl and then felt the dog's hot breath as Tiny sunk her teeth into his shoulder.

He let out a scream as he turned and swung the club down just behind the pit-bull's ear. The dog squealed, bit down even harder and started to shake his head back and forth. Sonny was rolling around like a rag doll. He yelled out in pain and wacked the dog as hard as he could again with the sap. He heard what sounded like a few rib bones cracking. This time the dog let out a cry, let go, and disappeared into the darkness.

Sonny scrambled to his feet. His left leg was throbbing. He tried to run between the houses, toward the back alley where his pickup was parked, but after a few steps, he slowed down to a fast limp.

Sonny heard sirens heading toward him. He scrambled into the truck and pulled out into the alley with his lights off. He drove down the alley for several blocks before pulling out onto the road. He could feel blood running down his wet pant leg. It felt like his calf muscle had been torn in half. Sonny switched on his headlights and used his good leg to

The Black Orchid Mystery

press down on the accelerator. Two miles down the road, an ambulance blasted past him with the siren wailing.

The next thing Luther knew, his back yard was awash in red and blue lights, and a paramedic was standing over him. He tried to sit up.

"Stay still, my man. We've got everything covered. We're going to get you onto this gurney and take you for a little ride to the hospital."

"Hospital? I ain't going to no hosp…" Again, Luther tried to push himself up. When he did, a stabbing pain ran across the back of his head. He lay back down. "What happened?" he asked.

A policeman bent over him. "Not sure, Mr. Johnson, but by the looks of it, you had someone sneaking around your back yard. We've found plenty of footprints. Do you remember getting your gun and coming outside? Your neighbor heard a shot and gave us a call. Did you shoot at anyone?"

Luther tried to remember what had happened. "I don't think so. The last thing I remember was reading the paper."

The policemen showed Luther a gun. "Do you recognize this, Mr. Johnson?"

Luther tried to focus on what the cop was showing him. "Sure, that's my gun."

"We found it next to you on the ground, and it's recently been fired."

The first medic was joined by another, and they both gently lifted Luther onto the gurney. "Away we go," the first medic joked, as they wheeled him out to the waiting ambulance.

At the hospital, the doctor stitched up Luther's head and took a series of X-rays. Two hours later the doctor walked into his room holding one of the films. "You must have a pretty hard head, Mr. Johnson."

"I've been accused of that most of my life. Let's see what you got."

The doctor held up the film. "Here's where you have a laceration from the blow. By the looks of it, you took a pretty good knock to the head. In fact, by looking at the damage, I thought for sure we were looking at a skull fracture."

He held the film in front of Luther. "But the good news is, nothing. Not even a tiny crack. I'd say you're one lucky fellow."

"When can I get out of here, Doc?"

"Let's see how you do the rest of the night. If your vitals look good in the morning, you can be on your way."

"Sounds good to me," Luther said. He watched as the doctor walked out of his room. He gingerly put his head back on the pillow and listened to the sounds of the hospital. He could hear machines working, coded messages from down the hall, and the snoring of another person in the room, who was hidden behind a curtain. He tried to remember what had happened. He had been reading the paper. But then what? How had he ended up outside? Luther tried to think. He reached up and touched the knot on his head. *A sound! Footsteps. That's right. He thought he heard someone sneaking around his place. Was it some random burglar or did it have something to do with that crazy skinhead he ran into down at the public fishing spot.*

Chapter 18

Sonny pushed himself up from bed and glanced out the window. A cold mist was hovering above the ground surrounding the trailer. He winced as he tried to get out of the bed. He limped into the kitchen and sat down at the table. "What happened to you?" Francine asked. "And what time did you get home last night?"

He ignored his wife's questions. "Just get me a cup of coffee, would ya."

She got up and poured him a cup. As she handed it to him, she saw the side of his hand was scrapped raw.

"Were you in another fight down at the Eight Spot? Oh, no…did the cops come?"

He blew on his hot coffee and gave Francine a cold stare. "I wasn't at the Eight Spot, and there were no cops. Stop asking so damned many questions!"

"Well, you know what Daddy said. You can't be getting into any trouble, and I don't know about this habitual felon thing, but…"

Sonny hit the table with his sore hand so hard the sugar bowl flew up in the air, did a spin, and broke into several pieces as it hit the linoleum. A pile of white crystals spread over the kitchen floor. He jumped up and headed for the door, his hand throbbing. Sonny had forgotten about his injured leg, and when his foot hit the floor, he winced in pain.

He limped down the porch steps and slowly made his way over to his truck. He climbed in and turned the key. The engine turned over weakly a few times, and then Sonny heard a series of clicks. He waited a few minutes and tried again. This time the engine only turned over once before it went dead. Sonny climbed out of the seat and slammed the door. He bent down, picked up a palm frond with his left hand, and started beating on the hood of the truck. He started yelling, "You damn piece of shit!" He hit the truck a few more times and then tossed the frond into the bushes.

Francine watched from the window as he tried unsuccessfully to start the truck. When he lost his temper, she went to Ronnie's room, told him to stay put, and shut his door.

Sonny headed back to the house and limped over to the steps. He only made it halfway up before he had to stop. The pain in his leg was killing him.

He held on to the railing and waited for the pain to subside. He climbed up the remaining steps and limped into the kitchen. "Call your old man. I need a new battery."

"I can't call him. He just forked over your bail money. That wasn't cheap, Sonny!"

He grabbed Francine by both arms. "Call your old man."

"Sonny, you're hurting me."

"Damn-it, Francine. Get over to the phone and call him. We need to get that truck going."

She broke free and rubbed her left shoulder. "Honey, I can't keep calling Daddy every time we need something. We've got to be able to take care of ourselves."

Sonny looked out the window and saw his truck standing immobile in the middle of a patch of weeds. He reached back and slapped Francine across the face. She fell sideways onto the sharp edge of the table. A pain shot through her abdomen as she rolled onto the floor. Immediately, she knew something was wrong. "Sonny, the baby…the baby…"

Sonny yelled, "We can't afford no baby!" He grabbed a kitchen chair and shoved it hard into the small of her back. Francine tried to crawl under the table. Jolts of pain were stabbing her in the abdomen. Sonny kicked at her under the table.

"Sonny, please!" she screamed.

Ronnie was in his room; his ear pressed against the door. He didn't know what to do. He heard his mother cry out something about the baby. Ronnie unlocked the door and ran into the kitchen.

He could see his mother on the floor, rolled up like a ball. There were bright red smears of blood on the carpet next to her. Ronnie ran toward his father, his fists swinging.

Sonny pushed him out of the way, sending him sprawling against the clothes hamper. It teetered for a moment and then crashed onto the floor. Sonny yanked open the door and hobbled down the steps into the yard. His leg was throbbing and his shoulder was starting to bleed again. He headed down the dirt road until he got to the black-topped county highway. Sonny walked along the edge of the road until he heard a car approaching. He turned around and stuck out his thumb.

Candace made it into the office before Archie. She felt bad about having to leave early the day before, so she wanted to make sure she got in early. It was almost an hour later when Archie walked in the door. "What are you doing here so early?"

"I thought I'd make up the time I lost yesterday."

Archie walked over to her desk. "Candace, are you crazy? Your son needed you. Don't ever worry about taking time off for him." He looked at the piles of paper surrounding her. "Find anything?"

Candace grabbed a folder and said, "I think so! First off, from some of these letters, I discovered Clara's maiden name was Thorsen. When I found that out, I did a search on Clara Thorsen, and I found an article written by Hedda Hopper. It was in a gossip column in the *New York Times* where she scandalously reported that a chorus line dancer with the same name was involved with a rich and famous Broadway backer almost twice her age. The column ran October 12th, 1953. I did a little digging and found that there was a dancer in the Broadway play Can-Can with Clara's name. How about that!"

Archie grabbed a pencil. "That would make her twenty-four years old in nineteen fifty-three. Okay, you've placed her in New York City. What about relatives? Were you able to find any?"

Candace pulled out another folder. "From everything I've looked at so far, I can't find any location where there could possibly be any relatives except one."

"And where is that?"

"Upper Michigan."

"Why there?"

"I think that's where she was born and raised. Well, somebody named Clara Thorsen was, and from some other digging, I'm pretty sure she has a sister who's about three years older."

"Hmm, a relative! Gloria will be thrilled. Well, maybe not so much. That would make her around eighty-seven."

Candace frowned. "I know. I'm hoping she may still be alive. If not, maybe there's some other relatives still around."

"Having her sister be alive would be a long shot." Archie said.

"I know, but it's worth a try. I've got a few phone numbers to try."

He looked at the clock. "A little early to start calling strangers. Why don't you wait an hour or two?"

Candace busied herself updating her notes with the new information Archie had given her the day before. At 10:30 a.m. she started calling. After half an hour, she walked into Archie's office.

He glanced up from his desk. "How's it going?"

"Not so good. I've made a few calls, but they're all dead ends." A smile broke out on her face. "I really made one guy mad. Sounded like I woke him up. He told me to go to hell and slammed down the phone." She glanced down at a yellow pad. "I've still got a few more calls to make."

Archie winced. "I don't know how you do it. Oh, I didn't tell you who I got a call from yesterday."

"Yes you did. Sanford's secretary, telling you that you were fired."

"No, I know I told you that. It was someone else."

Candace thought for a moment. "I know! It was Luther, and he wants to go fishing."

Archie laughed. "Great guess, but no. It was Amanda."

Candace pulled a chair over and sat down. "Oh, how did it go?"

"Not so good. She was crying. She's having problems with that boyfriend of hers."

"I told you he was a creep."

He paused. "And, she wanted to borrow some money." Archie looked over at her to see what her reaction was.

Candace didn't change her expression. "Ah...Really?"

"Yeah, not a big deal. She only asked for eighty bucks. She sounded all shook up. Something about her boyfriend going into her purse and taking her Christmas money."

"Went into her purse? You've got to be kidding."

"I know. Anyway, I'm trying to get her to come down here and visit. Maybe if she was here, we could convince her of what a jerk this guy really is."

"We?" Candace asked.

Archie turned around. "Yes, we. I'm going to need all the help I can get."

Candace laughed. "You're giving me way too much credit. But, I'll be happy to help if you think there's anything I can do." She stood up. "Now, let me get back to these calls."

Six inches of snow blanketed Michigan's Upper Peninsula during the night and thirty-mile-an-hour winds were creating four foot drifts as a Canadian Clipper blizzard blew in across Lake Superior. John Barrington was upstairs in his office when the phone rang. His daughter, Samantha, answered it before he had a chance. "I think you better take this, Dad," she shouted up the stairway from the kitchen below.

John reached for the phone. "Hello."

"Good morning. My name's Candace Muldoon. I'm trying to reach Thortis Thorsen. Do I have the correct number?"

John was surprised to hear his aunt's name mentioned. He hadn't taken a call for her since he had moved into the house over two years ago. "I'm afraid my Aunt Thortis has passed away. Is there something I can help you with?"

Candace sat up a little straighter at her desk and grabbed a pencil. "I'm sorry to hear that; but, yes, possibly you can. Can I ask who I'm speaking with?"

"My name's John Barrington. I'm Thortis Thorsen's nephew."

"I see. Thank you, Mr. Barrington. Well, let me explain. I'm working with a private investigator in Vero Beach, Florida, and we're trying to find relatives of Clara Silverman, which I believe may be your aunt's sister."

"Clara Silverman? No, I'm afraid you have the wrong number," John said.

Candace panicked when she thought he may hang up. "Wait. I'm sorry. You did say your aunt's name was Thortis Thorsen, correct?"

"Yes," John said, wondering what this was about.

Suddenly, it dawned on Candace. "Oh, wait a minute. I was using Clara's married name. Your aunt did have a sister named Clara, right?"

John hesitated. "Ah, yes…yes she did."

Candace wondered what the best way to continue would be. "As I said, I'm trying to find relatives of Clara Silver…er…Clara Thorsen. I've been going through a box of documents, and I've found some letters that appear to be from her sister. The letters were signed "Love, Thortis." The return address was Box 479, Rural Route 1, Garden, Michigan."

"Well, that's our address," John said. "You said you were working for a private investigator from Florida?"

Candace scribbled madly on a yellow legal pad. "Yes, his name is Mr. Archibald and…"

"Why is a detective involved? Has something happened to this woman?"

Candace paused. "Ah, she's disappeared."

"Disappeared?" John asked. He thought for a moment. "This woman would be quite elderly, right? Did she wander off? Is she suffering from dementia?"

"We don't know, Mr. Barrington. We're looking into all of those possibilities. So, based on our conversation, it sounds like you have not had any recent communications with your Aunt Clara or with anyone else asking about her. Is that correct?"

"I'm sorry, what did you say your name was?"

"Candace…Candace Muldoon."

"I'm sorry, but Ms. Muldoon, I don't remember hearing my Aunt Clara's name mentioned for at least twenty years. It's a little surprising to have someone call out of the blue and start asking questions."

"I certainly understand," Candace replied. "Oh, if I might add, this matter is of some delicacy, so this information is not public knowledge."

"A woman's disappeared and it's not public knowledge?"

"I know that sounds somewhat bizarre, Mr. Barrington, but Mrs. Silverman is quite wealthy, and she's a very private person."

John stood up from his desk. "So, what I think you're trying to tell me is that a very wealthy woman who may be my long lost aunt has disappeared, and you're wondering if I've been contacted by anyone in regards to this…disappearance?" *Like a ransom demand*, he thought to himself.

"That's correct."

John thought for a moment. "I see. Would it be possible for me to talk with the detective regarding this information?"

"Yes, I can transfer you over to him right now, if you'd like."

"What did you say his name is?"

"Archie Archibald. He's listed under Archibald Archibald."

"I'm sure they have licensing there in Florida, right?" John asked.

"They certainly do. Hang on a minute, I'll be happy to provide his state issued certificate number." Candace pulled out her drawer, found a copy of Archie's license and read it to John.

He said, "Thank you. I'll tell you what, if you don't mind, I'd like to give him a call in about half an hour. Would that be all right?"

"Sure." She gave John Archie's office and cell phone number. "Thank you so much for your time. He'll be expecting your call."

Candace hung up and ran back to Archie's office. "I found a relative!"

"Good job!" Archie exclaimed. "Who is it?"

"His name's John Barrington. He lives in Upper Michigan. He's Mrs. Silverman's nephew. Unfortunately, Clara's sister passed away a few years ago. That's about all the information I have. He didn't want to talk to me. I gave him your number; he said he'll call you back in half an hour. Probably wants time to check you out."

"How's he going to do that?"

"By your website, I guess. I gave him your Florida investigator license number so he can see that you're legit." Candace laughed. "He said he hasn't heard anyone mention Clara's name for twenty years."

"Oh, yeah. We do have a website, don't we? Remind me to look that up sometime."

"What? You haven't even checked it out yet?"

Archie looked embarrassed. "I was going to, but then something came up. I think Luther came by, and we went to lunch."

Archie went to the break area, poured himself a cup of coffee, and walked into his office. Mentioning lunch with Luther sounded like a good idea. He dialed Luther's number, and when he didn't answer, Archie left a message asking him if he wanted to have lunch around noon.

As soon as he put the phone down, Candace buzzed in and told him Mr. Barrington was on the line. Archie picked up the phone. "Thank you for calling me back, Mr. Barrington."

"You're welcome. From what your secretary told me, it sounds like a woman who may be my long lost aunt is living in Florida but she's disappeared. Is that correct?"

"I'm afraid it is. You mentioned your aunt was 'long lost.' When was the last time you heard from her?"

John laughed. "That would be never. My sister and I used to hear stories about her from my Aunt Thortis, her older sister. We've never met her. Frankly, I had no idea she was even alive."

"What kind of stories did your aunt tell you?"

John thought for a moment. "It seemed to be a topic that nobody in the family wanted to talk about. I remember the few times her name came up, it seemed like the conversation quickly changed to another subject. She got pregnant when she was quite young. I think she was around fifteen, and it shamed the family. Her father sent her away to have the baby." John paused. "Times sure have changed. From what my Aunt Clara told us, she never came back."

"Do you know where her father sent her?"

"No. Wait a minute. I think my aunt said it was New York City. I can't believe she's still alive.

You know, when my Aunt Thortis passed away, we didn't even try to notify her sister because we just presumed she was dead."

"So there wasn't any contact between Clara and her sister or any other family member that you knew of?" Archie asked.

"My aunt said they communicated for awhile when Clara first went away, but over time, they lost touch. I don't know of any other communication with anyone else. I'll check with my sister. She lives in Chicago. She'll be amazed to hear Aunt Clara's still alive. Like I said, we all thought she had passed away many years ago."

Archie jotted down a few notes. "Mr. Barrington, I don't know if my secretary mentioned this or not, but the disappearance of your Aunt Clara is a very sensitive topic to those associated with her, and we'd like to keep the details of this as private as possible. That would be your aunt's wishes as well, if I may speak for her."

"Really?" John said.

"So, you haven't been contacted in any way regarding your aunt. You know, someone asking about her or offering you information about her for a price?"

"No, you're the first person, outside of the family, to bring up her name."

Archie wrote a few more notes. "I see. Well, you have my number. I'd appreciate you hanging on to it and giving me a call if something new develops or if you happen to remember something that you feel could be important."

John paused for a moment, glancing down at the number. "I'll do that, Mr. Archibald. Good bye." He set down the phone and walked downstairs. Kit was reading a book in the living room. A fire was roaring in the fireplace, and the room felt cozy and warm. Samantha was sitting on the floor, in front of the coffee table, putting together a jig-saw puzzle.

"You're not going to believe that call," John said.

Both Kit and Samantha looked up. "Who was it?" Kit asked.

"It was a detective from Florida trying to find relatives of my Aunt Clara."

"Your Aunt Clara? Who's that?" Samantha asked.

"Aunt Thortis' younger sister," John replied.

Kit thought for a moment. "Oh, I faintly remember hearing something about her. Didn't she leave here when she was very young? She got pregnant or something?"

Samantha looked up from her puzzle.

John sat down on the couch. "Yes, that's what happened."

"She got sent away because she was pregnant?" Samantha asked, with a look of surprise.

"Things were different then, honey," John said. "Poor Clara, her father sent her all the way to New York to have the baby. Once she got there, she never came back."

"Why?" Samantha asked.

"I don't know for sure. Aunt Thortis said she was broken-hearted that her father sent her away. It tore Thortis up. She never got over it."

"That's awful!" Samantha said.

John looked over at Kit, "Let me fill you in on what else the detective told me."

Samantha got up from the floor and sat next to her dad. "A real detective! Are you kidding me?"

Archie hung up the phone and jotted down some notes. He picked up his pad and walked over to Candace's desk. "Good job! How did you find this guy?"

"I found three letters from Clara's sister, Thortis Thorsen, so I was able to get her name and where she lived. I did an internet search for Thortis and Garden, Michigan, and her name came up in an article from two years ago about some Halloween festival they were having on a farm up in Michigan. A huge corn maze, hay rides, and things like that. Anyway, in the article it also mentioned her nephew, John Barrington. For some reason, I couldn't fine Thortis' phone number, but I was able to fine Mr. Barrington's."

"What did the letters say?"

"They were all just about the same. Her sister missed her and kept asking when she was coming home."

Archie nodded. "According to Mr. Barrington, they lost touch shortly after Clara left Michigan. Your phone call must have been quite I surprise. I bet he's scratching his head about now, hearing from us, out of the blue!"

"Oh, Archie, there were more articles about that festival and maze thing. A girl got abducted, something about money being stolen, there was even a murder! I tell you, it was pretty awful."

"A murder?" Archie asked, surprised. "Could anything you found have something to do with our case?"

"I don't think so. It all happened two years ago and there was never any mention of a Clara Silverman. But I did find out that the house Mrs. Silverman grew up in has a name."

"A name? What do you mean a name?"

"I guess it's a landmark in the area. Everyone calls it 'The Four Chimneys'."

"Must be a big house." Archie said. He heard the front door open. "Luther! What the hell happened to you?"

Luther's head was wrapped in a huge white bandage. He seemed a little unsteady. Candace bolted from her chair and ran over to him. "My goodness, Luther! You're about to fall over!"

Chapter 19

Nancy Abbott sat in the living room and poured herself another martini. She heard the garage door open, and two minutes later her husband, Victor, walked into the living room. "Hi, honey. How was your day?" Victor asked.

"Not so damn good. It still didn't get here!" she snarled.

He sighed, walked over to the bar, and poured himself a drink. "What didn't get here?"

"Don't pretend you don't know what I'm talking about," she said, glaring at him. "I've only been asking you about the invitation for over a month now."

He walked back from the bar and sat down in a leather chair facing his wife. "Oh, that."

"Yes, that. Thanksgiving's over, and we still don't have an invitation to the New Years Eve Gala. I guess we're on the shit list instead, thanks to your stupid partner."

Victor took a sip of his drink. "You're probably right. I was hoping this wouldn't happen. So petty, so very, very petty. But, I know both the Ruggles and the Sterns received their invitations last week. I was hoping ours would have gotten here by now."

Nancy sipped her martini. "That stupid twit you call a partner. How long are you going to put up with Jonathan's shit? He botched Betty's boob job, and now we're left out of everything. It's like suddenly, we don't even exist."

"Why Frank is taking it out on us just shows you what a shallow bastard he really is."

"When you're the mayor, you can do things like that. I'm sure it's not Frank. He's going to do what Betty tells him to do," Nancy said. "Jonathan's cocaine habit is going to cost you the business some day. Why you won't confront him about it, I'll never know."

"Maybe I need to talk to that lawyer friend of yours. He owes me. He should give me a year's worth of free service, as cozy as you two are."

Nancy slammed down her drink. "Just what in the hell does that mean?"

"Oh, come on. Everyone's talking about you two. Sanford tries to screw every woman he comes near, and you two seem to be the toast of the town these days."

She jumped up from the couch and screamed, "You're an idiot! Are you really that stupid? Don't you understand I have to kiss his ass to make all these sales to Mrs. Silverman? He controls her and her money one hundred percent. You never seem to complain about all the commission checks I bring in."

Nancy walked over to the bar and refreshed her drink. "Don't forget, that's the money that helps us pay the damn house payment after you send out the checks to your three ex-wives. How dare you!"

She grabbed her glass and stomped off to the bedroom. Victor stood up, took a step toward the bedroom and then stopped. He was sorry for what he said, but the rumors were getting harder to ignore. He had a feeling that the more successful Nancy's gallery became, the more distant she was becoming. He didn't like it. And it was true; she was spending an awful lot of time with Sanford. Victor walked over to the couch and sat down. He grabbed the remote and turned on the television. *It's going to be another long night*, he thought.

Chapter 20

Kit stood up from the computer with a shocked look on her face. She walked into the kitchen where John and Samantha were eating. "You're not going to believe this!"

John looked up from the table. He saw a look on his wife's face that he had never seen before. "What?"

"Thortis' sister. She's rich, and I don't mean kind of. If you can believe what's on the net, she's like one of the richest women in the country!"

Samantha stopped chewing. "Really?"

Kit sat down at the table. "Oh, yeah. She's got houses all over the place."

"Well, that's where she probably is then. At one of her other houses," John said.

"I'd hope the detective thought of that already," Kit said.

"I guess. So, what are you trying to tell me?"

"I think you need to get down to Florida and see what's going on."

"I've never even met her," John said. "And, I don't want her money."

"It's not a matter of money. It's a matter of family. This is your Aunt Thortis' sister. Your aunt was nice enough to leave you and your sister this house and all the land. Do you think Thortis would want us to just sit around and do nothing if she knew her sister was missing?"

"No," John said. He thought for a moment. "I know Thortis' heart was broken when she lost contact with Clara."

"Exactly. That's why you should take a quick trip to Florida and see what's going on."

"They're just going to think I'm only interested in the money," John said.

"Sure they are. Who cares what they think. This is about family."

John listened to the wind howling across the fields and watched as the snow blew sideways outside the kitchen window. "Guess a trip to Florida wouldn't be such a bad thing, no matter what."

"Can I come, too?" Samantha asked. "I've never been to Florida. I'd love to see some of those palm trees."

Kit laughed. "And what about school?"

"I can always catch up!"

The Black Orchid Mystery

John looked at Samantha. "We've got a missing person here. Not quite your typical Florida vacation. I'm not sure what I'm getting myself into, Sam. So, I don't think this would be the best time for you to see Florida."

Sam frowned. "I could help. I watch all those crime shows on TV."

He smiled. "Not this time, honey." He turned to Kit. "Maybe you're right. Grab a calendar and let's see what would be a good time to head down there."

She pulled off a calendar that was hanging on the side of the refrigerator and sat next to John. "You've got a dentist appointment this Thursday, and your annual checkup is next Monday."

He looked over at the calendar. "Hmmm, what about a week from tomorrow?"

"That would probably work. Do you really want to wait that long?"

"I guess I'm going to have to. I don't want to reschedule those appointments. I'll call that detective guy and let him know I'm coming next Wednesday."

"Okay," Kit said, circling that date with a pencil. She looked at the calendar again. "John, the next day is the meeting the State's having at the county seat about the prison."

"Damn," John said. "That's the most important meeting they're having yet. Maybe I should wait two weeks?"

Kit shook her head. "I don't think so. Look, I'll go to the meeting and call you with the results when it's over."

"That sounds good. I really don't want to wait that long."

"Hey, I was just thinking. Maybe, before you go, you should talk to Iver Swenson."

"Who?" John asked.

"Iver Swenson. He's probably the only person around here that would remember your Aunt Clara."

"Why should I talk to him?" John asked.

"From what everyone around here says, he's the guy that got Clara pregnant."

"Really?"

"Yes, and the last I heard, he was living at the senior center in Rapid River. My cousin works there. He's her husband's uncle. She told me about him when we first started dating. She told me he still talks about her."

"I wonder what kind of reception I'd get," John said. "Can you imagine, some stranger stopping by opening up a bunch of old wounds. He'd probably hit me with his cane!"

She laughed. "Maybe, but what do you have to lose? At least you might end up with a story you can tell the detective down in Florida."

He thought about it. Since Kit was from the area, she had a good understanding of local residents. John had grown up fifty miles away, seven miles west of Escanaba, and he had moved to Chicago after graduating from college. He had just moved back two years ago. Maybe Kit was right. It would be nice to show up in Florida with some kind of information about his Aunt.

The Black Orchid Mystery

"Can you call over there and see if now's a good time to see him? I'm kind of anxious to hear if he's got anything to say."

A few minutes later Kit walked back from the phone. "He's taking his daily nap right now, but the nurse said he'd be ready for company in about an hour."

"Okay. Let me get ready."

Fifteen minutes later, he climbed into his truck and headed over to US 2. He turned left and drove twenty miles until he pulled up into the visitor parking area. John walked up to the desk and asked for Iver Swenson's room number. The day nurse seemed to be quite surprised. "Is he expecting you?" she asked.

"No, not really."

John could see a look of concern on the nurse's face. "Is something wrong?"

"I've worked here for five years, and Mr. Swenson's never had a visitor. This may be somewhat startling to him." She stood thinking for a moment. "Come on, I'll show you to his room. He's a bit hard of hearing, so you may have to talk a little loud."

"Okay," John said, already regretting his decision to come.

The nurse pushed open the door to room 36 and ushered him inside. A feeble old man was sitting in a worn chair, staring out the window.

"I have a visitor for you, Mr. Swenson." The old man turned with a confused look on his face. "What?"

The nurse stepped closer and raised her voice. "A visitor. Mr...." She gave John a quizzical look.

He took a step forward. "John Barrington."

"Mr. Barrington would like to see you."

The old man turned and looked at him. "Do I know you? Are you Fredrica's boy?"

John grabbed a chair that was next to the bed, moved it over by the old man, and sat down. "No sir, I live over in Garden. In the house they call 'The Four Chimneys'."

A glimmer of recognition crossed Iver's face. "Four Chimneys. That's Thortis Thorsen's old place."

"That's right," John said, somewhat relieved. "I'm her nephew. So, you knew my aunt?"

The nurse patted John on the back. "I'll leave you two to reminisce," she said, as she stepped out the door.

At the mention of Thortis' name, the old man's face lit up for a moment and then settled into a wrinkled frown. "What about her? Did she die?"

"Yes, almost three years ago."

Iver stared at him. "So that's what you're here to tell me? That your aunt died three years ago?"

John let out a laugh. "No, no. Nothing like that. I moved back up here from Chicago awhile back when I inherited the house, and I'm trying to learn as much as I can about my relatives. Someone told me you were friends with my aunt's younger sister, Clara, a long time ago."

The Black Orchid Mystery

Iver looked away. Finally, he turned to John. "Friends? I guess you could call it that."

John waited for him to add something to the conversation. Finally, John said, "I understand she left this area when she was quite young."

A dark look crossed Iver's face. "She was sent away. She didn't want to go."

John sat quietly, hoping Mr. Swenson would continue talking.

"That father of hers is the one who sent her away. I don't think that would have ever happened if Clara's mother had been alive." He adjusted himself in the chair, leaned forward and whispered, "She was carrying my child."

"But, she was quite young, right?"

"We both were. She was two months shy of turning sixteen, and I was seventeen."

"I see," John said softly.

Iver coughed. "But, so what? You know what? He never even asked me about it. He just packed her up and sent her away. Can you imagine?"

"Really?"

Iver twisted in his chair, his head closer to John. "Here it was, my kid, and he never even told me he was sending her away."

"I'm sorry," John said softly. "That must have been quite a shock."

"You know why he done it, don't you?"

"Ah, well, probably due to her age?"

"Hell no!" Iver exploded, banging the arm of his chair with a wrinkly hand. "Cause I wasn't good enough. That's why."

Again, John just sat there.

"No sir! We weren't good enough for that son-of-a-bitch. We didn't have a fancy car like he had. We didn't live in a big house. My father worked out in the woods. We lived down the road in a tiny house my father and grandfather built by hand."

John nodded.

"But you know what? That didn't matter to Clara. She loved me and I loved her. We could have made it just fine. But, before I knew it, she was gone, and I never got to see her again. Don't even know if she had a boy or a girl. Can you imagine?"

John didn't know what to say.

Iver continued. "I was so mad at her dad, I almost run him down with my truck one day over in Garden. He jumped out of the way and landed in the middle of a big mud puddle, fancy suit and all." Iver started to laugh. "You should have seen him when he stood up. He was madder than hell. But I was glad I done it."

His laugh turned into a loud, watery cough. The cough continued, and it got to the point where John was ready to run to the nurses' station. He pulled out a handkerchief and hacked into it a few times.

"Are you okay?" John asked.

"Yeah, I'm fine."

"Do you know where they sent her?"

He looked down at the floor and thought for a moment. "Someplace out east. Some kind of place they send girls off to. To have their kids. I think it was in New York City. They just gave the baby away. It about killed Clara. I got a couple of letters from her at first, but after awhile, they stopped coming."

"And she never came back?" John asked, "Not even for a visit?"

"Nope. She thought everyone around here would be talking about her. I think she got used to the big city and decided to stay."

John put his hand on his shoulder. "I appreciate you spending time with me."

He looked up at John. "Going so soon?"

"I told my wife I'd only be gone an hour."

"I'm sorry to hear about your Aunt Thortis passing. She was a real nice woman."

"Thank you."

"Can I ask you a question?"

"Sure."

"Do you have any children?"

"Yes. I do."

Iver looked out the window and seemed lost in thought. "Sometimes I wonder what my child turned out to be like. I'm hoping she had a boy. I always imagine it was a boy." He smiled. "Who knows, maybe he's a famous ball player, or maybe he went into the service. It's hard not knowing."

"From what I've heard today, Mr. Swenson, and getting to know you, I'm sure you could be very proud." John stepped toward the door.

Iver tried to stand up. He got half way and then sat back down. "Can you come back sometime? I don't get much company."

"If you want me to. I'd really like to do that. I promise."

On the drive back to the house, he thought about how two sisters could be so different. His Aunt Thortis has never married. She had lived in the family house her whole life. How did Aunt Clara go from being an young unwed mother, sent away from the family, to a very wealthy woman with houses all over the place?" *At least I have something to tell the detective.*

As he pulled up to the driveway, John saw Kit pull back the kitchen curtains and peek out. He knew she was anxious to hear what he had to say. Walking into the house, he smelled something wonderful baking in the oven.

"How did it go? Did he talk to you?"

"He sure did. The poor old man seemed starved for company. He couldn't believe someone was actually coming to see him."

"That's sad. What did he have to tell you?" she asked, with a look of anticipation.

He laughed. "We kind of got off to a rocky start. I only had to mention Clara's name and he got a little emotional." He spent the next twenty minutes relaying what Iver had told him.

"Hold on a minute," Kit said. "I need to pull a pie out of the oven." She grabbed a hot pad and pulled out a beautiful apple pie. She carefully sat it on a wire rack on the counter. "Want a piece?"

"Are you kidding?"

Kit cut two pieces and returned back to the table. "So, I bet that's why Iver never married. Sounds like he never got over losing Clara and the child he fathered. Clara's father was a powerful man in the community. He owned most of the timber around here, and he had political ambitions. I guess he just couldn't come to grips that his little girl would end up pregnant."

"By a guy from the wrong side of the tracks, don't forget."

Kit uttered a sigh. "So sad, because in the end, it cost him his daughter. He never saw her again,"

John paused to eat a forkful of pie. "Hmm, that's good." He looked over at Kit. "Do you think this is worth telling Mr. Archibald?"

"I don't know why not," she said. "It's not much, but it's something that was hushed up for over sixty years."

"Okay. I'll give him a call. Ah, right after I have another piece of that pie."

Chapter 21

Archie had taken one look at Luther and decided his friend should not be spending the night alone. He drove him over to his apartment and called for a pizza to be delivered. While they waited, Luther told him about what happened the night before.

"Who do you think it was? Was someone trying to rob you, or was it that crazy guy who picked a fight with you at the county park?"

"I don't know. I never saw anybody. I got hit from behind pretty good. Nobody went into the house and took anything. But the neighbor's dog was barking pretty loud. In fact, that's who found me. My neighbor came out when he heard the shot."

"Shot?"

"Yeah, I had taken out my gun, and I must have pulled the trigger when I went down."

Archie heard a knock at the door. As he walked by, Luther dug into his pocket and pulled out some money. "Here, Archie. Let me get the pizza."

"Don't be crazy. You're my guest tonight. I'm getting it."

He paid the man and carried the large steaming box back to the kitchen. He opened the fridge and pulled out two beers. Luther followed him back from the living room.

As the two men started eating, Luther asked, "Anything new with the Silverman case?"

"Not too much, other than I got fired."

Luther stopped chewing. "Fired? Are you joking? What the hell happened?"

Archie burst out with a laugh. "It's no joke, and I don't know what happened. Mr. Leeds' secretary called me and told me I was off the case. Just like that." He reached for another piece of pizza. "We're still working on it. Leeds gave me enough money for another month, and the housekeeper, Mrs. Rodriguez, keeps asking me to see if I can find any relatives of Mrs. Silverman."

"She does?"

"Yeah, and guess what? I think we found one."

"Do they know what happened to her?" Luther asked.

"Unfortunately, no. The guy lives way up north, in the Upper Peninsula of Michigan. . He didn't even know she was alive. "

Luther looked at Archie. "I don't know. Sounds kind of crazy to me. Oh, I forgot to tell you.

I called a friend of mine who's a cop. The guy coaches with me in Fellsmere. I asked about any disappearances we've had around here in the last few years."

"Really? What did he say?"

He reached into his pants pocket and pulled out a piece of paper. "Here's what the guy told me. A year ago, a girl going to the community college went missing. She was 22 years old and didn't seem to have any boyfriend problems. No drug issues that they know of. Her parents are from Ft. Lauderdale, and they don't think she's a runaway. Then, last September we had two missing teenagers, both sixteen. The cops think they ran off to Vegas. They were a mixed couple. A black guy and a white girl, and their parents were giving them some problems. They classified those two as runaways. Three months ago, a prominent banker's partner disappeared. The banker claims he ran away with another guy but, according to my contact, they're a little suspicious."

"Why's that?"

"The bank is in the process of undergoing a federal audit."

"That doesn't sound good!"

"Yeah. Maybe he's setting things up in the islands, or something."

"I wouldn't want the Fed's breathing down my neck," Archie replied.

"But wait," Luther said. "There's one more. Just two days ago, Irene Beaverton, age fifty-two, disappeared off a sailboat in the Malaleuca Harbor during the middle of the night."

"So, what do you think? Any similarities?"

"That's what I was looking for. The woman on the sailboat's got a few bucks. Nothing like Mrs. Silverman, but she's the daughter of Howard Beaverton, from Beaverton Industries. She's involved with the yacht club, and she was putting together the third annual Beaverton Sailing regatta."

"I saw something about that in the paper. You need lots of money to be putting that together."

Luther nodded. "This year they were sailing from the Bahamas to Vero." He thought for a moment. "From what I heard, she's quite the drinker. I really don't think this has anything to do with the Silverman case."

"Doesn't sound like it," Archie said. "You didn't mention anything about this case, did you?"

Luther's eyes got wide. "Hell no!"

"Good. But, I think you should stay in touch with your friend about Mrs. Beaverton, just in case." Archie stood up. "You need another beer?"

Chapter 22

Archie stretched and rolled over in bed. He opened his eyes and looked out the window. It seemed lighter than usual. He turned to the night stand and looked at the clock. It was almost nine in the morning. He threw off the covers and sat on the edge of the bed. His head hurt and he still felt tired. *How much had he and Luther drunk last night,* he wondered.

As Archie stepped out of the shower, he heard the phone ringing. *Probably Candace, wondering where I am.* Archie grabbed a towel, wrapped it around himself, stepped back into the bedroom, and grabbed the phone. "Hold your horses. I'll be there in half an hour."

"Hello?"

He stood there, stunned. "Amanda? I'm sorry, honey. I thought it was my secretary wondering why I wasn't at work."

"Oh, well, anyway, I was thinking about what you said, and if you still want me to come, I'd really like to get out of here for awhile and see you."

"Why, that's wonderful. When were you thinking of coming?"

"Looks like a big snow storm's going to hit right after the week-end, and I don't want to get stuck in that. It's kind of at the last minute, but do you think I could come this week-end? Saturday or Sunday? Is that too early?"

A jolt of excitement shot through Archie. "No…no…not at all!"

"That would be perfect!"

Archie broke out in a big smile. "Wonderful! I'll have my assistant make all the arrangements this morning. I'll call you and let you know what she puts together."

There was a moment of silence. "Okay…are you sure it's all right?"

"Are you kidding? This is great! I can't wait to see you again."

"Okay, then. See you soon and…thanks."

Amanda hung up, and he just sat there. After all these years, it was finally going to happen. He would be reunited with his daughter.

He finished dressing and walked into the kitchen. Luther had already made a pot of coffee and was sitting at the table, staring out the window. He could see Archie was in a great mood as soon as he walked in.

"Morning, Archie. You sure look happy this morning. Are you always so excited about going to work in the morning?"

Archie laughed, "No, that's not it. Amanda just called. She's coming for a visit. Can you believe it?"

"That's great! I hope I get to meet her. I remember her running around your office in Fort Lauderdale. That was a long time ago. She was just a kid."

"Of course you'll get to meet her, Luther. Yes, she was probably only around three then. She's all grown up now."

Luther drained his cup and stood up. "Thanks for putting up with me last night." He reached up and rubbed his head. "I'm not sure if my head's aching from all the beer we drank last night or that crack I got on it the night before."

"If you don't feel well, stick around. Stay here another day," Archie said, with a look of concern.

"Naw, I'm feeling fine. I gotta get home. I got the kids coming down to the park this afternoon for a ball game. I need to stop by the field and make sure everything's ready."

"You're sure dedicated. I hope those kids appreciate what you do."

Luther laughed. "I get a lot more out of it than they do. Them kids keep me young!"

He walked over to the sink and rinsed out his cup. "Thanks again, Archie, for watching out for me."

"Not a problem, my friend. Glad we had some time to talk and have a few beers."

Archie stayed in the apartment for another half hour after Luther had gone, straightening up the kitchen. He couldn't wait to tell Candace the news about Amanda.

When Archie walked into the office, Candace could tell something was up. Archie was beaming. "Guess what?" he asked her.

"Luther won the lottery, and he's taking us to Rio de Janerio?"

"Not quite. It's more like I won the lottery."

"Really!"

"You bet. I got a call from Amanda this morning, and she's taking up my offer to come down to Florida. I need you to make the travel arrangements, if you could. It's kind of last minute. She'd like to get here either Saturday or Sunday. See if you can get her into Melbourne from Sandusky, Ohio. If you can't, I guess Orlando would be okay."

Candace grimaced. "Oh, that's not much notice. A flight like that's going to cost you plenty."

"That's okay. The sooner, the better. I don't want her to change her mind. Let me know what you come up with."

Candace turned to her computer. "I'll work on it right now. How long is she staying?"

"I'm not sure. We didn't discuss that part of it. I was too excited about her coming. Just book it one way. We'll play the rest by ear."

"Will do. Oh, you missed a call from that guy in Michigan."

"I did?" Archie said, with a look of surprise. "What did he have to say?"

Candace looked down at a yellow pad. "Something about going to see an old man in a nursing home who knew Clara."

"Really? Did it have anything to do with her disappearance?"

"No. But, now we know why Mrs. Silverman ended up in New York."

"Why?"

"The person Mr. Barrington talked to got her pregnant. She was sent away to have the baby. Once she got to New York, she never came back home.

"I can see why," Archie said, with a smile. She seemed to do quite well for herself."

"I know! That's another mystery. How did a young, pregnant girl from a small town get sent away to the big city to have an illegitimate child and end up being one of the richest women in America!"

"No kidding! What made him go see that guy, anyway?"

"I'm not sure. We didn't talk that long. He'd like you to call him. Oh, and he's planning on coming down here."

"He's coming down here? When? Not next week, I hope. That's when Amanda's coming."

"He said something about a week from today."

Archie thought for a minute. "I guess that will work. That'll give me a few days to spend with Amanda before he gets here. I wonder why he decided to come."

"Probably found out how much his long lost Aunt was worth."

Archie laughed. "Yeah, that would get me on a plane, that's for sure. Do we have any aspirin around here?"

"Sure, I stuck a bottle back in the coffee area. It's in the cabinet with all the cups. Got a little headache? The boys have a big night?"

Archie rubbed his temples and walked over to the cabinet. "Yeah. I guess we drank a little too much beer last night."

Candace heard the door open. She saw a man, who appeared to be in his late forties, walk over to her desk. He was wearing khakis and had on a dark blue shirt.

"I'm here to see Mr. Archibald."

"Your name, sir?"

"James Harrow."

"Do you have an appointment?" she asked.

"Ah, no, I don't, but from what I've been told, he's quite interested in speaking with me."

Archie walked over to Candace's desk. "James, so nice of you to stop by. Come in, let's walk back to my office."

Archie led James back to his office and pulled a chair up next to his desk. He motioned for James to sit down. "Care of a cup of coffee?"

James hesitated for a second. "Ah…tea? Would it be possible to get a cup of tea?" Archie remembered Candace would make a cup of tea every now and then, but he wasn't sure how to make one. He walked out and asked if she could get Mr. Harrow a cup.

Once back in the office, Archie said, "Thanks again for stopping by, Mr. Harrow."

"Have you found out anything about Mrs. Silverman? We're all about going crazy with worry."

"I'm looking at a few angles, but nothing that gives a good indication of what happened to her."

"I'm sorry to hear that. This has been dragging on now for way too long. I'm about ready to call the authorities, even though I know Mr. Leeds would fire me on the spot, once he found out."

"You don't have any theories about what may have happened?"

"I wish I did. I've been with Mrs. Silverman for quite some time, and this is just devastating." He took a breath and moved his chair closer to Archie's desk. "Let's discuss the matter of why I'm here to see you, Mr. Archibald."

Candace walked in and handed James his tea. He glanced over, gave her the once over, looked back at Archie and continued. "I understand Gloria was in here the other day and mentioned that I was working with Mrs. Silverman on her memoirs. Is that true?"

The Black Orchid Mystery

Archie was in the middle of taking a sip of coffee. He set down his cup. "Yes, that did come out in a conversation, but I can assure you, Mr. Harrow, Gloria was quite upset that she mentioned it, and I'm not going to share that with anyone."

James glared at Archie. "I certainly hope not."

Archie continued, "But, I was wondering. Is there anything that Mrs. Silverman may have told you about her life, any secrets, any problems with someone in the past, that would give you an indication that some kind of foul play is involved here?"

"Certainly not!" James said. "If there was, I'd immediately tell you or Mr. Leeds."

He remembered what Candace had shared with him about John Barrington's call. "What about going way back to her childhood," Archie asked. "Any red flags there?"

James gave Archie a perturbed look. "Are you kidding? Clara refuses to discuss that part of her life. She insists that we start with her wedding to Mr. Silverman. I've beseeched her to reconsider, but she threatened to shut down the whole project if I ever brought it up again."

"She did?" Archie asked, with a note of curiosity.

"Can you imagine? How can I write her biography and leave out her early formative years? I know for a fact that she met some very important people when she danced on Broadway before she met Mr. Silverman."

Archie scribbled in his notepad. "She danced on Broadway?"

"Oh, yes. And in some popular shows, as well. Over the years, she's told me about some of them. She knew people like Abe Burrows, Gwen Verdon, Hedda Hopper. Can you imagine the stories? The list goes on and on, but she refused to let me include any of it. I have no idea how she got involved with dancing or how she found her way to Broadway. She simply won't discuss it."

Archie thought about what he had learned from John Barrington. It wasn't his place to share that information.

"I can hardly imagine how exciting it must have been young: living in New York City, and hanging around with so many important people of the day," Archie commented.

"My point exactly! It would make fascinating reading," James huffed.

"Something must have happened that she doesn't want to revisit."

"I know," James replied. "But, I have the utmost respect for her; and, if I knew what it was, I would never use it to paint a negative picture of Mrs. Silverman. Not after all she's done for me."

"Mr. Harrow, can you think of anything else that may shed any light on what may have happened to her?"

"No," he said abruptly. "This visit was to implore you not to mention to anyone my writing endeavor."

"Not a problem," Archie said. "Thank you for your visit."

Gloria sat in her car watching the entrance to Archie's office. She was parked almost a block away, but she had an unobstructed view of James' car parked right in front of the office. She made sure that when he drove off, he would be heading down the street away from her.

Enrique had helped her find the other box of documents she had seen up in the attic. She thought it best that James know as little as possible about her role in providing Archie with these papers. She feared that if Mr. Leeds ever found out what she was doing, he'd probably let her go, and she didn't want James to be caught up in something like that.

She saw the front door open. She watched as James stepped into his car and pulled away. Gloria waited a few minutes and then drove around the block so that she could pull up to the main door. She opened the back passenger door, grabbed the cardboard box, and struggled to the front door. She balanced the edge of the box on her hip and pulled the door open. Just then, a gust of wind caught it, and the door jerked open, causing Gloria to lose her balance. She fell backwards onto the sidewalk. The box fell on its side, and papers started blowing down the street.

Candace leaped from her desk and yelled, "Archie, come quick!"

He ran from his office and saw Candace running to the front door.

"What is it?"

"Gloria. She fell down!"

He ran over to the plate glass window and saw Gloria lying on the sidewalk.

Candace ran up to her. "Are you all right?"

Archie was right behind. He ran over and bent down. "What happened? Are you okay?"

Gloria took Archie's hand. "I'm okay." She looked around. "The papers, the papers!"

Archie flipped the box upright and slammed the top closed. Candace was already running down the sidewalk, scooping up as many documents as she could find.

"Come on, let's go inside." Archie picked up the cardboard box and stood waiting for Gloria. She bent down and picked up a small bundle wrapped in black tissue paper. He held the door open, followed her inside and guided her to a chair. "Are you okay?"

He noticed she was holding on to a small package. She seemed to be near tears. "Let me get you a cup of coffee."

Candace walked in with a handful of crumpled papers. "I'm pretty sure I got them all," she said, stuffing the papers into the box.

He returned and handed Gloria a cup. She was trying not to cry but he could see that her cheeks looked wet. "Take it easy, Mrs. Rodriquez. Just sit for a moment and relax."

She wiped her face, looked down in her lap, and handed the bundle to Archie. "This is for you. It fell out of the box, but I think it's okay."

The Black Orchid Mystery

Archie took the package, carefully unwrapped the tissue paper and smiled. "Is this one of those famous black orchids I've been hearing about?"

She gave him a weak smile. "Yes. I hope when you look at it, you will think of Mrs. Silverman and try and find her even more."

"Well, thank you so much. It's very beautiful."

Gloria looked down. "I probably shouldn't be coming here, but I'm only trying to help her. I brought you another bunch of papers Enrique found for me way up in the attic."

He looked over at the box. "Did you ever hear Mrs. Silverman mention being sent away when she was a teen-ager?"

"Sent away?" she asked, not quite comprehending.

"Yes. Did she ever mention being sent to New York when she was around fifteen years old?"

Gloria thought for awhile. "No, senor. She never say nothing like that."

Candace walked in and handed then both a cup of steaming coffee. She also tucked a tissue into Gloria's lap. "Gracias. If Mr. Leeds ever finds out I was here, he's going to be so mad."

"Actually, I'm very happy you came by today," Archie said.

"You are?"

"Yes, I think we may have located a relative of Mrs. Silverman's."

Gloria jumped from her chair and gave him a big hug. "You have? Oh, bless you…bless you."

He continued, "His name is Barrington, John Barrington. Mrs. Silverman's nephew. Have you ever heard Mrs. Silverman mention that name?"

She stopped to think. "It is not a name I have heard before, but I hope this is a nice man who can do good things for her."

"We've talked with him on the phone several times, and he seems very nice. But, then again, we haven't met him in person."

"How did you find him?"

"The first box of papers you dropped off helped Candace find him."

Tears formed in her eyes. "I think it's best for Mrs. Silverman to have some nice relatives," she said.

"I agree, but, don't get too excited. We don't know anything about this guy, and we still have to find her."

She frowned, "Si, we need to find her."

"Mr. Barrington will be arriving in Florida a week from today. I'd like to take him over to the Estate on Sunday so he can see the place and meet the staff. I'm going to have to call Mr. Leeds and let him know our plans."

Gloria grimaced. "He will not be happy."

Archie thought for a minute. "Maybe so, but if and when I introduce you to Mr. Barrington, it would probably be best to pretend that you are very surprised. You know, don't let on that any of our meetings ever occurred."

Gloria looked relieved. "Oh, yes…yes…thank you. I understand." She looked at her watch. "I better be getting back."

Candace waited till Gloria was out the door. "How are you going to tell Mr. Leeds about John? You're not even supposed to still be on the case."

"Easy," Archie said with a smile. "I'll tell him we initiated the contact when I was still on the case, and he just got back to us now. Which is pretty much what happened, by a day or two."

He walked into his office and called Sanford. Ten minutes later he walked over to Candace's desk, laughing.

"What's so funny?"

"He hit the roof! He's on his way over to see us now."

"To see us? You mean he's coming over here to see you." She paused, "So, Gloria was right. She knew he wouldn't be happy about this."

Twenty minutes later Sanford stormed into the office and demanded to see Archie. Candace buzzed him, "Mr. Leeds is here to see you."

"Thank you. Please show him back here."

Sanford stepped into the office. "Didn't my secretary tell you...."

Archie interrupted, "Sit down, Mr. Leeds." He pointed to a chair.

Sanford pulled out a monogrammed handkerchief from his pocket, wiped the seat of the chair a few times, and sat down. "I thought my secretary was very clear when she informed you that you were no longer needed on the case. So, what's all this about you finding some sort of relative?"

"She was…she was. But, like I told you on the phone, we had already reached out to this guy before I was asked to leave. He's just gotten back to us now. I really didn't even have to tell you about it, but I thought it was the professional thing to do."

"I'm not so sure about that. Anyway, who is this person and how did you find him?"

"Before we get into that, can I ask you a question?" Archie asked.

"What?"

"Why did you want me off the case? I read your statement in the press about Mrs. Silverman deciding to visit another one of her properties, but you and I both know that's a lot of bull-shit."

Sanford stared at him. "I have my reasons. You've been paid handsomely. Now, back to that relative."

"It's Mrs. Silverman's nephew," Archie said.

"Go on, how did you find him?"

"My assistant did some digging on the internet. She's very good at finding information."

"How do you know this isn't some imposter trying to cash in on her?" Sanford asked.

"From the digging we've done, I'm sure he's her nephew. We've established the connection to his other aunt who lived in the area. He was quite surprised to learn that his Aunt Clara was still alive. So surprised, he's already made flight reservations. He'll be here Wednesday."

"What are his intentions?"

"I have no idea, but I would imagine it's quite disquieting to learn that the aunt you thought was

The Black Orchid Mystery

dead for many years is still alive. And then to find out in the next breath that, yes, she's alive, but now she's disappeared."

Sanford stood up. "Why was this person even contacted in the first place? What does he have to do with Clara's disappearance?"

Archie sighed. "In any investigation, you need to talk to as many people as possible who had something to do with the victim. There's always a chance that they may have some knowledge of something that may have happened in the past that's critical to the case. Or maybe they've been contacted by someone."

"Impossible!" Sanford yelled. "Mrs. Silverman's been quite clear that she's never wanted anything to do with her family."

"Maybe her family doesn't feel the same way." Archie said.

"Oh, I'm sure they wouldn't once they get wind of her net worth. It'll be like feeding at the trough. I can't believe what you've done. You're introducing a total stranger into this mess who has absolutely nothing to contribute to a solution. I suggest you call this guy and tell him to cancel his travel plans."

"I'm not on the case. Did you forget that?"

Sanford shot Archie a look of disgust. "You certainly got paid enough to make one more damn phone call!"

"Look, it's still family. If this guy is actually concerned about his aunt, I can't tell him what to do or not to do. He can go anyplace he wants."

"I forbid him to step one foot on the property."

"Really?" Archie said with a smile.

Sanford thought for a moment. "How about this," Sanford said, as he pulled out his cell phone. "Let me check my calendar." His fingers fiddled with the phone. "You said he's getting here next Wednesday, didn't you?"

"Yes."

"Why don't you and ...what's his name?"

"Barrington. John Barrington."

"I need to meet him. Why don't we plan on you and Mr. Barrington having dinner with me at my club, the Palms. Plan on Thursday night around eight o'clock. I'll stop by and pick you up. I'm very interested in talking to him in person. I need to see what his intentions are."

"We can do that. We've booked him a room at the Sea Drift Suites on Ocean Avenue. Pick us up there. We'll be in the lobby."

"Fine." he glanced over at Archie. "Oh, just so you know, sport coats are required."

Sanford turned and walked out of Archie's office. He paused for a second as he passed by Candace, furtively glancing down at her ample cleavage. She looked up. "Can I help you, Mr. Leeds?"

Caught, Sanford mumbled something unintelligible, and headed out the door.

Candace had a scowl on her face as she watched him walk to his car. She got up and marched over to Archie's office. "Dirty old man!"

He panicked for a moment. "What?"

"That Mr. Leeds. You should have seen the way he was looking at me."

"Oh," Archie replied.

She sat down in the chair next to Archie's desk. "Would you mind if I came in a little early tomorrow? I'd like to keep working through the boxes Gloria brought over."

"That's fine," he replied.

"I'm a little confused," she said.

"About what?"

"About a few things. Sanford puts a statement in the paper that says Mrs. Silverman's taken a trip to visit another one of her properties; you get a call telling you you're off the case; but we know Mrs. Silverman's still missing. Does any of that make sense to you?"

Archie let out a chuckle. "No, sure doesn't. Maybe that's why he's so upset about us finding her nephew. There's a lot more going on here that we still need to figure out."

"I agree." She stood up and walked over to the doorway.

"Wait a minute," Archie called out. "How's Evan doing?"

Candace turned and the look on her face changed immediately. "Not so good, I'm afraid. He's in his chair all the time now. He doesn't have the strength in his legs to even stand up."

"Oh, no. What do the doctors say?"

"The same old thing. More tests. I swear we're both at the point now where we don't ever want to see another doctor's office."

"Maybe you need to take him somewhere else?"

"I know. That's what my sister keeps telling me."

"If you need some time off, just let me know." Archie could see she was close to tears.

"Thanks."

Chapter 23

The next morning, James Harrow finished his prep work for lunch and walked out to the foyer. He was carrying a baking tray with an unbaked apple pie on top. The pie was covered with a red and white checkered dish towel.

      James quickly glanced around to make sure he was alone before climbing the stairs to the second floor. He walked over to Sanford's office and tried the door, even though he knew it would be locked. He pulled a key out of his pocket and opened the door. Years before, Clara had given James a master key that opened every lock on the Estate. If Sanford knew that, he'd have a fit. James moved quickly. He knew Sanford could turn up at any time. There was no rhyme or reason to his appearances.

James walked over to a filing cabinet and pulled out the second drawer from the bottom. It had taken him three previous trips to get this far. He wondered how many times he would have to sneak back. He leafed through several manila folders until he found some papers that looked promising. He slipped the folder under the pie on the baking tray and covered everything up again with the dish towel.

Turning to Sanford's desk, he pulled out a drawer and quickly thumbed through several thick folders. Nothing seemed that interesting. As he stuck them back, James noticed a thin ledger book sticking up at the far end of the drawer. He pulled it out and started leafing through the pages. He could feel his heart start to race. This could be one of the things he was looking for. He shoved the book under the dish towel with the other folder. He carefully pushed the desk drawer closed and stood up.

Tip-toeing over to the door, he slowly pulled it open just a crack. He put his eye close to the opening and peered out. He stepped outside the office, shut and locked the door, and quickly walked over to the top of the steps.

"Are you doing your baking up here on the second floor now? Enrique asked, as he walked up behind him.

James jumped, almost tipping the pie off of the tray. "No, but it's not such a bad idea," he said with a nervous laugh. "Sometimes I wish we had another oven. I was walking up to my room and forgot I even had it. I'll tell you, it's hard for me to focus with Clara being gone. Do you feel it, too?"

The Black Orchid Mystery

"I know," Enrique said. "I don't understand why Mr. Leeds hasn't brought in the FBI or something."

"Who knows? Probably a little worried about what they'd find." James stopped. "That's not very nice. Oh, well. Guess we've got to do as Sanford says. At least for now, anyway."

Archie was in his office trying to catalog all the papers from the second box Gloria had brought in. He looked up as Candace walked in waving a piece of paper. "Archie, take a look at this. I found the place Clara was sent to!"

"Good job!"

Candace handed the paper to Archie. Archie read for a few moments and then glanced up at Candace, eyes wide. "Great find! It looks like some adoption release document. Ah, now we're getting somewhere. Where did you find it?"

"It was way toward the bottom of that first box Gloria brought over."

Archie read further. "It's an adoption form. Looks like she had a baby boy at the Trinity Lutheran Home for Unwed Mothers in Bedford-Stuyvesant, New York."

Candace bent down. "Hmm, very interesting. That's right around the time her sister Thortis started sending her those letters."

"Either Clara wasn't allowed to correspond with her family, or she didn't want too, because Mr. Barrington said they never heard from her once she had left. Boy, what James Harrow wouldn't do to find out about this. Make sure you don't mention this to anyone."

"I won't."

He looked over at the piles of paper he had created. "Look at this mess. Maybe I can turn up another nugget like the one you just found."

"Ma, I don't want to go to practice today," Ronnie said, as Francine was packing some of his clothes into a box. "I want to stay home and watch cartoons."

"Nonsense. You need to get out of this house. You've been mopping around all day."

"When's Dad coming back?" Ronnie asked. "I don't want to go stay at Grandpa's."

Tears welled up in her eyes. "I don't know, Ronnie. There's a lot of problems that have to be worked out." She reached down and felt her bruised stomach. "Get your stuff. We're leaving for the field now. And watch out, don't scratch the car. Grandpa will have a fit!"

He was in a foul mood when his mother dropped him off. He walked into the field house and threw his glove down on the floor. He looked up and saw Evan pushing the wheels of his chair. He was headed his way.

"Hi, Ronnie. Coach wants me to go over your stats before we get out on the field."

"Don't care about my stats. Leave me alone."

Evan looked surprised. "What are you talking about? I gotta cover these with everyone. Come on, I got four more guys to go."

The Black Orchid Mystery

"Get outta here!" Ronnie yelled.

Evan glanced down at his papers. "Hey, your numbers are getting better. Here, let me show you."

Ronnie turned and grabbed him by the arm. "I told you to leave me alone, you little freak. Now get away from me."

Evan's papers scattered onto the floor. He sat in his chair with a look of disbelief.

Ronnie walked over and started kicking the papers down the hallway. "Why are you even here? You can't run, you can't play ball…you're just…just weak."

Luther was in the office gathering up equipment when he heard Ronnie yell. He walked out to the hallway and saw Ronnie grab Evan. He ran over to the boys. "Hey, hold it! Hold it right now!" he said, pulling the boys apart. "What's going on out here?"

Evan looked away. "Nothing."

Ronnie was glaring at Evan, his hands clenched in a fist. Luther pointed to his office. "Ronnie, get over there. We're going to talk."

Ronnie slowly walked toward the office with Luther right behind him. When they got inside, Luther shut the door. "Okay, what was that all about?"

"Nothing."

He stepped closer and bent down. "Ronnie, I know better than that. Why were you yelling out there, and what could possibly have made you grab Evan like that?"

Ronnie looked up. "I didn't want to come today. My Ma made me."

"Okay," Luther said. "But that wasn't Evan's fault, now was it."

He didn't respond.

"I asked Evan to go over everyone's numbers with them before we hit the field today. Let's go back out, and he'll let you know what your stats are, okay?"

"No! Ronnie stepped back. The look of anger had reappeared on his face. "What's that freak even doing here? He can't even play ball!"

"Ronnie!"

Ronnie's face was getting redder. "Shut up! My dad says I don't have to listen to you."

"Ronnie, remember all the talks we had on good sportsmanship and fair play? I can't believe I'm hearing this from you."

"Well, it's true. Evan's weak and you…" He looked up at Coach Johnson with a rage in his face Luther had never seen before.

"Just never mind, Ronnie. If you don't want to be here, we can fix that. I'll give your mother a call, and we'll discuss your future with the team. You just sit in here until she comes and picks you up."

Twenty minutes later, Francine was in tears as she walked with Ronnie back to the car. She drove back to the trailer in silence. As she turned into the driveway, she saw Sonny sitting on the porch, smoking a cigarette.

"What's all the boxes for?" he asked, as she and Ronnie walked up the steps.

"We're moving out for awhile," Francine said, trying to keep her voice from cracking.

"Really?" He flicked his cigarette butt into the dirt and followed them into the kitchen.

"Where'd you get the car?" Sonny asked.

"Daddy lent it to me."

Sonny let out a laugh. "Now, that's just great. Let me get this straight. Your old man can get you a car, but he can't lend us the money to get a battery for my damned truck?"

"Don't start. Please, don't start," she pleaded.

He walked over and put his arm around her. "Come on, baby. I'm sorry. I know I got mad when that truck wouldn't start. Billy's bring me out a battery tomorrow. You can stop packing them boxes. Everything's going to be okay."

Francine pulled away. "No it's not. I'm tired of being your punching bag. You wanted to kill the baby. That's what you were trying to do." She picked up a box and started putting in some clothes that were piled on the living room couch.

"That's crazy talk. Come on, stop it." He reached for her.

She brushed past him, walked down to Ronnie's room, and grabbed him by the arm. "Come on, Ronnie. We're leaving right now."

As they got back to the living room, Ronnie pulled away and ran over to his dad. "I don't wanna go."

Francine tried to calm herself. "We're leaving, Ronnie. Go get in the car."

"Now wait a minute," Sonny said, putting himself between her and Ronnie. "If the boy don't want to go, he don't have to go. Besides, we've got a rally to go to tomorrow."

"I'm leaving, Ronnie. Please get in the car."

Sonny took a step closer and Francine backed up. "Tell ya what. Ronnie will stay with me tonight, and he'll come with me to the rally tomorrow. You go over to your dad's house, if you want, and I'll drop him off tomorrow night. How's that?"

Francine didn't like the arrangement, but she knew it was the best she could hope for. "Okay, but I want Ronnie over at Daddy's by supper-time tomorrow."

James searched the attic for the second time, with no success. He knew a couple of trunks were filled with all kinds of papers and old pictures, because he had stumbled upon them the year before. It was those boxes that had given him the idea to start his book about Clara.

He wanted to take advantage of Clara's absence to spend some time going through the trunks to see what light they could reveal about her early life. It was hard to find the time when she was present, and then he always ran the risk of somehow getting caught. He thought the timing would be perfect with her away, especially since Sanford wasn't stopping by quite as often anymore.

James shoved a coat rack to one side and peered behind it. Nothing but old clothes. *Where could they have gone?*

He walked over to an attic window and looked out. Enrique was riding around the front lawn on the mower. He walked back to the bundle of clothes and lifted it up. Underneath, he spotted a long, flat cardboard box tied up with string. He sat down and untied the string. Inside he found several old playbills, all wrapped in brown wrapping paper. He pulled out the top few and spread them open on top of the clothes. One was for a play called *A Pin to see the Peep Show*. According to the playbill, it opened at the Playhouse Theater on September 17, 1953. He didn't recognize any of the actors. He set it aside and smoothed out the next one. It was for the play *Charlie's Aunt,* which opened that December.

Another one slipped off the pile and fell to the attic floor. He reached down and held it up. It was for *Can-Can*. James saw that it opened May 7th at the Shubert. He knew this was one of the plays Clara had danced in because she had reminisced to him about it a few years before. Clara had told him that Hans Conried, who had a staring roll in the play, introduced her to his friend, Franklin Silverman. Hans knew Franklin had an eye for younger women, and Clara had stood out as one of the prettiest chorus line dancers.

James tossed the playbills back into the box. He decided to take the whole container with him back to his room. He could spend as much time as he needed learning about Clara's days on Broadway.

Chapter 24

Sanford pulled into his parking space and sat in the car with the motor running. He was upset after leaving Archie's office. He couldn't help thinking about the consequences of having one of Clara's relatives poking around in her affairs. He took a deep breath and tried to calm himself down. At least he had another week before the guy showed up. There should be no reason for the kidnappers to wait any longer than that. For all he knew, he may have a ransom demand waiting on his answering machine. By the time that nephew got there, the whole mess could be over and done with. Even then, he still didn't need any unwanted scrutiny into his handling of Clara's estate.

    He reached for his cell phone and punched in Nancy Abbott's number. "What are you doing?"

The Black Orchid Mystery

"I'm at the gallery, doing paperwork."

"Perfect, don't go anywhere. I'm pulling out of the office now and headed your way."

From the way Sanford barged in, Nancy could tell something was bothering him. She closed her notebook and looked up. "What's going on? It looks like you're going to jump out of your suit."

Just then a well dressed elderly man and woman walked in and started to look around. "Hold on a minute," she said, getting up from her desk. She walked over to the couple.

Sanford paced back and forth as she chatted with her customers. Sanford could hear her reviewing the biographies of several of her artists. Finally, they thanked Nancy for her time and walked out.

Sanford stepped over to the door, flipped the sign from "Open" to "Closed" and snapped the lock shut.

"What are you doing? I just opened up the shop."

Sanford ran his fingers through his hair. "We've got to talk, and I can't be interrupted a hundred times by a bunch of cheap tourists who aren't going to buy anything from you, anyway."

"Well, make it quick. You're costing me money, whether you know it or not."

"I'm not kidding. This is serious," Sanford said with a concerned look. "If we don't get this right, you'll know what losing money really means. And that might just be the start of it."

"What is that supposed to mean?"

"I don't see your pretty little face doing so well behind bars. They still send people to jail for fraud, you know."

Nancy sighed. "Sanford, just what are you talking about?"

"Look, I just came from that idiot detective's office and …."

"What detective's office?"

"The guy I hired when Clara went missing. Didn't I tell you about him?"

"No."

"Well, anyway, what's important here, he told me he'd found a relative of Clara's. Some nephew of hers. He's flying down here in a few days. I have no idea why he's coming, but we can't afford to have anyone poking around Clara's business. Especially now."

"What are you going to do about it?" Nancy asked with a look of alarm.

"I'm going to check him out and see what I can find. I'm picking him up at the Sea Drift Thursday night. I'm taking him and that muddling detective to the club for dinner."

"And…?" Nancy asked.

Sanford looked exasperated. "I need to know what this guy's true intent actually is. Is he a helpful relative concerned about a missing aunt he's never even met, or is he just a thieving relative who smells a big inheritance?"

"What has this got to do with me?" she asked.

"I hope you're kidding," Sanford stammered. "Clara's place is packed from top to bottom with

The Black Orchid Mystery

expensive art that she paid way beyond top dollar for. Who knows what this guy's background is? If he gets an opportunity to see what his aunt paid for some of those paintings, we've both got a lot of explaining to do."

Nancy looked exasperated. "The value of art is not quantitative. How do you explain someone paying two-hundred and fifty million dollars for Cezanne's *Card Players*? Who can say that price was too much? Would two-hundred and twenty million have been more ethical?"

He walked over to the door and checked that it was still locked. "There's an opportunity here I think you're missing."

She turned. "Oh?"

"We can't take a chance that those art works ever get inventoried by this guy."

"What do you suggest?"

"I think we need to get over to the Estate now and grab as many of those paintings as we can. I'm the only one who's got a record of what she's bought, so it's not like anyone will know what's missing."

"What about Gloria and the others?"

"They wouldn't know what was supposed to be there and what was missing in a million years. We can leave some of the less expensive ones, so the place won't look like it was looted." Sanford glanced at his Rolex. "Come on, we've got to get going. We need to take that SUV of yours." He handed Nancy a small handheld remote.

"What's this?"

"It opens the gate."

They drove over to the Estate in almost total silence. Sanford pulled a cigar out of his pocket, but Nancy wouldn't let him light it.

When they drove up to the Estate, she backed the SUV up close to the front door. Sanford walked up and pushed on the massive front door, but it was locked. He fumbled around in his pocket and pulled out a set of keys. By the time he had positioned the right key toward the lock, the door swung open and Enrique stood there. "Hello, Mr. Leeds. Hello, Mrs. Abbott. Come in."

Sanford ignored the welcome. "Where's Gloria?"

"She's in the kitchen."

"Okay, do me a favor, will you? Take the rest of the day off. Go to the movies or something." Sanford pulled out his wallet. "Here's fifty bucks. We need to get a few things done here, and it would be better if we could work alone."

Enrique looked surprised. "You sure?"

"Yes, yes. Please, go have fun. Oh, take Gloria with you. She needs a break. I know you both have been very upset from everything that's going on." Sanford pulled out his wallet and pulled out another fifty dollars. "Here you go. Oh, where's James?"

Enrique took the money and stuffed it into his pocket. "I haven't seen him all day, like usual."

"Really?" Sanford turned and headed for the kitchen.

Gloria looked surprised when she saw him in the doorway. "Ah, Mr. Leeds. Can I help you?"

"Yes. I know you and Enrique have been through a lot lately. I've asked him to get you out of here for a few hours. You know, take some time off. Maybe a movie or dinner. That's it. Go have a nice dinner. I gave Enrique some money."

"What? Go to dinner? I'm in the middle of…"

Sanford took Gloria by the hand. "Don't worry about it. Mrs. Abbott and I have some business to attend to. We really need some peace and quiet." He led Gloria out to foyer. "There you go now, have a good time."

Gloria stared at Sanford with a look that combined amazement and suspicion.

Enrique gave her a slight push toward the door. "Come on, let's go."

When they were gone, Sanford walked back to the foyer and found Nancy. She had already brought down three paintings from the second floor and had them stacked in a corner. They worked together for another hour. Finally, the van was full, and Sanford slammed the back doors closed. As Nancy drove back to the gallery, Sanford said, "I think we can get the rest in one more trip. I'd like to be able to finish this tonight. Do you have the time?"

She looked at her watch. "I wasn't planning to be away that long, but Victor and I are hardly speaking, so I'm sure he'd be delighted if I stayed away as long as possible."

"Good. When we get back to the gallery, I want to divide these paintings up. Since you've already been paid for them, and I'm the only one with the transaction information, they can all find homes with another group of clients. I'll let you know which paintings I want to sell."

Nancy glared at him. "What are you talking about? You already got your cut the first time. I should be able to resell them again."

Sanford smiled. "Keep your eyes on the road. If I hadn't thought of this brilliant idea, you'd be sitting here with nothing."

She was still seething as she pulled the van into the back of the gallery. Sanford opened the back door, and they transported the paintings to the storage area behind the gallery.

Sanford walked around pointing to pictures. "I'll take that one, that one, and that one."

Nancy could clearly see Sanford was selecting the most expensive works. "You're not getting away with this," she screamed. "I know what you're doing. I've worked too long and hard building this business to let you march in here and dictate what I get to keep after you've picked through the cream." She walked over and pushed him away from a painting he was about to pick up.

"And I also know about those pills you made Gloria give to Mrs. Silverman."

Sanford looked surprised.

"Oh, yeah, the pills that kept her in a twilight state so you could close up most of the mansion without her asking questions. Cutting that staff must have lined your pockets real good. You're lucky nobody gets in to see what the place looks like now." She shot him a disparaging look. "What's the problem? Are you worried the old lady's going to run out of money?"

She didn't wait for an answer. "We both know the answer to that. No, it's so you can divert even more of her fortune your way!"

Sanford spun around, his face in a rage. "I'll pick whatever damn paintings I want to. I didn't get to where I am by being stupid, and if you think you're going to threaten me about how I run the Silverman estate, you've got another thing coming."

He stepped closer and grabbed her by the shoulders. She wiggled out of his grasp and gave him a push. "Don't touch me!"

He stumbled backwards, pushed himself off a wall, and then lunged at her. Sanford slapped her hard across the face. She fell into a group of paintings that were leaning against the wall. Nancy grabbed a painting and slammed a corner of it into his crotch. He fell against a large stand holding a huge ceramic vase. He struggled to catch himself, his arms pin-wheeling in the air. Sanford's feet went out from under him, and he fell backwards onto the floor.

Nancy watched as the vase teetered back and forth before it slowly toppled over and crashed into many pieces just inches from his legs.

As Sanford scrambled back to his feet, Nancy saw blood oozing from the side of his hand. He approached her and swung at her head. A line of blood splattered on the wall behind her. He screamed, "You ungrateful bitch!"

She ducked and fell to her knees. Nancy could feel the broken vase fragments cut into her legs.

She looked up to see Sanford coming at her. His face was in a rage. He was on top of her, punching her face and pulling her hair. "I'll show you. Don't ever think you can go around threatening me, you little piece of trash."

As she threw up her arms to ward off his blows, she fell back down, and her left hand slammed down onto another sharp shard from the smashed vase.

Sanford stood up and took a step back. Nancy thought for a moment he was going to help her up. Instead, he kicked at her and then came raging at her again, both hands clenched into fists. She instinctively rolled to her side, trying to get out of the way of his blows. Her hand grasped a large piece of the vase. She closed her eyes and slashed upwards with the ceramic piece. She felt Sanford hit her on the shoulder, and then she felt the shard connect with some resistance. Nancy heard a muffled cry.

She looked up and saw a gaping hole in front of Sanford's neck. The shard in her hand was red with blood. He grabbed his throat with both hands and started slowly weaving back and forth. There was a look of shock on his face, and a low gurgling noise was coming from his neck. Blood was oozing out from between his fingers. Sanford collapsed on the ground, his eyes wide with fear. He was gasping for air, but only a sucking sound came from his throat.

Nancy scrambled to her feet and backed into a corner. Her legs were bleeding from countless scrapes and cuts. As she watched, Sanford continued to try to breathe. Red bubbles were forming between his fingers. After less than a minute, he stopped struggling for breath, and his arms fell limp to his side.

She ran to the front of the gallery and grabbed the telephone on her desk. She picked it up and hesitated. She thought for a moment. Who was she calling? Was it for help? Help for what, to save the bastard who was going to swindle her out of a fortune in art? The police? So she could show them the corpse of one of the most prominent members of Vero society that she had just killed?

Nancy slowly set the receiver back down. She walked back to the storeroom and peeked around the corner. Sanford was still on the floor in exactly the same position he had been when she left him. His eyes were wide open. She looked down at herself. She had blood on her hand and legs, but her clothes were free of any blood stains. She walked back to the gallery, went into the restroom, and watched as the cool water washed the red stains away from her hands. She bandaged her hand and legs from the supplies in an emergency kit and then leaned against the sink. She was starting to feel as if she might faint.

After a few minutes, she stepped back into the storeroom, stepped over Sanford, and went out the back door. Halfway to the van, she stopped. *Keys*, she thought. *I need his keys*. Nancy walked back into the storage area and stared at Sanford's body. She stepped over him, opened the door to the utility closet, and pulled out a mop and bucket. She took the handle of the mop and poked his body. He didn't move. She walked over and slipped her hand into his pants pocket. She couldn't bring herself to look at him. She fumbled around for his keys. It seemed like an eternity before she found them. As she eased the keys out of his pocket, a small remote fell to the floor. She scooped it up.

She ran back to the van and climbed into the driver's seat. Her hand was shaking, as she fumbled for a cigarette. She pulled onto Ocean Boulevard and headed toward the Estate. Her mind was racing. She had brokered those paintings in the first place and had shown them to Mrs. Silverman. In the beginning, she was the one who discovered what kind of art she admired. She took the time and effort to find items that would add value to Mrs. Silverman's collection. With Sanford out of the picture, Nancy figured the only person who could be a threat now was that relative Sanford said the detective discovered.

What was it Sanford had said? The nephew would be staying at the Sea Drift, and they were all supposed to have dinner sometime next week. She wondered when the nephew was going to make an appearance at the Estate. Nancy pulled up to the ornate gate and hit the button on the remote. She watched as the gate slowly swung open. She continued down the driveway and pulled up close to the front door. She sat in the car for a few minutes. Her whole body was shaking. She got out, walked up to the door, and tried to put the key into the lock. Her hand was trembling. She was in the middle of giving herself a calming self-talk when the door slowly opened. Gloria stood just inside the doorway looking at Nancy suspiciously.

She jumped back. Oh,…Gloria!" She tried to smile. "I…I thought you and Enrique were going out?"

"We did. We got some takeout, and then we came right back. Like I told Mr. Leeds, I have things to do." Gloria peeked out the doorway. "Is he coming in?"

"No. Not tonight."

Gloria pushed some money into Nancy's hand. "Here's what's left of our dinner money. Tell Mr. Leeds thank you very much."

Nancy was about to hand the money back to Gloria, but an image of Sanford lying on the floor of her storeroom, a raw, red, gaping hole where his throat was supposed to be, filled her mind. She started to tremble again. "Ah, okay. I'll tell him."

Gloria stepped forward, her hands on her hips. "Are you okay?"

Nancy smiled. "Yes. I'm fine, but it feels like I may be coming down with something."

"What happened to your hand? Look at your legs! Did you fall down?"

"Yes. I took a tumble in my storage room. When I was putting away…" Nancy realized Gloria wasn't supposed to know about the paintings. "Some new artwork." She looked down at her legs. "I'm fine. It actually looks a lot worse than it is."

Gloria looked past Nancy, out at the dark driveway. "I thought Mr. Leeds had some work to do here tonight?"

Nancy could see Gloria was getting very suspicious. She needed to change tactics. She sighed. "He was helping me. I have a big show coming up, and I need to grab some of Mrs. Silverman's art to exhibit. He helped me with the first load, and I told him to go home. I have a few more paintings to borrow. I'll only be a minute. I know where everything is, so I won't need any help."

Gloria glanced down at her hand. "He gave you his keys?"

"Ah…yes, yes he did," Nancy said abruptly. "Look, I need to get going." She brushed past Gloria and headed upstairs where Sanford had stashed the remaining canvases. She flipped through the stack and picked out a dozen of the most famous works. She carried them back out to the van, two at a time. She was careful to check the foyer before she carried anything down. She didn't need that nosy James chiming in with his own set of questions.

Nancy carefully set the last two paintings into the van. She slammed the back door shut and climbed into the driver's seat. All the way back to the gallery, Nancy dreaded having to go back to the storage area. She pulled into the alley and turned off the motor. She sat in the van and tried to think. She didn't want to go back in there. Finally, she walked to the back door and let herself in. She glanced over at the floor. He was still there. He hadn't moved. He was staring up at the ceiling, eyes wide open, exactly the same as when she had left.

Something had to be done with his body. She looked over at the utility closet. Maybe it was big enough to hold him. She walked over to the body, bent down and grabbed Sanford's hands. His fingers felt cold and stiff. She stifled a scream and overcame the urge to drop his hands and run out of the room. She tugged on his arms, but the body didn't budge. Again she pulled. Nothing. She lay his arms back down and backed away from the corpse, trembling.

Nancy ran into the gallery and sat at her desk, sobbing. She tried to think about what had happened. She was only protecting herself from his rage. She hadn't meant to kill him. *Hell*, she thought, *I had my eyes closed. How could I have known I'd slice at his throat like that?* How was she going to explain that to the authorities? He was a very powerful and prominent man in the community. And then there was their little art thing. *God knows, I don't want people digging into that mess.*

Nancy thought about the body. Sanford was a big man. She had pulled as hard as she could, and he didn't move an inch. She couldn't have him just lying in the middle of her storage area much longer. What could she do? She put her head down and rubbed both temples with her finger tips. She needed help. Calling her husband was out of the question. Who could she call about something like this? Suddenly, Nancy remembered that unsavory character that had barged into Sanford's office. What was his name? Sammy? No. Sonny! That was it. Okay, now what was his last name?

Nancy got up from the desk and started pacing back and forth. What was it? Sanford had only mentioned it once. She thought. In most instances, she was very good with names. Porter! That was it. Nancy pulled out a Vero phone directory and looked him up. She ran down the column. Porter, Anthony; Porter, Daniel; Porter, David… I hope Sonny isn't some sort of a nick name. There it was: Porter, Sonny. He had a Fellsmere address.

Chapter 25

Sonny pulled up to the gallery and parked. He couldn't imagine why the broad he met up in Sanford's office would want to see him. He remembered her. She looked pretty high class. That's what had him wondering what in the hell could she want from him. He walked up to the gallery and saw a *Closed* sign. Not surprising since it was almost eleven o'clock. He banged on the door a few times. Nancy yanked open the door, pulled him inside, and slammed the door shut again.

"What's going on?" He looked over at her and stopped. "Are you okay?"

Nancy's bottom lip was trembling. "No…I certainly am not." Tears streamed down her face.

"What's the deal?"

She steadied herself next to her desk. "Look, a terrible accident happened, and I need you to do me a favor. I'll pay you for your time, but I need you to keep this between you and me. You can't ever talk about this to anyone, agreed?"

He just stared. It looked as if she were going to come unglued any second. This woman didn't look anything like the composed, professional person he had seen in Sanford's office. "Well, I ain't agreeing to anything until I know what I'm getting myself into, lady. I mean, I don't know you from Adam. I only saw you once in Sanford's office. Did Sanford give you my number?"

Nancy pulled a cigarette out of her purse. She lit it with trembling fingers and took a long drag. "No, I remembered your name, and I looked it up."

Sonny smiled. "So, what's on your mind?"

She took a step forward. "Okay, here it is. I was fighting for my life with someone in the back, in my storage area. I hit him with a sharp piece of broken pottery, and I must have hit him just right, because now he's…he's dead." She took another long drag. "And…I need you to get rid of the body." She braced herself for his reaction.

Sonny just stood there and took it all in. "Okay…okay. So, if you was fighting for your life, why not just go to the cops?"

Nancy shook her head. "Let's just say this person is well-known in the community and has a lot of connections. And…there's some things we don't want looked into. That's all I can say about that."

"Okay, I get it. Ain't none of my business. It's not very hard to get rid of a body with all these swamps around here and all, but if I'm gonna do this, you need to write out a paper that says I ain't killed nobody. Okay?"

"Are you crazy?" Nancy said, raising her voice. "You want me to give you a paper that says you didn't kill anyone, which is really me giving you a paper that says I killed someone." She slumped down in a chair and buried her face in her hands. "I knew calling you was a stupid thing to do, but…but I had no other choice."

"Hold on, lady. I didn't say I wouldn't do it. I just don't need no murder rap, that's all." He thought for a moment. "Let's say I'm up for doing this. What did you think something like this is worth?"

"What do you think?" Nancy said, as she rummaged around her purse for a tissue.

Sonny scratched his chin and thought for a minute. "I'd probably do it for a couple of grand." He watched Nancy for a reaction. When he saw she didn't flinch, he said, "Yeah, five grand."

"How about this. I need to know you won't go talking about what happened tonight. So, I'll give you two thousand right now, and I'll also put away a painting for you that's worth sixty thousand dollars. If nobody finds the body in a year, and you keep your mouth shut, I'll either give you the painting, or sell it for you and give you the cash."

"Believe me, lady, I could dump a body so deep out in the swamp, ain't nobody gonna find any part of it. It's so thick with gators out there, they'll tear it to shreds within an hour."

Nancy turned away, thinking she may be sick.

"Sixty grand?" Sonny said with amazement. "That must be some painting. Can I see it?"

Nancy looked surprised. "You want to see it?"

"Yeah."

"Okay, it's right back there," she pointed down the hallway, "...with the body."

Sonny followed her from the gallery into the storage area. He looked down at the floor. "Holy shit, that's Sanford!"

She just stood there looking down.

He took a step back. "You never told me it was Sanford."

"Does it really matter?"

Sonny thought. "I guess not. Not for sixty grand. Let's see the painting."

Nancy walked over to several painting leaning against the wall that had just come from the Silverman estate. She pulled out a small abstract and handed it to Sonny.

"Come on, lady. Stop the crap," He said, pushing the canvas back at her. "I could do better than that with a box of crayolas when I'm totally shit-faced."

"Be careful!" Nancy said. "It's a Lemire. He's very hot now in New York. The only reason I could even get my hands on one is because he comes down here to paint in the winter. He's come into the gallery, and I know him."

"How about this," Sonny said, bending down to take a closer look at Sanford. "You keep your paintings. Give me three grand tonight and hand over the rest of the cash next year."

"It's a deal."

"I need to go get a rug and some tarps. I'll be back here around midnight."

Nancy paused. "The car!"

"What car?"

"Sanford's. You need to get rid of the car, too."

"Not a problem."

Chapter 26

Nancy spent a restless night in a motel on US 1 in Fort Pierce. She had called her husband and told him she was headed to Miami to pick up a few things for the shop, and she'd be home the next day. There was no way she could let him see what a wreck she was.

She got into the shower and let hot water run down her body for about twenty minutes. It seemed to help her control the shakes. The sun was bright, and it felt good on her body as she walked to the car. She had felt cold and clammy all night.

Nancy looked around the parking lot. No police cars. That was a good sign. She saw a Denny's Restaurant across the street and decided she needed coffee and some breakfast. She pulled a pair of oversized sunglasses out of her purse and walked across the street to the diner.

The coffee tasted good. Too bad she couldn't have a cigarette. She needed one. Nancy pulled out a pen and started doodling on a napkin. She wrote down Sanford's name and drew a line underneath it. Under that, she wrote *Clara Silverman, The Nephew, The Help, and The Detective*. She stared at the napkin for a few minutes, thinking.

She read Clara Silverman's name over and over. She knew Sanford must have been behind her disappearance and she had a few good reasons why. First, she had a strong suspicion he was funneling more and more of the estate's money into his accounts and into the charity he named for his father. Nancy laughed to herself. That was some kind of charity. Sanford had gotten drunk one of the nights when they spent the week-end together in Miami. They were in the penthouse suite of the Chateaux and she asked him how much a place like that cost. He told her not to worry about it, that it was a charity function, and that's where he was going to send the bill. Then he bragged about how he donated ten percent of the charity's money to the community, while the rest stayed with good, old Sanford.

He was always full of grandiose ideas. Like the artwork. At first, she thought the sales were all legitimate. Why wouldn't a rich old woman want to collect beautiful paintings? Then Sanford had approached her about how he was expecting a kickback from each sale. Initially, she had balked at that idea, but then her access to Mrs. Silverman was denied. What was she to do?

Nancy put a question mark next to *The Nephew* on the napkin. She wondered what would happen to the estate if Clara never turned up. Since he was a living relative, he'd probably fight like hell to get his hands on her holdings, no matter what the will said. What would he have to say if he ever found out that several million dollars worth of art was missing?

Nancy took a sip of her coffee. She wondered who else might pose a threat in regards to the missing artwork. Not the staff, and probably not the detective. Once this case fell apart, he would be on to something new. The long lost nephew was the only person that presented a threat to the several million dollars of artwork that was now sitting in her storage area.

Her eyes moved down to *The Detective*. Why in the hell did Sanford even hire this guy? Probably because, if word did get out that Clara was missing, he could say he was actually doing something about it.

Nancy asked for another coffee refill. With Sanford now out of the picture, all the dynamics of this whole deal were suddenly quite different. She and that scary skinhead Sonny, were the only ones that knew about Sanford. Once word got out that he was gone, everyone would probably think Sanford was behind Mrs. Silverman's disappearance. If something was to happen to the nephew, everyone would think that Sanford was behind that, too. Everyone would think that he did poor Clara in for her money, and that he, or someone he hired, would have been behind getting rid of the nephew, too. The obvious conclusion was that Sanford had probably slipped away to some tropical island where he was living the good life and living off the money he had siphoned off the Silverman estate.

Nancy tapped her pen on the napkin. Maybe she could arrange for someone to send her a letter from Sanford explaining what he did. She could have it sent from the Bahamas or Mexico. Nancy smiled. That would be perfect. It could be mailed directly to the newspaper.

This whole mess hinged on Sonny doing a good job of getting rid of Sanford's body. She buried her face in her hands. Her whole future and several million dollars were resting on that crazy red-neck from Fellsmere.

She finished her breakfast and paid the bill. On the way back to the motel, she kept her face down as she crossed US 1. Just her luck to be spotted by someone she knew. She checked out of the room and decided the best thing to do would be to go back to Vero, open the gallery, and try to live her life as if nothing had even happened. And wait for Mrs. Silverman's nephew to show up.

Around four o'clock, Archie decided he was too excited about Amanda's visit to concentrate on work. He told Candace he needed to go home and complete the finishing touches on his place, so it would be ready for tomorrow. Once home, he cleaned the bathroom, and put away some food he picked up on the way. By seven that night, everything was ready. Fresh linen was on the bed in the guest room; the house had been swept, mopped, and dusted, and the refrigerator had been packed with the most food it had ever held since he had moved in.

Chapter 27

Candace and Evan drove over to Archie's apartment the next morning. She had offered the use of her car since Archie's Miata was too small to hold everyone going to the airport.

She was surprised to see what a great job Archie had done with his place. He opened his refrigerator. "Look at this. Normally, I only have some cold meat and a six pack in here. Now, you could hardly fit another thing in!"

Evan rolled his wheelchair over to the television and clicked it on. "Wow! The picture's so clear now. Last time I was here, it looked kind of dusty."

"Evan!" Candace shouted. "That's not very nice!"

Archie laughed. "But it's true."

They arrived at the airport at quarter after eleven. Candace had never seen Archie so nervous. "How do I look?" he asked, checking out his reflection in the big plate glass windows of the terminal.

Evan wheeled himself over to the window and stared at the only airplane that was sitting at the gate.

"You look fine, Archie. Just fine," she said.

At five minutes to twelve, people started walking into the terminal from the main concourse. Archie strained to get a glimpse of Amanda.

"How are you going to recognize her?" Candace asked. "You haven't seen her since she was four or five years old, right?"

"I've got this," he said, pulling out a photograph. "She emailed me a picture and I printed it off this morning."

As Candace was looking at the picture, he shouted, "There she is!"

Candace looked up to see Amanda walking down the concourse. She was taller than Archie, and she was thin. Almost skinny. She was wearing a warm winter jacket, and her blonde hair was sticking out of a cute, gray, furry hat. She walked up to Candace and Archie. "Dad?"

It almost seemed that, even with the picture, Archie hadn't recognized her. He let out a loud "Oh," wrapped his arms around her, and held her tight. Candace dabbed at the tears that were forming in her eyes.

Finally, Archie let loose his grasp and took a step back. "Let me look at you. It's been so long."

"Do I look a little different?" Amanda asked, with a smile. She glanced over at Candace and Evan with a puzzled look.

"Oh, goodness!" Archie said, "I'm sorry. Amanda, I'd like you to meet my secretary, Candace Muldoon, and her son, Evan. Candace is the one who was able to find you after I'd given up."

"Thank you, Ms. Muldoon. I'm so happy I'm here."

"You're very welcome. Oh, please call me Candace. It's nice to see Archie so excited. I hope you have a wonderful visit."

"Let's get your luggage," Archie said. "Are you hungry? I thought we'd stop for lunch at a nice beachside restaurant."

"That sounds great," Evan said. "I'm starving."

"You're always starving," Candace said.

Amanda seemed to enjoy the drive back to Vero Beach. She marveled at all the palm trees they were passing and how blue the ocean looked. "I can't believe how warm it is here," she said, peeling off her jacket. "It seems unreal that it was five below zero this morning when I got on the plane in Cleveland. Look outside. No snow, and it has to be in the eighties."

Archie laughed, "That's why I don't live up north anymore."

After a wonderful lunch at the Ocean View Grill, he drove everyone back to his apartment.

"Here we are. It's not fancy, but it's home," Archie said, unlocking the door. "Come on in. I'll put your suitcases in the guest room, Amanda."

"And it's a lot cleaner than it was yesterday!" Evan piped up. Candace turned and shot Evan a dirty look.

Archie set down the suitcases and surveyed the room to make sure everything was perfect.

Amanda saw a photograph of her was sitting on the nightstand. She walked over and picked it up. "I remember this!" She turned to Archie. "How old was I?"

"You were five. Look how cute you were!"

His cell phone rang, and he fished it out of his pocket. "Hello?"

"It's Jennifer from Mr. Leeds' office."

The last time he had heard her voice was when she unceremoniously fired him. This time her voice was completely different. She sounded somewhat hesitant. Archie wondered if she was going to tell him he was back on the case. "What can I do for you?"

"I…I just wanted to know if you've heard from Sanford recently?"

"No, I haven't," Archie replied. This was not the question he was expecting. "Is there some news I should be aware of?"

There was a pause at the other end of the line. "Ah, no. I was just wondering."

"I left the office a little early yesterday, but I had my cell phone with me. He hasn't called me."

"Okay, I'm sorry to have bothered you. Thank you. Good bye."

Archie stared at his phone. He went back into the living room and walked over to Candace. "I just got a very strange call."

"From who?"

"Sanford Leeds' secretary. She wanted to know if I'd heard from Sanford recently. I told her no and asked her if there was some kind of news that I should know of. She just said 'No' and hung up."

"So, she just wanted to know if Sanford had talked to you, but she didn't say what for?"

"Right."

"That is crazy." Candace said, with a puzzled look. "Maybe he's going to ask you back on the case, and she thought he had already made the call?"

"I don't know. I didn't get that feeling." Archie turned to Amanda and Evan, "Who wants something to drink?"

James walked out of the kitchen and looked around. The foyer was empty. He was nervous. After his last discovery in Sanford's office, he couldn't wait to return and see what other interesting documents he could find. But, after almost being caught by Enrique the last time, he knew he had to be careful. And besides, Sanford was overdue for a visit. James glanced at his watch. *No time like the present; let's get this over with.*

Nancy paced back and forth in her gallery. She wondered how long it would take before someone noticed that Sanford wasn't around. She thought about calling his secretary and making something up about him getting some kind of phone call and having to leave in a hurry. She pulled out a cigarette. That wouldn't be such a great idea, she thought. It would just connect her to his absence.

She walked back to the storage room and looked around. She had talked Sonny into cleaning up after he loaded Sanford's body into the BMW's trunk. She slowly circled the room, checking for anything Sonny might have missed. This was the fifth time that day she had conducted this ritual.

All of the paintings they had taken from Clara's place were under several black plastic tarps. She knew she had to get them out of there. Maybe she should rent a storage unit someplace out of town. Before she did that, she would have to write down every picture they had taken so she could keep track of them.

She suddenly stopped. Sanford kept a ledger of every painting she had ever sold Mrs. Silverman. It had the date, the price, and a detailed description of each painting. It was someplace in Sanford's office at the estate. What if Clara's nephew stumbled upon it?

Nancy ran to the front of her store and flipped her sign around to *Closed*. She grabbed her purse and walked out the back door to her van. *I've got to find that ledger*, she thought in a panic.

On the ride to the Estate, Nancy tried to remember where Sanford kept it. She had seen him use it so many times. After each transaction, she would follow him up to his office where he would

The Black Orchid Mystery

update the book. She tried to think of where he kept it. Sometimes it would be on top of the desk, and other times he would take it out of his desk. She had seen him do this countless times, but she had never really paid that much attention. She knew her time in Sanford's office would have to be kept to a minimum. She remembered all the questions Gloria had asked her the last time. She knew Gloria would think that she shouldn't be in his office without him.

Gloria answered the door. When she saw who it was, she stood in the doorway with the door opened slightly. "Oh, Mrs. Abbott. Can I help you?"

"Hello, Gloria. Sanford wants me to get one more painting. He's not able to come today but he gave me his keys again." She held up his keys and gave them a little shake. "It's in his office. I'll just be a minute." She smiled.

Gloria didn't move. "Maybe I should give Mr. Leeds a call?"

Nancy frowned. "Don't be silly. I told you, he sent me here to pick up a painting."

Gloria stepped away but didn't open the door any wider. "Go, then. You know the way."

Nancy's high heels echoed through the foyer as she walked over to the staircase. She watched as Gloria walked back to the kitchen. She knew Gloria was going to make a call to Sanford's office.

She continued up the steps and walked over to the door. She pulled on it, just in case, but wasn't surprised to find it locked. She got Sanford's key ring out of her purse and looked at the jumble of keys it contained. After six tries, she found the right one.

James was bent down behind the desk, flipping through a stack of papers. He froze. It sounded like someone tried to open the door. Then he heard keys rattling. He stuffed the papers back into the drawer and frantically looked for someplace to hide. There was no closet, and trying to crouch down behind the desk was out of the question. He desperately tried to think of some excuse he could tell Sanford. All he could think of was that stupid joke with Enrique about looking for another oven.

Nancy pushed open the door and stopped. "James!"

James was surprised to see it was Nancy Abbott opening the door and not Sanford.

"Nancy?"

Nancy stared at him. "What are you doing in here?"

"Er,...I...ah, Gloria asked me to come up here and see if I could get this window open." He walked over to the window behind Sanford's desk and pushed it open. "Damned cigars. Gloria's trying to air the office out. Get some fresh air in here for once."

Nancy gave him a suspicious look. "Really?"

He just stood there. Finally, he said, "Is Mr. Leeds here?"

"No. He asked me to pick up a picture to have it reappraised."

James stepped toward the door. "Well, nice seeing you again."

Nancy closed the door after he left the room. She knew she didn't have much time. She didn't want Gloria snooping around upstairs once she wasn't able to reach Sanford. She walked over to his desk and pulled open the top drawer on the right. That was where she thought she had seen him pull out the ledger. The drawer contained a few spiral notebooks, a pad of paper, and a box of cigars. There was no ledger book.

She opened the drawer underneath and started leafing through the contents. This drawer was stuffed with manila folders. She quickly glanced through them, but, again, there was no ledger. She continued until every drawer in the desk had been searched. There was no book. *Maybe he took it to his office*, she fumed. She looked over at the large filing cabinet behind his desk. It would take weeks to go through that, and she couldn't remember him ever getting the book out of there. He had always pulled it out of his desk.

Nancy stormed out of the room and walked down the stairs.

From the kitchen, Gloria could hear her heels clicking on the wood as she came down the stairs. She walked out to see Nancy at the door. "No picture?"

"What?" Nancy said.

"I thought you were picking up a picture for Mr. Leeds?"

"Oh, that. It wasn't up there. He must have taken it before and not remembered."

"Oh, that's too bad." Gloria said. "You had to make a trip for nothing."

Back at Archie's apartment, the afternoon was going by too fast. Candace and Evan had Amanda mesmerized with their Florida stories, most of which revolved around snake and alligator encounters they had with Candace's sister.

"I can't believe she drives air-boats in the swamp!" Amanda said with a laugh. "You wouldn't catch me going out there!"

"I'd rather go out there than get stranded in a snow-drift!" Evan said. "What's the worst blizzard you've ever seen?"

Amanda shared her up-north adventures of snow storms, being snowed in, and cross- country skiing stories. Archie just sat back and enjoyed every moment.

Candace glanced down at her watch. It was four-thirty. "Evan, we need to get going."

"What?" Archie said. "I thought you'd stay and eat with us."

She shook her head. "Not tonight. Evan's got some homework he needs to work on, and I think the two of you need to spend some time alone." She turned to Amanda. "It was wonderful meeting you, Amanda."

Once they left, it got quiet in Archie's apartment. Amanda looked over at him. "Can I ask you a question?"

"Sure, what?"

"Is she your girlfriend, too?"

Archie looked surprised. "What? Candace? No, she works for me and that's it." He paused. "Are you kidding? Did you see how young she is?"

"What difference does that make? I think she likes you, and you can tell her son thinks the world of you."

He smiled. "You must be overly tired from your trip. Evan's a wonderful kid. He's as smart as can be, just like his mother. Come on; let's figure out what's for supper."

Amanda followed him into the kitchen.

He opened the refrigerator. "I hope you don't mind if we eat in tonight. I bought all the fixin's for a homemade pizza. I thought it would be nice if we just stayed in and talked."

"Mind? Not at all. I feel so comfy here. I don't think I could even get myself motivated to go out."

"Good." He handed her a package of cheese. "Give me a hand. Let's see what kind of creation we can throw together."

After dinner, they sat in the living room and spent the next several hours catching up on all sorts of topics. During a lull in the conversation, Archie got up to get another glass of wine for her. When he returned, he caught her in the middle of a yawn. He glanced down at his watch. It was quarter after twelve. "You must be exhausted! Here I am, talking away, and I completely forgot what a long day you've had."

He walked over to Amanda and pulled her up from the couch. He gave her a big hug. "Thank you so much for coming. I'm so glad you're here."

"Thanks for letting me come on such a short notice."

Archie kissed her on the cheek. "Okay, tomorrow's another day. Get a good night's sleep."

After she had gone to bed, he sat for another hour, just thinking. He was too happy to fall asleep.

Amanda slept in until a little after nine o'clock. When she got up, Archie cooked a big breakfast of pancakes and bacon. After everything was cleaned up and put away, they walked over to the pool for a few hours. The afternoon was spent talking and getting ready for the barbeque Archie was going to cook.

Candace and Evan showed up around three in the afternoon. "Where's Luther?" Candace asked.

"He decided to stay home and rest, today. I think he's still a little sore from the other night."

"Oh no. He wanted to take Evan fishing tomorrow. I hope he doesn't feel obligated. He should take care of his health, first."

"Fishing?" Archie said with a laugh. "That's pure medicine to Luther."

Archie put the steaks on around six o'clock, and it was a little before eleven o'clock before everyone left.

Archie yawned. "It's been quite a day. I hope you had fun."

"Oh, I sure did. That Evan is so funny!"

"He sure comes out with some crazy stuff for his age. Tomorrow you can come in with me to the office. Don't worry about getting up early. We get there when we get there. I'm not planning on putting in a full day."

"Okay. That sounds good," Amanda replied.

The next morning, Candace walked into the office. Evan was right behind her, pushing his wheelchair in front of him. Archie had just finished showing Amanda around. He was in the coffee area, brewing a fresh pot.

Evan walked over to Amanda. He was wearing his deer slayer hat but had left the pipe and magnifying glass home. "So, you had the tour, did you?"

She smiled. "Well, good morning to you, too! Yes, I did."

"Didn't take long, did it."

Candace gave the back of his chair a little shove. "Evan! I swear. What's the matter with you!"

Archie turned around. "What are you doing out of school, anyway?"

"Teachers' work day. You know, it's the day they all sit around and eat doughnuts and don't have to put up with us kids."

"I'm sure they're a little more productive than that," Archie said with a laugh. "So what are you going to do? Hang around the office all day?"

"No way," he said with a look of excitement, Mr. Johnson told Mom he'd take me fishing today."

"Fishing? Aren't you the lucky guy." Archie said.

"Why don't you come with us?" Evan said.

"It sounds like a great time, but I have some work to do this morning. Then I'm going to show Amanda around Vero for awhile in the afternoon."

Evan looked around the foyer. "Where's Coach?"

"He'll be here, honey," Candace said, looking at her watch. Don't be so impatient."

Evan turned and stared at the front door.

Archie looked over at Amanda. "I'm going to ask Luther to drive you back to the apartment on the way to the lake. I'm sure you'd like to have a little bit of time to yourself."

"I want to take some pictures of your complex. Those palm trees outside your apartment look so cool."

"There he is now!" Evan said, pointing out the window.

Luther pulled up in front of the office, and Archie was happy to see he looked like he was walking much better.

Luther walked in and looked around. "Who's ready to do a little fishing?"

"Me!" Evan shouted. "Let's go!"

"Hold on, not so fast," Archie said. "Luther, I'd like you to meet my daughter, Amanda."

Luther walked over and extended his hand. "My goodness! Look how you've changed. I know you won't remember, but the last time I saw you, you were probably only about two years old."

Amanda smiled, "You're right, I'm sorry, I don't remember. Nice to meet you, Luther."

"Your father and I go back many years," Luther said, slapping Archie on the back.

"Yeah, yeah, yeah…let's go fishing!" Evan said.

"Evan!" Candace said. "Now I know why they say children should be seen, not heard."

Luther walked over to Evan and put his arm around him. "The boy's just like me. We both get excited about fishing. Let's get going."

"You got that right!" Evan said.

"And, I'm taking you back to the apartment, right?" he asked Amanda.

"That's what I understand," she said.

"I'll pick you up around two o'clock," Archie told her.

Once outside, Luther walked behind Evan as he pushed his wheelchair in front of him. Once they got to the truck, Luther folded up the chair and set it next to the fishing gear. Amanda climbed in next to Evan.

When they got to Archie's apartment, Luther walked Amanda up to the front door. "You can go fishing with us, if you'd like." he asked.

"Thanks for the offer, but I think it'll be fun to walk around the complex and take some pictures of all the tropical plants. Something I can look at for the rest of the winter when I go back up north."

She pulled the key Archie had given her out of her purse and opened the door.

"Okay. It was nice meeting you. I'm sure we'll be seeing each other sometime soon." "Thanks for the ride. Have fun fishing. Maybe we'll fry up your catch sometime?"

"Let's go!" Evan yelled out the window.

Luther turned toward the truck. "That boy's got to learn some patience."

Amanda shut the apartment door and turned the deadbolt. She walked into the kitchen and poured herself a glass of orange juice. As she was walking over to the table, she heard a noise coming from Archie's bedroom. She froze. It sounded like a drawer being closed.

Amanda frantically looked around the kitchen. She spotted a wooden knife rack on the counter. She pulled out a long knife and held it in front of her as she backed her way over to the front door. Suddenly, a man walked out of Archie's bedroom. Amanda screamed and fumbled for the door knob.

"Hey, knock it off. It's me!"

She stopped. It was a familiar voice. "Travis?"

"Hey, baby! Welcome to Florida!"

"What...what are you doing here? And...how did you get in here?"

Travis smiled. "I missed you, baby. The more I thought about you being in warm, sunny Florida, the more I thought I needed to be here, too."

"How'd you get in here?"

Travis laughed. "Oh, come on, Amanda. That's my thing, remember. It was easy. I jimmied the sliding glass door on the patio. What's wrong, baby? You don't look too happy to see me."

"I'm just shocked, I guess. Why didn't you say something before I left?"

"Didn't know I was coming. Let's just say I came into some unexpected cash and thought I might like to spend a few days on the beach with my honey."

"Where are you staying?"

Travis looked surprised. "Well, here. Where else?"

"I don't think my dad will go for that. He doesn't even know me yet." Amanda flung herself down on the couch. "Travis, you gotta get outta here. This looks bad. It looks like I set up my dad. He's going to think I knew all about this."

"That's crazy talk. I'll tell the dude I just decided to pay you a visit, like I did. Think of all the fun we can have." He walked over to the living room window. "Look, there's frickin' palm trees out there. No ice, no snow, just frickin' palm trees. I can't wait to get to the beach."

She glared at him. "When I walked in, you were in my dad's bedroom. What were you doing in there?"

"Just checking out the place," Travis said with an exaggerated smile.

"I hope you weren't…"

"Come on now. You don't need to go there. Relax, baby." Travis grabbed her by her arm and pulled her toward the spare bedroom. "Come on, I missed you. Let's have a little fun. We're on vacation!"

"I saw you yesterday morning. It's not like I've been gone two weeks."

"I know, I know…" Travis said, pushing Amanda down onto the bed.

Candace looked out the window and saw Luther's truck pull up. She glanced at her watch and wondered why they were back so soon. It was only quarter to one. She sprang from her desk and met Luther outside, as he was helping Evan get into his wheelchair. "Back so soon?" she asked.

"I'm afraid the boy doesn't feel too good," Luther said with a look of concern. "We put the boat in the water and had just started to fish when Evan said he wasn't feeling good. I took a look at him, and he didn't look well."

Candace bent down and looked at Evan. "What's wrong, honey?"

"I'm kind of tired, Mom. I feel like I could throw up."

Archie stepped out of his office when he heard the door open. He looked out the window and saw Luther's truck parked in front of the building. He walked outside and asked Luther, "What's going on? I thought you guys were going fishing?"

"We did. For a little while. Then Evan said he didn't feel so good, so I turned the boat around, and we came back."

Candace pulled her cell phone out and made a call. "If you don't mind, Archie, I'd like to take Evan over to my sister's."

"Why don't you just take him home?" Archie asked. "I think that would be better for him."

Candace thought for a moment. "You don't mind?"

"No, not at all. He needs to be home."

Candace gave Archie a quick hug. "Thank you. Thank you so much."

As Candace was driving away, Archie tuned to Luther. "So what happened?"

Luther scratched his head. "I think the little guy got too excited. I never saw anyone so pumped up about going fishing. Everything was fine until we got in the boat. Then his energy just started to fade away."

"Do you think he got sea sick from the boat?"

"Naw, it was flat as glass out there. We went out to the stick marsh. You know there ain't no waves or anything out there."

"I really feel sorry for Candace," Archie said. "I know she's been worrying a lot about Evan lately. He seems to be getting worse, and the doctors can't find anything."

"That's a shame," Luther said, shaking his head.

Archie glanced down at his watch. "I need to get out of here. I told Amanda I'd pick her up around two o'clock."

"You better get going," Luther said, as he headed for his truck.

At 1:50 p.m., Archie pulled up to the apartment. He was anxious to pick up Amanda and show her around the area. He thought he would take her to Pelican Island. After all, it was the first national wildlife refuge created in the United States. Or, since she had talked about taking pictures of the palm trees around the complex, he thought they might stop at McKee Botanical Gardens. He had never been there, but he had seen signs advertising it around the area, and it looked beautiful.

Archie unlocked the front door and stepped inside his apartment. "Hi, I'm back." He looked over and saw Amanda sitting on the couch with a strange man. "Oh!" Archie said, somewhat startled.

She had a sour look on her face, but the young man was sitting there with a big grin. Actually, a kind of stupid grin, Archie thought. She got up from the couch. "Dad, this is my boyfriend, Travis. Travis Engstrom."

"Really?" Archie said, as he walked over to him. Archie expected Travis to stand up and shake hands, but he just sat and looked up at him. Looked up with that foolish grin.

Amanda walked over to Archie and whispered, "Can I talk to you in the kitchen?"

Once out of the living room, Amanda grabbed him by the arms and said, "I swear I didn't know he was coming here. He never said a word to me that he was coming. I'm really sorry. I don't know what to do."

He looked into her eyes. "Do you want him here?"

She teared up. "I don't know. I was mad at him when I left, and I just wanted to spend some time with you. You know, just the two of us."

"Okay, I need to understand what's going on here. Since he's here now, we can't be rude; but I don't want him to spoil our time together, either. Don't worry; I'll take care of this."

Archie walked back to the living room. "We're going to take a drive so I can show Amanda around the area. Would you like to join us?"

Travis pushed himself off the couch. "Sure, I've never been to Florida before."

As they headed toward the front door, Archie suddenly stopped. "This isn't going to work. We'll never all fit in my Miata. Let me call Luther and see if we can switch cars for a few days."

Twenty minutes later Luther pulled up. Archie walked up to him. "Hey, I really appreciate this. I hope you don't mind."

Luther smiled. "Hell, no. I got me a fancy sports car for a few days." He looked over at Amanda. "Who's the guy?"

"We've got a little situation going on here. It's Amanda's boyfriend. He showed up unexpectedly."

"Oh, not so good. What're you going to do?"

Archie grimaced. "I'm not sure. But I'll tell you what; I'm not going to let this guy ruin her trip."

Luther climbed into the Miata. "Good luck!"

"Thanks, I'll need it." Archie watched as Luther drove off.

"Okay, come on. Let's head out," Archie called out to his daughter and her unexpected guest.

As they got into the truck, Amanda sat next to Archie, and Travis sat next to the window. "Did you see how that guy peeled out with your car, man?" Travis said. "I really think he dug it big time."

Archie looked over at him. He was wearing that stupid grin again.

Archie headed down Route 60, crossed the Merril P. Barber Bridge, and drove through the quaint seaside shopping area. He got onto A1A and drove south to Fort Pierce. Archie turned east onto North Beach Causeway Drive and crossed over to the mainland where he turned north on US 1 and headed back to Vero. As they crossed into the Vero Beach city limits, Travis piped up, "Is anyone besides me starving to death?"

Amanda shot him a dirty look. Archie turned to his daughter, "Good point. Let's stop and get something to eat. He headed back to the beach, and they stopped at a rustic café right on the water's edge. Once they got a table, they ordered a round of drinks, and Archie proposed a toast, "Here's to getting acquainted again with my beautiful daughter after all these years."

When the waitress appeared again to take their orders, Archie ordered the blackened Mahi fish sandwich, Amanda ordered the grouper sandwich, and Travis ordered the hearty fisherman's platter. The one that came with a Maine lobster.

"I never had lobster before, either," Travis announced to the table, looking around with that irritating grin. Amanda shot a look over at Archie. He had a strained smile on his face, "Is that right?"

When the bill arrived, Amanda dug into her purse and tried to give Archie some money. "No, no. Don't be crazy. I'm getting dinner."

Travis asked if anyone was getting dessert. Archie looked over at him. "I bet you never had Key Lime pie before, have you?"

Amanda cringed.

The evening was spent with Archie trying as hard as he could to talk to Amanda, but every time they got a conversation going, Travis interrupted with what he wanted to do the next day. He wanted to go to the beach. He wanted to see alligators. Then, he asked Archie if he could take off work and charter a boat so they could go ocean fishing. Finally, Archie couldn't take it any longer. He gave up and went to bed.

The next morning he and Amanda sat in the kitchen having breakfast. Travis was still sleeping on the couch. Archie enjoyed having some time with her. "What do you want to do today?"

"I'd like to go to the beach and take a nice long walk," she said, glancing out the kitchen window. "It looks like a beautiful day."

"That's a great idea. You can drop me off at work. I've got a few beach chairs in the garage. I'll throw them in the back of the truck. Grab a couple of beach towels from the linen closet." Archie looked up at the kitchen clock and then over at Travis. "We need to leave in a little while."

"I'll wake him up."

Archie walked out to the garage. As he grabbed the beach chairs, his cell phone rang. He struggled with the chairs and finally tossed them down on the grass. He pulled his phone out. "Hello."

"Oh, thank you for answering, Mr. Archibald!" It was Sanford Leeds' secretary, Jennifer.

Archie immediately noticed a different tone in her voice. Gone was the condescending attitude she had always exhibited when she was in his office.

"Have you heard from Sanford?"

He was surprised at the question. "No, I haven't. What's going on? You asked me this same question just a few days ago. Has something happened that I need to know about?"

"Um, no. Not exactly."

"Jennifer, the last time I saw him was when he came to my office." He thought for a minute. "That was almost a week ago."

"Ah, he's…he's…not been here in the office for a couple of days, and I haven't been able to reach him." He heard a muffled sob. "This has never happened before, and I'm worried sick. I've called just about everyone. You were my last hope."

"I'm sorry I can't be of any help. When was the last time you heard from him?"

"Last Wednesday. After work we stopped by the Ocean Club for a few drinks. The next morning, I came in late, and he never showed up. He called me from the road a few times, but he never came into the building."

He could hear the quiet desperation in her voice. "Where are you now?"

"I'm up in the office. Every day I come in hoping I'd see signs that he's been here, but his office looks exactly the same as when he left it Wednesday night."

"Do you want me to stop by? I'm heading over beachside right now. I'll be right in your area."

There was a slight pause. "Would you?"

"Sure, no problem. I have something to do, but after that, I can stop by in about an hour."

"Thank you, Mr. Archibald."

The Black Orchid Mystery

Archie shoved his cell phone back into his pocket. He wondered what was going on. He had never heard Jennifer sound so unsure of herself.

He picked up the beach chairs, threw them in the back of Luther's truck, and walked back to the house. Travis was sitting on the edge of the couch rubbing his eyes. His hair was going in all directions.

"Why so early?" he asked.

Archie ignored him. Amanda walked over with a bowl of cereal and a banana. "You need to eat something before we go."

On the drive to the beach, Archie told Amanda and Travis that something had come up, and he needed to see someone. He explained that he would drop them off and meet them in about an hour. As Archie drove over to Sanford's office, he wondered what could possibly have caused Sanford to be gone from the office so long without informing his secretary.

He walked into the reception area and saw Jennifer's desk was empty. He looked through the window to Sanford's office and saw her standing at the end of his desk. Archie walked into the office, and he could tell something was wrong. When Jennifer turned to greet him, it looked as if she had been crying.

She dabbed her face with a tissue. "Thanks for coming, Mr. Archibald."

Archie glanced around the office. Nothing looked out of the ordinary. "What's going on?"

She motioned for him to sit down.

"Like I told you, I haven't seen or heard from him all week, and I'm worried sick about it."

"Have you mentioned this to anyone?"

"I've asked a few other people if they've heard from him, like I asked you, but I haven't told the authorities, if that's what you're asking."

Archie thought to himself, *Oh great! Another person's gone missing and nobody contacted the cops.*

"Is this unusual behavior for him?"

"Yes and no. He used to have a drinking problem, and it wasn't that unusual for him to be gone for a few days. But that was years ago. He hasn't pulled anything like that for about four years. And besides, it would never be for almost a whole week."

Archie thought for a moment. "So, the last time you saw him was last Wednesday night, right."

Jennifer hesitated, "Um…yeah."

Archie could tell from her response that it was probably really early Thursday morning, but he didn't see the need to press the issue. "And you've reached out to anyone you could think of to see if they've heard from him since, and no one has, right?"

Jennifer nodded in agreement.

"What about his wife? Any kids?"

"Sanford's got three ex-wives, and, quite frankly, I think they'd all be tickled pink if they heard he had disappeared. He has a step-daughter from wife number two, but they don't communicate. If the alimony payments stopped coming, that would get their attention, I suppose."

"What about close friends?"

"I called Oliver Patnaude, a lawyer friend, and Nancy Abbott. She owns a gallery downtown, but neither of them have heard from him."

Archie looked over at the top of Sanford's huge mahogany desk. It was completely empty. He looked back at Jennifer. "Was he working on any other cases?"

Jennifer shook her head. "No, running Mrs. Silverman's affairs became a full time job."

"What about enemies?"

She let out a laugh. "Come on, he's a lawyer! That list is long and probably growing."

He stood up. "I don't know what to tell you. Now we seem to have two people that have disappeared into thin air. If you ask me, I think it's time to notify the authorities."

Jennifer thought for a moment. "I know. But Sanford would have a fit if I did that and he's really off on some drinking binge." She walked over and gazed out the window. "I think I'll wait to see what happens this week-end. If I don't hear from him by Monday, I'll talk to one of the guys I know on the force."

"Okay. Call me if anything comes up." He walked over to the door.

"Mr. Archibald."

Archie stopped. "Yes?"

"I just want to say thank you for coming by. I know you didn't have to with that phone call I had to make. It wasn't my idea, he…"

Archie interrupted. "No need to thank me. I understand. Please, let me know if any new information comes up."

On the drive back to the beach, he wondered if Sanford's absence could be connected with Clara Silverman's disappearance. What was the chance that he was actually in the middle of some wild drinking binge?

Candace glanced at her watch. She wondered when Archie was going to show up at the office. She was anxious to hear how his time with his daughter was going. Just then, she saw Luther's truck pull up in front of the building, and Archie got out. She was expecting him to be in a great mood, but one look at him when he walked in told her to expect something else.

"What's the matter?"

He flopped down in a chair next to her desk. "Where do I start?"

"What do you mean…is it Amanda?"

"Well, not really. Before I get into that, how's Evan?"

"He seems to be much better today. I think he got a little too excited about that fishing trip. I could see he was getting all wound up. When I got him home, he was exhausted. He went to bed and slept until seven o'clock. Anyway, he seems rested today. Thank you for letting me get out of here." She took a deep breath. "So, tell me about your time with Amanda."

Archie sighed and rolled his eyes. "It's a long story. Yesterday, when I got home, that derelict boyfriend of hers was in the apartment. He had decided to surprise her and come down and spend time with her."

"Oh, no! What's he like?"

"Just like you told me. He's a complete ass! He won't let me get a word in with Amanda. He's got to be the center of every conversation. But that's not the worst of it." Archie paused.

From the look on his face, Candace knew he was upset. "What?"

"I'm missing some money."

"Are you kidding me?"

"No. This morning I went to my drawer where I keep my cash for the week. When I opened it, I could see someone had rummaged through it, and when I counted my money, I was two hundred and twenty dollars short."

"Oh, Archie."

"I've got to get this guy out of there. I can't really confront him, since I didn't see him take it, but I know he did."

"That's terrible!"

"I know. But, that's not all. I've got some more bad news."

She braced herself for what was coming

"We've got to keep this quiet, but it looks like Sanford Leeds is missing."

Candace bolted from her desk. "What?"

"I just came from his office. His secretary, Jennifer, is beside herself. She hasn't seen him since…ah, sometime late Wednesday night."

"You've got to be kidding. What's that all about? First Clara and now him!"

Just then, the front door opened and Luther walked in. "Morning, everyone!" He walked up to them and pulled over a chair. "How's the visit going?"

"It was going great until the boyfriend showed up."

"Boyfriend?"

Archie explained the surprise waiting for him when he got home and his concern about the missing money. He didn't mention anything about Sanford.

"That's too bad, Archie. I hope this creep doesn't ruin your daughter's visit."

Archie shook his head. "I'm not about to let that happen." He looked over at the clock. "I need to head over to the beach and pick them up. I'm half an hour late already."

Archie drove back over to the beach and started walking along the shore, searching for Amanda and her uninvited guest. He couldn't bear to refer to him as her boyfriend. It didn't take long to spot them, thanks to the lime green beach umbrella Archie had found in the garage. He walked over and saw Amanda sitting in a beach chair by herself.

"Having fun?" Archie asked.

Amanda turned with a start. "Oh, you scared me."

The Black Orchid Mystery

He froze. He could see that she had been crying, and there was a wide, red welt along the right side of her face.

"Amanda, what happened?"

"Uh… the…the umbrella. It got caught in the wind, and it hit me."

"Really? Where's Travis?"

"He's…he's walking down the beach."

Archie could feel his temper rising. "He hit you, didn't he?"

"No. It was the umbrella like I told you."

Archie kneeled down and looked at her face. "Looks like a slap from an open hand to me. There's no way the umbrella would leave a mark like that."

She reached up and grabbed his hand. "Dad, please. I'm okay. I don't want to start anything."

"This is unacceptable, Amanda. I'm not sure what you see in this guy, but I'll tell you what, he has to leave and leave now."

"It was my fault, Dad."

"Your fault? Nonsense. There's no excuse for anyone to hit you. I can't put up with that. This guy has to go."

"He's going. That's what we were talking about. Please, it may take a day or two, but he's leaving. Let's not make a scene. It's almost all worked out."

Archie looked down the beach and saw Travis walking back up from the ocean. As he got closer, he saw Archie standing there. Travis sat down on the sand, gazing out at the ocean.

Archie walked over to him. "Stand up."

Travis stood up and took a menacing stance. "What?"

"Dad!" Amanda shouted.

"Look, I don't know what happened here, but let me be perfectly clear. You were not invited on this trip, you just showed up. If you ever lay a hand on my daughter again, I'll either beat you to a pulp or press charges against you. I want you out of my house by Sunday evening. It's time for you to go back to Ohio."

Travis was about to say something, but Amanda jumped in between them. "Like I said, he's making plans to leave. That won't be a problem. Come on, let's all get along. I don't want to ruin this beautiful day."

Archie turned. "See that restaurant? I'll be sitting at the bar. When you're ready to eat something, just come and meet me."

As he walked over to the building, his blood was boiling. He found a seat at the bar, pulled out his cell phone, and called Luther.

Luther listened while Archie explained what had just happened. He had never heard Archie so upset. "Look, I'm out running errands, but I'm only about two miles from you. How 'bout if I come by and I'll buy you a drink?"

"That would be great," Archie said. "I may need somebody to hold me back from taking a swing at that two-bit loser."

"Now, don't do that. I'll be right there."

Archie ordered another drink for himself and one for Luther. By the time the drinks arrived, Luther was walking in the door. He pulled up a stool next to Archie. "I sure am enjoying that little car of yours. It handles real good."

"Thanks for lending me your truck. You can get it back sometime Sunday. That's when I told that creep he has to be out of here."

"You're letting him stay that long?"

"Only for Amanda's sake. I have to give him some time to figure out how he's going to get home."

"I suppose," Luther said, taking a sip of his drink.

"Another thing, but this can't get around."

Luther gave Archie a puzzled look.

"I came back from Sanford's office right after all this must have happened," Archie said.

"And how is the pompous ass?"

Archie lowered his voice. "Missing."

Luther paused, his drink halfway to his lips. "Missing? Are you kidding me?"

"No. I've been getting a few calls from his secretary asking me if I had heard from him. I found this a little strange, since the last time I heard from her was when she fired me. But, from the tone of her voice, I could tell she was upset. She asked me if I could come by, and she said she hasn't seen or heard from him for almost a week."

"Geeze!" Luther said. "What the hell's going on?"

"She said he's been known to go on drinking binges in the past, but they never lasted this long."

"He's missing, Mrs. Silverman's missing? What's going on?"

"I don't know, but we've got John Barrington coming to town tomorrow. We better make sure he doesn't go missing, too."

Archie saw Amanda and Travis walk into the restaurant. He motioned for them to come over to the bar.

"What are you drinking?" Luther asked them. "Let me get it."

Amanda sat next to Archie, and Travis stood next to Luther. Luther pulled out a bar stool. "Sit down." Travis took one look at him and moved over to the stool.

"My name's Luther. I'm a good friend of Archie's."

"Hi. I'm Travis."

"How long you staying?" Luther asked, somewhat nonchalantly. The barmaid set a drink down.

"Thanks." Travis picked up his drink. "Supposed to head back home Sunday or Monday, but I may hang around a little longer. I'm kinda digging this warm weather."

"Really?" Luther asked.

"Might as well. How often do I get to Florida? Not very."

"I'll tell you what," Luther said. "How'd you like to go fishing with me tomorrow?"

"Fishing? Hell, yes!" Travis said, with a look of surprise on his face. "Are we going to go out in the ocean?"

"No. I got me a bass boat, and I like to go to Blue Cypress Lake. It's real pretty, and the fishing's pretty damn good."

"Sure, that'd be great."

"I'll pick you up around seven."

"Seven? As in the morning?" he asked, somewhat taken aback.

"That's right. It'll take us an hour just to get there."

"How about nine o'clock?"

"You ain't done much fishing, have you," Luther laughed. "How about eight o'clock?"

"Okay."

A waitress walked over to Archie and told him a table was ready. Luther picked up the bar tab, and they all walked over and sat down. The table was next to two large glass patio doors, and it had an unobstructed view of the ocean. Archie and Luther let their guests sit facing the view. The waitress took their order and walked back to the kitchen.

"Guess what, Amanda? I'm going fishing with Luther tomorrow," Travis said.
Archie was in the middle of taking a drink of water and almost choked. After coughing a few times, he looked at Luther. "What?"

Luther smiled. "Yep. Boys day out. I thought it would be fun to take the lad for some real Florida fishing. Let you two get some father-daughter time tomorrow. You don't mind, do you?"

Amanda looked over at Archie. "I don't mind," she said, with a look of relief on her face.

"No, fine with me. You don't have to do this, Luther."

Travis looked over at Archie. "Hey, don't talk the dude out of it."

"I'm always looking for a fishing partner," Luther said. "And you've been too damn busy lately. We'll have a great time," Luther said with a big smile, winking at Archie. "Oh, by the way, I'll need to take the truck home tonight so I can pick up my boat."

"Oh. Sure, that's not a problem." Archie could hardly believe what he was hearing. After all he had told him about this guy, how could he want to take him fishing? Luther must be an even bigger fishing fanatic than he realized. "Don't forget, Luther. Mr. Barrington gets here tomorrow, and I need you to pick him up at the airport and keep an eye on him."

A look of panic crossed Luther's face. "Damn, I almost forgot. What time is he coming in?"

"Candace has him getting into Melbourne around four o'clock."

"Not a problem," Luther said, relieved. "I'll be back in plenty of time."

Chapter 28

Clara glanced over at the clock. It was almost five. The woman would be coming in with her supper and a freshly laundered pair of black pajamas any time now. She slipped her legs out of bed and pushed herself up to a standing position. For the last three days she was feeling more like her old self. This morning she had decided she had to do something, and she finally felt strong enough to make an attempt.

She walked over to the door and stood behind it. She waited several minutes and then heard the key turn in the lock. *Right on time*, Clara thought to herself. The door slowly swung open, and she waited until the woman stepped into the room. She was holding a tray of food with one hand and had the folded pajamas in the other.

Clara shoved the door against the woman as hard as she could. She fell against the night table and then slid down to the floor next to the bed. The tray of food flew into the air, did a s0mersault, and came crashing down onto the wooden plank floor. The tray bounced off the floor and hit the woman against the side of her face. She cried out in pain.

Clara stepped through the doorway, swung the door shut, and fumbled for the key that was still in the lock. She heard the woman scramble to her feet. The door knob in Clara's hand started to twist just as she was able to turn the key. As Clara stopped to catch her breath, she heard pounding from behind the door. "Open this door! Let me out! Mrs. Silverman, please!"

Looking for a way out, Clara walked down a hallway and stepped into a small dining room. French doors were open on the wall to the right of the dining room table, but they led to a living room.

She could see a television set was on in the next room. She approached the open doorway and peeked in. She could see the back of a man's head as he watched TV. To the left was a side door. She could faintly hear pounding coming from her room, but the sound of the television masked most of it. She tip-toed over to the door, grabbed the handle and turned it. She pulled the door open and took a step outside. The smell of fresh-air engulfed her. She breathed in deep.

"What the…"

Clara felt a strong hand grab her shoulder. "What do you think you're doing?"

The Black Orchid Mystery

Clara turned around and saw a middle-aged man behind her. He had on brown pants and a green sweater that zipped up the front. He was balding, but had a neatly trimmed gray moustache. "Please, I need to go home. People are looking for me. I need to get back to Gloria and James. They will be worried."

The man put his arm around her and turned her toward the open doorway. "Not quite yet, Mrs. Silverman. Not quite yet. Come, dear, let me walk you back to your room."

Clara stopped walking. "No! No!" She looked around. "Help! Help me!"

The man gently pushed her back into the room and shut the door. As he guided her back down the hallway, she asked, "Do you want money? I'll pay you what-ever you want. Please, I need to go home."

"Now, now Mrs. Silverman," the man said softly. "Looks like you're feeling much better!"

Clara stopped midway down the hallway. "How can I be feeling better when you keep me locked up in a room all the time?"

"I know. I know. I'm sorry about that. But just look at how much more energy you have."

As they approached the door to Clara's room, the pounding noise got louder. "Let me out! Open this door!"

The man walked over, unlocked the door, and pushed it open. A plate of meatloaf and potatoes was turned upside down, and green beans were scattered under the furniture.

"Am I bleeding?" the woman said. She pulled her hair away from the side of her face. "Look. Am I bleeding?"

"No. There's a red mark, but you're not bleeding. Go upstairs," he said, "I'll clean up this mess."

"She almost killed me!" the woman said, as she stomped out of the room.

Chapter 29

John Barrington's alarm went off at 4:00 a.m. He rolled over and turned it off. Kit yawned, got out of bed, and looked out the window.

"What's it look like?" he asked, as he forced himself to step out from under the warm covers.

"It's snowing."

"That's what I was afraid of," he said, walking over to the window. "It's pretty light. Let's hope that doesn't change and the wind doesn't pick up."

They left the house at 5:05 a.m., giving them two hours to drive the forty-five miles to Escanaba. There were one-foot snow drifts around Saint Jacques, but other than that, the drive was uneventful.

At the airport, John got his boarding passes, checked his luggage, and turned to Kit. "This should be interesting. Wish me luck."

She gave him a tight hug. "Be careful. We don't know what's going on down there."

He picked up his carry-on bag. "Watch out on the drive home. Those drifts are only going to get bigger."

She gave John another hug. "I will, but the plows should be out by now. Bye, honey. Be safe, and call me when you get there."

The flight to Detroit took a little over an hour. John got off the plane and headed to a restaurant for breakfast. He had two and a half hours to kill before his flight to Atlanta. He spent his time people-watching and wondering what he was going to find out about his Aunt Clara when he got to Florida.

Just before eight o'clock, Luther pulled up to Archie's apartment. Archie walked out to greet him with two cups of coffee, one in each hand. "Why are you doing this?" Archie asked. "That bozo doesn't deserve one second of your time."

"Now, now," Luther said, taking a cup from Archie. "Thanks. You never have time to go fishing anymore, and it's a lot more fun than going by myself."

"Suit yourself," Archie said. "But, after spending a few hours with this guy, I bet you change your mind about fishing alone. I really don't get it."

Travis walked out of the house looking as if he had just gotten up. His hair was uncombed and he had missed matching the buttons on his shirt with the buttonholes, so his shirt was buttoned all wrong.

Luther took one look at him and smiled, "You're gonna fit in with all them crackers just fine."

"What?" Travis asked.

"Ah, nothing."

Archie had to turn around to hide his laughter.

The hour drive to Blue Cypress Lake was uneventful. Travis slept the whole way. When they got to Middleton's Fish Camp, Luther backed the boat into the water. Travis was no help. He climbed out of the truck, and ran into the bait store to buy a pack of cigarettes. Luther parked his truck and they both walked over to the boat. Luther started the engine and they glided down the channel that led to the lake.

"Gator!" Luther said, pointing to a five foot alligator basking in the sun on a muddy bank.

"Nice!" Travis said.

"There's another one," Luther said, pointing to a spot twenty feet from the first one.

"And there's one swimming in the water!" Travis called out.

"This lake's full of them," Luther said. "I had eighteen of 'em around my boat a few weeks ago. But it's the water moccasins you need to watch out for."

"Water moccasins?"

"Yeah, they're mean and aggressive."

"Will they kill you?"

"Nah, but you'll wish you'd be dead. Let's just say, whatever they bite on you, you're gonna lose. Your arm, your leg…your private parts."

"Private parts?" Travis said, with a wince.

Luther turned a hard right, and they headed to the far northern end of the lake. There were a few other fishing boats near the boat launch, and a few were scattered toward the middle of the lake, but the farther north Luther went, the more desolate it got. Finally, he cut the motor and they drifted to a stop.

He handed Travis a fishing rod. "Here you go."

They spent the next hour fishing, almost in silence. Luther had brought a cooler full of beer, and Travis didn't seem shy about helping himself. After his third beer, Travis said, "I gotta pee."

"Not a problem. Pee off the back of the boat."

Travis looked surprised. "Right out here?"

"Where do you think we're gonna go? To a Holiday Inn? Yeah, just pee off the back."

Travis finished, sat back down, and reached for another beer.

Luther threw out a cast and asked Travis, "You got a record?"

Travis spun around. "What?"

"A record. You got a record?"

Travis set down his beer and picked up his pole. "Yeah, I've had a few scrapes with the law, that's for sure."

Luther nodded. "You do know that Archie's one of my best friends, don't you."

"Yeah, I know," Travis said, casting his line.

"I hear he was missing a little money right around the time you showed up in his apartment."

"I don't know anything about that," Travis said, somewhat defensively. "He never said anything about it to me."

Luther nodded. He reeled in his line and cast it out again, this time from the other side of the boat.

"You ever hit a woman?" Luther asked.

"What?"

"I asked you if you ever hit a woman," Luther repeated.

"Why the hell would you ask me something like that?" Travis said. He looked over at Luther out of the corner of his eye.

"I understand you hit Amanda yesterday at the beach."

Travis reeled in his lure and tossed down his pole. "That's a bunch of bull-shit. Take me back to the marina. I'm done with this crap."

Luther slowly pulled his revolver out from under his shirt. "I don't think so."

A look of panic crossed Travis's face. "What the hell are you doing, man? Are you crazy or something?"

"Get in the water," Luther said.

"What?"

"Go ahead, slip over the side there and get in the water."

"Mister, you must be nuts. I'm not getting in that water."

Luther pointed the gun at his head and squeezed off a round. Travis felt the bullet wiz by his left ear.

"Get in the water."

"Look man, I don't know what pissed you off, but I don't wanna drown out here."

"You're not going to drown. If you do as I say, you'll be just fine. If you don't, you'll end up being gator bait. I just needed to talk to you, that's all. And I want to make sure I have your undivided attention. Now, get going."

Travis grabbed the side of the boat and slowly slipped his legs over. He felt cool water inch up his body as his feet sank deeper into the lake. He was hanging onto the side of the boat with both hands. The water was now up to his neck.

"Feel anything nibbling at your toes?" Luther asked.

Travis let out a yell and wildly looked around. He jerked his knees up.

"Those gators can be real sneaky, and those damn water moccasins can slip right up your pant legs."

"What the hell's wrong with you?" Travis pleaded.

"Tell you what," Luther said. "You want to get out of the water? All you got to do is agree to a few of my terms and get back in the boat, or you can say no, and we'll start trolling for gators."

"What do you want?" Travis asked.

"First, I want to know where Archie's money is."

"I didn't take no money!"

Travis pushed a button and the motor kicked in. "Hang on! We're gonna go gator hunting."

The Black Orchid Mystery

He felt the water around his legs start to move. "Wait…wait…I got it right here in my pocket."

"Okay, you'll be giving that to me so I can get it back to Archie. Next, you're going to let me drop you off at the Greyhound Bus terminal in Ft. Pierce, and you're going to buy a one-way ticket and head back up to wherever the hell you came from."

"What about all my shit? It's over at the house."

"Don't worry about it. We'll send it to you."

"But I'll be all wet." Travis said.

"We'll set your ass in the back of the truck, and you'll be dry as a bone by the time we get there."

"I'll smell like an old fish," Travis said with a scowl.

"Then you'll fit in real good with everyone else on the bus."

Travis looked over to his left. "Shit, man, there's a gator over there."

Luther looked over. "There sure enough is. Take your time deciding. You just may save me the drive."

Travis watched as the gator disappeared under the water. "I'll go…I'll go," he said, reaching out his hand. "Help me get in the boat, damn it!"

Chapter 30

Sonny finished his second cup of coffee and walked outside. He listened to the birds flitting around the bushes surrounding the trailer. He thought of how quiet it had been since Francine and the boy had left. He didn't think she would stay away that long. She had stormed off before, but it normally only lasted one or two nights.

He headed to the wooded area behind the trailer where Sanford's car was hidden. Before he tried to get rid of the car, he needed to do a major cleaning of the trunk. When Sonny pulled Sanford out, before he buried him back in the woods, he noticed several clumps of his hair had stuck to a large pool of dried blood. Sonny pulled off the camouflage tarp that was draped over the car.

The Black Orchid Mystery

He stepped back and stared. That was one hell of a good looking car. It made no sense at all to bring this car over to the car crushing machine in Orange City. He had already made plans to drive it over there after hours and have it crushed, no questions asked. His friend Billy knew the guy that ran the place. But, hell, this was at least a sixty thousand dollar car. Why sell it for scrap?

Billy had told him he was crazy when Sonny had called him to set it up. Maybe it made sense, what Billy had said; drive the damn car down to Miami and get rid of it there. Billy said if he did that, it could be on a barge to Haiti the next day, and who the hell could find it then? At least he'd be able to put some extra cash in his pocket while he waited to get the money from Nancy. To hell with Orange City; he was taking it to Miami.

Sonny started the BMW and drove it up next to his truck, in front of the trailer. He popped the trunk and stepped back, coughing. The trunk was reeking. A putrid smell of decay washed over him. He turned and bent over in the tall grass. He spit and coughed a few times, trying not to throw up. He slammed the trunk shut and walked back toward the house to get a pail of water and some bleach.

As he neared the trailer, he noticed a car was headed down his driveway. He stood at the end of the road and watched as Francine pulled up and parked next to his truck. Ronnie jumped out and started walking toward the BMW. "Wow, where did you get the cool car, Dad?"

"Get away from there!" Sonny yelled. "Hey, come over here and give your old Dad a hug." Ronnie turned, ran over, and leaped into Sonny's arms. He gave him a big hug. "Boy, I sure missed you, buddy."

"Is that your car, Dad?" Ronnie asked.

Sonny stood up. "No. I'm selling it for a friend. Pretty nice, huh."

Francine started walking to the trailer.

"Where you going? Can't you even say hello?" Sonny, called out.

"I need to pick up a few more things," Francine answered. She kept walking toward the trailer.

"What the…" He ran over to her and grabbed her by the shoulder. "Come on, baby. You've been gone long enough. I thought you were coming back."

She pulled away and stared at him. "I'm not coming back. Daddy got a lawyer…"

Sonny interrupted. "A lawyer? What in the hell did he get a lawyer for?"

She could see his face was getting red, and the cords in his neck were standing out. She backed up a few steps. "It's over, Sonny. I can't live like this anymore."

"It's your old man, that's the problem," he yelled. "He's feeding you a bunch of bull-shit. He's poisoning you against me."

"Leave Daddy out of this. I'm done and I need to move on."

He grabbed her, twisted her arm around her back, and pushed her up the trailer steps. "You're

The Black Orchid Mystery

staying here tonight. We need to talk. I don't want you near that lying bastard."

Sonny pushed open the front door and threw Francine inside. She fell to the floor and grabbed her stomach. "Sonny, the baby, the baby…"

Ronnie ran up the steps and jumped in front of his mother. "Dad, stop!"

Sonny pushed Ronnie aside. "Go to your room. This don't concern you." He reached down and pulled Francine up by her hair. He grabbed her and started shaking her. "You listen to me…"

"Sonny, stop it!"

Ronnie ran down the hallway to his room and slammed the door shut. He listened from his room and heard bangs and crashes through the door. The floor of his room was shaking. He heard his mother cry out and then a sound that sounded like a loud slap. He pushed open his door and crept down the hallway to his parents' room.

"Damn you, Francine. You listen and you listen good…"

Ronnie heard another slap. He walked over to the nightstand and pulled out a .22 caliber handgun. He held it behind his back and walked out into the living room.

Sonny was reaching back to slap Francine when he saw Ronnie step out of the shadows, the gun pointed at his head. "Ronnie, you put that…"

Francine heard a loud blast and watched as a small red hole appeared just to the right of Sonny's nose. She felt his grip on her blouse loosen and watched as he crumpled to the floor.

Ronnie threw the gun onto the couch, ran over and wrapped his arms around her. "I'm sorry, Momma. I'm sorry!"

By the time Luther pulled up to Archie's apartment, he didn't have much time to spare before he needed to head over to his house, unhook the boat, and get cleaned up. It was almost time to pick up John Barrington from the Melbourne airport. He quickly walked over to the front door and pushed the door bell. Archie opened the door, and Luther walked in alone.
Amanda was sitting on the couch, reading a magazine. She looked up. "Where's Travis?"

"Ah, the boy decided to head back home," Luther said in a somber tone.

"What?" Amanda asked.

Archie looked up in surprise.

"Yeah, we got to talking, and he thought it best to head back home. I dropped him off at the Fort Pierce bus station."

Archie continued to have a look of amazement on his face.

Amanda stood up. "Now wait a minute, what's going on?"

Archie turned toward her, "I'm sure everything's just fine, Amanda. Travis wasn't invited, he just showed up. After all that's happened, I think it's probably best for everyone that he decided to go back home."

"Yeah, with a little convincing, I'm sure," she said.

Luther looked at his watch. "Hey, I need to go home and get ready to pick up Mr. Barrington."

Archie said, "I'll walk you out." As they walked to the truck, he asked, "Okay, how in the hell did you manage that?"

"Don't ask any questions," Luther said with a low laugh. "You don't want to know." He reached into his pocket. "Oh, by the way, here's your money."

Archie stopped. "What?"

"Here, take it," he said, pushing a wad of bills into Archie's hand.

"There're wet!"

"Like I said, no questions."

"What the hell are you, some kind of miracle worker?" Archie asked. "Not only do you make that creep disappear, but you get back my missing money!" He paused. "He is alive, isn't he? He really did get on the bus, right."

Luther laughed. "Come on, Archie. Are you serious?"

He watched as Luther drove away. While he was relieved that jerk of a boyfriend was out of his hair, Archie didn't look forward to walking back into the house with no answers.

Amanda was waiting for him at the door. "Okay, I know your friend Luther was really enjoying himself, but I need to know what happened to Travis. There's no way he'd just get up and head to the bus station without telling me."

"I really don't know, Amanda. I tried to get more information from Luther, but he stuck to his story."

"That's a bunch of bull-shit!" she screamed.

"I'll call Luther and see…"

"I can't believe this…." Amanda started crying. She pushed past him and ran into the guest room, slamming the door behind her.

An ambulance, two police cars, and a van from child services were parked in front of the trailer in Fellsmere. Francine sat on the steps, holding Ronnie tight. She looked up at one of the policemen. "Please, please don't take away my son!"

Francine had dialed 9-1-1, and it seemed like forever before the police arrived. She had repeated what had happened over and over to the various patrolmen and detectives that had arrived on the scene. Then, once the social workers showed up, she explained to them what happened. She knew they were going to take Ronnie away, but in her heart, she just couldn't face it.

One of the two policemen, who had been standing over her, bent down. "I know this is a very difficult time, but can I ask you a question?"

Francine nodded her head.

"What do you know about that BMW parked out front?"

"Nothing. I moved out of here a week ago. It wasn't here then. I just came back to pick up a few more of my things, and we saw it then."

The Black Orchid Mystery

John's plane was delayed about an hour because of an ice storm in Atlanta, but just as planned, Luther was waiting for him when he landed. He was holding a sign that had John's name on it. John laughed when he saw it.

"Luther P. Johnson at your service," he said, shaking John's hand. "Mr. Archibald asked me to meet you and take you over to your hotel. He apologizes that he couldn't be here in person."

After picking up John's suitcase from the baggage claim area, they headed out the door. Once outside, John stopped and looked around. "Amazing! No snow and the temperature's above zero!" He took a deep breath. There was a humid, earthy smell in the air. He gazed at the lush tropical landscaping that decorated the airport perimeter. "It's nice to be back in Florida. Especially coming from where I did."

"Upper Michigan, right?" Luther asked.

"Yes, the Upper Peninsula. It was eight below when I got in the car this morning. It was a long drive to the airport. Blowing snow and one foot drifts. I'm lucky I made it."

Luther shuddered. "Makes me cold just hearing about it."

He set John's suitcase into the bed of the pickup while John peeled off his jacket. "I forgot how warm it gets down here."

"It's only in the mid-seventies."

John laughed, "Only? That's about an eighty degree difference for me!"

"Stick around awhile, you'll get used to it."

On the drive back to Vero Beach, Luther said, "I'm sure you have some questions. Archie wants me to brief you as to what's happening with your aunt." Luther spent the next twenty minutes getting him up to speed.

John stared out the window and then turned to Luther. "I hate to say it, Luther, but it seems that nobody really knows much at this stage of the game."

He nodded. "Yeah, that's how I see it. We're hoping you might be able to think of something that could point us in a new direction."

John frowned, "That's highly unlikely. As I've said, all I know about my Aunt Clara comes from stories I've heard from her sister over the years, and then what the man in the nursing home had to tell me just a few days ago. I can't see how any of that has any relevancy."

"Probably so, but Archie was very happy when he heard you were coming."

"When it comes down to me providing anything useful in her disappearance, I think he's in for a big disappointment."

Luther pulled into a driveway off Coral Avenue and stopped under a covered walkway. "Here we are."

John looked out the window. Thick green Arica Palms lined the walkway to the lobby. "This looks beautiful!" John said, as he stepped out of Luther's truck.

"I hope you like it. It's not a real big place, and it's kind of out of the way. Quiet and secluded. I know the owners. They'll take good care of you while you're here."

John grabbed his suitcase and walked with Luther toward the lobby. They stepped onto a low bridge that crossed over a small pond. John looked down and saw the water was filled with huge orange and yellow koi. Tall thick strands of bamboo ringed the water. "I wish my kids could see this," he said with a smile. "They'd really get a kick out of it."

"Now you know a good place to stay. Bring the whole family next time," Luther said, as he held open the lobby door.

John checked into the hotel, and, as they waited for a bellboy to take him to his room, Luther mentioned, "I almost forgot. I'll be back at seven to take you to dinner."

John looked surprised. "That's not necessary. I'll be fine."

"No, no. I insist. Archie feels terrible that he can't join us, but, his daughter is visiting. He's having dinner with her tonight."

"I hate to trouble you," John said. "I'm sure you have other things to do."

"Not one more word. I'll meet you right here in the lobby at seven o'clock sharp."

"Okay, thank you for picking me up. I'll see you then."

John walked up to his room and started unpacking his suitcase. He just finished hanging up the last of his shirts, when his cell phone rang.

"Hello."

"Hi, Honey. How was your trip?" Kit asked.

"Pretty smooth. The plane got delayed for an hour coming out of Atlanta, but Mr. Archibald had a friend waiting for me. He just dropped me off at the hotel about twenty minutes ago. It's really warm here. You wouldn't believe what a difference from this morning. How did the meeting go?"

There was a pause. "Not so good. Looks like it's a done deal. There were about thirty people there. Twenty of us wanted the land to be left alone, but it didn't make a difference. They're going to start clear-cutting as soon as the first spring thaw."

John let out a long sigh. "Maybe we should sell the house."

Chapter 31

James Harrow walked across the driveway and took the steps up to the recreation room. He was carrying a brief-case stuffed with three more folders from Sanford's office. He made sure nobody would see him. He had seen Gloria go to her room, and he knew, from Enrique's ceaseless bragging, that he had a hot date with someone he had met down by the beach, and he was planning to spend the night at her place.

James made his way through the recreation room and the office. He stopped at the door to the living quarters and knocked softly.

"Come in," a voice softly responded.

He pushed open the door and walked up to the woman who was sitting at the kitchen table.

"Find anything new?" she asked.

"I've pulled out a few more folders. Not sure if they'll add much to what we already have."

"I'll take a look. James, I've been thinking about what you said about how that Abbott woman caught you in Sanford's office."

"Yes?"

"Do you think she actually believed your reason for being there?"

He frowned. "I don't know. At first, I fumbled around for something to say. I doubt I was very convincing. Why?"

"I hope she didn't get suspicious when she caught you in there. We're getting close. With the ledger you brought me, we may have more than enough evidence to put her and that Leeds chap away."

James sat down at the table and sighed. "Margaret, I can't thank you enough. If you hadn't been willing to come over and look into this for me, I don't know what we would have done."

She walked over and gave him a hug. "That's what families are for, cousin! Actually, this was a perfect mission to test my training. I needed a new environment after university."

"It was so good of you to come. Sorry we had to keep you holed up like some prisoner."

Margaret laughed. "And they say Economics is boring! Prisoner? I prefer to think it was more like a British spy."

"I'm sorry, but with all that was going on, I knew this had to be done very discretely. I don't think Sanford would take it too kindly if he knew someone was snooping into his affairs."

"Well, mission accomplished. I probably don't even need the files you've brought with you. I've plenty of proof that Mr. Leeds was fleecing Clara out of millions. I suspect those files will just be the icing on the cake. Care for a cup of tea? I was just going to heat up a kettle when you arrived."

He smiled. "I'd love some."

James and Margaret spent almost an hour talking about their families, home in Brixham, their favorite pubs in Cornwall, and how they spent their youth traveling the beautiful seaside towns along the English Riviera. He glanced down at his watch and stood up. "Look at the time! I better get back, or Gloria will think I've been snatched up like poor Clara!"

"I'll take a look at the papers you brought and let you know what they tell us."

James stopped. "All right. Oh, we've got some visitors arriving. Quite exciting, actually. Mr. Archibald, that detective I told you about, found Clara's nephew. When Gloria found out, she almost went crazy with joy. I hope he's not interested in just her money like everyone else seems to be."

He walked over to a window. "They just pulled in now. I'd better get down there and welcome them." As he headed down the stairs, he watched as Archie and two other men got out of a truck. He walked over to the group. "Hello, Mr. Archibald. Right on time, I see."

"Good morning, James. Yes, eleven o'clock, just like I told Gloria." Archie stepped back. "I'd like to introduce you to John Barrington, Mrs. Silverman's long lost nephew."

"Oh, yes," James said, shaking his hand. "Nice to meet you, Mr. Barrington."

"And this is my friend, Luther Johnson," Archie continued.

"Hello, Mr. Johnson. Welcome. Do come in, will you, gentlemen?"

As James pushed open the door, Gloria was hurriedly walking toward them with a huge smile on her face. "Come in, come in!"

Archie introduced her to John and Luther. John briefly explained how he fit into the family. He talked about Thortis, Clara's sister, and the family home in the Upper Peninsula of Michigan. Gloria stood there beaming, taking it all in.

James motioned toward a door. "I have a bit of refreshments set out in the dining room. Please, this way…we'll tell you all we know about your aunt, and then I'm sure you would be interested in taking a look at the house and grounds."

The dining room was paneled in a dark, rich mahogany. The long table had been set with six places at the far end of the room. Several black orchids were arranged along the table as centerpieces. Gloria made sure everyone was seated and then came around with a sterling silver coffee pot. James set out a plate of freshly baked chocolate chip cookies.

John was fascinated at the things he was hearing about his aunt. He wished Kit could have been with him to hear it, too. He knew he would never remember all the details when he got back. He looked around the room and could only imagine what the rest of the place looked like. Kit was right. His aunt was loaded.

"When I heard you were going to pay us a visit," James said, "I did a little research on your part of the world. I must admit, I'm a little confused, and I have a few questions."

John smiled. "I hope I can answer them. What confused you?"

James walked over to a bookcase and pulled out a huge atlas. He flipped a few pages and opened the book to a map of Michigan. He pointed to the top of the page, "If you look, you can see the peninsula you live on here."

"That's right," John said.

"But for the life of me, I can't figure out why it's not part of the state they call Wisconsin. Look, down here. It's attached to Wisconsin. Its not even close to the other part of Michigan!"

John laughed. "I hope you don't want me to explain that! I would bet the majority of us Yoopers wonder the same thing."

"What is Yoopers?" Gloria asked.

"Oh, I'm sorry. That's what we call ourselves. Anyone that lives in the Upper Peninsula. We call it the U.P. for short. You know, U.P. kind of sounds like Yooper."

"From what I've read, it does look sort of wild. Lots of wilderness, bears and deer. That sort of thing." James continued.

Oh, you've got that right. There are lots of forests in Upper Michigan. We've got a huge problem right now where I live. The state wants to build a big prison down the road from us, and the locals are fighting it. But, from what my wife told me, the last meeting wasn't very encouraging. It looks like it's going to be built, regardless. We really hate to see so much land mowed down for a prison. It will completely change our way of life."

"That's not good," Gloria said.

"I'm sorry to hear that," James said. "So sad."

"Not good at all," John said. There was an awkward pause.

Archie jumped in. "John, both James and Gloria have been working for your aunt for quite a long time."

"She's a wonderful woman," James said, ignoring the fact that she was missing.

"I only wish her sister could be with me now." John looked around. "She would never believe it."

"It's very sad that the sisters were not close," Gloria said, shaking her head.

"It was sad. It broke my aunt's heart when Clara went away and they lost touch. And I have a wonderful sister who lives in Chicago. I think Clara would enjoy meeting my lovely wife and our great kids." He stopped. "It's…it's very difficult to be here and not know where Clara is. But, from all I've been hearing, she's very blessed to have you around."

"Why, thank you, John," James said, standing up. "I know I'm also speaking for Gloria when I say

The Black Orchid Mystery

we appreciate your kind words. Shall we take the tour?"

"Before we do that," John said, "I have a question."

James sat back down. "What is it?"

"I'd like to ask everyone here what they think happened to my aunt. She's been gone now for…"

"Sixteen days," Archie volunteered.

Gloria got a look of discomfort on her face, and she looked over at James. James glanced toward Archie and said, "I wish we knew, John. From the little we know, it seems she was taken in the middle of the night; but, as far as I know, there has been no demand for money. We've combed the grounds thoroughly several times, and we know she's not in the house. Perhaps Mr. Archibald can update us on any new developments."

Archie had a concerned look. "Well, besides Mr. Barrington joining us, there is a recent development I'd like to discuss. It may or may not be significant, but it appears that Sanford may be missing now, also."

Both James and Gloria bolted from their seats. A plate of cookies fell from Gloria's lap. "What?" they cried, almost in unison.

"Like I said, it may be nothing, but Sanford's secretary has been trying to reach him for several days now, and she hasn't been successful."

"How long are we talking about?" James asked. "Just a few days ago, Nancy Abbott was here looking for a painting based on a request from Sanford."

"That's interesting," Archie said. "What day was it, can you remember?"

James thought for a moment. "This past Saturday."

"Really!" Archie said, with a look of surprise. "I'll have to let Jennifer know about that, because she claims the last time she heard from him was over a week ago." He pulled out his notebook and wrote down the date. "Anyway, please don't mention anything about this to anyone."

"What about Enrique?" Gloria asked.

"Probably not. I don't see why he would have to know about this." Archie could see that she was not happy with that answer. "Hey, I think it's about time for the tour. James, are you ready?"

"I am." He led the way, talking with John as they walked. From the dining room, they went to the library, the music room, the kitchen, the solarium, and the great room. From there they went up the steps to the second floor. James pointed out Clara's room, her balcony, and the other bedrooms and baths along the corridors. He indicated the door to Sanford's office as they walked by. James briefly discussed how the third and fourth floors had been shut up by Mr. Leeds, and he described the different rooms that were found up there.

He then led them outside and across the driveway to the huge garage. From the end of the driveway, they looked over at the grounds and the pond.

"Is that an alligator?" John asked.

Everyone turned toward the pond. James said, "Yes, he's been living there for a few years now. Every now and then, Enrique has to chase him off the grass and back into the water."

"Where is Enrique?" John asked. "I'd like to meet him."

"Right here," said a voice from behind them.

Enrique had walked over from behind the garage when they were all staring at the pond. James introduced John and Luther to him and then pointed to the staircase. "All right, up the stairs we go." Everyone except Enrique proceeded to the second floor above the garage. When everyone was inside the recreation room, James explained why Mrs. Silverman was so interested in having it constructed. "Unfortunately," he said, looking directly at Gloria, "It really isn't used much. Back there, Mrs. Silverman had a small office suite constructed with two offices, a conference room, and small living quarters in the back."

John, thinking that was the next stop on the tour, took a few steps toward the office door. James put a hand on his shoulder. "Ah, we've had some termite issues recently, and the area's just been fumigated, so I'm afraid you'll just have to take my word for what's in there."

Enrique turned to James. "It was?"

James gave him a big smile. "Yes, Enrique. Must have been during one of your famous gallivanting escapades."

"Oh, okay," John said.

They all turned and followed James down the stairway and back out into the bright Florida sunshine.

Archie turned to Gloria and James. "Thank you both for taking the time to show John the Estate. I really appreciate all you've done for us today."

"You're not leaving?" James asked with a puzzled look.

"Well...yes. We've seen everything, and John has met..."

"Nonsense," James interrupted. "Gloria and I have put together a wonderful lunch for everyone. It's all ready. Come, please."

Archie looked at John and Luther. Luther shrugged his shoulders. "I got nowhere to go," he said with a smile.

"And you know I don't!" John said with a smile. "What about you?"

"I was going to have lunch with my daughter. But it's fine. I'll just call her and tell her I'll be back in a little while."

"You'll be glad you stayed," Gloria beamed.

Everyone followed James back to the dining room. When they arrived, a table had been set and Enrique entered, pushing a wheeled cart filled with food.

Archie said to John, "Excuse me for a moment." He stepped out into the hallway and dialed his home number. He let it ring until the answering machine picked up. "Amanda, this is Dad. I thought I'd be home around now, but it looks like it will be about another hour or so. Go ahead and have lunch.

I'll see you shortly." *She must be at the pool*, Archie thought as he walked back into the dining room.

"We're serving an all-Florida lunch," James said with a big grin. "Hearts of palm salad, clam chowder made from Indian River clams, catfish fillets also from the Indian River, and Florida lobster tails."

Luther sat down next to John. "I'm glad we stayed!"

James poured everyone a Chardonnay, and Enrique and Gloria set out heaping plates of food. The conversation started out quite subdued, but after a few more wines and another helping of lobster tails, everyone in the room became quite talkative. Gloria asked John what Mrs. Silverman's family home was like, and John explained how the house got its name, The Four Chimneys. Everyone in the group was mesmerized when he started telling them stories about the infamous maze they had opened to the public on Halloween, two years earlier.

Just when everyone thought they couldn't eat another bite, James walked out of the kitchen holding a home-made key lime pie. Gloria cut it into pieces, and James walked around the table, serving a large piece to everyone.

When he put one down in front of by Archie, he leaned over and said, "Could I have a word with you after dessert?"

"Certainly," Archie said, as Gloria poured everyone Cuban coffee.

Luther held up his cup. "We're going to need this to stay awake the rest of the afternoon."

When everyone was finished with the pie, Gloria and Enrique started clearing the table. Archie, Luther, and John walked out to the foyer. James approached the group. "May I have a minute of Archie's time?"

He led Archie back to a small office just off the kitchen. "I think I have a good idea of what happened to Sanford, if he's actually missing."

"You do?"

"I certainly do. Look, I know the others are waiting, but this won't take long. I thought you'd like to know what I've discovered," James said, pulling out a small key. He bent down, unlocked a drawer, reached in, and handed Archie a ledger book. "Take a look at this."

He opened it up and started leafing through it.

"This book keeps track of every painting Mrs. Silverman purchased for the last five years. As you can see, eighty percent of them were bought through Abbott Galleries."

Archie was looking at the prices Mrs. Silverman had paid. There were sums of sixty thousand dollars, eighty-five thousand, one hundred and twenty thousand, and three hundred thousand. It went on and on.

"If you turn to the last five pages, you'll see she's paid over two million dollars for paintings in the last year and a half."

Archie flipped to the back and started counting.

"But guess what?" James asked.

He looked up from the ledger. "What?"

The Black Orchid Mystery

"First of all, when you start looking at what the real value is of the paintings, you'll find that Mrs. Silverman paid way too much. But there's more." James waited for Archie to ask.

"And?"

"You won't find most of those paintings anywhere at the Estate," James said. "I know, because I've looked."

"Where are they?" Archie asked.

"They were carted out of here during the last few weeks by Sanford and Nancy Abbott."

"You saw them do it?"

"Some of them. Gloria and Enrique saw them move some, also."

"They removed expensive paintings right in front of you?" Archie asked.

James laughed. "We're the help, Mr. Archibald. Don't you understand? Gloria, Enrique and I, we hardly exist. As far as Sanford and that pretentious art dealer of his are concerned, my only worth is to whip up meals for Mrs. Silverman and the staff. Sanford doesn't have a clue that I've published three historical novels or that I'm quite a well-known author in the British Isles." James slammed his hand down on the desk. "He doesn't know and he wouldn't care! To him, we're just the hired help."

James paused to collect himself. "But Mrs. Silverman knows. She's provided me with a lifestyle that is conducive to my work. If it wasn't for her, I would never have had the time or the resources to spend on my craft. It's ironic. She could buy and sell these two idiots a thousand times over, but still, she has more class in her little pinky than they could ever hope to have."

"If you're saying that once Mrs. Silverman disappeared, Sanford and Mrs. Abbott had free reign to loot the Estate of its treasures, do you think they are behind her disappearance?"

James thought for a moment. "I've had a suspicion for several years that Sanford was skimming from the Estate, and I don't just mean the art. I've actually got someone looking into this right now, but I don't want to say anymore about that, and please don't mention this to Enrique or Gloria. As to the disappearance, maybe he's just taking advantage of the situation. But here's what I do know, last week Sanford and Nancy were pulling paintings out of here like mad. Then, Nancy came back by herself and took another load."

"What day was that?" Archie asked.

"Thursday. You know what I think? I think Sanford's made off with the artwork. When you told me he seems to have disappeared, it all came together. Think about it. Last week they both come and grab the most expensive artwork. We're talking millions of dollars. Nobody's seen Sanford since. Then, his partner in crime comes by and gives me a flimsy excuse about needing to pick up another picture for his charity. I think he's probably already out of the country and she's not far behind.

Archie handed the ledger back to him. "Thanks for sharing this with me. Looks like I've got a few more stops to make today."

The Black Orchid Mystery

James locked the book up, and they walked back to the dining room. Everyone said goodbye.

As they were driving back, Luther asked, "What was that meeting with James all about?"

Archie wasn't worried about sharing James' news with Luther, but he didn't feel it would be a good idea to burden John with more problems. At least not before he could check them out. He replied, "James, like all of us, is quite worried about Mrs. Silverman. He's got a few ideas about what may be going on, but I'm afraid I need to check out a few things before I can say one way or the other."

"Okay," Luther said.

"In fact, there's something I want to check out right after I drop John off."

"Do you need any help?" John asked.

"Not yet, but thanks."

It was almost three-thirty by the time they pulled up to the Sea Drift . "We had a dinner reservation with Mr. Leeds at his club tonight for eight o'clock," Archie said to John, "but I doubt that's going to happen. How about Luther and I pick you up at the same time?"

"Are you sure I can't help you guys out?"

"Not right now, but thanks for your offer."

"Okay. Yes, eight o'clock sounds good," John said. "After that lunch, I'm ready for a nap."

Archie walked with John up to the hotel lobby. "Do me a favor, will you? Stay in your room until we get here. Don't open the door for anyone, and don't go roaming around. Not that I think anything would happen. I just can't take a chance."

John looked surprised. "Really? Okay, if you insist."

Luther dropped Archie off next to the Miata, which was parked in front of Archie's office.

"I'll see you back at the Sea Drift tonight at eight," Archie said.

He pulled out his cell phone and dialed his home number. The phone rang five times, and, again, the answering machine kicked in. "Honey, I'm on my way. Sorry this took so long. I'll be home in five minutes."

Archie wondered why Amanda wasn't answering the phone. He hoped she wasn't mad at him for missing lunch. Archie parked in front of the apartment and walked up to the door. It was locked. Archie unlocked the door and pushed it open. "I'm home!"

The apartment was silent. He glanced around the apartment. She wasn't in the living room or kitchen. He walked into the guest room. It was empty. He pulled open the closet door. There was nothing hanging on the hangers. Her suitcase was missing. Archie walked back into the kitchen and saw a note on the table.

Dad, I'm sorry to take off like this, but after what happened with Travis, I didn't feel much in a vacation mood. I have unfinished business I have to take care of back home, and things will only get worse if I don't start dealing with them as soon as possible.

Thank you so much for letting me come and stay with you. I love you, and I hope I can come back real soon when things are different. Please don't be mad, Amanda.

Archie pulled out a kitchen chair and sat down with the note still in his hand. He read the note again. Archie walked over to the wall phone and dialed Candace's number.

"You're not going to believe what happened," he said.

"What?"

"Amanda left."

"She left? What do you mean?"

"I just got home, and she's packed up her things and gone back home. Here, let me read you the note she left me." He read her the note.

"What does that mean?" Candace asked.

"I don't know. Does it mean she's going to go back to that jerk, or does it mean she's going back to break up with him?"

"Hard to tell," Candace said. "But it sounds like she'd like to come back, so I guess she's not mad at you, or anything."

"I sure hope not," Archie said. "I sure wasn't expecting this!"

"How are you doing, Archie? I know you've got that dinner with John tonight. Do you want me to take your place?"

"Oh, no. But, thank you. I'll be fine. Going to dinner will give me something else to think about."

"If you hear anything more from Amanda, let me know," Candace said.

"Thanks, I will."

"Oh, how did the visit to the Estate go?"

"Very well. They welcomed John like the long lost relative he is. James served us a lunch that was out of this world. I think John was very impressed. Now, we just have to make some progress finding his aunt, and I have a few ideas about that."

"You do?"

Archie's cell phone started to ring. He pulled it out of his suit coat. "It's Sanford's secretary. I better take this. I'll see you tomorrow." Archie answered the phone.

"Archie, it's Jennifer."

From the sound of her voice, Archie could tell something was the matter. "What's going on?"

"I just got a call from the police. They found Sanford's BMW."

"Was it at an airport?"

"No," Jennifer said, breaking down. "They...they found it way out west of Fellsmere at that horrible Sonny Porter's place."

"It sounds like you know this guy?"

"Oh, I certainly do. He's some crazy skin-head that Sanford would give money to."

"Wait a minute. Sanford was giving money to a skin-head?" He could hear her sobbing.

"I hated that guy. He always gave me the creeps. Yes, Sanford said he was some kind of informant, but I never knew about any information he ever gave us."

"Do you think Sanford asked him to hide his car?"

Jennifer sobbed. "No...they...they started asking me all kind of questions. They really didn't come out and say anything, but I don't think this is good news for Sanford."

Archie looked at the clock. "Do you want me to come over there?"

"No. I'm heading home. I just thought you'd want to know what's going on."

"Okay, well, thank you for calling me. If you hear any more about this, let me know."

At 6:30 p.m., Nancy walked out the back door of the gallery. She was wearing a man's dark suit that she had picked up at a Fort Pierce Salvation Army store. The handgun she normally kept in the top drawer of her desk was now concealed in the suit coat's right pocket. Her hair was stuffed under a baseball cap turned backwards.

Nancy bent down and unscrewed the back license plate of the black Acura she had rented in Fort Pierce. On top of the real license plate, she put a copy of an Illinois license plate she had taken a picture of in front of her shop. She screwed it on tight and stood back up. Glued to a piece of stiff cardboard, it looked pretty good, even in twilight. When it got dark in an hour, nobody would be able to tell it wasn't real.

She didn't know what Clara's nephew looked like, but it didn't matter. She had two pictures of that detective, and she knew they would probably be going out to dinner together. Nancy had staked out Archie's office three times and had managed to take several good pictures of him.

At 6:50 p.m., she drove six blocks over to Banyan Road and parked the car. The side street provided a direct view of the hotel's lobby door. She remembered that Sanford told her he made dinner reservations for eight o'clock. She knew they wouldn't be going to Sanford's club, but she hoped they would be going to dinner around the same time.

She drank coffee and smoked cigarettes to pass the time. She tried not to think about everything that could go wrong. This was her only chance, and it had to work.

At 7:50 p.m., she saw a truck pull up in the hotel driveway. She watched as two men got out. One was black, and the other guy looked as if he could be the detective. She glanced down at the photographs. The truck was facing north in the driveway, and, lucky for Nancy, that meant the driver had to get out in her line of sight. But, they pulled up and got out so quickly, Nancy couldn't be sure it was the detective or not. *Why would he have a big black guy with him,* she wondered. *For protection?*

Nancy stepped out of her car and pulled the gun out of her pocket. She walked closer to the truck and stood behind a thick Royal Palm. She could feel sweat forming under her suit, and her heart was starting to pound. She tried to see into the lobby. After a few minutes, she watched as a man got off the elevator and joined the two others. *That must be him*, Nancy thought. In the light of the lobby, she could see one of them was definitely Archie. Archie held the door open, and the other two men walked out.

Nancy inched herself from behind the tree, took aim at the guy who was in the middle of the group, and steadied her gun hand with her left arm. She waited until they got halfway to the truck.

Archie turned to John. "I hope you like seafood. We're going to take you to…"

"Archie, watch out!" Luther bellowed. He gave John a shove, knocking him to the ground.

A shot rang out, and Archie could see the darkness light up from a bright muzzle flash. It was close. Very close. He ducked down next to John and pulled a revolver from his shoulder holster. "Are you okay?" he asked John.

"I think so!"

Archie heard someone running and then the sound of a car door slamming shut. He ran to Ocean Boulevard and saw a black car head north, its tires screeching.

"Archie! Luther's been hit! He's bleeding!"

Archie ran back to the truck. He bent down and saw a dark red circle of blood forming on Luther's shirt.

By this time, the desk clerk and several other people had come running out of the hotel. "I called 9-1-1," the clerk shouted.

Archie pulled out his handkerchief and held it down on Luther's wound, trying to stem the bleeding. Luther was coughing weakly, and Archie could hear him trying to breathe. *Please get here fast*, Archie said to himself.

Finally, the sound of sirens could be heard heading their way. Once they had loaded Luther into the ambulance, Archie called out to John. "Stay here and talk to the police, I'm riding with Luther to the hospital."

Nancy drove ten blocks north and then turned west onto Live Oak Road. She followed it until it turned into Indian River Drive and took it all the way to State Road 60. She pulled off the ball cap and struggled out of the suit jacket as she drove. She turned right onto A1A, and just before the intersection at 17th Street, she pulled into a bank parking lot. She got out and tore off the paper Illinois tag. She tore it into several pieces and tossed it into a garbage can. She slipped off the suit pants and threw the clothes into a black garbage bag. A block away from the car rental place, Nancy pulled behind an office building and tossed the garbage bag into a big green trash bin.

She sat in the car and tried to collect her thoughts. At first, it felt as if everything was happening so fast, but then toward the end, it seemed like everything was moving in slow motion. She remembered having a good line on the nephew, but right after she fired, she remembered a lot of shouting going on.

Nancy drove to the car rental lot and turned in her car. She walked several blocks back to where she had parked her car and drove home. *Just act normal*, she kept repeating to herself over and over. *Pretend nothing has happened.*

It was almost midnight. Archie was sitting in the hospital waiting room with John. After talking to several detectives, one of them had driven John to the hospital, where he had spent two hours talking with Archie.

The waiting room door opened, and a solemn-faced doctor walked in, followed by a nurse. "We did everything we could, Mr. Archibald."

Archie stood up. A cold sweat enveloped him, and he thought for a moment he may pass out. "What?"

"I'm sorry to tell you, Mr. Johnson did not come out of surgery."

John stood quietly, not knowing what to do or say.

Archie moved back over to a chair, sat down, and put his head in his hands. He fought back tears.

A nurse walked over. "Can I get you something? Do you want me to call someone for you?"

He shook his head and mumbled through his fingers, "I'll be okay."

After what seemed like an eternity, he turned to John. "I have to call Candace."

"Would you like me to make the call?"

"Thanks, but no, I have to do it." Archie pulled out his cell phone and walked into the hallway.

A few minutes later, he walked back into the room, brushing away some tears. "She's going to meet us at the office. Let's go."

Archie and John sat next to Candace's desk, waiting for her to show up.

"Let me make some coffee," John suggested. "Do you have a coffee area?"

Archie pointed down the hallway. "Everything's in there. Thanks."

John busied himself looking for the coffee and filters. Just as he hit the brew button, he heard the door fly open, followed by a female voice crying out, "Oh, Archie!"

Candace ran into the office and hugged Archie. "I...I...can't believe it," she said between sobs.

Archie held her tight. He could feel her trembling.

John walked in with a small tray holding three cups of steaming coffee.

Archie stepped back. "Candace, this is John Barrington."

Candace pulled a tissue out of her purse and wiped her eyes. "I'm sorry. Hello. I...I wish we were meeting under better circumstances."

"Me, too," John said, handing her a cup.

"I'm going to get to the bottom of this," Archie said. "I owe it to Luther."

"I'm sure that shot was meant for me," John said. "If it wasn't for Luther's quick action, I'd probably not be here now. He saved my life."

"That's how Luther was," Archie said. "He was highly trained in the military and very brave." He walked back to the coffee area and wiped his face with a napkin. He stood quietly for a few moments, trying to compose himself.

When he returned, Candace asked, "Whoever did this knew John was staying at the Sea Drift, and they must have known you'd be picking him up tonight."

"I'm registered under my real name," John volunteered. "I had no idea there would be any chance of danger."

"We didn't think so either, John. Probably not a good idea, now that I think about it," Archie said. "But, you're right Candace. Let's think of who would know that." Everyone was silent until Archie spoke again. "Sanford set up the time and place. So, he would know. If he knew, his secretary probably knew it, too."

"What about Gloria or James?" Candace asked.

"They met John this morning." Archie turned to John. "Did you tell anyone where you were staying?"

He shook his head. "No. Nobody even asked. Do you suppose Luther may have mentioned it to anyone?"

Archie shook his head. "No way. He understood completely the importance of discretion in this business. The leak didn't come from him."

"Why do you think it was meant for you?" Candace asked John.

Archie interrupted. "Unfortunately, I think he's right. I know of two, possibly three, people who would find your visit threatening."

"Who would that be?" John asked.

"Sanford!" Candace cried.

"Yes," Archie said. "And Sanford's partner in crime."

"Who's that?" Candace asked.

"Nancy Abbott from the gallery."

"That's two," John said. "Who's number three?"

"Clara's kidnapper, if there is one."

"What do you mean, if there is one?" John asked.

Candace blurted out, "So, do you think Sanford made himself disappear for a week or so in order for him not to be a suspect in the shooting?"

"I'm not sure about that," Archie said. "Wouldn't it be better for him to be seen around the area and have an iron-clad alibi? If he suddenly show's up now, right after this, it's going to look very suspicious. Besides, if he was behind this, he would have hired someone to do it. I can't see him risking everything by attempting it himself."

"Where would he find someone like that?" Candace asked.

"Are you kidding?" Archie said. "He's a lawyer. They come across all types of people in their business. In fact, somebody named Sonny Porter would be a perfect candidate."

"Let's go back to who would know where I was staying," John said. "I never mentioned where I was staying to anyone at the Estate." John turned to Candace, "Did you?"

"No."

"Nor did I," Archie added. "I set up the meeting date and time for our visit to the estate, but I never mentioned where you were staying. I need to pay Sanford's secretary another visit tomorrow. For all we know, maybe he's back in the office, and she never let me know."

"What about Luther's family?" Candace asked.

"I'm not sure. I know he had a brother, but he was killed in a car accident when I knew Luther down in Fort Lauderdale. Let me think for a minute. I remember he had a sister, but there was some kind of problem. I don't think they were speaking."

"He didn't seem to have any family to go to for Thanksgiving," Candace said, trying to hold back a sob.

"You're right. Well, I'll make the arrangements if nobody comes forward," Archie said. "Now I think it's time we all went home and got some sleep."

Candace gathered the empty coffee cups and brought them to the back.

"You're coming to my place for the rest of the night," Archie said to John. "I'll take you back to the hotel tomorrow to get your things, and you're checking out. You can bunk with me for the rest of your stay."

A cold, damp, swirling salt fog was blowing in from the ocean when they walked out of the office. As Archie was locking up, Candace said, "I'm sorry to hear about Amanda."

"Thanks. It was quite a shock when I got home; but you know, with all that's going on now, I'm glad she went back home. Until we figure out what the hell's going on, I wouldn't want her here. And you need to be very careful, too."

"I will."

"In fact, we'll follow you home and make sure you get into the house okay."

"You don't need to do that!" Candace said.

"It's not negotiable. Come on, we'll walk you to your car," Archie said as he pulled out his gun.

Chapter 32

Archie was having a nightmare. A shadowy figure with a gun was chasing Luther and him through a narrow back alley in Fort Lauderdale. They were running as fast as they could, but the gunman was always right behind them. They ducked behind a dumpster and watched as the man walked by them. Just then his cell phone rang, and the gunman spun around. Try as he may, he couldn't get the phone to stop ringing.

He rolled over. The cell phone on his nightstand was ringing. He picked it up. "Hello?"

"Oh my God! I just saw the morning news. I'm so sorry about what happened to your friend, Mr. Archibald."

It was Sanford's secretary.

The sudden jolt of reality hit Archie, and he felt the blackness of the night before wash over him. "Um, thank you. What time is it?"

"It's nine-thirty. Oh, I'm sorry. Did I wake you?"

"You did, but it's okay. I need to get back to the office."

He sat on the edge of the bed and took a deep breath, trying to clear his head. "I'm glad you called. Actually, I was going to see if I could stop by. I've got a few things to ask you." He paused, "Any word from Sanford?"

"No, nothing. Yes, please come over. I'm in the office now. Come whenever you can."

"I'll try and make if before noon."

The damp mist from the night before had turned into gray skies and a steady drizzle. The temperature was around 57 degrees. When he got out of the shower, John already had the coffee made. They stopped by the Sea Drift Hotel on the way to the office, where they packed up John's belongings and checked out. The area outside of the lobby was strung with yellow crime scene tape.

It was eleven o'clock before everyone reassembled back in the office. They all sat around Candace's desk. "I talked to Sanford's secretary this morning. According to her, still no sign of him. I'm heading over there now. Lock the door behind me, and if someone shows up that you don't know, don't open it." Archie walked back to his office and came out with another revolver. He gave it to Candace. "I don't know who's a better shot. Whoever feels the most comfortable should keep this."

Candace and John looked at each other. She reached for the gun. "I'll take it, if you don't mind."

John gave her a weak smile. "Fine with me."

When Archie walked into Sanford's office, he could see Jennifer was almost beside herself. She ran over and gave Archie a hug. "This is awful. I'm so sorry about your friend. Are you all right?"

"I'm doing the best I can…under the circumstances," Archie slowly replied.

"This has to have something to do with Sanford. Maybe he's dead, too." Jennifer slumped down into a chair. "I don't know what to do, Mr. Archibald. I can't stall off his clients any longer. I'm completely out of excuses. These people are getting nasty. They're positive Sanford ran off with their money. They're threatening to call the police." Jennifer wiped a tear from her face. "Who knows? They may already have. I've been called every name in the book. I really don't know what to do. And now this!"

Archie thought that if this was an act, Jennifer should be up for an Academy Award. "I've got a question for you. I brought John over to the Estate yesterday, and both James and Gloria mentioned that Nancy Abbott was there Saturday picking up several paintings based on Sanford's direction. Do you know anything about that?"

"No. Why wouldn't Sanford pick them up himself?" Jennifer asked. "What day did you say that was?"

"Saturday."

"Saturday? They must be wrong. I haven't heard from him since Wednesday. Why would he ask Nancy to pick up something he needed and not ask me?"

"Maybe he had asked her before, and she was just getting around to it," Archie proposed.

"Well, maybe," Jennifer said, sounding doubtful.

Archie walked over to the window and gazed out at the Atlantic Ocean. "I need you to level with me, Jennifer. I know you have loyalty to Sanford, but we're in a situation now where people are disappearing and getting killed. I've got a few ideas I want to discuss with, you but I need you to be honest with me." Archie turned from the window. "Can you do that?"

She dabbed her red eyes with a tissue. "Yes."

"What if Sanford and Nancy were running a scam in regards to all that artwork Nancy was selling Mrs. Silverman. What are the chances that Sanford grabbed money or even some paintings, and took off to South America or someplace, where he's waiting for Nancy."

Archie stared at her, expecting her to vehemently deny his theory.

She didn't say anything. Finally, after an awkward silence, she said, "I don't know. Do I think Sanford was the most ethical person I ever met? No. And, I do know he was quite chummy with Nancy. But, I really can't see him abandoning his business,

The Black Orchid Mystery

all his things, and everything, to run off with Nancy. She can be a real bitch."

"Interesting," Archie said. "Did you notice, you didn't say my theory was insane?" He walked over to the door. "The majority of his business was Mrs. Silverman, right?"

"Yes. It's turned into that."

He nodded. "When's the last time you saw this Sonny Porter?"

Jennifer shuddered. "I don't know. I think it's been a few weeks. He barged in here when Sanford was meeting with Mrs. Abbott. I tried to keep him out, but Sanford told me to send him in. I think he tried to steal my purse. He's a horrible person."

"You said he was in there with Sanford and Nancy?"

"Yes. I tried…"

He interrupted. "Okay, looks like I need to talk to Mrs. Abbott. What's the address of her gallery?"

"It's only a few blocks from here on Cardinal Drive."

Sonny groaned and tried to move. A monitor beeped in the nurses' station, and two orderlies ran to his room. At first, he was confused by the green curtain surrounding his bed. He saw a tube coming out of his left arm. He tried to speak. "Where…am I?"

A nurse leaned over him. "You're in the hospital. You've been unconscious for awhile. Just relax."

Sonny glanced around. He turned and saw a uniformed police officer sitting next to his bed and a man in a grey suit standing near the window.

"Feeling better?" the man asked.

Sonny groaned. "No. What happened?"

"From what we could figure out, you got into an argument with your wife."

Sonny looked puzzled. "Oh? What's different about that?"

"Then somebody shot you."

"I got shot?"

"That's what your wife told us."

Sonny tried to remember what had happened. "So, who are you?"

"Detective Beam."

"What are you doing here?" Sonny asked.

"I've got a few questions for you about that BMW that was parked in your driveway."

"A what?"

"A fancy BMW."

Slowly, a sinking feeling washed over him. He turned away from the detective and looked out the window. "Yeah. What about it?"

"Is this your car?"

"Ah, no. It's a friend of mine's."

"And who may that be?" the detective asked.

"A lawyer from Vero."

Sonny felt perspiration start to break out on his forehead.

"Why was it parked in front of your trailer?"

"Ah, he's thinking of selling it. He wanted me to bring it down to Miami and see what its worth. You know, they get better prices down there."

"What's your friend's name?"

Sonny coughed and winced in pain. "Ah, Leeds. Sanford Leeds."

"I talked to his secretary this morning, and she tells me he's been missing for a few days. What can you tell me about that?"

The perspiration turned to a cold chill. "Ah, missing?"

"Yeah, missing," the detective answered. "I've got another question."

Sonny continued to stare out of the window.

"It's about the trunk of that car. You know, the dead body smell, all the blood, the hair?"

Sonny didn't reply.

The detective opened a folder and pulled out a few pages. "I see here that you've done some time. Not so good for you to be getting into more trouble. We've got you in possession of a car belonging to a missing person, and then we find evidence that a body was in the trunk. This is not looking so great for you, my friend. Why don't you help yourself and tell me what's going on? Here's your chance to tell your side of the story."

Sonny rolled over toward the officer. "You got a smoke?"

Detective Beam shook out a cigarette, lit it and handed it to him. Sonny took a long, deep drag.

"Look, I got some news. But you need to work with me here."

"No promises, but tell me what you know, and I'll see what I can do."

Sonny wiped his brow and took another drag. "First off, I didn't kill nobody. I only moved the body. That bitch, she called me out of the blue, and asked me if I could get rid of a body. I didn't even know her. I only met her once at Sanford's office. I'm not involved here. I just did some lady a favor. You gotta believe me."

The detective pulled out a small recorder. "Okay, let's start over. What bitch gave you a call? Who's body are we talking about, and where is it now?"

Archie pulled up in front of the Abbott Gallery and walked in. Nancy was sitting at her desk, talking on the phone. She recognized him immediately. She tried to concentrate on her phone conversation. "Yes, Mrs. Moul, I can open up tonight at seven o'clock, if you'd like. No, I promise nobody else will be here. Very private, just like you prefer."

Archie looked around the place, waiting for her to finish. It didn't take very long to see that there was nothing in this gallery that would soon be hanging from his walls.

Nancy put down the phone and walked over to him. "Hello, is there anything I can help you with?"

"Actually, there may be." He tried to smile, but nothing happened. "My name's Mr. Archibald, and I've been hired by…"

Archie could see a change in her face immediately. She took a step backwards and interrupted him. "You've been hired by Mr. Leeds to look into what happened to Clara Silverman." She smiled and presented her hand. "Sanford's told me some wonderful things about you, Mr. Archibald."

Yeah, I bet he has, Archie thought to himself, shaking her hand. *Now I know you're lying.* "Why thank you." He glanced around the gallery. "You have some very nice things here, Mrs. Abbott." He walked over to an abstract painting and pretended to study it. After a few minutes, he turned back to Nancy. "Oh, I was wondering. When was the last time you saw Mr. Leeds?"

Nancy knew the day was coming when she was going to be asked this question. She was prepared. "Hmm, let's see…I think it was a week ago. Yes, it was. Mr. Leeds and I went over to the Silverman Estate together."

He was waiting for her to finish her statement but she stopped talking. "And why was that?"

"Ah, we picked up a few paintings for a charity auction he's putting together."

"A week ago? Could you be more specific? Exactly what day would that have been?"

She walked over to her desk and grabbed a calendar. "Thursday, yes…it was a week ago last Thursday."

"Have you been back to the Estate since then?"

Nancy smiled. "Back to the Estate?"

Archie watched her. She seemed nervous, but she was doing her best to hide it. He didn't say anything. He just stared at her.

"Well, as a matter of fact, I have." She reached into her purse for a cigarette. "May I ask why so many questions?"

"Have you seen the news this morning?"

"I haven't," she said, giving Archie an inquisitive look. "Have I missed something?"

"My best friend, Luther Johnson, was murdered last night, right in front of the Sea Drift Hotel." Just having to say those words made him grow cold.

A look of shock crossed Nancy's face. "Did you say your friend…was murdered?"

"Yes."

She blinked and coughed out a little puff of smoke. "Ah, why… that's terrible, Mr. Archibald. Did you say the Sea Drift? Right here in Vero Beach?"

"I'm afraid so," Archie said.

"Was it some kind of robbery? Did they catch anyone yet?"

"I'd classify it more as an assassination, and no, they haven't arrested anyone yet."

She pulled a tissue from her purse and dabbed at some moisture that was forming over her upper lip. "Can I get you a cup of coffee?"

"Yes. Black, please." Archie was pleased at the offer. It gave him more time to interact with her. He noticed her hand was trembling slightly as she poured his cup.

The Black Orchid Mystery

"Your questions are all about Sanford. Do you think there is some kind of connection?"

"I certainly do," Archie said, trying to read anything on her face. "Mrs. Silverman's nephew was with us at the time of the shooting. I'm sure he was the target, not my friend."

"And you think Sanford had something to do with this? Is that why you're asking me all these questions?"

"Who knows? When did you say was the last time you went over to the Estate?"

She was still trying to comprehend that she had shot the wrong man and that Mrs. Silverman's nephew was still alive.

"Ah, I may have…"

"Excuse me," Archie said. He felt his cell phone buzz in his pocket. He pulled it out and saw it was Candace calling. "Hold on, I need to take this." He stepped outside the gallery and shut the door. "Hello."

"Are you sitting down?" Candace asked.

"Ah, no. I'm at Nancy Abbott's gallery, listening to her lie to me. Why?"

"You're not going to believe this…" There was a long pause.

Archie was impatient. He wanted to get back to Nancy. "Yes?"

"Enrique just called. You're not going to believe this, but Mrs. Silverman's back."

He was sure he had heard her wrong. "What did you say?"

Candace laughed. "I told them you wouldn't believe it. I said Mrs. Silverman's back at the Estate. Safe and sound, back in her room."

"Enrique told you this?" Archie asked. "When did this happen? How did this happen?"

"I don't know all the details. He said Gloria asked him to call. She was with James making sure the old lady was okay. Seems like she's fine."

Archie leaned against the doorframe. "You're right. I wish I was sitting down! I don't know what the hell's going on with this case, but I do know Luther's dead, and somebody's going to pay for that. I'm about done at the Gallery. I'll head over to the Estate now. Keep John in the office. I don't think now is the time to introduce him to his aunt. I'll call you when I get there."

"Okay, Archie. Be careful."

Nancy was sitting at her desk when he stepped back in.

"That was interesting!" Archie said.

She looked up but didn't respond.

"Apparently, Clara Silverman's back at the Estate, doing just fine!" Archie said.

Nancy leapt from her desk. "What!"

He took a step back in surprise. He wasn't expecting that. "That's what I've just been told."

"Well, how...who had her? Who brought her back? How...how is she?"

Nancy's tone of voice didn't radiate happiness and relief. It sounded more like despair and anger.

"At this time I don't have any answers. I told you what I just heard from my secretary. This should make Sanford's day."

She gave him a weak smile. All in the mouth, nothing from the eyes. "Oh…yes. Poor Sanford. He was going crazy about this. And you said Mrs. Silverman seems to be okay?"

"Like I said, I don't know any details. I'm heading over there now." Archie finished his coffee and handed the cup to her.

On his way over to the Estate, Archie kept thinking of various scenarios explaining how Clara Silverman could have possibly reappeared back at the Estate. Had she been dropped off? Had she been there all the time? Why had Enrique called and not Gloria or James? Nothing made any sense. Then he started wondering why Nancy Abbott had exhibited such a profound reaction at the news.

He pulled out his cell phone and punched in Candace's number. "Do me a favor. Can you and John go over and keep an eye on Nancy Abbott? She's involved with this somehow. She was clearly lying to me about Sanford, and when I told her Mrs. Silverman was back, she almost came unglued."

"Sure, we can head over there."

"Be careful. Don't approach her and don't let her see you. Just watch the gallery. Let me know if anything happens."

"Will do. Where are you?" Candace asked.

"Just turning into the Estate road now," Archie said. He bounced and swayed down the tree lined road and pulled up to the gate. He pushed the button and asked Enrique to let him in.

As the gate slowly opened, he picked up his phone and called Sanford's office. When Jennifer answered, he asked, "Have you heard any news?"

"No. Nothing. Why?"

"Ah, no reason. Just checking in. I'll call you later, okay?" He jumped out, ran up the steps and rang the doorbell.

After a minute or two, Enrique opened the door. "You weren't joking, right?" Archie asked. "Mrs. Silverman's back?"

"Yes, can you believe it?" He said with a huge smile.

"What happened?"

"Right before breakfast, Gloria just happened to walk past Mrs. Silverman's room, and she heard her call out. She went in and found her sitting up in her bed."

"Where's James?" Archie asked.

"He's upstairs with Gloria, in the bedroom."

"Thanks." Archie turned and headed toward the staircase. He walked down the long corridor to Mrs. Silverman's room and stopped just outside the door. He peeked into the room and saw Gloria sitting next to the bed. James was standing just inside the doorway. When he noticed Archie, he stepped out and quietly closed the door behind him.

"Okay, what's the story?" Archie said briskly.

James was startled. "You don't look happy she's back?"

"I don't? Maybe it's because my best friend was murdered last night. All because of her disappearance. And now, all of a sudden, she's back."

James looked shocked. "Your friend…murdered?"

"Yes, doesn't anyone in this town watch the news?"

"I'm sorry," James said. "Um, we've been somewhat preoccupied. Who was killed?"

"Luther. Last night when we took John to dinner."

James turned pale. "No…not the gentleman that was here yesterday!"

"Yes."

"What about Mr. Barrington?"

"He's fine." Archie pointed to the bedroom. "So, what happened?"

"It's the strangest thing. Gloria was making her rounds, like she does every morning before breakfast, and happened to walk by the bedroom. She heard a noise, and when she looked in, she saw Mrs. Silverman sitting up in bed. I heard a scream and ran up."

"Has she told you what happened? How she got back?"

"Yes. From what she related, two people, a man and a woman, delivered her back to the Estate sometime early in the morning. We think Clara might have been given some type of mild sedative that seems to be slowly wearing off. Other than that, she seems to be in remarkably good condition. Actually,

Gloria and I both feel that she's better right now than when she disappeared."

"How do you think they were able to get her in without you knowing about it?"

James thought. "We've been wondering about that, too. It probably occurred early, maybe three or four o'clock. They must have had a key."

"Can I speak to her?" Archie asked.

"I don't know. I think it would be best if we wait awhile."

Archie tensed. "Look, James. We're not just talking about someone playing games with a rich old lady. My best friend was gunned down last night, and I know it had something to do with what's going on here. I think I need to talk to her now."

James stepped back. "Ah, I see. Yes, certainly. Please, let me talk to her first and let her know who you are."

"Keep the door open so I can hear what you're saying."

James looked hurt. "But you certainly don't think…"

Archie gave him a slight push. "Come on, get in there."

James stepped into the room and left the door open. "Clara, I'd like you to meet Mr. Archibald. He's a detective who's been working with us to try and find you."

Archie stepped into the room and looked over toward the bed. A tiny woman was sitting upright in bed. A stack of pillows were behind her. A thick array of whitish-gray hair surrounded her face. She

The Black Orchid Mystery

was wearing black silk pajamas. Clara turned to Archie. "So why didn't you?"

"Pardon me?" Archie asked.

"Find me. Why didn't you find me?"

Archie thought for a moment. "That's a very good question. It seems you just disappeared like smoke. Do you remember who took you? How they were able to get you out of here?"

"I felt like I was in some kind of twilight most of the time before they took me, so I can't remember much. I do remember being lifted out of this bed, but like I said, it felt like a dream."

"So you can't remember what they looked like? Was it two people? A man and a woman?"

Clara thought. "I don't know who took me, but there was a woman who was watching me. She would come in and bring me food on a tray. After a while she brought me a TV, but I didn't think anyone even knew I was gone. There was nothing on the news, not even a peep! I kept waiting to see something on the television."

"You've been watching the news?" Archie asked, somewhat amazed.

"Yes. Why weren't the police involved? Don't they get involved in kidnappings anymore? Was there a ransom paid?"

James leaned over the bed and patted Mrs. Silverman's hand. "Mr. Leeds thought it best not to get involved with too much publicity."

"Publicity? I was taken from my home, for goodness sake. Didn't anyone even care?"

Gloria stood up. "Oh, yes…yes…yes. We were all looking for you. We searched everywhere."

"Do you remember anything about where you were kept?" Archie asked.

"Of course I do," Clara snapped. "I was locked in a room someplace."

Archie took a step closer to the bed. "You can't remember what the people looked like who took you, but do you remember anything about the people who were caring for you?"

"Like I said, I can't remember who took me; and at first, I was quite weak and I felt confused. It was hard to focus. After a few days, I started feeling better. I saw a woman and a man. They would come in and check on me and feed me. I begged them to let me come back home."

"You didn't recognize them?" Archie asked.

"No, never seen them before."

"But they kept you locked in the room?"

"Yes. But I almost escaped. I started feeling stronger, and a few days ago, I hit the lady a good one with her food tray. Knocked her right down!" Clara smiled with a look of pride. "I made it all the way out of the house, but that man grabbed me and took me back."

"Did they ever ask for money?" Archie asked. "You know, a ransom to bring you back?"

Clara thought for a moment. "No, I even told them I'd pay whatever they wanted.

"What happened this morning? Do you remember?"

The Black Orchid Mystery

"The lady came in early and told me to drink a glass of orange juice. I did, and then I got so tired. I must have fallen back to sleep. The next thing I knew, when I woke up, here I was…back home."

Gloria turned to Archie. "I need to tell her about Mr. Barrington." Archie winced. He didn't think this was the correct time, but it was now too late.

"Tell me what?"

"Something wonderful. Mr. Archibald found your nephew. He's such a nice man. He came down here from up north to help us find you."

Clara turned to James. "My nephew? Is this some kind of joke?"

The joy and happiness in Gloria's face turned to hurt. "No, wait…it's good. Mr. Barrington is…"

James interrupted. "Mr. Archibald was responsible. I had no idea. But, Clara, we've met him. I think you should talk with him and hear what he has to say."

Clara waved her arms. "No…no…no. I've had nothing to do with those people ever since I got sent away." She glared at everyone. "Get out, all of you. Out…out…out."

"Please," Gloria pleaded. "It's a good thing!"

"Out!" Clara screamed.

Chapter 33

Nancy stubbed out another cigarette. The ashtray was overflowing. *Was it true that Clara was back at the Estate, or had that detective just said that to see my reaction?* She went over to the door, flipped her sign over to 'Closed', walked back to the storage area and started counting. Leaning against the back wall were a total of sixteen paintings. She estimated the total worth was over two million dollars, all sitting in her storage area. Just waiting to be discovered.

She covered the paintings back up with the black plastic, went back to the office, and looked up several different storage places. She made a call to a company on 10th Avenue, and reserved a five foot by five foot air conditioned bay.

Candace hung up the phone. "Archie wants us to run over to an art gallery near the beach and see what the owner's up to."

"Okay. What's she got to do with all this?" John asked.

"Apparently, she sells a lot of art to your aunt. Let's go."

She slowed down as they drove past the gallery. "Look!" John said. "There's a woman locking the front door. Is that her?"

She glanced over at the shop. "Could be. I've never met her. I'll swing around again. Let's see what she's doing."

They went around the block and drove by the gallery again. John peered out the window. "There's a *closed* sign in the doorway. She's getting in a van. Yes, that must be her, because the van has Abbott Gallery painted on the side."

Candace slowed down and pulled into a parking space near the corner. "Where did she go?"

"She turned at the corner, and now she's headed into the alley. Looks like she may be going to the back."

"Let's get out here and walk behind the building. Just be careful. We don't want her to see us."

As they made their way around the block, John pointed, "Over there, a van with Abbott Galleries on the side, parked up close to the back of the building."

They walked behind the store next to the gallery and crouched down behind a big green dumpster.

"There she is," John whispered, "Looks like she's loading paintings into the van."

"Why would she be doing that in the middle of the day and have her gallery closed?" Candace whispered.

"Maybe she made a big sale, and she's got a lot of art to deliver?"

"Could be."

They watched as she made several more trips to the van. John stepped closer to Candace and whispered, "I'm wondering, since Archie wanted us to come over here and see what she was up to, maybe these paintings belong to my aunt, and she's stealing them."

"Anything's possible."

"If that's the case, we should really know what these paintings look like before she drives away."

"How are we going to do that?" she asked.

"I've been timing her. It takes her about five minutes between trips. I could run over there and take a peek when she walks back into the store."

"Bad idea," Candace said. "Archie made a point of telling me we need to be careful."

"But what do we know?" he asked. "She's moving paintings from her store to her van. This is telling us nothing. Once she drives away, we'll know absolutely nothing."

The Black Orchid Mystery

John watched her make another trip. "See, that time it took her five minutes and ten seconds. I'm going to run over there and snap a few pictures with my phone. That way, we'll have some real evidence, if we need it."

Candace turned, "Please, I don't think…"

John watched as Nancy walked back into the building. He pulled out his cell phone and dashed over to the van. He glanced behind him to make sure the back door was close. John held his cell phone up and snapped a picture of the painting nearest him. He tilted the painting forward and took a picture of the next one. He repeated the process two more times.

Candace held her breath. She watched him as he clicked away with his cell phone.

He was about to take one last picture when he heard the back door of the gallery open. "Hey…"

He heard footsteps and then, "Can I help you?"

"Shit!" Candace said to herself.

John spun around. "Oh…hello. Help me? Yes…yes you can."

Nancy recognized him from the night before as they guy who was between the detective and that black guy. "What are you doing back here?"

"I'm…er…I'm redoing my condo, and I just happened to see these beautiful paintings sitting here in the van. I was thinking…."

"Where do you have your condo, Mr. Barrington?" Nancy asked. "Is it anywhere near your aunt's estate?"

He was taken aback. *How did she know his name?* "Er, my condo…"

"Yes, I know who you are, Mr. Barrington. There's no need to be sneaking around." She looked around. "Who else is here with you?"

"Ah, nobody. I learned that my aunt was doing business with you, so I decided to come and see your place. You were locking up when I got here, so I just followed you to the back."

"Why don't you come into the gallery? I'd love to show you my place. I'm dear friends with your aunt. Are you a collector?"

"Well, not to the extent that my aunt is." He glanced around to see if he could see Candace and then followed Nancy into the gallery.

"Damnit!" Candace thought. *"Archie's going to go ballistic when he finds this out!"*

Nancy walked him through the back room, down the hallway and into the gallery. "Sit down," she offered, pulling a chair over to the front of her desk. She walked behind the desk and sat down.

"So, Mr. Barrington, why would I find you sneaking around the back of my gallery and taking pictures of paintings in my van?"

"That's a good question, I must admit," John said. "I'll be honest with you. I knew you sold paintings to my aunt, and the thought crossed my mind that, perhaps, some of these paintings could be my aunt's property. I thought I'd take a few pictures just to make sure."

"Why would that thought even cross your mind?" Nancy said, slipping open the top right drawer of her desk.

He stood up. "I'm sorry. It seems I made an error in judgment."

She pulled out her revolver and aimed it at John's chest. "Maybe you did, Mr. Barrington, maybe you did."

"Now look," he said, staring at the gun. "There's no need for anything like this!"

Candace was staring at the back door, wondering what she should do. Suddenly, a voice behind her asked, "What's going on? Where's John?"

She let out a high squeal and spun around. "Archie! You half scared me to death!"

"I saw your car parked on Bougainvillea. Where's John?"

"You're going to kill me, but he ran over to the van to take pictures of the paintings Nancy was loading up. I tried to talk him out of it. Then, she walked out and caught him. They both walked back into the gallery."

Candace saw the concern on Archie's face. "How long ago?"

"Just now…a couple of minutes at the most."

"We've got to get him out of there," Archie said. "Here's what I need you to do. Go to the front door and see if you can see anything. Pretend to be a customer. Knock on the door like you don't even see the closed sign. Cause a distraction. But be careful.

Don't actually go in, and don't let Nancy get you, too."

"Okay!"

"We're going to take a little ride," Nancy said, gripping the gun. "I want you to see where I'm storing these painting, so you'll know I'm not a crook."

John looked at the gun pointing directly at him. "I don't think that's necessary. Like I said...."

Nancy stood up from behind the desk. "You need to know something, Mr. Barrington. I have nothing to lose. You need to do exactly as I say. Believe me, at this point, I won't think twice about putting a bullet in your heart."

He understood that she was serious. He had never heard anyone speak with such coldness before. She was completely devoid of any emotion. He stood up.

Candace walked up the front steps of the gallery and peered inside. Just as she was about to knock, she saw Nancy standing with a gun leveled at John.

Nancy noticed someone at the door and turned just in time to see a woman running back to the sidewalk.

"Come on!" Nancy said, motioning for John to start walking.

Candace ran around the building, back to the dumpster. "Archie, she's got a gun...." She looked around. He wasn't there.

Archie pressed himself against the wall of the storage area and pulled out his gun. He could hear talking, but he couldn't hear what was being said. He slowly moved to where he could look down the hallway. He saw Nancy holding a gun on John.

Archie pulled his head back when John turned around. He listened as footsteps started coming down the hall. He pressed himself tight against the wall and held his breath. The steps were getting closer, and then John walked by. Archie turned and swung his gun down against Nancy's forearm. Her gun fired into the floor, as it flew out of her hand. She dove down for the gun, grabbed it and pointed it at John. Archie gave him a push just as Nancy squeezed off a round. John yelled out in pain and fell to the floor.

Candace flew around the corner. "Archie, I heard a shot!"

Nancy grabbed Candace around the neck and pressed the gun to her head. "Back off, Archibald."

Archie took a step back and lowered his gun. Nancy started walking backwards, her arm still tight around Candace's throat. "Stay where you are, and she doesn't get hurt."

Nancy continued to move slowly down the hallway, one arm tightly around Candace's neck, and the other holding the gun to her head. They came to a corner of the hallway, and Nancy stopped. "Stay put for twenty minutes, or she gets it."

Archie waited until he heard the back door open. He ran down the hallway, into the storage room and pushed open the door. He saw Nancy dragging Candace toward the van, the gun still pointed at her head. Archie squatted down, raised his gun with both hands, took aim, and squeezed the trigger. A blast of red flew from Nancy's head, and she collapsed on top of Candace. They both tumbled to the ground. Candace pulled herself out from under Nancy and dove behind the green dumpster.

Archie ran over and kicked the gun out of Nancy's hand. He bent down and felt for a pulse. He didn't feel one. He got up and ran over to the dumpster. "Are you okay?"

Candace's blouse was covered with blood. "Yes, I'm fine."

Archie turned. "I've got to check on John."

She followed Archie as he ran back into the gallery. John was leaning against the wall in the hallway, holding his shoulder.

"Are you hit?" Archie asked.

"She grazed me. Some bleeding but no real damage. Burns like hell, but I'll make it."

"Candace, call the police."

She ran into the gallery, grabbed the phone, and punched in 9-1-1 with trembling fingers. "Please, there's been a shooting at the Abbott Gallery on Cardinal Drive."

Archie walked John into the office and sat him down. A few minutes later, they heard sirens and then saw two police cars racing down the street. They pulled up to the curb and squealed to a stop. Four cops leapt out, guns drawn, and ran into the gallery.

"We've got a man wounded here and a body out in the back." Archie said. He had put his gun on the far side of the desk. "That's my gun. I'm a private detective."

One of the officers picked it up. "Is anyone else armed?"

"No," Archie answered.

"Who's dead?" one of the cops asked.

"Nancy Abbott, the woman who owns this place."

"Who shot her?"

"I did. She shot him," Archie said, pointing to John, "and then she was holding a gun to my assistant's head."

Two ambulances pulled up, and a group of paramedics ran into the building. "Check this guy out," one of the officers said. "And take a look in the back. We may have a body back there."

"Who can tell me what's going on here?"

"I'm a private detective. I've got a concealed weapons permit. That was my gun you found on the desk. I've been working with attorney Sanford Leeds and Clara Silverman's Estate regarding suspicions about Nancy Abbot and her business dealings with Mrs. Silverman. The woman on my left is Candace Muldoon, my office manager, and the man on my right is John Barrington, Mrs. Silverman's nephew."

"Okay," the officer said, slipping handcuffs on Archie. "We'll check all this out, but right now, you're going to be restrained."

"Understood," Archie said. "I have my PI license in my wallet, if you want to take a look."

The officer fished out Archie's wallet, took out his PI license, and stuck the wallet back in his pocket. "Give me a few minutes to call this in."

A few minutes later, the officer returned. He unlocked the handcuffs and said, "Okay, looks like your license checks out. Tell me, what's going on?"

Archie thought quickly. He knew that even with Mrs. Silverman back home safe and sound, the story of her disappearance had to come out eventually. With his part in all of this, and the amount of time Mrs. Silverman had been missing, his PI license was probably going to be history. Archie took a deep breath, "Okay, I was hired by Sanford Leeds to look into the disappearance of the Black Orchid. That was a name that was used …."

"Hold it right there!" the detective interjected. "I've got a dead body outside and a guy shot in here, I can't be bothered by some missing plant."

"Let me try again. As I said, I was looking into some things for Mr. Leeds. I had talked with Mrs. Abbott earlier in the day, but I had to leave and go over to the Silverman Estate. Some things she told me this morning raised a red flag, so I asked my secretary and Mr. Barrington to come over and keep an eye on her until I could get back. When I returned, she was holding John at gun point. I knocked the gun away from her, she grabbed it back up, shot John, and then took Candace hostage with a gun at her head. I waited until they went out the door and then fired at Mrs. Abbott."

Candace looked out the window and saw another car pull up in front of the store. Two men in suits got out and walked up to the front door. One had on a dark blue suit, and the other man was wearing a rumpled gray one. They both pulled out

The Black Orchid Mystery

badges, as they approached the policeman next to Candace.

"We're Santiago and Reynolds from homicide. What's going on?" the man in the blue suit asked.

"We got a call about shots fired. We're sorting it out now. There's a dead body outside in the back, and the paramedics are checking out a guy who's been hit in the shoulder."

Reynolds, in the gray suit, stepped forward. "Who's dead outside?"

"The owner, Nancy Abbott."

A disappointed look crossed the homicide detectives' faces. Reynolds said, "Really? There's a crime scene lab on the way for something we're looking into. It should be here in a few minutes. We need to clear everyone out of here." He pulled the cop aside and talked to him in private for a few minutes. When he was done, the cop nodded and said, "Okay, I'll move them all downtown." He walked over to Archie and pulled him aside. "We're going to have to wait to hear the rest of your story about what happened here, Mr. Archibald. This morning they found that lawyer friend of yours' body buried out west of Fellsmere. They think he may have been killed here. We need everyone to clear out."

Candace gasped.

"I'd like you both to come down to headquarters. These guys from homicide want to talk to you, too. They're taking Mr. Barrington to the hospital, so they can patch him up. He should be out by the time we're done with you."

Just then the crime scene van pulled up in front of the building. Four more people got out and walked into the gallery, three men and a woman. One of the men started stringing yellow crime scene tape around the front entrance. The other three walked by, heading to the storage room. One of the lab technicians started spraying the storage room floor with Luminal. "Geeze! Look at this! It's lighting up like a Christmas tree! There's blood everywhere."

Chapter 34

The next morning Archie, Candace, and John were sitting in Archie's office. Candace brought in a coffee cake and was pouring coffee for everyone. John's arm was in a sling.

"What happened after they took me to the hospital?" John asked.

Archie laughed. "Two detectives and a van of crime scene techs showed up. They were investigating Sanford's murder, and they wanted to clear the scene for that. They took Candace and me down to headquarters to get our statements. Stupid me. I thought it was only going to take a short time, and then I'd be able to pick you up at the hospital. Oh, that was a wrong assumption. I didn't get out of there until just before midnight; and I swear, for a few hours I thought they were going to arrest me for murder."

"From the questions they were asking me," Candace added, "I thought that was going to happen, too."

Archie took a bite of his danish and waited for everyone to get coffee. The phone rang. Archie answered it and listened for a minute or two. "That's great news, James. Thank you. I'll relay the message. Oh, by the way, after that meeting would it be possible for you, Gloria, and Enrique to meet with us? It should only take about half an hour or so."

John gave Candace a quizzical look.

"Thank you, I appreciate it very much," he said before hanging up the phone.

"What was that all about?" Candace asked.

"Great news, actually," he said, with a big smile. "James convinced Mrs. Silverman to meet with you today, John."

"That is good news!" Candace said. "What about the other part? Our meeting with them?"

"I think it's time that we all met and discussed a few things as a group. With Sanford gone, and what we know about Nancy Abbott, I think it's time to talk about what happened to Mrs. Silverman and to understand who killed Luther."

"You do?" John asked. "Do you have enough information?"

"I think so. Some of what happened is quite predictable, but I think I've figured out the rest. It will be interesting to lay it all out and see what kind of reaction we get this afternoon."

"What time am I supposed to meet with Mrs. Silverman?" John asked.

"Two o'clock." Archie paused. "I'm not sure what to expect from that. I couldn't read James to see if he felt this was going to be a good thing or not."

"I'll just have to do my best to convince Aunt Clara I'm not out to steal her fortune," John said with a serious look.

"Good luck with that," Candace said. "Seems like just about everyone else around her thought otherwise."

"I know," John said. "I've been thinking about that."

They pulled up to the Estate a few minutes before two o'clock. Archie looked over at John. Archie could see he was nervous.

John's sport coat almost hid the sling that was cradling his right arm. Archie helped him out of the car. "Just be yourself, and don't expect miracles. Clara's spent her whole life mad at her father for sending her away. You've got over sixty years of stubbornness and resentment toward her family. There's only so much you can do. Meet us in the study when you're done meeting with Clara."

Candace gave John a hug, watching out for his right side. "Good luck! Oh, don't forget your papers."

James and Gloria greeted everyone at the door. James looked at John. "What happened to you?"

"We'll cover that later," Archie answered. "Have any of you seen the news last night or today?"

James looked somewhat puzzled. "No. We've been quite busy tending to Mrs. Silverman. We're not big television watchers. Well, Enrique is, but I don't think he watches the news. Why?"

"I'll bring you up to speed when we have our little meeting," Archie said with a smile.

James looked perturbed. "If you insist." He turned to John and smiled, "So nice of you to come. Mrs. Silverman's waiting for you. I'll take you up to see her." James paused and turned to Archie. "Gloria will take you and Candace to the study, as you requested."

Once inside the study, Gloria escorted them to plush leather seats. "Can I get you something to drink?"

Both Archie and Candace asked for coffee.

Walking over to a table where a silver coffee pot had already been set up, Gloria poured two cups, placed them on a tray, along with cream and sugar, and walked back to Archie and Candace. "Here you are."

James didn't say anything as he escorted John up to Mrs. Silverman's room. John didn't interpret his silence as a good omen. James knocked softly at the door. There was a soft "Come in," and James swung open the door. "Mr. Barrington is here to see you, Mrs. Silverman."

She was sitting in a chair next to a small writing table. "Thank you, James." He escorted John into the room. "Please sit down," Clara said, pointing to a chair next to hers. She looked up. "You don't have to stay, James. Thank you for showing Mr. Barrington up."

James nodded with a slight smile. "When you're finished here, Mr. Barrington, please join us downstairs in the study."

"I will." He glanced down at a large manila envelope he was holding on to. As James walked out and closed the door, Clara turned to him and asked, "I'm wondering, Mr. Barrington, what made you come all the way to Florida?"

"That's a very good question. A few weeks ago, I got a call from a private detective agency here in Vero Beach. Based on some research they had been conducting, the detective thought that you and I may be related. I talked with him, and he told me that you were missing. He wondered if I had heard from you or knew anything about what may have happened to you."

Clara looked at his shoulder. "Have you been injured?"

"Slightly. It's a very long story we'd like to discuss with you at a later time, if that's okay."

"If you wish. So then, back to the detective. What did you tell him?"

"First of all, I was quite surprised to hear your name mentioned. Years ago, I had heard Aunt Thortis talk about you. About how she missed you, how she had tried to contact you, and that after you had left, she never saw you again."

"Really?" Clara said, with a quizzical look. "I'm surprised to hear that. She said I had left? It was more like I was sent away." Clara paused, lost in thought. "Well, how is my dear sister, anyway?"

John looked at her. "What?"

"How is Thortis?"

"Oh. I'm sorry, but she passed away a little over two years ago."

Clara glanced out the window. "She did? Such a shame."

"Yes, it was quite a loss. She was very close to my sister and me. She left us the family homestead."

"I'm so sorry she passed."

"I live there now with my daughter and my wife. It gave me an excuse to leave Chicago...to get out of the city. Upper Michigan's a much healthier environment to raise children." He reached down to his envelope. "I have some pictures of the house. Would you like to see them?"

"You do?" she said.

John pulled out several pictures of the house and handed them to her.

Clara took the pictures and leafed through them one by one. John saw a tear form in the corner of her eye.

"Its...its been so long," Clara said, looking through the pictures again. "It looks almost the same as I remembered, though."

"Here are some shots of the inside," he said, handing her another group of photographs.

She slowly shuffled through them, one by one. Suddenly she gasped. "Oh, here's my room!" she said, staring intently at one of the pictures. "It…it looks just the same."

"It is the same. Aunt Thortis kept it like that. She wouldn't let anyone in except the cleaning lady. She wanted it to be exactly the same if you ever came back."

Clara stared at the picture again. "She did? After all these years?"

"Yes. She never gave up hope."

Clara looked at each picture again and then handed them back to John.

"No, keep them. I made them for you."

"You did?" She took the envelope and set it on the table next to her. She sat in silence for awhile and then turned to John. "What do you want, Mr. Barrington? Why are you here?"

He thought for a moment. He knew this may be his only opportunity to try to convince his aunt of his true intentions. "I'm only here for one reason and one reason only. Here's the reason." He reached into the envelope, pulled out an 8 by 10 portrait of Thortis, taken a year before she died, and handed it to Clara.

She took the picture and stared at it.

"I'm here for Aunt Thortis. What would she think, if she knew I was aware you were in serious trouble, and I didn't do a thing to help? Often, I feel her looking down at us as we enjoy living our new life on the family homestead. I couldn't live with myself if I sat home and did nothing after all the times I heard her talk about what a broken heart she had because the two of you had completely lost touch."

Clara sat silently with downcast eyes. Finally she said, "You said Thortis had tried to find me?"

"Several times," John said. "From what I remember, she said she had written you letters, but she didn't think you got them because she never got one back. She knew you went to New York, but she didn't know where."

"Went to New York?" Clara said, with a tone of resentment in her voice. "I'll have you know, Mr. Barrington, I did not run away. I was sent away by my father. He said I had shamed the family. If that was true, how could I come back? I missed them all so much, but I could never forgive my father for what he did."

John sat quietly.

"You know what they call me behind my back, don't you?"

John thought for a moment. "Ah, no."

"The Black Orchid."

He had heard that from Candace, but didn't want to mention it. "And that's because of those beautiful orchids that grow on the property, right?"

Clara smiled. "Yes and no. When my husband died, I started dressing all in black. That's when the newspapers started calling me that." She looked at him. "And you know what? I kind of liked it. I didn't really have a past. I had given up my roots. I needed a new identity, so I continued to dress in black long past the mourning time. All because I wanted to forget about my past." She stood up and

The Black Orchid Mystery

walked over to the balcony. "You know I'm a wealthy woman, don't you?" Clara asked.

John glanced around the room. "That's quite apparent."

"Are you interested in my money, Mr. Barrington? Do you think you should inherit my house, too?"

He thought for awhile. "I'm sure you'll find this impossible to understand, but I'm not the least interested in your money, and that's not why I'm here. Look at the photograph I just gave you. That should answer your question. I'm sure plenty of people are interested in your money, Aunt Clara, but I'm not one of them. I live a comfortable life, with a family I love, in the house you grew up in, and that's where I plan to stay. I would like to have you in our lives again, as my aunt, as Thortis' sister. You probably don't believe me, but that about sums up my interest in coming to Florida."

Clara didn't say anything. She walked back to the desk and stared at the picture of her sister. Finally, she turned to him. "Gloria told me I should talk to you, Mr. Barrington. She begged me. For so many years, she would tell me to try and reunite with my family. It always hurt me when she told me that. It reminded me that they sent me away. They said I shamed them." Tears started rolling down her cheeks. "I have a lot, but I was never able to forgive my father for sending me away."

He watched as she wiped a tear off of Thortis' photograph with a thin, wrinkled finger.

She looked up at him. "Maybe Gloria was right. James told me he thinks my attorney has been stealing my money, stealing my art. I…I just don't know who to trust anymore."

"From what I've been able to see, it seems like you have a wonderful staff that truly cares for you and looks out for your best interest, as well as they can, under the circumstances. If Gloria has been telling you that, I'd really like you to think about it. You have family. We live in the house you grew up in. We'd like to have you enter our lives. I think you would enjoy getting to know our children. I know a lot has happened recently, but I'm asking you to seriously consider giving your family another try."

Clara glanced down at the picture of her sister again. "Thank you for your time, John. I'll do that."

He stood up. He could tell the conversation was over. He wanted to give her a hug, but wasn't sure of how that would be interpreted. He took her hand. "That's wonderful. I appreciate it. Thank you for listening to Gloria and giving me the time for our talk."

He stepped out of her room, closed the door and leaned against the wall. He thought things had gone quite well, but only time would tell.

As he walked down the stairway, he looked around and wondered what Aunt Thortis would think of this place. He chuckled. If she had only known. When he entered the study, Gloria jumped up. "How was she? How did it go?"

"I…I think it went very well. Thank you for all of your support."

The Black Orchid Mystery

Gloria smiled. "Family! She needs her family. Money doesn't make you rich."

He nodded. "Let's see what happens." She walked over to the coffee table and poured John a cup. "Here, take this."

He grabbed the cup and found an empty seat next to Candace.

"Okay," Archie said, surveying the room. "Looks like everyone's here." Archie waited for Gloria to return to where she was sitting, between Enrique and James. "So much has happened in the last few days. Some wonderful things, like Mrs. Silverman coming home, and some unspeakably tragic." He paused and blinked a few times. "Anyway, I thought it would be a good thing for us all to review, as a group, what we know, and to discuss some possible scenarios for the things we're not quite sure of. Does everyone agree?"

Everyone nodded their heads.

"Fine," Archie said. "First, I don't think anyone would be surprised to find out that Mr. Leeds was involved in an embezzlement scheme and has been siphoning off money from Mrs. Silverman's estate for quite some time. Do we all agree on this?"

Enrique looked surprised. "He was?"

"Yes, he certainly was," James stated. "I've been looking into this for quite some time. Actually, I started wondering what was going on when Mr. Leeds started reducing the staff and closed off the third and fourth floors."

Archie turned to face the staff. "I should have said the *late* Mr. Leeds, since he is no longer with us." He watched the shock on their faces.

"What happened?" James asked in disbelief. "I thought he had run off with the art and the money? Do we know this as a fact, or is this conjecture based on his disappearance?"

"Oh, it's a fact," Archie said. "Maybe running off was what he had planned, but that got interrupted when he was murdered by Nancy Abbott."

Gloria stood up. "Mrs. Abbott?"

"One and the same," he said. "You noticed John's arm is in a sling. Yesterday, he was shot by Mrs. Abbott."

"What!" Gloria said. "Oh, Mr. Barrington!"

John nodded. "But, you don't know the half of it. She also grabbed Candace and had a gun to her head. Archie - I don't know how he did it - was able to follow them out of the building and shoot her. As she fell, Candace was able to get away."

"So, she's in custody now?" James asked.

Archie frowned. "Ah, no. She's dead."

Gloria shuddered and wiped her eyes.

"I see," James said, somewhat subdued.

Archie looked around. "So, that explains Sanford's disappearance. He was murdered. Let's talk about the other disappearance, Mrs. Silverman's."

"Yes! Enrique said. "What the heck happened to her?"

Archie smiled. "Maybe you should ask the people sitting next to you."

Candace and John both turned to Archie. "What?" Candace said.

"James, would you like to comment?" Archie asked.

"I can't imagine what you're talking about. Why don't you continue? I'd like to hear what you've got to say."

"I'll do that. We know that, on many occasions, Gloria asked me to see if I could find relatives of Mrs. Silverman. Why?" Archie didn't wait for an answer. "For several reasons. First of all, she could see that the Estate wasn't being managed correctly. Staff was let go and the house and grounds were starting to show the effects of the reductions. Secondly, she, along with James, probably had a good idea Sanford was siphoning money off for his benefit. And the most important reason, she could see that Clara's health was deteriorating. Clara's health worried her the most. She hoped that a concerned relative could be found to step in and take charge of things for Clara's benefit. Since a relative wasn't looming on the horizon, and Clara's health was rapidly deteriorating, something had to be done."

Archie stood up and walked over to the coffee urn. He felt everyone's eyes on him as he filled his cup and slowly walked back to the group.

"And?" Candace asked, sitting on the edge of her chair.

"Gloria shared her concerns with James, and as a last resort, they both came up with a plan to smuggle Clara out of the Estate, to a place where she would be safe."

James stood up. "Preposterous, Mr. Archibald! This is pure speculation, nothing more." His face was getting redder. "And quite damaging, I may add. Do you intend to throw us in jail for kidnapping?"

Enrique glanced at both of them with a look of shock. "What!"

"Hear me out, James," Archie said with a smile. "And, to ease your mind, I don't think you or Gloria have anything to worry about. Clara's back, safe and sound. Nobody outside of this circle even knows she was missing." He paused. "Well, Nancy Abbott did, but she won't be communicating with anyone. Hear me out." Archie took a sip of coffee. "Anyway, when I started reviewing my notes of the conversations I had with both of you, you almost never mentioned Clara in the past tense. It was like, in your minds, she was never really gone. That's because you knew where she was. You knew, not only was she in a safe place, but because she wasn't taking the medicine Sanford was bringing for Gloria to give to her, she was actually growing stronger every day she was away from the Estate. You both probably saved her life. So, there should be no reason for concern."

Archie looked around the room. "Anyone want to add anything before I continue?" Nobody said a word. "A few days after I first visited the Estate, Gloria showed up at my office with a bunch of documents about Mrs. Silverman's past. Why? Was this really going to help me locate Mrs. Silverman?"

Again, Archie glanced around, waiting for an answer. "Not at all. But that wasn't a problem because Gloria knew where she was. But, she did see this as an opportunity to finally locate a relative of Mrs. Silverman. A much needed relative who could step in and make things right."

James stood up. "Again, this is all guesswork. Here you are accusing us of a very serious crime, Mr. Archibald. A crime that could put us both in jail for a very long time, and you have absolutely no proof."

"It's the only scenario that makes sense," Archie replied. "Other than wandering off, and we know now that that didn't happen, why would Clara go missing? We know Sanford had nothing to do with it because he went crazy when that photograph appeared in the paper. Remember? He had to make up some bizarre statement for the press that she had decided to visit one of her other properties. We all know that was a lie. Not only that, but there's been no ransom demand. And then, miraculously, she shows up back in her room, in better shape than when she left, like nothing ever happened!"

Archie surveyed the room. "People just don't disappear and reappear."

Gloria looked down at the floor. "I know, I know. I take her away. If I go to jail…"

James flew from his chair. "Gloria, stop this!"

She glared at him. "No, I do it to save her life. But, if I do wrong, I go to jail. Don't you worry. I do this, not you."

"Nobody's going to go to jail," Archie said. "Based on what we all know was happening, something had to be done. Maybe there could have been another solution, but what was done was done in the spirit of helping Mrs. Silverman, and we can't fault that."

He looked over at James. "I doubt that Gloria could have pulled all of this off without assistance, but if that's what's going to be the story, then I guess that's what we accept."

James looked over at Gloria. "Of course she didn't do this alone. We were frantic. We could see her fading away right before our eyes. Sanford insisted Clara take the pills he had brought, and we were convinced they were killing her. It got to the point that he didn't trust Gloria to give them to her. He was doing it himself. We had to do something quickly."

"My cousin and her husband said they would watch her," Gloria said. "She's a nurse. So, we brought Mrs. Silverman there in the middle of the night." She turned to Enrique. "I'm sorry we didn't tell you, but we were scared, and we didn't want you to get into trouble. You're too young to have problems with the policia."

James looked back at Archie. "I hate to even ask this question, but what about your friend Luther?"

"Nancy Abbott." Archie said. "It had to be her. After all, Sanford was already dead. She now had all the stolen art. The only person that posed a threat to her was a concerned relative. I'm sure the shot that killed Luther was meant for John. But, Luther, being who he was, made sure John was out of harm's way."

"I cannot believe that woman," Gloria said quietly.

Archie glanced down at his notes. "Well, I think that wraps everything up."

"Just a minute!" a voice said from just outside the doorway. Everyone turned to see Clara slowly walk into the room. James ran over and offered his arm. He guided her to a chair. "James mentioned some sort of meeting down here when he brought Mr. Barrington in to see me. I wondered what was going on." She looked around the room. "I've been listening at the door. It seems like I've caused a whole lot of people a considerable amount of trouble."

"Oh, don't think of it…" James interrupted.

"Please, let me continue," Clara said. "If you think about it, this whole mess was caused by me putting faith in people who didn't really have my best interest in mind. And why should they? Sanford was only interested in my money. And that Abbott woman was only interested in selling me things. And why shouldn't they be? I don't mean anything to them. It's my own fault. I've been stubborn my whole life. Maybe it's time I listened a little more to the people around me. The people who have had my best interest in mind for many years."

Clara looked directly at Gloria. She held up a photograph. "Look, Gloria. Mr. Barrington brought me a picture of my dear sister Thortis. It was taken only a few years ago. It was shocking to see how much she resembled my mother. The mother that probably would have refused to let my father send me away, if she had been alive. I looked at that picture, and it makes me sad to think my stubbornness robbed me of so many wonderful years we could have had together."

She blinked back the tears. "What do I have? I have lots of money. With money comes power. I had the power to keep myself isolated from life. Now, I'm a bitter, old prisoner in my own little world." She looked over at John, "Gloria was right. I would like to have a family again, if you could find it in your heart."

John walked over and gave Clara a hug. "That's why I'm here, Aunt Clara. That's why I'm here."

Chapter 35

By 6:00 p.m. Wednesday evening, cars were lined up for blocks along 17th Street all the way back to Old Dixie Highway. The funeral home parking lot had been filled by five o'clock.

The funeral director peeked into the lobby. "We need to get more chairs," he said to his assistant.

"Again? I think we've only got about ten more left. Where are all these people coming from?"

"I don't know…I just don't know."

Archie, Candace, Evan and John were sitting in the third row from the front. Archie turned around to survey the crowd. He watched as another group of young people walked through the door.

"This is amazing," Archie said to Candace. "He must have touched the lives of hundreds of kids in Fellsmere. I don't know where they're going to put any more people."

Candace turned around. She was dabbing her eyes with a tissue. "Seeing all these young people just makes it even harder. Now, there's so many children Luther won't be able to reach. Oh, James, Gloria and Enrique just walked in." Candace glanced over at Evan. "You doing okay?"

He nodded.

At the end of a very moving service, the minister asked if anyone would like to stand and give a tribute to Luther. Archie hesitated for a second and then stood up. "I first met Luther almost twenty years ago, when we both lived in Fort Lauderdale. We became good friends almost immediately, and it was because of Luther that I decided to move up here. Looking out at this crowd, it's very apparent I'm not the only person he has touched. I'd like to share a story about the first day I met him. I had just rented a small office space in a strip mall in Fort Lauderdale to start my own business. I was moving in some office furniture, and I was quite nervous about the whole process, because for the first time, I was leaving the stability of working for someone else. Starting my own business was a very daunting project for me at the time. While I was backing up the moving van, I misjudged how big the truck was, and I put a ding into Luther's new truck. He was the strip mall super.

I watched as he got out and walked over. As we all know, Luther was a big man, and he could look somewhat intimidating. I was anticipating the worst. He just stuck his hand out, welcomed me to the plaza, and asked if he could help me unload the van. I asked him about the dent and offered to pay for whatever it would cost to have it fixed. He just laughed and said he knew a guy who had a body shop and told me not to worry about it." Archie dabbed his eyes with a handkerchief and paused for a moment. "That was the first day of a friendship that lasted many years. Now that I think of it, I'm grateful that I backed into his truck. Because of it, I met one hell of a man."

Archie wiped his eyes again and sat down. Several more people stood up and talked about Luther. The minister said a final prayer and the service was over. As they were walking out of the funeral home, a woman walked up to Archie.

"Excuse me, sir."

He stopped. "Yes?"

"I understand you were the one who made the arrangements for my brother?"

Archie looked at the woman. "Oh, my goodness. You must be Esther. Yes, I did. I'm sorry if I…"

The woman shook her head. "No, no…please. I just want to thank you for all you've done."

He breathed a sigh of relief. "Thank you, but it was the least I could do."

She stepped closer. "Luther and I haven't been speaking for the last few years. It's my fault, and I'll never forgive myself. I'd like to try and repay you for what this must have cost. I can't give you all of it right now, but I'm hoping we can work out some kind of arrangement."

"You don't owe me anything, so please put that out of your mind. I'm just pleased that you were able to come today. Luther's spoken of you often."

The woman looked relieved. "Thank you, Mr. Archibald. My brother thought the world of you, and now I know why."

"Where are you living?" Archie asked.

"I have me a place over in Eatonville."

"I don't want to speak out of turn, but from what I understand; Luther wanted you to have his house in Fellsmere."

"That would be a blessing, Mr. Archibald. A true blessing."

The next day, Archie helped John load his suitcase into Candace's van. At the airport, the two men shook hands. John looked at Archie. "I really don't know what to say. I'm happy I've been able to find my Aunt Clara, but to do that, you've paid a very heavy price. Luther…he was such…." He stopped and turned away.

"I know," Archie said. "I know exactly what you're feeling. Somehow, we just have to move on and concentrate on the positive."

He nodded in agreement. "I better get to my gate. Again, thank you for all you've done."

The flight back to Upper Michigan went by quickly. John slept during most of the flight from Detroit to Green Bay. Kit was waiting for him when he arrived. She ran up and was about to wrapped herself around him. "Wait a minute!" he said, showing her his sling.

Kit stepped back with a look of fright. "What happened? You've been hurt? You never told me that on the phone!"

"I'm fine. It's a long story. There was so much going on. If you even knew half of it, knowing you, you'd have jumped on a plane, and it was way too dangerous for that. I'm sorry, but I'll tell you what happened on the drive back home. By the way, I knew you wanted to bring the kids, but this is why I asked you not to." He looked over at her. "A lot of things happened down there that I don't want them to hear."

From the look on his face, Kit suddenly got a knot in her stomach. She reached up and kissed him. "I'm so glad you're home!"

John didn't start talking until they crossed the border from Wisconsin into Michigan. It was a bright, sunny, winter's day. The sky was a clear blue, and the temperature was 24 degrees. Finally, he turned to her. "The good news is, I got to meet Clara, and I think she's interested in getting to know us. She's been bitter her whole life about being sent away, but I think she's finally had a change of heart."

"That's good. What was her place like? Do you think she's as wealthy as they say?"

John laughed. "Not a doubt about it. Her place was huge. There was a big iron gate blocking the driveway in the middle of a tropical forest. You had to press a button and talk to someone before you could go any farther."

"No kidding! Tell me more!"

"It had about fifty rooms. I think they said there were fourteen bedrooms. Anyway, it was very impressive, but it looked like it needed some work; and the top two floors were boarded off, so I never did get to see them."

"Boarded off? Why, was it too expensive to air condition them?"

"No. Nothing like that. It turns out; the lawyer who was in charge of her estate wasn't keeping it up."

"That's not right. Is she going to fire him?"

"No."

"Why not?"

"He's dead."

"Dead? What happened?"

"He got murdered by the woman who was selling Aunt Clara tons of expensive paintings."

Kit looked over at him. "Murdered? Is she in jail?"

"No."

"She's not?" she asked. "Why?"

"She's dead."

"She's dead, too? What happened to her?"

"Archie, the detective that found us, shot her in the head after she shot me; and she had a gun pointed to his office manager's head."

Kit pulled the car into the driveway of Schloegel's restaurant. She started to shake. She grabbed his hand. "John, what in the hell did you get yourself into down there?"

"There's more. Poor Luther. Come on, let's get something to eat. I need a pasty and a cup of strong coffee."

By the time they pulled up to the Four Chimneys, John was exhausted. He grabbed his suitcase out of the trunk and walked into the house. Samantha and Sneaker ran up to him.

"Oh, Daddy," Samantha said. "I'm so glad you're home!"

"Me too," Sneaker said with a big grin. "Did you bring me anything?"

John smiled. "You know, this wasn't really a vacation. It was a very serious trip I made."

Sneaker's face fell.

"But I did find a little time to pick you up something."

Sneaker smiled.

John opened his suitcase, pulled out a book on Florida alligators, and handed it to Sneaker. His eyes lit up. "Cool!"

"And I've got something for you, Samantha," John said, pulling another bag out of his suitcase.

"What is it?"

"Open it up,"

Samantha reached into the bag and pulled out a coral necklace. "It's beautiful! Thank you."

He handed Kit a package. "Here's something for you, too."

Archie walked into the office and saw Candace surrounded by Christmas catalogs. "What are you looking for," he asked.

"Nothing in particular. Just a few last minute things for Evan." She looked up from her desk. "Are you finished shopping for Amanda?"

"Oh, yeah. I shipped her things up to Ohio a few days ago. Thanks for helping me pick out those clothes."

"You're welcome. It was fun!"

"Oh, before I forget. John called me last night. He made it back home just fine. His poor wife was really upset when she saw his sling and when she heard about everything that had happened."

"I'm not surprised. I was wondering how that conversation was going to go."

Archie's cell phone rang. "Hello, Gloria. I'm fine thank you."

Candace watched as his expression turned to a puzzled look. As he put his phone down, she asked, "What was that all about. You should have seen your face!"

"She said Mrs. Silverman would like to see me tomorrow and wondered if I would be interested in going to New York City in a few days."

"New York City? What's that all about?"

"I don't know. Gloria said Mrs. Silverman will discuss it with me when I get there."

"Tomorrow's Saturday. She wants to see you on a Saturday?"

"Guess so. I can't wait. This has to be good!"

She paused. "Speaking of Mrs. Silverman, can I ask you a favor?"

"Sure, what is it?"

"Evan's been driving me crazy about seeing the Estate. He's heard us talk about Mrs. Silverman and her big house and everything, and he'd love to see it."

"I don't think that would be a problem. I'll give Gloria a call and see if you can both come with me."

Chapter 36

The next day, at 1:00 p.m., Archie drove Candace's van down the narrow road that led to the Estate.

"That's so cool!" Evan said, as they pulled up to the gate.

"It was so nice to let Evan and me come with you," Candace said, as Archie waited for the gate to open.

"About half an hour after I had asked James if it would be okay to have Evan come with us so he could see the place, James called back and said Mrs. Silverman would be delighted to meet him."

Candace pulled Evan's wheelchair out of the back of the van. "Hear that, Evan.? You need to be on your best behavior. No wisecracks. Do you understand?"

"Yeah, I get it."

"Do you want to walk with your chair or sit?"

"I'm kinda tired. I think I'll sit."

Candace frowned. "Okay. Now don't forget, your best behavior!"

Gloria answered the door and ushered them to the back of the house where Clara was having coffee in the solarium. It was a bright, sunny day, and when they walked in, Candace gasped. Clara was sitting at a large table completely surrounded by black orchids.

Archie introduced Candace and Evan to everyone. Candace walked over and looked at the orchids. "Beautiful! Absolutely beautiful!"

Clara smiled. "Aren't they magnificent? Thank you so much for coming." She looked over at Evan. "And you must be Evan. I hear you wanted to see my house."

Evan smiled. "I've never seen a real castle before!"

Clara chuckled. "It's hardly that, young man."

"It's big," James said, "but I don't think we'd call it a real castle."

Clara turned back to Candace. "From what Archie tells me, you're the one who found my nephew. Is that correct?"

"I was able to do some digging on the internet, and after a few phone calls, I got lucky and was able to locate him."

Clara smiled. "I just want to thank you. It was wonderful meeting him."

James could see Evan was getting a little restless. He walked over, "How would you like a tour of this place?"

His eyes lit up. "Oh, yeah."

James grabbed the handles on his chair. "Come on, I'll show you around."

Once Evan and James left the room, Clara turned to Candace. "May I ask you a question, dear?"

"Certainly."

"What's the condition that's put your son in a wheelchair?"

"That's a good question. We've been working for over two years to get an answer to it. Just a few weeks ago, the doctors told me they think it could be a rare form of Guillain-Barre disease."

"I see," Clara said. "What's the prognosis?"

Tears welled up in Candace's eyes. "I'm sorry...." She pulled a tissue out of her purse and wiped her face. "Not so good, from what they tell me; but then again, they aren't one hundred percent sure of what it is he has."

Clara reached over and took her hand. "I'm so sorry I've upset you. Please forgive me."

"No, no...I appreciate your concern. It's just that we've been trying to figure out what's been making his legs so weak for so long now."

Clara leaned closer to Candace, "May I ask you what doctor you have been working with?"

"His name's Doctor Freed, at Saint Francis."

"I see. Well, let's hope things start to get better. Would you excuse us? I'd like to discuss something with Mr. Archibald."

The Black Orchid Mystery

"That's fine."

Gloria walked up, as if on cue. "I've got some refreshments set out in the dining room. James will meet us there with Evan."

When everyone had left the room, Clara turned to Archie. "Mr. Archibald. There's something I would like you to do for me, if you aren't too busy."

"What is it?"

She pointed to a large wicker chair next to the table. "Please, sit down. After having a few weeks to ponder all of the things that recently happened," she said, looking over at him, "and once again, I'm so very sorry about your friend."

Archie mumbled, "Thank you."

"Well, I've been telling Gloria and James about how wonderful it was to meet John. Did you know we talk on the phone now?"

Archie smiled. "No, I'm so glad to hear that."

"Yes, yes. I've talked with his wife and his daughter Samantha." She laughed. "I've tried to talk to his boy, but I don't think he likes to talk on the phone much. Anyway, it's been such a pleasure." She patted him on the hand. "Forgive me, I seem to be rambling. Actually, I'm quite curious to learn more about the baby I gave up for adoption. I was wondering if you would be so kind and take a trip to New York and look into this for me."

Archie could hardly hold back his amazement. "I'd be very interested in looking into that, Mrs. Silverman, but I must caution you, the outcome of what we find out could be quite disappointing. Are you prepared for that?"

"That's why I'd like you to look into this first. I think you're quite capable of analyzing what you find out, and I would expect you to bring me the results of your findings first, before any actual contact was made."

"Good, good," Archie said. "We're on the same page."

"Another thing, Mr. Archibald. It dawned on me that my child would also be a cousin to John. I'm sure he's wondered about this, too."

"I'm sure he has, Mrs. Silverman. But, you do realize that the state agencies won't be opening up their sealed records to me, even if I'm working on your behalf."

"Oh, goodness. I don't think my name should be mentioned at all. I want this done as quietly as possible. I know it won't be easy, but let's see what you can find out. What do you say?"

"I'd be happy to see what I can find out for you."

She took his hand. "Wonderful. Please see James when he's done showing Evan around. He has some money to get you started. Just keep track of your expenses and let him know what you need in regards to finances."

Archie stood up. "I'll let you know what I find out as soon as possible." He walked back to the dining room and saw Gloria sitting with Candace. Ten minutes later, James wheeled in Evan.

"How was it?" Archie asked.

"It was cool. I want to live in a house like this!"

The Black Orchid Mystery

Candace laughed. "Me, too! We better start buying lottery tickets!"

Archie pulled James aside. "Looks like I'm going to New York."

"Great news! I was hoping you'd be interested in doing this. Let's head up to the office."

Once upstairs, James opened a drawer, pulled out an envelope, and handed it to Archie. "This should be enough to get you going."

Archie laughed. "You sure were able to change Mrs. Silverman's way of thinking. Now she's asking me to go dig up all her secrets!"

"I know," James said. "But I can't take any credit for it, much as I'd like to. You finding John Barrington made all the difference in the world. I swear she's like a different person."

"I'm glad that worked out so well," Archie said.

"Oh, while you're in New York, can you do me a favor?"

"What's that?"

"The Fitzgerald Theater holds a special place in Mrs. Silverman's heart. It's where she started working as a dancer. Her generosity was responsible for a complete renovation last year." James paused.

"And…" Archie said, waiting to hear what the favor was.

"I'd like you to stop by. The manager's name is Irving Schuck. I'd like you to see if you can gather a few anecdotes about Mrs. Silverman's years as a dancer. Who she met, what shows she was in…things like that."

"And this is okay with Mrs. Silverman?" he asked.

"Yes, it's fine. We discussed it when she told me she was interested in having you try and track down her child."

He pulled out a pad of paper. "Fitzgerald Theater and the manager's name is Irving…?"

"Schuck."

"Oh, yeah. That's it."

As they returned to the dining room, Archie looked over at Evan and saw that it was time to leave. He walked over to Gloria. "Thank you for your hospitality. Please tell Mrs. Silverman we had a wonderful time."

Chapter 37

Three days later, Archie was on a Delta Airlines flight headed for JFK Airport. The sky was bright blue and cloudless as they approached the city. As the skyscrapers rising up from the city grew closer, he watched the Statue of Liberty pass by his window. He could see the green expanse of Central Park, ringed by a border of gray concrete.

Thank God for my carry-on bag, he thought, as he walked right past the crowded baggage carousel and headed out the door. He took a cab to his hotel on West 92nd Street and checked into his room. He unpacked his bag, sat down in the chair next to a small writing desk, pulled out his cell phone, and dialed Irving Schuck's number. The phone rang four times before Archie heard it pick up.

"Mr. Schuck? Archie Archibald. I'm in my hotel, and I was wondering if I could come by sometime this afternoon as we discussed last night." He listened for a response. "Okay, that would be fine. I'll meet you in your office around five o'clock. Wonderful. See you then."

Archie thought Mrs. Silverman must have had some incredible memories of the Fitzgerald if she had spent so much money renovating it the year before. He had lunch at a deli, walked around Broadway for two hours and then headed over to the theater. He roamed around the lobby and then sneaked a peek into the main theater. It was amazing. It had been restored to what it must have looked like during the thirties of forties. One of the ticket sellers directed to him to where Mr. Schuck's office was. He walked down a dark, narrow hallway until he came to the office. The door was partially open. Archie knocked.

A booming voice told him to come in. Archie stepped inside and saw a short, portly man wearing a brown suit, sitting behind an old wooden desk. The office was a mess. Playbills and assorted papers were lying all over his desk. Two ashtrays filled with cigar buts were sitting between several paper cups half filled with old coffee. Archie walked over and held out his hand.

"Mr. Archibald. How nice to meet you." He pushed a pile of newspapers off a chair and motioned for Archie to sit down.

"Thank you for agreeing to see me on such short notice."

The Black Orchid Mystery

"Not a problem. What can I do for you?" Irving didn't wait for an answer. He held up his hand. "But first, how is dear Mrs. Silverman?"

"She's doing very well. Thank you for asking. It's a pity she couldn't accompany me and see what a magnificent job they did with the theater."

"Have you seen it?" Irving asked.

"Only a little. I poked my head in before I came to your office. It looked amazing."

"Thanks to Mrs. Silverman. She was the one that made everything happen. After we're done here, I'll give you a proper tour. Show you backstage and everything. I think you'll really enjoy it."

"Thank you," Archie said. "I'm looking forward to it. But, from the looks of it, business seems to be strong. There was a crowd of people outside the doors when I came in."

Irving rolled his eyes. "Oh, that. Yes. Did you notice we have Nicholas Savage performing here?"

"The Nicholas Savage from *America's Greatest Voice*?"

"The one and only," Irving said with more than a hint of sarcasm.

"What's the problem? Can't he sing?"

Irving laughed. "It's not that. But, this is his first play, and I think it's a bit overwhelming for him. Think about it. Just a few months ago he was singing in his bedroom on some *You Tube* videos. Now he's on Broadway. Well, pretty damn close to Broadway." Irving let out a laugh. "And that damn tongue ring of his! He refuses to take it out even though it gives him some kind of strange lisp. I swear, we can't understand half of what he's singing."

Archie smiled. "There's no telling the power of popular culture these days."

"I should worry," Irving said with a shrug. "He's filling up the house every night. Come on, let me show you around."

As he guided Archie around curtains and cables, Archie asked, "I know Mrs. Silverman has a special place in her heart for this place. As I explained last night, I'm wondering if you know anyone who can give me some anecdotes of when she performed here."

"Watch your step. Anecdotes? Hmm, it's been quite some time since she actually danced on this stage. I don't think anyone who works here now would even have a clue that she ever set foot in this theater."

Archie tripped on a roll of rope and grabbed Irving for support. "I know, it has to have been over sixty years ago."

Irving guided Archie out onto the stage. "The whole stage and all the rigging have been replaced. We were able to locate some photographs of what the theater looked like when it opened, so we tried to restore it to exactly the same look."

Archie looked around. "It's magnificent. You've really done a great job."

Irving showed him some of the dressing rooms, and on the way back to his office said, "I thought Mrs. Silverman always wanted to keep all the details of her life private."

"She did. But there have been some recent developments that I really can't go into, that seem to have given her a change of heart."

Irving stopped for a moment. "Freda Mountjoy! She worked here for years. Did all kinds of things. She retired a few years before I started, but she still stops in now and then to look around."

"What's her connection to Mrs. Silverman?"

"Roommates way back when."

Archie's eyes widened. "Really!"

Irving got a sheepish look on his face. "I kind of slipped one day. Freda was here, and she noticed all the remodeling work that was being done. I know Mrs. Silverman didn't want her name mentioned, but it just came out; and besides, Freda has a long association with the theater. When I mentioned Mrs. Silverman was funding the restoration, she got very excited. That's when she told me they'd been roommates back in the fifties."

"That's amazing!"

"Freda told me how she got Mrs. Silverman her first dancing job. It was in the Mae West play *Diamond Lil*. Freda had been called, and they needed more dancers. She let Mrs. Silverman know, and then they hired her, too. Oh, the stories that woman has about Mae West. It must have been a magical time to be hanging around Broadway back then."

"Do you think she would talk to me about her memories?" Archie asked.

"I'm sure she would. She loves to talk about the good old days." Irving guided Archie back to his office. "Sit down."

"That was wonderful. Mrs. Silverman will be thrilled when I tell her what a wonderful job they've done."

Irving beamed. "Thank you. I just wish she was able to come and see the place for herself. We sent pictures. But they don't capture the feel of the place."

Archie looked at his watch. "Are you busy? Can I buy you a drink?"

"A drink? Certainly. Let's head over to O'Malleys." Irving stopped. "Before I forget, let me give Freda a quick call."

Irving chatted a few minutes and put down the phone. He picked up a pencil and scribbled on a piece of paper. "It's all set. She's got a place in Bedford-Stuyvesant. Here's her address and phone number. She asked if you'd give her a call in the morning to set a time. Old people! They never know how they're going to feel the next day."

"I really appreciate this. Thank you so much."

The next morning, Archie woke up with a splitting headache. *What time was it?* He sat up and glanced at the clock radio. It was almost nine o'clock. His throat was dry, and he felt as if his head had been clamped in a vise. He rummaged around in his luggage for some aspirin. It had been quite the night. It must have been close to 2:00 a.m. when he

The Black Orchid Mystery

finally got to bed. Nothing like bar hopping in the city with someone every bartender seemed to know.

He dragged himself into the shower and spent the next half hour under a cascade of steaming hot water. He got dressed, ordered room service, sat back down on the bed, and closed his eyes.

Archie felt much better after breakfast. He poured himself a second cup of coffee, pulled out his phone, and called Mrs. Mountjoy.

"Good morning. This is Archie Archibald. Mr. Schuck called you and mentioned something about me coming by for a few minutes."

Archie listened as a frail voice came over the phone. "Yes, I remember. You've got some questions about Clara Thorsen."

"Yes, that's right. I understand you have some wonderful stories about when you both were dancers down at the Fitzgerald."

He heard her chuckle. "Yes, I certainly do. What time is it?"

"It's ten-fifteen."

"You can stop by, Mr. Archibald. Would it be possible to bring me some lunch?"

"Lunch? Yes, certainly. I'd be happy to pick up some things for lunch. What would you like?"

"I'd like some cold cuts and cheeses. You know. A variety."

That should be easy enough. "That's fine, Mrs. Mountjoy."

"And some wine."

"Wine? You want me to bring wine?"

"Yes."

"Ah,…okay, what kind would you like?"

"A nice Merlot would be good. Oh, and some bread for the cold cuts. Pumpernickel. And get it at the S and J Deli. It's just down the street. They have the most magnificent bread."

"All right, Mrs. Mountjoy. I'll stop at the S and J Deli and pick up some cold cuts, some cheeses, a loaf of pumpernickel bread, and a bottle of Merlot."

"No!"

Archie paused. "Did I get something wrong?"

"A case," Freda snapped back.

"Excuse me?"

"I want a case of Merlot."

Archie took a deep breath. "Okay, a case it will be."

"And don't dawdle in the lobby when you get here," she added. "It's not safe."

As she gave him her address, he scribbled it down on some hotel stationary.

Oh, wonderful, Archie thought, as he hung up the phone. He was headed over to some dangerous neighborhood to spend an afternoon with a wino. He hailed a cab in front of the hotel and gave the driver Freda's address. The cabbie looked at Archie. "Bed-Stuy? Really?"

He didn't know how to answer. "Ah, yes, but first we need to find the S and J Deli which is supposedly right down the block."

As the cabbie merged onto Interstate 495, heading east, he asked, "You fixen' up one of them old Brownstones?"

"No, just visiting someone."

The driver nodded. "Couple of years ago, you'd never find a cabbie that'd take you near there, but now yuppies are buying up those places like crazy." He chuckled. "Who'd a thought it, eh?"

Half an hour later, Archie looked out at the buildings as the cab turned down Monroe Avenue. The street was lined with trees. A few blocks before, he could see that many of the old Brownstones had been completely redone. Unfortunately, that was not the case for the neighborhood where Mrs. Mountjoy lived.

He spotted the deli. "Pull up here, please. I need to pick up a few things."

"Not a problem. The meter keeps running, buddy."

Archie ran into the deli and ordered the lunch items. The man behind the counter had to go to the back room for the case of wine. Archie lugged everything back to the cab. They drove another two blocks and pulled up to a dilapidated building. Archie stepped out of the cab with his groceries, pulled out the case of wine, and paid the driver. As he was walking up the steps, three teenagers walked over to him.

"Looks like the man be having a party," one of the boys said.

"Yeah, and he need to be sharing some of that wine," another said.

Archie felt his heart begin to race. He tried to ignore them as he glanced at the list of names in the lobby. He spotted Mountjoy and pressed the buzzer. Laughter broke out behind him when the group saw where he was headed. "Look at that big fool. He be partying with that old drunk upstairs."

"He gonna need all that wine before she be looking good!" Archie heard more laughter as the elevator door closed behind him. He pushed the button for Mrs. Lovejoy's level and waited as the elevator jerked and swayed to the seventh floor. As the elevator door opened, he said a little prayer of thanks. He walked down the hallway, found her door and knocked. There was no response. *Are you kidding me? What am I going to do with all this stuff?* He knocked harder. Suddenly, he heard several latches and locks being turned, and then the door slowly opened. Archie peered into the darkened apartment. Freda Mountjoy was short and slightly stooped over. Her hair was sparse but died a dark black. He noticed her hands were wrinkled, and her fingers were skinny, except where arthritis had swollen her knuckles to twice their normal size. She glanced up and gave Archie the once over. Her gaze moved to the case of wine that was resting on the floor next to him. She smiled. "Come in."

She motioned for him to sit on a small settee as she slowly eased herself into a tattered chair opposite him. "So, what do you want to know?"

"Not much, Mrs. Mountjoy. I promise not to take too much of your time."

"The wine," Freda said. "Glasses are in the kitchen. Can you pour us a glass? It's hard for me to get out of this chair."

"Certainly." He walked into the kitchen and looked around. There was a dirty coffee cup on the counter and a few plates and bowls sitting in the sink, but he didn't see any wine glasses. Freda must have read his mind. He heard a thin voice call out from the living room, "They're in the cabinet over the sink."

He opened the door and took out two glasses. "Do you have a corkscrew?"

"Drawer under the counter. On the right."

He rummaged in the drawer and pulled out an opener. He popped out the cork, poured out two glasses, and walked back to the living room. "Here you go."

Freda took a sip. "Why the interest in Clara? I thought she'd died years ago, until Mr. Schuck told me about her fixin' up the theater."

Archie thought for a moment. "She's decided to put together some stories about her life, you know, to share with the younger relatives. I was told you were a very dear friend of hers and that you might have some stories to share when you were roommates."

"Did those hooligans bother you?"

"Who?" Archie asked.

"Those hooligans downstairs."

"Oh, the greeting committee? Yes, I met them."

"You're lucky you made it up here in one piece. Especially with that wine."

He wanted to steer the conversation back to Clara. "They didn't bother me much. You were roommates with Clara, is that right?"

She smiled. "I got her her first job. We were just chorus girls, you know, dancing in the back. But we got to see some famous people."

"Mr. Schuck mentioned that you both danced in a Mae West show."

She smiled. "Oh, yes. How could anyone forget that! When Ms. West came by, there was always sparks flying with her and the director. Oh, the language she would use!" Freda took a sip of wine and smiled at Archie.

"How did you meet Clara?"

"Let me think…it was so long ago. Oh, I remember. I was dancing down at another theater and that show closed. It only played about two weeks. I had met Clara, she was working behind the lunch counter at Fine's Drugstore. I used to stop in there for lunch because it was the cheapest around. Well, Clara was so pretty. They were always looking for new girls to put in the chorus line, you know. Anyway, we became friends." A sad look crossed Freda's face. "Oh, she was going through some bad times. You know about the baby, don't you?"

"The one Clara gave up for adoption?" Archie asked.

Freda looked relieved. "Yes, did she ever get back with her family?"

He thought for a moment. "Yes, she did. It took quite some time, but yes, she did."

Freda drained her glass. "When I knew her, she was quite upset with them. She didn't want anything to do with them."

The Black Orchid Mystery

"Well, you know, that was a long time ago," he said.

"Sending the poor dear off like that. Times certainly have changed, haven't they."

Archie just nodded.

"Did she ever reunite with her son?" Freda asked.

Archie set his wine glass down on the table. "No, but she would really like to find out about him. Do you know anything about him?"

"Oh, poor Clara. Whenever she had a few drinks, all she did was cry. It was a big mistake to have her give away that child. It just tore her to pieces." She handed Archie her glass. "Can you be a dear and fill this for me."

When he returned, he asked, "Do you remember when she had the child?"

"It was a few years before she met me. The poor girl was only fifteen. Sending her off to the Lutheran Home like that. You'd think her family could have taken it in."

"Yes. It's quite a shame."

She took a sip of wine and pushed herself up from the chair. "What about lunch? Are you hungry, Mr. Archibald?"

"That's a good idea. You sit back down. I'll put something together for us."

Ten minutes later he walked out with a platter of cheese and crackers and a plate of sandwiches.

"Here we go. Did you two meet anybody else that was famous, other than Mae West?"

Freda let out a laugh. "Surly you jest, Mr. Archibald. You have no idea. Let me tell you about…."

For the next hour, she regaled him with stories of Noel Coward, Gertrude Lawrence, and many other Broadway stars. Finally, during a lull in the conversation, Archie stood up. "This has been a delight, Mrs. Mountjoy. Thank you so much for your time. Could you call a cab for me?"

Back at the hotel, Archie tried to write down as much of the conversations as he could. He was sure, after confirming with Mrs. Silverman, that James would have plenty of Broadway anecdotes for his biography. Now he had to work on the hard part. How was he going to get any information on Clara's adopted son?

He walked over to the writing desk next to his window and pulled out a phone book. He flipped through the pages until he found "New York State Agencies." He ran his finger down the page and stopped at "New York State Department of Health, Adoption Information Registry." He scribbled down the address on another piece of hotel stationary.

Archie started pacing his room again, waving the paper as we walked. He knew nobody would talk to him about Clara's son's adoption. He racked his brain for a solution. *I can't get this close without finding out more about her son. Who adopted him? Where is he now?* Suddenly, Archie had an idea. It was a long shot, but at least he thought it had some

The Black Orchid Mystery

chance of working. Archie picked up the phone and called Irving Schuck.

The next morning Archie had a leisurely breakfast. Afterwards, he went back to his room for some final preparations. At 10:30 a.m., he walked down to the lobby and hailed a cab. He was hoping to get to the Health Department office on Worth Street around eleven o'clock.

He paid the cabbie and walked into the huge, white marble state building. It took him a few minutes to figure out where the Health and Vital Statistics offices were located. He walked in and took a seat. There were about twenty people waiting to get a number from the receptionist, who then set an appointment with a case worker.

The caseworkers were situated along a long row of plate glass windows with small cutouts in them. Archie watched as the workers moved behind the glass partitions. He tried to be as inconspicuous as possible. After half an hour, he had picked out two people who fit his profile. Both were females, about twenty to twenty-four years old. The first one, a brunette about five feet, four inches tall, scurried about, going from a computer to a huge row of filing cabinets. The other had bleached blonde hair. It was impossible to guess how tall she was because she stayed at her desk, typing on a computer.

Archie glanced at his watch. It was three minutes to twelve. He watched as the brunette got up and walked out from the glass partitioned office into the waiting room. He stood up as she walked out the main door. He kept a reasonable distance behind as he followed her to a row of elevators. He slipped in behind her just as the door slid shut. He stared down at the floor, not saying anything. The elevator made several stops, but it wasn't until they got to the basement floor, that the girl got out. He exited the car, hung back, and watched as she walked into a cafeteria. He let a few people get ahead of him before he picked up an empty tray and got in line.

Archie picked out a bowl of soup and a cup of coffee, paid for his lunch, and surveyed the seating area to see if he could see where she was sitting. The cafeteria was crowded, and it took a minute before he located her.

Archie walked up to her table and asked, "Mind if I sit here?"

She glanced up at him. "What? Oh, sorry, my friend's on his way." She gave him a look that may as well have screamed "Get the hell out of here, creepo!"

He panicked. This wasn't going as planned. He searched the room for an empty table. He stopped. Sitting on the other side of the cafeteria, was a girl who looked like the blonde he had picked out upstairs. He hadn't seen her leave, but maybe she went to lunch right after he had followed the brunette down to the cafeteria. He made his way over to her table. Archie could feel little beads of sweat on his forehead. This had to work. He walked over to her table and pretended to stumble. She looked up.

"Can I set my tray down for a minute? I need to get some water and take a pill."

The Black Orchid Mystery

She could see he looked overheated. "Sure."

He put down his tray and walked over to the soda machines. He grabbed a cup and filled it with water. He came back and sat down. Archie pretended to pop a pill. He took a long drink of water and asked, "Mind if I sit here for a minute?"

The girl looked around, saw that all the tables around her were filled. Hesitantly, she said, "Aw, I guess."

He took a few sips of coffee, waited a minute and then asked, "You work here?"

She finished chewing a bite of her sandwich. "Yeah."

He looked surprised. "Oh, I think I just saw you up in the Health and Vital Statistics office."

The girl nodded.

"What do you do up there?"

"I'm just an intern. I'm going to City College. Computer Science. I'm helping them update their records. I get college credit." She paused. "It's good experience."

"They sure aren't very friendly up there, are they," Archie said. "Oh, my name's Archie."

"Hi, I'm Ashley. What do you mean?" she asked with a puzzled look.

"I was just up there trying to get some information for my friend, but they wouldn't give me the time of day."

"Really? What kind of information?"

"My friend's mother found some information on *Ancestry.com* that looks like she may have had a brother that was adopted out. He asked me to see what I could find out about it."

"It's an adoption? No, they won't give out anything to you. Maybe your friend should just come over himself." Ashley paused. "I'm not sure if they'd even help him then. They're pretty strict about adoption stuff."

He chuckled. "I told him the same thing, but it's impossible for him to come here."

"Why? Is he disabled?"

Archie stared at her with a straight face. "Oh, hardly. He's in a play on Broadway. He's Nicholas Savage. He'd be mobbed if he tried to come over here."

He watched as she dropped her fork. "What! You know Nicholas Savage!"

"Oh, yes. Good friend of mine. But, he'll probably stop speaking to me now, when I come back with nothing for his mother."

"I can't believe it! Wait until I tell my girlfriend. We tried to get tickets, but they sold out in like twenty minutes." Ashley paused, beaming. "You really know Nicholas Savage!"

"It's a shame you couldn't get tickets," Archie said. "I've got two front row seats I'm not using."

"You do!" she said. Her eyes wide.

"Yeah," he said. "Too bad about not being able to get that information. You know, if there was some way to look up what he's looking for, I could probably get you and your girlfriend backstage."

Her face fell. "Are you kidding me?" She thought for a moment. "Do you know what would happen if I got caught? I'd get fired like that." She snapped her fingers.

He gave her a serious look. "I know. That would be asking a lot. What was I thinking?"

She took another bite of her sandwich and glanced around the room. "You know, I could probably try. I have access to all the databases. What is it he's looking for?"

Archie grabbed a napkin and pulled out a pen. "It should be easy. Probably would only take you a few seconds. The woman's name is Clara Thorsen, and she gave birth to a baby boy at the end of 1946. Nick's mother just wants to know who adopted it. You know, maybe send some money to the family anonymously."

He scribbled Clara's name and the date on the napkin, along with his cell phone number and handed it to Ashley. "If you find it, call me. You and your girlfriend can meet me in the lobby of the Fitzgerald at quarter to seven."

She looked worried. "I don't know. I'll see if I can try, but I'm only going to try once. If I find it, I find it."

"That's good enough for me," Archie said. "How about this, if you try and can't find it, you still get two front row seats. If you try and you do find it, you get to go backstage and meet Nick."

"I'll find it!" Ashley said with a huge smile. She grabbed her tray and stood up. "Wish me luck."

Twenty minutes later Archie was still down in the cafeteria finishing his coffee. His cell phone rang. It was a number he didn't recognize. His heart was racing as he answered the phone. He heard Ashley whisper, "The baby was named Ronald John Thorsen. He was born October 14, 1946 and adopted by William and Diane Verch, 237 Pine Ridge Way, Cedarhurst." The phone clicked dead.

He grabbed another napkin, wrote down what she had just told him, and headed outside to hail a cab.

"Where to, buddy" the cabbie asked him.

"Allerton Plaza Hotel, on West ninety-second."

"You got, it." The cab pulled out into traffic. Archie thought for a moment. "I've changed my mind. Drop me off at the New York Public Library instead."

As Archie walked up the steps, he admired the two famous lion sculptures, Patience and Fortitude. He entered the building and walked over to the row of computers. Everyone was occupied. He kept repeating *Ronald John Thorsen* over and over, as if he was afraid of forgetting the name. After a twenty minute wait, he was finally able to sit down at a computer. He started searching for the name Ronald John Verch.

An article popped up listing the members of the varsity football team for Lawrence High School in Cedarhurst, New York. Archie found a small picture of Ronald. He squinted at the screen. Ronald was sitting third from the right in the second row. He had short black hair and appeared to be somewhat stocky.

Archie continued his search. Another article showed up, this one announcing his engagement to Kathleen O'Conner. They were both eighteen years old. The article said she would be attending beauty school in New Rochelle and he was enlisting in the United States Marines. From the picture, it looked as if Kathleen had red hair and an abundance of freckles. *A pretty Irish lassie,* he thought.

Archie clicked on the next article and felt a shock of disbelief. It was a title from the *Daily News*, "Another Local Boy Dies in Vietnam." He read how Ronald had been killed November 17, 1965, in the battle of Ia Drang just northwest of Plei Me in the central highlands of South Vietnam. It told how the 7th Cavalry suffered heavy losses in a firefight that lasted sixteen hours. Several of the survivors credited Ronald with heroic action when he stormed a large group of enemy soldiers during a surprise attack. There was a picture of Mr. and Mrs. Verch at the funeral. Mr. Verch was reaching out for a folded American flag. His wife had her face buried in her husband's shoulder. Ronald John Verch was only nineteen years old when he died.

Archie printed a copy of the article, then took a cab back to his hotel and spent the afternoon thinking about what he had learned.

At six-thirty, Archie was standing in the lobby of the Fitzgerald Theater. Over the crowd noise, he heard, "There he is. I told you he'd be here." Ashley and her friend ran up to him. "You weren't kidding, were you?"

"No, not at all. Here are your tickets. After the show, just stay in your seats. I'll have someone take you backstage. One thing, please don't mention any of the information you found today when you meet Nicholas. Too many reporters. We don't want this out in the public. Okay?"

"Not a problem," Ashley gushed. She grabbed the tickets from Archie and gave him a hug. "This is awesome! Thanks!"

Archie had mixed feelings as he returned to Vero Beach. He had some wonderful stories for James about young Clara dancing on Broadway, but he didn't have good news about the baby Clara had given up for adoption, and he wasn't sure how to break the news to Clara.

Candace picked him up from the airport. On the drive back to his house, she asked, "How did it go?"

Archie told her about his trip and his mixed feelings about what he had found.

"I see what you mean. It's hard to tell how Mrs. Silverman will take your news."

"I wish you could have met Mrs. Silverman's old roommate." Archie laughed, and shook his head.

"Why?"

"I don't even know where to start. She was such a character."

Candace stood next to Archie as he was taking his carry-on bag out of the trunk. "Tomorrow's Christmas Eve. Would you like to come over and have dinner with us? It's only going to be my sister, her two kids, Evan and me."

"Sure, that would be great. I have a few things for Evan that I was going to give you now, but I'll just bring them with me when I come over. What time?"

"I think we'll eat around six- thirty."

Chapter 38

It was 10:30 a.m., December 24th, when Archie pulled into the Estate. He wasn't sure how he was going to break the news to Mrs. Silverman about her son. Gloria greeted him at the door. "Come, she's sitting on the patio getting some fresh air."

Gloria led Archie into the solarium and pushed open a huge set of French doors which opened to an area that resembled a small tropical paradise. Clara was sitting in a large rattan chair and motioned for Archie to sit next to her.

"Iced tea or lemonade?" Clara asked.

"Hmm, lemonade sounds perfect."

Gloria walked over to the table and poured Archie a glass. She made him a small plate of fresh fruit and brought everything over.

The Black Orchid Mystery

"I was surprised to hear from James that you were back from New York so soon. Were you able to find out anything? James mentioned something about a report you've written."

Archie took a deep breath. "Ah, well, yes. I did make some progress. I have it here, if you'd like to review it."

Clara held up her hand. "That's all I need to know. Just leave it with me. I'd much prefer to read it when I'm alone. If I have any questions, I'll give you a call."

He breathed a sigh of relief. "Oh, that's not a problem. In fact…"

"Now, for our second topic of discussion," Clara interrupted. "That Evan boy. What can you tell me about him?"

Archie thought about the conversation he remembered between Candace and Clara the week before. "Nothing more than what Candace has told you. Unfortunately, it's been quite an ordeal for them with not so many good answers."

"Well, I've taken the liberty to contact some people and to put some things in motion, but I'd like you to make sure Ms. Muldoon isn't offended by me poking my nose into her private business."

"What do you mean?" Archie said, confused.

Clara chuckled. "Sometimes I can't help myself. Anyway, after our conversation last week, I asked James to find the best doctor in the world associated with Guillain-Barre disease. We found Doctor Hebbard in Los Angeles. He seems to be the leading expert. Then, I had James contact Doctor

Freed at Saint Francis on my behalf." She paused for a sip of tea. "Not a difficult task when one of the wings of the hospital is named for my late husband. Anyway, the two doctors are now comparing notes, and we're working on a time, in the very near future, when we can send Evan to Los Angeles, accompanied by Doctor Freed. She won't have to worry about the cost. Everything will be paid for." Clara paused. "Do you think I've overstepped my authority, Mr. Archibald? Do you think Ms. Muldoon will be offended?"

Archie bolted from his chair and gave Clara a spontaneous hug. "Are you kidding? What a fantastic thing you've done. But, I can't give her this wonderful news. It has to come from you!"

"No, no, no!" Clara said, "Please, you just tell her the best way you can. Don't even mention my name. Tell her Doctor Freed arranged everything and found the funding."

He took a step back. "I'm sorry, but I'm not going to lie. I'll be happy to give her the news, if that's what you want, but I'm also going to tell her what you've done."

Clara reached over and picked up a cookie. "Well, if that's the case, then I insist on one condition."

Archie's heart stopped. "Okay?"

"If you insist on telling her, I don't want this to leak out to the press. This has to be just between us. Do you understand?"

"Completely. You have nothing to worry about. Thank you. Thank you."

The Black Orchid Mystery

It took Archie two trips before he transported all the presents from his car to under Candace's tree.

"Have you lost your mind?" she asked.

Archie laughed. "Don't get too excited. There're a few things for Evan and a couple of things for you."

"Archie, you shouldn't have!"

"I'm just happy I'm not sitting at home alone. I had a nice talk with Amanda when I got home from Mrs. Silverman's. Sounds like everything's fine. The old boyfriend's been convicted of robbery. Looks like he'll be doing five to ten years in prison. I think she saw him for what he really is when he showed up down here."

After a wonderful dinner, Candace put off opening the presents as long as she could, but Evan was quickly running out of patience. Around eleven o'clock, after the presents had been opened, he had fallen asleep on the couch, and Estelle and her kids had gone home.

Candace looked around at all the crumpled wrapping paper and empty boxes. "This was wonderful. Would you like a drink?"

"One more. Oh, there's something I need to tell you, but I had to wait until your sister left."

Candace poured out two drinks and handed one to Archie. "You…you do?"

Archie couldn't stop smiling. He took a sip of his drink. "First, what I'm about to tell you is strictly between you, me, and Mrs. Silverman. It can't be discussed with anyone else. Understand?"

"Ah, okay." Candace had a puzzled look on her face.

"Okay. Clara wanted me to tell you that she's working with Doctor Freed to have Evan fly to Los Angeles and meet with one of the world's experts on Guillain-Barre disease, Dr. Hebbard. After the two doctors consulted with each other, they seem very hopeful that progress can be made with Evan's condition. All expenses will be covered. The flights, hotel, hospital, everything."

Candace sat there staring at him. Suddenly, she threw herself into his arms and burst out crying. "Oh, Archie. Thank you, thank you!"

"Don't thank me. I'm just passing along the news."

Candace couldn't stop crying. "This…this is the best Christmas ever!"

Chapter 39

Monday, December 26th, started out rainy and gray. On the drive into the office, Archie had an idea. He smelled coffee as soon as he opened the door. "Great morning for some coffee," he said to Candace as she was pouring a cup.

"No kidding. It's nasty out there. Here, take this." She handed him a cup.

"I've got an idea."

"What's that?"

"Mrs. Silverman paid me very generously to take that trip to New York. We're in the middle of the holidays. Nobody's going to be coming around now. Why don't we take a few weeks off? When you think of all that's happened. We sure earned it."

A look of concern came over Candace. "A few weeks?"

"Yeah. Two weeks off, paid."

"Come on, Archie. That's…"

"Accepted. I'm glad you agree. Make a sign for the door that says 'Open January 9th'."

"Really?"

"Yes. Make the sign and go back home."

"What are you going to do with all this time?" she asked.

"I think I'll head up to Ohio and see Amanda."

"Oh, that would be nice."

The phone in Archie's office rang. He walked back to his desk and picked it up.

"Mr. Archibald? James here. Do you have a moment? Mrs. Silverman would like to talk with you."

Archie listened as James handed over the phone. "Mr. Archibald?"

"Yes, good morning."

"I was wondering if you could do me a favor."

"I'd be happy to. What can I do for you?"

"Would you call my nephew and tell him you're going to send him the information you found on my son?"

"If that's what you would like me to do, sure. I'll call him right now."

"Thank you. I think it's important for him to know what happened, but I just can't bring myself to talk about it. And…if you don't mind. Don't tell him what the news is; just tell him you'll be sending him your report."

"All right. Whatever you wish."

Two days later, John opened a Fed-Ex box and pulled out Archie's report. He walked to the kitchen and sat down at the table. "Here's the information Archie told me he was sending."

Kit pulled up a chair. "Oh. What do you think?"

"I'm not sure. From the sound of his voice, I don't think it's going to be great news. He didn't sound excited when he told me Aunt Clara wanted me to read it."

John read each page. When he finished each one, he handed it to Kit. He heard her say, "Oh, goodness." He waited until she had finished reading the last page. "I had a feeling it wasn't going to be good."

He gathered up the papers and said, "I'll be up in the office. I need to make a copy."

"Why?"

"Mr. Swenson needs to know what happened."

"It's just so sad."

"I know, but I think he'd be very proud when he reads the article."

When John got to the nursing home, he didn't see anyone at the front desk. He waited for a few moments and then headed down to Room 36. When he got there, he noticed the door was partially open. He pushed on the door and called out, "Mr. Swenson. I'm back."

He looked into the room. It was empty. The bed was made, and there was nothing of Mr.

Swenson's on the top of the dresser. No pictures hung on the wall. John stepped out of the room and saw a nurse walking toward him down the hallway.

"Excuse me. Do you know where Mr. Swenson is? Is he in the recreation room?"

The nurse looked at the door number. "Mr. Swenson? The man who lived here?"

"Yes…"

She looked at him. "I'm so sorry. I'm afraid he passed away Christmas Eve."

Her words hit him like a hammer.

She looked at John again. "You're the man who came and visited him before, aren't you?"

"Yes. My name's John Barrington. I promised him I'd come back."

"Come with me," the nurse said.

He followed her back to the main desk. She pulled out a filing cabinet drawer, reached in, and handed John a large envelope. "Mr. Swenson suffered a heart attack around eight o'clock. But, a few days after you left, he gave me this and asked me to make sure you received it if anything ever happened to him."

He took the envelope.

"Well, thank you. Thank you very much," John said.

"My pleasure," the nurse said. "When you showed up the first time, we were so happy to see someone was here to visit Iver. He was such a nice man."

John walked back to his car and set down the envelope he had been carrying. He opened the package he had been given and looked inside. He tilted the package and watched as Iver's World War II medals poured into his hand.

John glanced back down at Archie's report. *If only I had gotten this a few days earlier.*

Chapter 40

It was a sunny day, the third of April, when John heard the noise. He stopped raking and listened. It sounded like a fleet of big trucks moving along M-183. John got into his truck and drove down to the county road. He watched as large earthmovers, bulldozers, and dump trucks headed south toward Fairport.

John drove back home and walked into the kitchen. Kit was pulling cookies out of the oven. "They're starting to widen the road down at Fairport."

"Oh, no. Is that what I was hearing?"

"Yep. I drove down to the county road and saw a whole convoy of vehicles headed to Fairport. Must have been waiting for the frost to get out of the ground."

The Black Orchid Mystery

Kit handed him a warm cookie. "We'd better get used to it. Once that prison's built, there's going to be all kinds of traffic on that road."

"I still can't believe they're going to clear cut all that land."

Two weeks later John put the phone down and found Kit shaking rugs on the back porch. "It's official. Aunt Clara's coming to visit us next week."

She picked up another rug. "Good thing I'm starting this cleaning early!"

"I'm a little nervous. I hope she's not expecting to be staying in something really fancy."

Kit laughed. "She's coming back to her childhood home. It hasn't really changed much since she left. I'm sure that's what she wants to see." Kit paused. "She's not coming alone, is she?"

"Oh, no. Gloria's traveling with her. And Archie, his secretary, and her son are coming, too."

"Wow!" Kit said. "Where are we going to put them all?"

"Clara can stay in her old room. Evan can share Sneaker's room. We've cleaned the spare rooms. I'm sure we'll find places for everyone," John said with a smile. "I'm excited!"

"Don't forget, next week's the big meeting down at Fairport where the state's going to announce final plans for the prison."

"Good," John said. "This will give me a good reason not to go. It's a done deal. I don't need to stand there and listen to bad news."

"You don't want to go? I thought we'd wave our signs one last time."

"I don't know about that. Too damn depressing, if you ask me."

The week flew by as John and Kit stayed busy with all of the preparations for the visit.

At a quarter after six in the evening, they watched as a rented SUV pulled into the driveway. They hurried out to help everyone with their luggage. John introduced everyone to Kit and led the way up the front porch steps and into the house.

"As we drove from the Green Bay airport," Archie said, "we watched as it seemed like civilization kept getting farther and farther away. We took M-35 like you suggested and hardly saw a car the last fifty miles before we got to Escanaba."

"Do you like living out here in the woods?" Gloria asked Kit.

"What about bears?" Evan asked. "Do you think I'll get to see one?"

"It's very peaceful living out here," Kit said to Gloria. She turned to Evan. "Bears are quite shy. I know people who have lived here their whole lives who have never seen one." She saw the look of disappointment on his face. "But, you never know."

John carried Clara's luggage up the stairs. Gloria watched as Clara stepped into her old bedroom. She looked around. "I don't believe it. I don't believe it. It hasn't changed at all!"

"How long has it been since you've seen this room?" Gloria asked.

The Black Orchid Mystery

Clara thought for awhile. "Almost seventy years, if you can believe that." She turned to John. "It feels like I stepped into a time machine."

"I only wish your sister was here to see you come home. She's the one who insisted your room stay exactly the same."

After supper, John, Kit, Gloria and Clara sat around the kitchen table. Samantha and Sneaker had taken Archie, Candace and Evan out to the barn to see the two horses. Candace had mentioned she would like to go horseback riding the next day.

Clara glanced around the room. "This is where Thortis and I would do our schoolwork. Right here." She took a deep breath. "Even the smell of the trees outside brings back memories. There's something about that Great Lakes air. Oh, how I've missed it."

There was a clattering noise on the back porch as everyone returned from the barn. "What did you think of the horses?" Kit asked.

"They're beautiful. I can't wait to go riding tomorrow," Candace said.

"Are you going riding, too?" John asked Archie.

"What? Me? No. I haven't been on a horse since I was about ten or eleven. I'm going to have to pass."

"I'll go!" Evan shouted.

Candace looked at Kit. "It should be fine," Kit said. "They're used to the trails around here."

Evan stared at Clara for a few moments and said, "My mom said you grew up in this house, and this is the first time you ever came back. Is that true?"

Candace got a panicked look on her face, and she glanced over at John.

"Why, yes…yes it is," Clara said.

"Didn't you like it here?" Evan asked. "I think this is a neat old place."

"Evan!" Candace interrupted. "We don't ask people personal questions like that!"

Clara smiled. "No, it's fine." She thought for a moment. "You know, Evan, I think this is a neat old place, too. And I think it's quite a shame that it took me so long to come back."

"Okay, but it's not as neat as your castle." He turned to Sneaker. "You wouldn't believe her house in Florida. It's got a big gate that opens up. There's like a hundred rooms and it's got a pond filled with big alligators!"

Sneaker's eyes got wide. "Really?"

Clara laughed. "It's not quite that big, Sneaker. But I do have an alligator. Only one. So, what plans do you boys have now that we're done with supper?"

Sneaker looked down at the floor. Evan said, "Sneaker told me about a trail through the woods we're going to take. He saw a bear on it last year. I hope I get to see one!"

Clara laughed. "Oh my, a bear! Wouldn't you be scared?"

The Black Orchid Mystery

"No, he said the one he saw just ran away." He looked over at Sneaker. "He's an expert in the woods. He took me out before, and he knows just about everything."

"I have to agree," John said. "Nobody knows their way around the woods around here better than Sneaker."

"Let's go!" Evan cried.

"Now, you boys be careful," Candace said, as the boys raced out to the back porch. She had a worried look on her face. "Should I let him go? Won't it be dark soon?" she asked John.

"He'll be fine. Sneaker really is an expert in the woods. Evan couldn't be in better hands. Oh, in the summer it stays light around here till about ten-thirty."

Candace walked over to the window and watched as the boys raced down the stairs and disappeared into the woods. She turned to Clara. "Did you see that? It's like Evan never had a problem. How can I thank you?"

"Now, now…just watching him run fast like every young boy should, is all I need."

Archie walked in the back door. "I saw Sneaker take Evan onto a trail. Anyone up for a walk with me?"

"I'd like to go," Candace said. "Just don't get me lost." She turned to Clara, "He has no sense of direction."

"I'll walk with you," John said. "I'd like to get some fresh air."

They had been walking for about half an hour when Sneaker and Evan ran into them on their way back. Archie glanced at his watch. "It sure does stay light a long time up here."

John laughed. It's another story during the dead of winter. It gets dark pretty early then."

Clara excused herself and headed up to bed after everyone had returned from their walk. "It's been a long day. I'll see you all in the morning."

Gloria got up to help Clara up the stairs. "I'm tired, too. It's been a very exciting day!"

Around ten-thirty, John saw that Archie and Candace were starting to yawn. "I think it's time we all headed for bed. I'll have coffee going around eight a.m., if anyone's interested."

The next morning, everyone was sitting in the kitchen having breakfast. "Last night Kit told me today's the big rally and announcement about the prison," Archie mentioned to John.

"Sure is," John replied with no enthusiasm.

"Are we going?" Candace asked.

"No. Who wants to hear a bunch of bad news," John said.

Candace kicked Evan under the table. "Oh, I really want to go!" Evan piped up.

John turned with a look of surprise. "You do?"

"Uh, yeah. Should be kind of interesting. You know, with big officials and those protesters. Maybe a riot will break out."

"Probably a good reason to stay home," Kit chimed in.

"If the boy wants to go, I say we take him," Clara said, looking over at John. "If you don't want to go, we can take him; but you'll have to tell us how to get there."

"Oh, no. If you really want to go, we'll take you. I just thought it would be kind of boring for you all."

"Okay, it's settled. We'll all go," Clara said. She glanced at Evan. "Feeling better?"

He smiled. "Yep!"

At one o'clock, everyone piled into Kit's van and John's truck, and they drove fifteen miles south on M-183 to Fairport.

When everyone was out of the vehicles, Kit asked John, "Do you want the signs?"

"No. Let's just find a place to sit and get this over with as quickly as we can."

He walked the group over to an area in front of a makeshift podium where about seventy-five folding chairs had been set up.

Evan poked his mother. "What's that?" he asked, pointing to a large object covered by a sheet of white fabric.

"I don't know? Let's ask John." Candace leaned over and repeated Evan's question.

"Looks to me like it may be some kind of statue," John said.

"Why would you need a statue at a prison dedication?" Kit asked.

John laughed. "Maybe it's John Dillinger. I heard he came through this area in the thirties."

Twenty minutes later, a man in a dark blue suit approached the podium. Almost all of the chairs were now occupied. He walked up and tapped on the microphone a few times. "Hello, hello, can everyone hear me? My name's Thomas Ferguson. I'm your state representative. I want to thank you all for coming today. I have several exciting announcements to make that you're probably not expecting. I think you all will be very pleased, and I'm happy to be the one to share them with you today."

John leaned over to Kit. "Do you know what he's talking about?"

She shook her head. "No, I sure don't."

Representative Ferguson continued, "As we're all aware, there has been some controversy over the proposed new prison. The prison would create a lot of much needed jobs, but many acres of pristine wilderness would have to be destroyed." He paused and looked over the crowd. "I'm happy to announce an exciting new development that should provide a win-win solution for everyone. After a flurry of last minute negotiations, I'm proud to announce that all of the land selected for the prison has recently been purchased by an anonymous donor, and today it will be dedicated as a memorial forest."

Representative Ferguson walked over and pulled the covering off the statue. A six foot bronze soldier stood on a three foot granite pedestal. "I'm proud to announce the dedication of the Ronald J. Verch Memorial Forest."

The Black Orchid Mystery

John looked over at Kit and Clara with a surprised look. Clara had a huge smile on her face.

Representative Ferguson continued. "Mr. Verch gallantly gave up his life protecting this country on November 17, 1965, in Vietnam. Although he was from Illinois, he had strong ties to this area, and it was because of the generosity of an unnamed donor that we were able to purchase this magnificent piece of property." He paused as the crowd applauded. "Also, if you look toward your left, next to that large pond, you will see another marker." Representative Ferguson waved his hand above his head, and a forest ranger pulled off a white tarp that was covering the monument.

"I'm pleased to announce the formation of the Luther P. Johnson Memorial Fishing Site. We have a beautiful stone pillar with a plaque honoring Mr. Johnson. Mr. Johnson was an avid fisherman, and our generous donor has set up funds for the creation of a boat ramp and the purchase of fishing equipment that will be loaned out to all children at no cost."

Archie was dumbstruck. He couldn't believe what he had just heard. He looked over at John. "Did you know about this?" From the shocked look on his face, Archie knew the answer.

"But, that's not all…" Representative Ferguson continued, trying to speak over the noise of the crowd. "There will also be a job training center, the Ronald J. Verch Job Center, set up in Garden, already funded with a million dollar donation by the same anonymous donor." He waited until the murmur of the crowd died down. "So, I'm sure you can understand how excited and happy I am to share this wonderful news with you. This clearly is a wonderful solution guaranteed to not only preserve this pristine section of land, but to also create much needed jobs at the same time."

Archie and John leapt from their chairs and stepped closer to Clara.

"Don't look at me, don't look at me," Clara said, as everyone started to crowd around her. "Didn't you hear? The man said anonymous. That means nobody knows anything about who did this!"

On the ride back to the house, Candace and John ended up in Archie's truck. He asked them, "Did you have any idea this was happening?"

"Are you kidding me?" John said. "I had no clue!"

"A little bit," Candace said, looking somewhat guilty. "James called me and told me that Clara wanted to do something in memory of her son and Luther. He asked me a few questions about Luther and then said not to mention anything to you because they weren't sure what they were going to be able to accomplish. Then, a few days later, Clara told me that during a conversation with John, he had mentioned how upset he was that this prison was going in. She asked me what I knew about it, and when I said I really had never heard about it, she hung up and I forgot all about it. When we got here, she told me to make sure everyone ended up at the dedication, but she didn't say why."

"And I almost ruined everything when I told everyone we weren't going," John said, shaking his head.

Candace laughed. "I was one step ahead of you. I told Even that if it looked like we weren't going, he should have a fit and say he really wanted to go. He was amazing."

"Maybe he should get into acting," John said.

Archie wiped his eyes. "I still can't believe it. It won't bring Luther back, but it's a wonderful legacy that thousands of people will get to enjoy for a long time."

After dinner, everyone crowded into the living room. Kit walked in with a fresh pot of coffee and topped off everyone's cup. Samantha watched as Clara looked around the living room.

"Does it feel funny coming back to your house after so many years?" Samantha asked.

Clara smiled. "Yes. Yes it does. So many little things bring back memories. Like the wallpaper in this room." Clara stopped for a moment. "It's hard to walk by Thortis' room. I would like so much if she could be here."

"I'm sure she's looking down at all of us right now," John said. "And she must be smiling from ear to ear to have you back with your family in the old homestead."

Clara glanced up at the ceiling and gave a little wave. Everyone started to laugh.

"Hey, what ever happened to the corn maze my mom told me about?" Evan asked John.

"It was quite something. The maze was about fifteen acres, and it took an hour to walk through it. We opened it up to the public, but it just got too huge to manage. We had cars lined up half a mile down the road trying to get in."

"That sounds cool!" Evan said. "Are you going to have another one?"

"After what happened last time, probably not. Maybe we'll make a small one some year, just for you and the family."

Clara said, "John took me out to the barn and showed me the horses. They're so beautiful. Thortis and I had a horse we called Buddy. We loved him so much."

Around ten o'clock a thunderstorm blew in from Lake Michigan, and John walked around shutting all the windows. While he was busy with that, Kit went into the kitchen and popped a big bowl of popcorn. Around eleven o'clock the party broke up and everyone headed upstairs.

Gloria followed Clara up the stairs and helped her get into her nightclothes. As she sat on the side of the bed, Clara grasped both of her hands. "I want to thank you for knowing what was right, for not paying attention to the ranting of a bitter old woman."

She looked around the room. "The few nights I've spent up here in my old room have pushed all the bad memories out of the way." She squeezed Gloria's hands even tighter. "And it's all because of you."

Gloria smiled. "Thank you. I'm so happy I could be here with you to see everything." She pulled

The Black Orchid Mystery

a homemade afghan up under Clara's chin and walked over to the door. "Good night."

As Gloria walked out of the bedroom, John pulled her aside. "Is she sleeping?"

"Not yet."

"Okay. I have something for her." John walked in, sat on the edge of Clara's bed, and handed her a small box. "Aunt Clara, I have something for you."

She took the box and flipped open the top. She looked up at John with a puzzled look.

"I'm not sure where to start," John said. "But when I found out you were still alive but had disappeared, my wife suggested I talk to Mr. Swenson." John waited for Clara's reaction.

"Iver? Oh, my goodness. Is he still alive?"

John frowned. "Um…I'm sorry. He passed away last December. But before he did, he gave me this box. Those are the medals he won during the war. I thought you should have them."

Clara stared at the box for a few minutes. "Such a wonderful boy." She looked up at John again. "Today has been a long day. Perhaps you could tell me more about Iver tomorrow?"

"I understand. I'll be happy to. I just wanted you to have those medals. Good night."

Early the next morning, Kit and Archie were sitting in the living room watching John try to make a fire in the fireplace.

"If I ever get this going, it will take the chill out of the house. With all that rain last night, it feels damp in here," John said, striking another match.

They heard footsteps running down the stairs and then the kitchen door flew open. Gloria looked around the kitchen and then dashed into the living room. "She's gone!"

Archie got up from the table. "Who's gone?"

"Mrs. Silverman! She's gone!"

"What?" Kit asked.

"Not again?" Archie asked, with a look of disbelief.

John threw his kindling down and walked over to Gloria. "What do you mean, gone?"

Tears started streaming down her face. "She's...passed away. I just checked on her. Mrs. Silverman's dead."

Both John and Archie bounded up the stairs. Archie ran over to the bed and grabbed her hand. He didn't feel any pulse. "She's right," he said, turning to John. He put her arm back onto the bed. "She's gone."

John reached over and closed the door. "I don't want the kids coming in here and seeing this." John walked back over to her bed. Clutched in her hand was the box he had given her the night before.

Two days later, John received a call from the medical examiner. "Okay, thank you. I appreciate you getting back to me." He put down the phone and turned to Archie. "Nothing conclusive. She just died in her sleep sometime during the middle of the night."

Archie smiled. "I don't think she wanted to leave here. The Black Orchid finally came home."

Ackowledgments

This book is dedicated to my sister, for always being there.

This book would not have been possible without the tireless input from:

> Julia Beam
> Gordon Anderson
> Duncan Hebbard

Other Novels by James R. Nelson

The Butterfly Conspiracy
The Maze at Four Chimneys
The Peacock Prophecy

Made in the USA
Charleston, SC
05 December 2013